Death at
Painted Cave

ALSO BY B A SMITH

NONFICTION

Psychology of Sex & Gender

Death at Painted Cave

B A SMITH

A ROBIN CRANE MYSTERY

An Imprint of *Rough Waters Press*

www.robincranemysteries.com

Copyright © 2013 Dr. Barbara A. Smith
ISBN-10: 0615771491
ISBN-13: 9780615771496

DEDICATION

*In memory of those difficult days and nights during which
you taught me the meaning of hope and of courage.*

To My Beloved Son
Morgan Christopher Smith

PROLOGUE

Sara Castillo, 2006

It **was dusk** when a distraught Sara Castillo made the rash decision to flee her apartment for the safety of her brother's arms. Johnny, who lived in Monterey, was not expecting his sister. Her protective parents did not realize their daughter had left Santa Barbara. The only member of her family to be in the country legally, she would be their first college graduate, and now her mad dash jeopardized that goal. Their pride and her happiness seemed a lifetime ago.

The coast highway, shrouded in dense fog, made the stomach-churning switchbacks a nightmare, but Sara continued driving north despite a growing panic that she would plunge into the ocean or cross the path of an oncoming car. In a desperate attempt to keep her eyes open and to divert her mind from burning neck and shoulder muscles, she shut off the radio, only to find the quiet more unnerving. But worst of all were the disquieting seconds when another car's brake lights abruptly materialized ahead of her. Sara knew that if she failed to reduce her speed in time, she would plow into a helpless driver, yet braking too suddenly meant some-one hitting her from behind. Conversely, *only* when car lights appeared, did the frightened young woman know she was in her own lane.

Sara quickly realized the enormity of her mistake. *If* she'd had her head on straight, she would have called her brother and left early the next day. She had considered stopping for the night but there was little lodging along the road and when a place did appear, a red neon *No Vacancy* sign glowed. The desire for sleep became irrelevant once she stopped for gas and something to eat, only to realize she had left her wallet at home. Gas and coffee were finally paid for with the little cash she managed to dig out of her jacket pocket and the console.

Once back on the road, an anxious fifteen minutes passed before Sara remembered that when her parents gave her the car, her mother had tucked an "emergency" fifty-dollar bill into the glove compart-ment. Relieved something was going right, she was looking for a place to get a sandwich when a harsh jolt thrust her forward: the thud of metal smashing metal reverberated throughout the car. In the face of utter terror, Sara recalled her father's lesson ... pump, breathe, pump, breathe ... she repeated the mantra but the car continued skidding and, worse, the lights of the following vehicle blinded her. When they dimmed, Sara saw she had crossed the yel-low line. The slight young woman wrenched the wheel to the right with all the strength she could muster, but the Hyundai continued its unrelenting slide toward the cliff. At last, by some miracle, Sara gained control over the car. Yet, within seconds, the blinding light once again enveloped her.

As the car vibrated with the next blow, she understood this was not an accident. All he'd had to do was follow her and she had given him his opportunity without a single thought. The car shuddered and veered sharply to the left. The petrified girl shot forward, prevented by the seatbelt from crashing through the window. Sara struggled to regain control, knowing that if she failed, she would pay with her life.

Within seconds, Sara Castillo heard a woman's heart shattering screams—for mami, for papi ...

>>   <<   >>   <<

Shortly after daybreak, thirteen year-old Jeremy Richardson took off for the beach, hoping to catch some good waves before school. Early enough that his mother was not yet up, telling him to forget it. Sam, his yellow lab, *was* up with tail wagging; he had almost bowled Jeremy over as he pushed through the screen door.

As boy and dog made their way down the rocky path, Sam tore out of sight. Worried, Jeremy repeatedly whistled and called out to no avail. Knowing Sam would not be coming back on his own, the teen hurried down the rest of the difficult pathway, periodically losing his balance as he clutched his favorite shortboard, a Firewire Dominator.

Once on the beach, Jeremy saw Sam leaping up and down while madly barking at a wrecked car. For a few seconds, he thought he was imagining things. Gathering up his courage, he leaned his board against a rock before moving closer to see whether anybody was inside the crushed metal. Unable to tell, the shaken boy tried to corral Sam. Finally, leaving his pet behind, he raced back to the house, surfboard forgotten.

A scared, flushed, and out-of-breath Jeremy burst through the front door and ran right into his mother. Her cup flew, coffee splashing all over her white terrycloth robe before shattering on the tile floor.

"Jim!" she screamed. "Jim, for God's sake, something's wrong with Jeremy! Oh my God, what's wrong honey? Was Sam hit? I came down to feed him but couldn't find him—I've told you so many times he can't run free." She reached out for her son. He pulled back.

"Mom, you've got to listen—it's not Sam! Well," he paused, "I can't get him, but he's okay."

He stepped on a piece of her cup and yelped.

"Oh my God, now you're hurt! Sit down and let me take care of your foot."

"Sal, what in the hell is going on? I didn't finish my project until 2 a.m. and I need some fucking sleep! Goddamn better be important because I've got to present the damn thing this afternoon!"

"Jim, you've got to get down here. *Now!* Something's wrong with Jeremy. He was down at the beach and the dog is gone. Now he's cut himself!"

"What in the hell was he doing on the beach this early in the morning? Oh, don't bother!" The sounds of his Dad angrily pounding his way down the stairs accompanied the yelling.

"Jeremy, I don't know how often I need to tell you before you finally listen—no surfing before school! And for Christ's sake, keep that damn dog on a leash!"

"Jim, listen to me. Something's wrong with Jeremy. God, can you please stop the yelling!" She flung herself into her husband's arms, almost knocking him down the last stair.

"*What* is going on here? Jeremy, sit down, catch your breath for a minute, and then tell me what's wrong." Without waiting for an answer, he continued where he had left off. "Did something happen to Sam?"

Sally tried to examine her son's injury but he wrenched his foot away.

"Dad, it's really bad! You have to come down to the beach! I think the car fell off the cliff ... from the highway. Please, can you help whoever's in the car? Oh, maybe they crashed and left. Right? You have to get Sam—he won't listen to me! He won't stop barking—someone must be alive. Please, Dad, you gotta hurry!" Cradling his foot, Jeremy began to cry.

"I'll call the California Highway Patrol," his father said, "and then we can go down to the beach. The foot looks okay—just a scratch. Sally, for *God's sake*, calm down. You're upsetting the boy. What in hell have you got all over you?"

"Jesus Christ, what *does* it matter? It's only coffee."

>>   <<   >>   <<

The two CHP officers were on patrol when the call came in from dispatch.

"Hey you bums, you need to head over to a possible crash site. A thirteen year-old boy told his parents a wrecked vehicle is on the beach. No surprise—it was damn foggy last night; I couldn't see two feet in front of me. The boy can't tell whether anyone's inside the car. The caller—the father—said the emergency vehicle entrance is obvious. Either of you familiar with the area?" He proceeded to give them directions to a beach on the Big Sur coastline, not far from the Esalen Institute.

"Tom! Steve here. I used to go surfing at that beach. Had a hot girlfriend who lived around there—man, I can still visualize that chick in her bikini. Strange the boy can't see anybody—the airbag should have completely deflated. Those cliffs are pretty steep, so it's unlikely there are survivors."

"Kid said the car is small and banged up."

"Possibly kids having a night out—too much alcohol or drugs and they walked away," Steve suggested. "When they wake up, they'll be wondering where their bruises came from. Where their car is."

"The father and son are going back down to the beach because the boy couldn't get hold of his dog," the dispatcher warned.

"Shit! Just what we need—an animal disturbing the scene."

"Steve again. I'll tell you what, call back and notify them we're on our way. Both parents are to go down the beach with their son: one parent can stay with the car, while the other takes boy and dog back to the house."

"Will do! I'll send out a bus to be safe."

Steve laughed. "Sounds like we're past needing the EMTs, but go ahead and call. Might as well keep everyone employed."

CHAPTER 1

Young Female At Painted Cave:
October 2011, Day One

"Chief, a call came in you should be aware of. A tourist discovered a body up in the hills—at the Painted Cave, across from the shoulder where you pull off to park. You know what I'm talking about?" prompted Sonia Rodriguez, assistant to Division Chief Bartolo, part-time dispatcher, and self-appointed mother hen for the Criminal Investigation Unit of the Santa Barbara Police Department. Sonia had been with the Chief for years and considered the whitewashed mission style building to be her second home. She actually showed the dedication of a mother wolf, rather than a hen, when it came to protecting those she considered as family, which was just about everyone in the unit.

"Been awhile but, yeah, I know the Painted Cave. Sex of the victim?"

"Young female. Who should I send?"

"Hmmm—Sonia, those caves also fall under the jurisdiction of the Park Service—contact them first. They'll be able to get someone out there faster than we can to secure the scene."

"Will do."

"What else?"

"Well, Jefe, the tourist said he went to the cave and before getting back to his car he took pictures. That is how he spotted the woman. Bueno, en realidad, a leg. I guess a bush or rocks hide the victim, but while taking pictures he saw the leg. He was difficult to understand."

"Sonia, tell me the guy didn't screw around with things."

"Lo siento, Jefe. The caller—he was a médico in Iraq—climbed down to see if the victim was alive. She is dead. He is careful not to disturb anything and is waiting in a red Porsche. Chief, he's the only one there. Bueno, except for the dead victim."

"Shit! Sonia, the caller shouldn't be out there alone. Jesus Christ, only in California would a tourist rent that color Porsche, nothing like advertising his status! Name?"

"Berkley Stilts."

"Berkley? Stilts? Odd name, maybe an actor. A con man."

"He talks fast and his phone breaks up."

"Got it. Well, he should not be at the scene, so call Mr. Stilts back and ask him to return in an hour. Probably nothing to worry about but we need to protect him and the crime scene. When he returns, he should park only if an official vehicle has arrived. Oh and tell him we appreciate his cooperation. Sonia, make sure the Park Service gets out there ASAP!"

"Will do Chief. Who should I send?"

"Painted Cave—I guess that would be Detective Crane—she hikes in those hills and is probably familiar with the area better than most. She should stay alert—the caller might just as likely be the suspect. On second thought, radio Detective Debayle, and tell him as soon as he finishes up with the domestic dispute he's to head up to the Pass."

"What if he wants to interview and book the husband?"

"Detective Tyler can bring him in. Hmmm—Robin's been doing fine work and she'll be first on the scene—tell her she's the primary on this one, but be sure to give Doug a heads-up. Later, if they need more help, send Deputy Chief O'Donnell or Detective Tyler, depending on who's free."

"I'll make the calls," Sonia said, trying to corral her long curly black hair streaked with grey, strands of which kept falling in her eyes.

"You'd better call Doc. If you need anything, I'll still be in my office. Damn, if these stats the Commander wants for Mayor Campbell aren't going to do me in."

"The joys of being the big honcho! Could turn the job over to the Deputy Chief and go deep sea fishing in Hawaii."

"Good idea, though Sheila hates fishing. I guess she can read her mysteries and lie in the sun, happy finally to have time with her contented husband. Rachel's soccer team certainly can use more coaching. Bet you'd like that, eh Sonia, Ken O'Donnell as Chief?"

"Por favor, you *know* I am kidding! Un café? Pie? The work will go better."

"Thanks. A cup of fresh coffee with pie would be great, but make the calls first." Bartolo hung up.

CHAPTER 2

Detective Robin Crane:
Day One

Robin's radio crackled to life with its typical fits and starts—a portent of what was to come—so much for enjoying the midday peace and quiet. Sonia Rodriguez, with the drama only the middle-age Latina dispatcher could muster, spiritedly requested she respond to a tourist who had called in a DOA, young female, at the Painted Cave. He had been taking pictures when he spotted a human leg down the hillside. The patrol unit had requested a detective because of the distance—the Chief wanted Robin to head out to San Marcos Pass immediately.

Lunch was over. Two overlapping but emotionally dissonant thoughts came to mind: A murder. Another day she would not be home for Sean after school.

"Robin, the Chief doesn't want the caller up at the cave alone because the killer may be hanging around, and the scene needs to be protected. The witness' name is Berkley Stilts—he is a tourist. I called back and told him to return in an hour, but not to park unless an SB cruiser or a Park police vehicle is at the location. The M.E. has also been notified."

"Thanks Sonia, I'll head out there right now. Doug?"

"Dougie will join you when he finishes up with a domestic in Isla Vista." Sonia then added ever so casually, knowing what the impact would be, "Robin, Chief Bartolo said you're the primary on this case." Without pause, the dispatcher signed off with "Honey, watch that cute little backside of yours."

Robin flinched and remembered telling Doug that on the East Coast Sonia would be the target of a discrimination suit in a flash with such a remark. "Go with the flow is the West Coast message," he had said with a rowdy laugh.

Anxious to get going, Robin wrapped up the remaining half of her powerhouse sandwich—sprouts and bits of Muenster cheese escaping. She capped her aloe-wheatgrass juice, switched on the lights, nosed her cruiser out of the parking lot and pulled into the steady stream of traffic. She knew Painted Cave Road was located three miles south of the San Marcos Pass. While driving toward Highway 101 and 154 she went over the route in her mind. The final leg of the drive was up a precipitous and narrow road with dangerously tight switchbacks, so to be safe, she turned into the Texaco gas station on the corner of Anacapa and East Figueroa to fill up and grab a much-needed coffee.

As Robin pulled up to the pump, it sunk in that the Chief had sufficient confidence in her abilities as a detective that he had given her primary responsibility for a murder, a first. Well, she guessed it was a homicide, but figured it wasn't wise to start the investigation by jumping the gun. There was always the chance it had been an accident or suicide.

It was going to be a long day. Well before dawn, Sean awakened crying from a nightmare. Subsequently, neither of them got enough sleep before the alarm went off at 6:30 a.m.—so much for reading *Harry Potter* to a six year-old at bedtime. Nevertheless, this was not the first time she had gotten too little sleep and faced a difficult day, and it would not be the last. Robin was relieved that she had made plans for Denise, her sitter, to pick up Sean after school because it was anybody's best guess what time she would finish up. When she was late, Denise fed and bathed Sean and her five-year-old, Francisco, and put both boys to bed. The only problem with the arrangement was that Robin had to scoop up a sleeping child. All too often, he wanted to play by the time they got home. On the other hand, that scenario would not last much longer because Sean would soon be too heavy for her to carry down Denise's stairs and up their own to his bed.

After the Detective paid for her coffee and the gas, seatbelt in place, she flipped on the local oldies station, 106.3, and the calming sounds of Crosby, Stills, Nash, and Young accompanied her as she swung onto the highway and once again turned on the lights. Even though the victim was a non-breather, she doubted the witness would drive around aimlessly. Worse, he might muck up her crime scene. Still, the siren would be over the top this far out.

The day was sunny. No clouds in the sky. There had been enough rain to green up the plant life. Robin was tempted to finish her sandwich but given the speed at which she was traveling, stuck to the coffee. As she left the city and drove up into the hills, she thought about how much she'd come to love Santa Barbara, home in a way L.A. never was—especially since she now had her son and an extended family courtesy of the SBPD.

Ken O'Donnell was the first of her colleagues to become a friend. Nothing ever romantic, which made for an especially comfortable relationship. More importantly, he and Sean got along well. Ken encouraged Robin to sign him up for the local t-ball team and routinely appeared unannounced to cheer the boy on *and* provide a steady stream of advice at top volume, puffing away on a cigar, much to the disgust of anyone in the immediate vicinity.

Robin appreciated knowing O'Donnell had her back—particularly a couple of months earlier when Stewart, her son's father, had shown up unannounced in Santa Barbara. The next day, Sean had mentioned being sad because his dad left before his game. Robin had called Ken and he appeared before the end of the first inning. Sean's team won the game, and when she reached out to hug Ken, her sleeve rode up. He noticed the bruises and had looked at her inquiringly. She shook her head, hoping he would take the hint and say nothing. He had taken them for dinner, and after Sean went to bed, rather than leaving as he usually did, Ken asked for a cup of coffee and settled himself on her living room couch.

When she finally sat down, he asked the inevitable question, "Robin, what's going on with Sean's father?"

"I guess I owe you an explanation." She took a sip of her wine. "I'll try and make a long story short but, I'm warning you, it's not pretty."

"I'm not trying to be nosy. I'm asking because I care about you and Sean. Anything you tell me stays between us."

"I know. Then again, this is difficult to talk about ... to anyone."

Robin thought about it. Her friend remained quiet.

"Whatever. Ken, Stewart never wanted the responsibility of a family. Instead, he wanted and wants a possession. After we separated, he would show up at my apartment unannounced. Once, I had a male friend over and from then on, he acted surly every time I saw him. Another time, again without warning, he came over and claimed the baby I carried was not his, so he 'wouldn't be giving me a dime.' Stewart then went from leaving nasty messages on my answering machine to following me. There would only have been more trouble if I stayed in L.A., so I applied to San Diego, San Francisco, and Santa Barbara PDs without telling him. Unfortunately, thanks to the internet, he found us anyway."

Jaw tight and fist clenched by his side, Ken offered to tell Stewart to back off, but she reminded him they were discussing Sean's father, and insisted she could work things out for herself. When Robin had not heard from Stewart for several weeks, she wondered whether her friend had made good on his threat. At the time, Ken was the only one in Santa Barbara aware of Stewart's history of abuse and his repeated threats to take her son away.

Notwithstanding her friendships, Robin missed her parents, Sean's only grandparents. Though she made the trek back East as often as possible, financially and job-wise, she wanted more. Robin kept trying to convince her parents to visit, but her mom seemed to be stuck on the star gazing she'd done when they visited Robin in L.A.—the local stars were pretty low-key and she had no plans to stalk the Montecito hills for the rich and famous, even for her mother. Robin thought the real problem was that her mom resented the fact that her daughter had not returned to Baltimore with her grandchild—a decision reflecting on them as parents. Her career shift made things worse: "So much money went into your education. We didn't have much but we always tried to help. First a psychologist and now a cop. You need to think about Sean. What happens to him if you are hurt or killed? He's not even going to know us."

Nothing she said brought her mother around. On the other hand, Robin knew her father would be interested in the region's history. Since Beth Steel went out of business her Pop had single-mindedly pursued his fascination with Atlantic Coast Indian tribes. She thought if she got him out of his safety zone, the California Chumash tribe, complex hunter-gatherers who had settled the area some 13,000 years ago, would intrigue him. The Chumash had adorned sandstone with elaborate artwork still visible inside the Painted Cave, the location where the witness had discovered the body. It would be ironic if a murder took place where she had enjoyed the peace of the cave, pleased to learn the Chumash did not emphasize war as did many other tribes with which she was familiar.

Regardless of family complications, here she was, Robin thought, a Santa Barbara detective on her way to a murder scene as the primary investigator. She sped along the Chumash Highway until she saw the small sign for Painted Cave road and took a sharp right. As the road rose precipitously, the twists and turns became increasingly more difficult to negotiate. Two bicyclists came whizzing down the road at a harrowing speed. She concentrated on her driving.

>>   <<   >>   <<

After making calls to all the relevant parties, except for Detective Debayle, whom she would talk with when he called in, Sonia advised a fellow dispatcher that she was taking a break and went to make a fresh pot of coffee. While waiting for it to brew, Sonia laughed as she thought about Chief Bartolo's disdain for paperwork: she loved the man and although retirement was almost certainly on the horizon, she avoided thinking of the day he would step down. They had worked together for two decades; the day he left would be the day she would apply for a transfer to another agency. It was common knowledge Deputy Chief Kenneth O'Donnell, the only person on the force she did not get along with, *at all*, would become Chief. Taciturn, long past the age when he could retire with healthy pensions, including one from the state of New York, O'Donnell stayed on the job to the frustration of everyone *except* Robin Crane. Much to Sonia's surprise—her shock really—he'd invited Robin to lunch when she was first hired, something he had never done with anyone else, before or since. The two continued to eat lunch together once a week.

Despite protestations to the contrary, Sonia prayed that the Deputy Chief would retire and Doug Debayle would replace the Chief. Pretty much everyone, except O'Donnell, liked Doug, a seven-year veteran of the SBPD. After the Chief, Doug was Sonia's favorite—not only because of their shared Latino heritage but also because of his relentless teasing and flirting. Ken laughed whenever the topic of retirement came up, insisting that the only way he would leave the job was feet first. *Nobody* doubted that would be the case. In sotto voce, Sonia declared she would willingly help him along. Debayle told Sonia to forget it: he liked being a detective and disliked admin duty. He was happy with his life as it was.

"Here you go Chief," Sonia said, entering his office without knocking, her large silver and turquoise bracelets jangling. She set the steaming mug of black coffee on his desk, as well as a generous slice of warm apple pie.

"I made the calls—Robin Crane's on her way. The Park Service is sending someone up there. Doc will head out after she finishes up an autopsy." She turned to go.

"Thank you," he told his unfailingly cheerful assistant—short, a bit heavy herself, always on a diet of some sort, she nonetheless was driven to feed everyone else. "Sonia, you are without a doubt an absolute wonder of a cook! Take it from an Italian such as myself who loves food and wine."

"Gracias," she smiled at her boss. In front of her sat a man with his ancestor's olive skin, pleasing features that invariably conveyed a cheerful nature, heavy brows shading his large brown thick-lashed puppy dog eyes, a head of abundant wavy white hair, and a bushy gray mustache Sheila was always after him to shave. He was of average height and muscular, but with the beginning of a paunch and developing jowls he attributed to too much paperwork. Given the Chief's aversion to exercise, Doug attributed the extra pounds to Sonia's homemade pies and her meat, bean, and cheese empanadas. She assured him he would be next and the detective laughed heartily, agreeing that would probably be the case.

At one time, Sonia thought something was going on between Doug and Robin. That would have been fine with her—she wanted her boy to settle down, but nothing seemed to have worked out. She remembered Doug's response to the twenty-something woman when she had arrived late for her interview, blushing and apologetic. He had not tried to hide his interest and Sonia watched with some amusement as Robin shifted the strap of her purse from shoulder to shoulder while Doug made small talk. He had been reluctant to leave, but Sonia knew Doug had a lunch date with an aspiring actress and shooed him out with a surreptitious wink.

While Sonia chatted with the young woman sitting on the other side of her littered desk, it occurred to her Dougie and Ms. Crane would make a striking couple, though workplace gossip might present a problem—one incident, in particular, came to mind: the morning an angry girlfriend stormed into Doug's office, calling him a player and more. Much more. When she had started throwing things, all the while screaming at Doug, others came out to see what was going on.

O'Donnell had laughed on witnessing the chaotic scene and told Sonia not to interfere. "The woman has it right! The pretty boy is getting his just desserts," he had declared with obvious satisfaction and continued laughing for all he was worth as he returned to his office.

He is simply "a man who appreciates women," she'd called out to O'Donnell's retreating back. Sonia had thought Doug was misunderstood—he wasn't coming on to somebody else like the crazy woman was yelling about.

The morning after Robin's interview, Doug had appeared in Sonia's office, curious as to the outcome. He had laughed that some might hold her Baltimore accent against her, and explained to a confused Sonia that Californians are not always big fans of East Coasters. Given his time at Yale, he expected they shared much in common. After some prodding, he admitted that he definitely found her "sky blue doe-eyes" attractive; he loved the "wide-eyed innocence of them." The light spatter of freckles that ranged across ivory skin and fine flaxen hair barely clearing her ear lobes were the frosting on the cake.

Two weeks later, the department welcomed Robin Crane as the newest officer on the Santa Barbara Police force.

Doug Debayle, with his raven hair and dark brown eyes, had appealed to Robin the first time she met him. He was good looking and a sharp dresser who wore impeccably tailored clothes—a typical outfit consisting of a black leather jacket, black button-up shantung silk shirt, fitted designer jeans and, the only item that introduced color each day, a silk tie. Smart and witty, he had a great sense of humor, albeit one she soon learned tended toward the sardonic. Sonia thought the attraction seemed mutual.

CHAPTER 3

Cecilia Hernández:
August 2010

C ecilia Hernández woke up slightly hung over after a night out with a friend. Having overslept, the diminutive graduate student quickly threw on a black turtleneck sweater cinched at her slim waist with a wide leather belt, faded jeans, and scuffed black ankle boots. While walking across the parking lot, she put small pearl earrings in her pierced ears. The Volkswagen's dashboard clock said 9:27 a.m. The rearview mirror showed she needed lipstick and mascara.

Cecilia arrived on the USB campus with a few minutes to spare. She went to her favorite bench, shaded by a stately eucalyptus tree, to look over her schedule: After her 10 o'clock child development class was the anthropology seminar she'd registered for after reading the rave reviews about the professor; then, a 1:30 appointment with her advisor to discuss ideas for her research project and funding opportunities. Cecilia was relieved to note that after the meeting she would have time to grab a nap in the library until her dreaded advanced stats class.

First in her family to attend college, Cecilia had wanted to be successful for as long as she could remember. Her parents had entered the United States from Mexico as migrant laborers, and the family lived wherever the jobs took them, mainly in the Pacific Northwest: California, Washington, and Oregon. When she was in the fifth grade, they had settled in the Salinas Valley where her father had steady employment in a small vineyard and her mother cleaned houses. Cecilia and her brother made friends and attended local schools.

Cecilia was well aware that her parents' lives had never been easy. Now they were no longer young and still illegal; she figured they would be ineligible for social security even though her father paid taxes. Cecilia's long-term professional plan was to develop a non-profit for at-risk children. An education, she hoped, also would enable her to care for her parents in their old age, a need intensified by her brother's recent death from leukemia. Cecilia took a deep breath and, despite her headache, went on with her day.

CHAPTER 4

Mr. Hollywood:
October 2011, Day One

S oon after pulling onto Painted Cave Road, Robin turned on her siren and in less than a mile pulled in behind a snazzy bright red Porsche Boxter Spyder positioned on the shoulder that served as parking for the isolated tourist attraction. A honey of a car, the Porsche was real competition for her beloved Nissan Sentra. Just as quickly, she put car envy aside. It dawned on the detective that the caller had not listened, despite Sonia's request for him to leave the immediate area until law enforcement arrived. Worse, no Park Service vehicle was in evidence. She removed her seatbelt and made sure her gun was hot.

When Robin opened the door, a slender man she figured for mid-40s got out of the Porsche and with long confident strides headed in her direction. She quickly exited the cruiser, leaving it locked behind her. Of medium height, he had movie star good looks—longish brown hair giving him a cultivated, unkempt surfer appearance, intense hazel eyes, and a strong square jaw. This was Southern California and Robin had learned the hard way to be careful until she knew with whom she was dealing. The paparazzi vultures were extremely unpleasant when several cases had landed the SBPD in the tabloids. In addition to her concerns about the rich and famous, Robin was well aware of the meth labs on national park land, though social skills and sartorial splendor were not typically associated with those folks.

Dressed in what had to be clothes by a designer whose goal was to create a mien that promised women a good time, her witness had the overall appearance of someone who had come into the world well swaddled and had been cared for accordingly. As he approached, too close for professional *and* personal reasons, Robin picked up a whiff of Hugo Boss *Dark Blue*, her favorite men's fragrance. Coincidently, at the mall, a young man at the Macy's counter assured her, with an unexpectedly languorous wink, the scent promised pleasure and seduction … and, in this case delivered.

"Officer, I'm Barclay Stalts; I made the call to the Santa Barbara Police Department. I found the body." He extended a hand in better shape than hers, obviously having been recently tended to by a manicurist. Hers, in contrast, were lucky if they ever received attention.

"Sir, I need for you to return to your car. Please don't get me wrong, we appreciate your cooperation. I'm aware you've been waiting for a while and—"

"Merely trying to help," he said. Nevertheless, Mr. Stalts acquiesced, returning to his car and closing the door with a bit too much force for her taste.

Robin approached the open window on the driver's side and attempted a more conciliatory approach. Last thing she needed was to start the investigation with a complaint.

"Sir, we're grateful you waited until someone arrived. I am Detective Robin Crane of the Santa Barbara Police Department. Sir, your license and registration?"

"Sure thing Officer Crane. Sorry about the adolescent display of temper—I'm pretty stressed out—it was mildly disconcerting to see the young woman in such a horrible state," he said sarcastically, negating the apology. Then he took a deep breath and began again.

"I am sorry, I do want to help. My name is Barclay Stalts," he drawled with an inflection she and Ken characterized as southern California cool. He took his license out of an expensive-looking wallet and removed his registration from the black leather console.

He handed her both documents. "Here you go."

Robin's antennae went up: Sonia had given her a different name. The State of California had issued the license in the name of Stalts. The dispatcher had also referred to him as a tourist, but the man sitting in the car sure did not seem to be a vacationer.

"Thank you, Mr. Stalts." She jotted down the relevant information and returned his license, but held onto the registration.

"Are you passing through or staying in Santa Barbara?"

"Living at a friend's place in the Hope Ranch area," he said, referring to an upscale bedroom community in Santa Barbara. "My buddy and his wife are filming a documentary in Africa. Wait a minute … I'm pretty sure I have their address." He pulled out his wallet again and handed her a business card.

Robin again wondered why Sonia thought a tourist called in the body. On the front was printed, *Ana Maria Solarno, Documentary Filmmaker*; she wrote down Solarno's contact information before flipping over the stylish chocolate brown card. Stalts' friend had scrawled across the back, *Enjoy!* (*Ana says to wash the dishes!*) *James.*

"Thank you for your cooperation," she said, handing back the card. "Sir, can you tell me where you were when you thought you observed a body?"

"I was standing in front of my car—not where I'm now parked, but behind that sign," he said, pointing in the direction of an information sign about the Painted Cave. "She's maybe 25 yards straight down the hill. Directly across the street. Shrubs, large rocks, and leaves mostly conceal the poor girl—all you can see from up here is a leg. To be honest, without the telephoto, I wouldn't have even seen that. Officer, you want me to show you?" he said with an appealing smile any woman *over* thirty would know to avoid.

"I appreciate your cooperation, sir. I'll need additional information from you, but I'd appreciate your remaining in the car while I examine the scene. It won't take too long—the medical examiner is coming with another officer, and a Park Service ranger is on the way, so we should be able to get you on the road shortly."

Robin vacillated, wondering whether she should wait for someone else to arrive, but then decided the man was what he said he was—a witness—only to be feared for his attitude. More importantly, she needed to confirm she had a non-breather.

"Sure, just trying to help." His reply again dripped with sarcasm.

"Sir, I understand your frustration, but there are procedures to be followed. Won't take long and, as I said, others are on the way."

"Not a problem."

Robin was a little suspicious of his most recent attempt to cooperate, but he stayed put while she returned to her car to get a jacket.

CHAPTER 5

Cecilia Hernández:
October 2010

After a hectic week of exams, Cecilia and Linda finally managed to get together for lunch at the deli in the Student Union. Over turkey sandwiches and iced tea they caught up with each other's personal lives—pretty boring they finally concluded—and went on to the inevitable discussion of their courses. Linda griped about an advanced lit class she was taking. Cecilia countered her stats course sucked but she loved Plask's anthropology seminar.

"Yeah, I took his class a couple of years ago. He *was* great!" Linda said.

"He is! I've become totally interested in the indigenous populations of Nicaragua."

"Plask's baby—he must love that! What are you doing for the final project?"

"Well, I thought I'd do something on the Miskito culture, but he gave me grief for a too broad thesis."

"Sounds like the Prof."

"Well, I was, like, embarrassed. Anyway, I'm working on it. There's been more written about the Miskito than any of the other groups of Nicaraguan indigenous populations, so I should be okay. Most of it written, as you know, by our esteemed Dr. Plask. Linda, admit it—he is so smart *and* so hot!"

"True, my friend, but you'd better stick to the academic topic. Plask has got quite the rep."

"Yeah, well, I guess so," she said, sounding doubtful.

"You're not hearing me Cecilia. He has a serious reputation for coming on to his female students—pretty well-deserved as far as I can tell."

"But, then, he's *so* amazing."

Shortly after that exchange, the two women made plans to get together over the weekend. Cecilia then headed to the sixth floor of the USB library, which held the special collection she needed. Seated in a comfortable armchair situated in front of a sunny window, she continued reading for Plask's class, typing up notes on her MacBook. Tired, Cecilia checked her e-mail and then closed her laptop and went over to the coffee bar to order a latte from the barista.

Once the caffeine kicked in, Cecilia resumed her work. According to Plask and other anthropologists, 17th Century Miskito men had assisted the English, French, and Dutch pirates by crafting dugouts for transportation, serving as guides, and providing food. They rendered such services in return for iron tools, guns and ammunition, the acquisition of which eventually enabled them to establish an independent state. Cecilia also learned the Miskito captured runaway slaves who fled from Spanish mines and English plantations, which perhaps accounted for the diversity of language in the region.

After the outlawing of buccaneering in 1685, many of the pirates had settled down with the Miskito and their African slaves. As reported by an article published in the *American Journal of Physical*

Anthropology, the Miskito people considered themselves a protectorate of the United Kingdom and later the United States, with Nicaragua deemed an alien government. That information clarified for Cecilia not only why the Indians failed to support the leftists during the 1980s revolution, but also why they continued to revolt against the Nicaraguan government, a state of affairs apparently persisting until the Sandinistas allowed for their autonomy.

Cecilia found much of her reading interesting but ultimately decided to concentrate on the social issues, since she wanted the credit for Dr. Plask's course applied toward her degree in psychology. By midafternoon, she felt confident she had developed the topic sufficiently and left to meet with Dr. Benson, her academic advisor.

CHAPTER 6

Domestic In Isla Vista:
October 2011, Day One

D etective Doug Debayle arrived at the Pasado Street address in response to a neighbor's anonymous report of a home invasion, although it sounded like a domestic to him. Pasado is located in Isla Vista, one of Santa Barbara's outlying communities, where both the university and a community college are situated. A high number of calls come in from that immediate area.

When the dispatcher called out on the radio, Doug took it since no patrol unit was available and he was in the area. Hungry, he hoped the problem was nothing more than a simple misunderstanding. Once there, he knew he would not be eating anytime soon. Although he had arrived with siren and lights, the man on the porch continued yelling through the open front door. Doug heard him despite parking twenty-five yards down the street, protocol to avoid finding himself in the line of fire.

As he approached the house, a woman leaned out of an upstairs window, "*Señor*, my husband said he will chop me up and dump me into the ocean to feed to the sharks! The children are very scared! He can do it. Roberto hangs around with *very* bad people!"

Doug held his badge up in the air. "Señora, are you hurt?"

"No. We are hiding."

"We'll take care of things, but you need to stay inside."

"I won't leave this room until a policeman is with me." The window shut with a resounding bang and the shade came down. Meantime, Andy Tyler showed up and Doug returned to the sidewalk to discuss the situation. He explained the woman was not hurt but refused to come out without protection. Once he got a handle on the dude, he would bring him out and then return to check on the woman. They agreed Tyler would update Sonia and request a couple of patrol officers for crowd control. He would also stay back to minimize the possibility of further escalation and to keep an eye on the neighbors while Doug, fluent in Spanish, attempted to mediate the conflict.

With a plan in place, Doug walked up the porch stairs, hand resting on the grip of his gun, and introduced himself to a livid man, about five feet five, 120 pounds, wiry build, much of it muscle. He was wearing faded jeans and a washed-out Carlos Santana T-shirt. His black hair, slicked back with product, framed a broad face with angular features and lips pulled cruelly thin.

After Doug got the dude to tone down the racket, he did an exterior pat down. Assured the suspect was clean, he continued. "Señor, I need you to tell me what happened here and I can't get your side of the story if you don't calm down."

The husband kept yelling.

"¡Ya, tranquilízate¡ ¿Qué pasó hombre? Take a breath and explain what's going on."

Without a second's hesitation, as if Doug had not said anything, or wasn't anybody to worry about, at top volume, his voice layered with a heavy dose of arrogance, the angry man assured the detective: "No judge is going to tell me I can't go into *my* house! In this country,

I have rights! The *Law and Order* tells me I have fuckin' rights. *No fuckin' judge is going to tell me if I see my own children. My own blood!* My own DNA. No *puta* of a fuckin' woman is going to tell me what I can or cannot do. The Bible, the Constitution, says I am the man of my family. *God* says I make the decisions! Even if the woman is a bitch, she is *my* bitch, and cannot keep me from my children. I *never* went in the house. I did nothing wrong."

Doug was relieved when the man stopped talking long enough to take a breath. The detective read him his rights, figuring he might have to bring him in on a disorderly. It was always better to play it safe and he was unsure whether an assault had been committed. It was a shitty feeling and worse: there could be serious consequences when a prosecutor refused to take one of his cases to court or a judge threw out a bust for something over which he had had control. With a firm grasp on the angry man's elbow, Doug led him off the porch and away from the house.

"Señor, please calm down. What is your name? Your wife's? Let's talk together like men should—this yelling is not good for your children." Doug figured the guy must have consumed a few beers given his yeasty breath and loud arrogant behavior.

"Roberto Ortega Jr. Susana is my wife." The man's breathing quickened. "You are right—a father should not make his children scared."

"Sir, you been drinking?"

"No. It is the daytime."

"Mr. Ortega, do you work?"

"For six years I work at a taquería on Milpas. *I* take care of my children," he said proudly.

"The name of your boss?"

"Señor Castillo."

"Do you mind if I speak with Mr. Castillo?" Doug hoped the question would serve as a dash of cold water on the man's fury, although he knew the query might set him off again.

"You can't show I did wrong. I need my job. I have a family."

"Only to verify employment—I'll be careful not to cause you any problems Mr. Ortega. Nothing about what happened here—well, as long as there is no more trouble," he quickly added as an afterthought.

"Bueno. If this is your legal promise. I want my rights—I'm legal."

"Sir, I understand you are in this country legally. Where do you live?"

"A little place. Two blocks from my work."

"Thank you, sir. May I see your license?"

"I don't have my wallet."

"Your address?"

"State Street—433 East State Street. I live at the house with an amigo who also works at the taquería."

The name Castillo, in conjunction with a taquería, raised a red flag for Doug but nothing came immediately to mind. At that point, he felt reassured a weapon was not involved in the dispute and continued trying to talk Ortega down. After Doug figured he had gotten the gist of the story, at least from the assailant's perspective, he took hold of the man's elbow and walked over to where Andy stood.

"Hey buddy, I've got to see to the wife and kids. Ask Sonia if she can get Laura McCann out here. Keep Mr. Ortega with you. No cuffs needed," Doug said. Without sufficient cause, he would have a lawsuit on his hands if they cuffed or put the husband in the patrol car.

Ortega leaned against the vehicle; he remained quiet, heavy lids drooping. Meantime, two patrol officers had arrived and were keeping an eye on the onlookers. The neighbors apparently decided it was safe and had gathered in small knots, chatting among themselves.

Doug entered the house. Contrary to Ortega's protestations, he had not remained on the porch: chairs overturned, dishes smashed, and the dining room table pushed against the wall indicated otherwise. A large mirror lay shattered in the entryway. Scattered in the midst of the detritus were children's toys and books. With a sharp pang, Doug realized he should have turned Ortega over to Andy immediately and checked on the wife and kids, regardless of the woman's assurances.

After talking with the dispatcher, Andy radioed Doug. "Hey, man. Sonia knows what's up. Laura is on her way. Mr. Ortega is under control. Everything cool in there?"

"No problem, dude."

"Keep the radio on."

"Roger."

After surveying the damage on the first floor, Doug started up the stairs, well aware that domestic calls are not only dangerous for the family but put anyone who attempts to intervene at risk, in part because emotions run high and it's not always clear from where or whom the danger is coming. The victim, usually a woman, could be armed and acting out of fear. Alternatively, the husband has an armed buddy in the house holding the wife and children hostage.

"Señora," he hollered up the stairway. "I want to make sure you're not hurt." No answer. Now, he was sure he had made a mistake in not entering the house first thing. He broke into a sweat.

"Your husband's not in the house," he called out again. "Susana, he's with another officer and can't hurt anyone now." *Fucking shit*, he added under his breath.

Doug unsnapped the retention, removed the gun from his holster, and held it in a firing position as he slowly moved up the inside of the stairwell, ready for whatever might come at him. Susana Ortega must know he had entered the house—she expected him after all. A child cried—the real losers in domestic violence situations. Doug prayed nobody was hurt, only frightened, which was bad enough. He hoped the baby's cries had drowned out his voice and not something worse. As he second-guessed his decision not to call for a bus, Doug made a mental note to talk to the Chief about getting the SBPD involved in a domestic violence prevention program.

He approached the bedroom, rapped lightly on the door and quickly moved to the side. "Ma'am, please open the door. I'm the detective who spoke with you from outside. Everything is under control. Your husband is with another detective." For good measure, he tried Spanish. "¿Por favor, podría usted abrir la puerta? Soy un oficial de policía y tenemos todo bajo control."

When the door cracked open, he repeated she was safe, but the crying woman asked to see Doug's badge. It took a good five minutes to convince her to let him into the room. Finally, he heard the scraping movement of a heavy piece of furniture. Once inside, he found himself face-to-face with a frail red-haired woman in her mid-thirties; flushed, she appeared on the verge of hysteria.

"Señora, are you physically hurt? Did your husband hit you? Threaten you with a weapon?"

"No, but he *would* have, if I had not gone to hide." Her voice bordered on shrill.

Doug took stock of his surroundings. Susana Ortega had barricaded herself and her three children into what appeared to be a baby's bedroom with its crib, rocker, and a wallpaper pattern resplendent with clouds and sheep naïve to what now faced this child newly born into the world. Despite the earlier cries, there were no children in sight. He felt as if he'd been punched in the gut, until he heard the muffled sobbing coming from a closet on the other side of the room.

"I want to check on your children," Doug said quietly, gently sitting the woman down on the bed. He reached the closet in a few quick strides, removed a barricade comprising the crib and rocker, and opened the door. In the furthest reaches of the small space, a little boy crouched in the corner. In his arms, he held a baby wrapped in a blanket. Both crying. In reality, the baby was screaming, but a pillow over the baby's face muffled the sound.

"Hijo, you're safe," Doug said, lifting up the baby and extending a hand to the boy, the pillow falling to the side. "Vaya a dónde su mamá." The boy flew into Susana's waiting arms.

"Ma'am, you have three children?" Doug asked, juggling the crying baby.

She shook her head affirmatively but failed to move.

"Your little girl?" With her free hand, the woman silently pointed to a plastic clothes hamper on its side and partially under the bed.

He handed her the baby, gently pulled out the container and took off the cover. Inside, a tiny girl with her mother's wild strawberry red hair. Half asleep, she sucked on a fluffy white blanket while looking at Doug.

Susana gently lifted the boy off her lap, placed the baby on the bed, and removed the toddler from her hiding place. Doug glanced over at the boy who had become scarily silent. He stared vacantly at nothing and nobody, seeing God only knows what. The child had the straight black hair, wide dark eyes, and sharp bone structure of his angry father. A conference Doug once attended on cross-generational abuse flashed across his mind and he cringed. He radioed Andy and gave him an update.

"Laura McCann's out here."

"Great. Andy, you'd better have her wait until I clear the rest of the house."

>>　　<<　　>>　　<<

After doing a walk-through of the second floor, Doug called Andy. "Hey, buddy, Laura can come in now. We're on the second floor. I'd like for her to take the children to the kitchen while I talk with their mother."

Doug turned around. "Señora, is that alright with you? Laura McCann is our community liaison. I am sure your children would like something to eat and drink. She always has juice boxes and cookies with her."

"Yes, that is better. Gracias."

A few minutes later, Laura entered the room with some trepidation but the little girl, white blanket clutched tightly, scrambled into the psychologist's open arms. Once she settled the wide-eyed child on a hip, Laura looked over at Doug and gave him a small smile before leaning over to pick up the baby. The boy began to cry. His mother wrapped the baby more tightly before settling her into Laura's other arm and then knelt down to hug her little boy, assuring him his sisters would be happier if he went downstairs with the nice lady and helped her with the baby. Susana kissed the obviously traumatized little boy and cautioned him to hold tightly onto the lady's skirt while going down the stairs.

Doug thought about that long-ago lecture in an undergraduate psychology class: "Nature or nurture … does biology or environment account for relational violence?" he'd naively asked.

The professor had replied, "Children learn from their parents how to respond to stress. If one parent hits another to make a point, the probability is high that their child, when faced with relational problems as an adult, will hit his or her partner if frustrated."

Doug was willing to bet he was right.

"Thanks Laura. You're an important part of the team."

"I'm glad you called. I'll talk with you later."

After Laura left the room with the children, Doug directed the still shaken woman to the rocker and gently asked her to tell him what happened.

Susana Ortega told a story not much different from the story her estranged husband had recounted, although it was the distinctions between their two accounts that mattered most. She claimed Roberto came inside uninvited, threatened her, and tore up the house.

"Susana, have either of you filed for divorce?"

"I did. But, but, I—" she stumbled over her words and began to cry.

"I can be more helpful if I know as much as possible," he said, suspecting Susana was leaving out important information.

She picked at her thumbnail. "I have a boyfriend," she mumbled, looking down at the floor.

"Susana, that's your right. Would you mind telling me his name?"

"Joel Stein. He works with my cousin."

"Where does Mr. Stein live?"

"Los Angeles."

"He works in L.A.?"

"Yes, at Universal Studios. Joel is an assistant to a screenwriter who stays in Santa Barbara—the man's friends are out of the country.

Before, Joel could come here only once or twice a month. I couldn't go to Los Angeles because of the children."

"Is your husband aware of your relationship with Mr. Stein?"

"I did not think so." There was a long pause before she continued.

"How would he be? Joel never comes here. When the children are with me, he meets us at the zoo, the park—bumps into us. If they are with their father, we stay outside of town."

Doug didn't have to give the scenario much thought. Possessive and angry, Ortega seemed the type to follow his wife. His little boy may have said something about the nice man at the zoo, the man at the park, the man who bought them ice cream or a toy, any number of good times and good things. The husband would have checked out the situation, eventually catching Susana with her boyfriend.

Relieved to see that the woman was calming down—her face less rosy, fewer tremors, Doug asked, "Susana, why don't you tell me what happened today? From the beginning."

She sighed, closed her eyes and bowed her head. "The fight started when Roberto came to the house and said he owned me. If I valued my life, I had better think twice about having his children around another man. I said there was no other man but he got angrier and angrier and called me a liar."

"Let's back up a little Susana, what was your husband doing here?" When Sonia initially spoke with Doug, she had said Susana was flagged in the system for previously having been issued a protective order. The protective order had been in place to avoid just this type of confrontation and he wanted to know how events played out in such a volatile manner.

"Roberto came because I said he could spend time with the children at the park and then take them for pizza. Just the older children. Officer, I am afraid to let him take the baby—I think he does not believe she is his."

That was a new piece of information. Not a concern Roberto brought up, although hardly a rare argument made by a disgruntled spouse facing a child support order. "Wasn't a protective order issued against your husband last year?" Doug asked, making a concerted effort to keep the frustration out of his voice. The courts and the police could not do much without the cooperation of the abuse victim. He wondered why Susana had not petitioned for a new one. They then could have placed Ortega under arrest for violating the protective order.

"Yes. Even when we had the order, my husband demands entrance and I am afraid. I have small children—the baby is crying—I want to keep the peace."

"Susana, you don't need to tell me, but it would be helpful to know whether Roberto is the biological father of your three children?"

"Yes. Each time I am pregnant, I hope things will be better. I have known Roberto for many years and he is difficult. Life is bad after the birth of my baby. Then, he started accusing me of being with another man. He left us."

"Señora, have you separated before? You probably feel like I'm invading your privacy but the more I know, the more help I can be."

"Others ask the same question only because they are curious. Every time I leave, Roberto finds me and makes threats. I would like to stay away, but life is difficult when I am on my own. He has the car even though he can walk to the taquería."

"Susana, I appreciate your honesty; I'm sorry things have been so tough. Should we stop?"

"No, it's okay." she replied, with a definitive shake of her head.

"What happened when Roberto came over to pick up the children?"

"I asked him to leave and said I would bring them to the park. I closed the door. Señor, I thought Roberto went away, but after only a few minutes, he knocked on the door. I asked him to wait outside while I got the children's sweaters. I did not lock the door because it makes him more angry. A few minutes later Roberto came into the house and began screaming about 'the boyfriend.' I told him to leave or I would call the police—he would go to jail." At this point in her story, Susana began crying again. "He became very, very angry ... even for him."

Doug made a note to talk with Stein. "Did you tell Roberto about your boyfriend?"

"No—I am afraid he will kill Joel. My husband is a very possessive man. I keep saying I have no boyfriend and that Roberto is crazy, doing drugs, or drinking too much, but he maybe followed me and found out. When he started throwing the toys and chairs, the children began crying. I was frightened he would hit me and demanded he go away. Roberto refused to go without the children, but I would not let him take them. On *Nancy Grace*, I see what fathers do to their children to get back at their woman."

"Nancy Grace?"

"On the television."

Doug figured he had better check out *Nancy Grace*.

"Not letting the children go was absolutely the right thing to do."

Susana continued crying, her shaking again intensifying. Yet Doug persisted, aware of the fragility of memory. "Señora, can you keep going?"

"I am okay." She blew her nose and put the tissue in her pocket. Doug got up and went into the bathroom. When he returned, he handed her a glass of water and she took a couple of sips before continuing.

"My husband is very angry. He screams at me I am in *his* house and God is *his* witness, he will not go anywhere. He scares me. I told him to sit at the table while I got the children ready. Roberto let me go upstairs, but maybe he heard me moving furniture because he went crazy throwing things. He screamed as he came up the stairs, the children cried. I hung a chair off the knob to hold it closed, and then finished pushing the dresser and bed in front of the door. He started yelling he would kill me; I hid the children and prayed to God to have somebody call 911."

"Susana, you are not to blame. We'll do our best to keep him away from you and the children, but please know you will be safer if you apply for a new order. Do you want to press charges against Roberto?"

"No. No. I can not do that."

She looked terrified. Doug decided to drop the question of charges for the moment. It would be worth interviewing the husband and see where he could get with him. The detective had enough experience with domestics to know she might not survive a next time. Her children might not survive. However, he decided to leave that message to Laura who would more effectively deliver it. Maybe *Nancy Grace* could help.

"Susana, you can join your children. Laura works with victims and she is able to help you figure out what to do next. She can make an appointment for counseling—that is, if you wish to talk with someone. Laura will also go to court with you to request a protective order and ask that it include a stipulation that safe arrangements can be made for when your husband picks up the children." He waited patiently through the next minute or two of silence.

Susana wiped away her tears. "I need help or Roberto will kill me one day. He *will* feed me to the sharks." Despite the grisly warning, she gave Doug her first real smile. "Thank you."

"No thanks are necessary." His radio buzzed. "Excuse me. Susana, you can go downstairs to be with your children. They are in the kitchen with Laura. Please stay inside until we leave with your husband. I need to talk with the other detective before that happens."

"What's up man?" Doug asked Andy. "Why's Ortega in the car?"

"Insisted. Says he's tired—appears repentant. Knows he's detained for security reasons, not arrested. For some unknown reason, he agreed to be cooperative. Recorded the conversation. Between you and me, probably too much alcohol. Oh, and Sonia wants to talk to you."

"Thanks man. Won't question my blessings. Things are pretty much wrapped up inside. We need to get him out of here though—take him back for an interview."

As soon as Doug unlocked the door of his own car, Sonia raised him on the radio. He once again wondered if she had him on webcam.

"Dougie, the Jefe asked whether you are almost finished up in Isla Vista."

"Hola, Sonia, mi amor! What happened to a civilized greeting? Ready to party?"

"Ay Douglas, such a flirt—bet you say the same thing to all the mujeres! Bueno, a man called about a dead female. He is at the Painted Cave and saw a body down a hill. The Jefe sent Robin. The M.E. is leaving as soon as she finishes her autopsy. Park Service should already be there to secure the scene. He wants you to head out as soon as you are finished. Dougie, you know where I'm talking about, don't you, mi amor?"

"I've passed by Painted Cave road when going to Lake Cachuma but have never been up there. Sonia, I assume I'm the primary. Despite having to catch up," Doug hastily added the caveat.

"Umm, Dougie, the Jefe said to tell you Robin's the primary on this one."

He hesitated for a few seconds too long and Sonia guessed she had caught Doug off guard. She knew for sure when he let slip a vigorous, "Damn!"

"Okay, Sonia, but first I've got to bring this piece of shit guy in. He's agreed to cooperate. Want to send Gordito instead? He has his own ride. Laura's with the wife and children, but someone needs to put the fear of God into Ortega. He is still living in the dark ages—dude believes a home is a man's castle to do with as he wishes. What this piece of shit wishes to do is terrify his family: feed the little woman to the sharks. Charmer, I tell you. Sonia, these women gotta learn not to give an inch."

"You're right but it's not so easy. No, mi hijo, the Jefe wants Gordito to bring the guy back to the house. You are to join Robin at the Cave. I'll send O'Donnell, if more help is needed."

No love lost there, Doug thought, *O'Donnell did not warrant a nickname.* Sonia's pet name for Andy Tyler was Gordito, or little fat one. When the Chief had tried to put a stop to her use of pet names, she explained that in Latin America people typically refer to those they care about using obvious physical characteristics. She continued to use descriptors such as flakita (little skinny one), gordito (little fat one), negrito (little black one), chinito (little chinese one), and machito (little white one) despite being told she was in California, not Latin America. He could only laugh.

"Ken O'Donnell, my favorite person! What did I do to deserve such an outstanding day? Well, I had better tie this thing up. Lunch a no go?" he asked, cognizant of what her answer would be. Sonia had a soft spot for Doug, but put him up against Bartolo and he lost every time.

"Forget the stomach, mi amor." She never disappointed.

"I guess that'll work. I'll let Tyler know what's up. Por favor, do *not* bother sending O'Donnell up to the Pass. If we need more help, tell him to take care of Ortega. I'm tired of the hump anyhow. Send Gordito out instead."

"If Gordito isn't available, the Jefe would probably be happy for any excuse to get out of paperwork. Be safe mi'jo. Don't give Robin grief about the primary thing."

"Who, me? Later, mamacita!"

"Hey man, what are we doing with this prize?" Tyler called out. "I'm famished."

Finished, Doug went to talk to his buddy. "I'm with you there—headed to this fiesta before I got some grub. Robin tells me to stockpile power bars but they sure as hell don't work for me!"

Of medium build, stocky going to pudgy, Doc and Doug kept telling Andy to exercise and to keep an eye on his food and liquor intake or he would find himself in the ICU. His friend's brashness and irreverence were characteristics that worked for Doug—they had gone to school together since the fourth grade and enjoyed each other, both on and off the job. O'Donnell was another story. Him, Doug did not trust. It was a two-way street.

"Bad news, Tyler. No food. The Chief says for you to bring in Mr. Ortega. You know the drill. I've got to meet up with Robin at the Pass—report of a female body."

"Damn! Watch yourself pal." Gordito returned to his car none too pleased. It would not be a pleasant ride for the mutt!

Doug called out, "Thanks. I'll send my notes to Sonia before I take off."

He typed up his observations on the laptop, making it clear this was a domestic, *not* a home invasion. The Chief insisted on categorizing domestics and home invasions as the same, but in Doug's mind, there was a world of difference between the two. Living day after day with a partner whom you love, whom you should be able to trust but who, instead, threatens your well-being, your very life, has to be a unique fear. Unfortunately, any effort to convince Bartolo of this argument went down in flames.

Doug was much too familiar with the data showing women are much more likely to be killed when they try to leave their abuser than if they stay. Unfortunately, that was usually when the detectives from the criminal investigation unit were called in. He and Bartolo generally got along well, but when it came to this issue, they'd had some vociferous arguments. Laura suggested it might be a generational thing, which he guessed made sense. Susana Ortega had tried to leave her husband, more than once, and his threats had probably escalated accordingly. Doug noted it was incumbent on the SBPD to keep Laura involved and to track the case, and advised Sonia that Gordito would bring Ortega in, signed off, copied the document to the patrol unit, and hit *send*.

He took off in the direction of 101, relieved at the light traffic. A glance at the gas gauge showed almost a full tank. He could not figure out lunch or, for that matter, could not figure out how he had lost his primary status—the power shift put him and Robin on distinctly different footing. That, he knew, would be something else to work out.

CHAPTER 7

Body At Painted Cave:
Day One

Although sunny, it quickly cools down in the mountains after midday; the breeze would make it almost chilly. Robin put on her Blauer jacket and surveyed the immediate vicinity. The shoulder of the road where she had parked would hold three, perhaps four cars if not too big, but nothing as big as the RVs that once roamed California like the dinosaurs of old. That all changed with the skyrocketing gas prices; though on second thought, they probably would have avoided the narrow twisting road all together. More recently, bicyclists and groups of motorcyclists favored the hills.

Relieved that the witness had remained in his car, Robin went to examine the area where he had spotted the body. On the other side of the narrow road, there was a sharp drop-off into a ravine; brush and scrub oak grew erratically along the top, and thicker toward the bottom. The creek bed was dry. When she tried to spot the body, Robin was unsure of what she was looking at and returned to her vehicle to get her evidence bag. Organized, she locked up and returned to the overlook.

Using her beloved Nikon 7 x 42 EDG binoculars, Robin made out what seemed to be a blue-jean clothed leg bent at an unnatural angle—a pink and grey sneaker half on and half off of the foot. Robin found it difficult to believe someone had carried a body down the embankment while managing to stay upright and without leaving slide marks. There had been no rain to wash them away. She reminded herself again that there was no evidence suggesting a murder rather than a hiking accident. After all, Robin spent plenty of time in the area and was well aware of the human, animal, and environmental threats in the mountains. On one occasion, she'd left her water and phone behind and then proceeded to get lost—it wasn't until sunset, dehydrated, dizzy and nauseous, she'd found her way back to the car, grateful Sean hadn't wanted to go hiking. With that self-cautionary note, Robin reverted to the murder theory. If carrying her down the hill was too difficult, maybe the killer rolled the body down the embankment before climbing down to hide it, though that seemed unlikely given the trees, shrubs, and the numerous boulders in the area. Anyhow, wind, if not Mr. Hollywood, may have removed evidence of disturbance to the hillside. Still, if she was dealing with a murder victim, Robin wondered why the killer disposed of her at a tourist stop. Leaving the victim in a public area suggested a lack of planning and a crime of passion. Although, she reflected, the killer might have gotten away with the crime if the witness had not observed the body before scavengers efficiently disposed of it.

Stalts' presence at the scene was problematic—though to be fair, she knew that if the victim was alive and he hadn't gone down to check, the outcome would have been worse. Despite being concerned about minimizing further disruption of the scene, Robin began the climb down to the body. Getting down the hillside was a slow go— small rocks and soil showered down at every step, causing her to grab periodically at scrub brush to stay upright or balance against a boulder, all the while trying to avoid the abundant poison oak. Once she reached the victim, and after pulling on a pair of the blue surgical gloves the M.E. insisted they use, Robin carefully pulled back a handful of prickly branches to reveal a young woman she could only imagine had been beautiful before death. Scavengers had taken their tragic toll. The amount of fluid emanating from her nose, eyes, and mouth suggested the girl had died within the last few days. *If*, she had been murdered, Robin believed in Doc's ability to obtain justice for the dead woman. She smeared Ben Gay under her nose and put on a surgical mask.

The female lying on a bed of rocks and dirt was small as a child. The short layers of her now dusty black hair enhanced the delicate bone structure of her face. A tiny pearl rested in an exposed ear. A brutal slash across her high-boned cheek betrayed a visible eye in peaceful repose. Blood had trickled down her cheek and crusted, forming a pathway of tears. Twisted unnaturally, her nose appeared broken. Only one leg and arm were visible.

A cold gust of wind caused Robin to shudder—a precursor of what she knew was to come. Those who loved the young woman would suffer terribly. That is, if they identified her—the detective immediately corrected herself—*when* they identified her. DNA made a cold case outcome less likely than ever, particularly with the advent of CODIS, the Combined DNA Index System funded through the FBI that compares and exchanges DNA profiles. The Chief insisted all samples be processed in a reasonable period, and the results be entered promptly into SBPD database. He was determined to close the unit's two unsolved cases and not acquire any new ones.

Robin stepped back and scanned the area for human footprints, but found only one set, which she assumed belonged to the witness. She observed plenty of animal tracks, yet nothing indicating the dead girl had done anything other than drop from the sky. Robin drew a diagram of the immediate area and made notes. She then removed her camera from the case and took photographs, attempting to disturb the scene as little as possible.

Dried blood matted much of the dead woman's hair. Robin hunched down to take a closer look and saw a nasty wound in the temporal region of the girl's head. Although the victim had probably not been in the ravine for more than two or three days, scavengers had been at her and the exposed part of her neck appeared chewed on. An analysis of the insects at work on her neck, the gaping cheek wound, and the seepage from facial orifices would be helpful in determining how long she had been dead. Robin searched but found no blood on the rocks.

She removed her gloves, put them in a baggie on which she noted the location, and then dropped it into the storage section of her evidence bag. She did a last visual inspection, knowing she would get hell from Doctor Genoa Taylor if she did much more. The M.E. did not suffer fools *at all*. As Robin looked around, it occurred to her getting Doc to the scene would be a problem; 61 years-old, extraordinarily intelligent, cranky, she was notoriously out of shape.

Concerned about any further degradation of the scene given the presence of at least two people and scavengers, Robin pulled on fresh gloves and looped the yellow crime scene tape around the surrounding brush, sapling trees, and several boulders, until she covered a 20' x 15' area. If the crime had been committed in the spur of the moment, she anticipated the perp had made a mistake of some sort. After removing her gloves, Robin slowly worked her way back up to the road several yards north; about half way up, she spotted a silver lipstick tube partially covered with dirt. She re-gloved and picked it up—the label on the bottom identified the lipstick as Revlon Blush Glitter. Relieved to find something sure to have DNA and a fingerprint, she bagged the item along with the surrounding dirt, sealed it shut, and noted the date, a description, location, and case ID on the label. She pushed an evidence flag into the ground.

Robin returned to the road and dusted off her pants. Before she had even caught her breath, Stalts was out of his car, a look of genuine concern having replaced his earlier heartthrob smile.

"Officer, tell me I wasn't wrong, maybe I somehow could have gotten her medical help. I hope I didn't jeopardize your case but I had to do *something*!"

"Mr. Stalts, no need to worry," the detective said a little more sympathetically this time. "Sadly, the woman is dead. As much as we try to avoid disrupting a crime scene before the M.E. arrives, you did the right thing. After all, you could just as well have saved her life. I'm afraid too many people would have looked the other away."

"That's a bit cynical on your part, don't you think?"

So much for the sympathetic approach, Robin thought.

"I don't believe I'm all that different from most people," he said.

She failed to reply and he threw her a bone. "Well, I imagine cynicism is unavoidable in your line of work. What a horrible thing someone did to such a beautiful girl."

Robin found herself caught up by the possibility she was becoming cynical. Yet, she thought, the guy need not be so condescending. After all, somebody has to do the job and there are bound to be costs if done well. It appeared Mr. Hollywood did not know much about paying a price for *anything* but his clothes and manicurist. With that thought, Robin reined herself in, realizing now was not the time to get snarky or to carry on a discussion of the personal price paid by law enforcement professionals.

The detective modulated her voice, needing for Stalts, who was definitely a person of interest, not to lawyer up. "Mr. Stalts, if you don't mind, I'd like to get a formal statement from you. Be assured that you can come to the Santa Barbara Police Department tomorrow to make any changes."

"Officer, call me Barclay. Better, my friends call me Bark. I'll do anything to help get the person or persons who killed that poor girl. What time would you like me to be the station?"

"Late morning is best, but I realize the day's been stressful for you, so come at your convenience, although sooner is better than later as memory quickly degrades. Here's a card with my phone number and the address."

Despite her suspicions regarding such a good looking, suave, and wealthy man who just happened to spot an attractive young woman hidden by brush and rocks, some 30 yards down an embankment, in an isolated area, her gut told her Barclay Stalts had not committed the murder. Her head knew better, however; his DNA was at the crime scene *because* he had purportedly gone down to find out whether the victim was alive. She had long since learned to be wary of suspects with neat answers. She had acquired her most important lessons from her disastrous relationship with her son's father. Stewart was inevitably convinced he knew it all, but as she had learned the hard way, he was usually talking pure bullshit.

"Not a problem. One o'clock?" Stalts answered, interrupting her reverie.

"That's fine. Mr. Stalts, why don't you tell me what happened: How you came to be here? How you happened to see the victim? Did you see anything suspicious? Either before you left or when you returned. Anybody suspicious? You've told me some of this, but I'm writing it down this time."

"Detective, truly, I'm glad that I can be of help."

"Sir, by any chance do you have another pair of shoes with you, so I can take the ones you are wearing to match prints? To rule you out." She'd ask for a DNA sample when he came in to sign his statement.

Surprised, he slowly kneaded his right shoulder with his left hand but finally, without a word, returned to his car and popped the trunk. The quiet was striking: only two bicyclists had passed by. Robin was beginning to get nervous—it was the first time she had worked a crime scene alone, never mind a possible murder. She couldn't understand where the ranger was, so decided to touch base with Sonia while Stalts changed shoes.

"Sir, I'm going to update our dispatcher. It'll only take me a minute or two." Robin returned to her car and put the camera and evidence she had collected in a locked container installed in the trunk, but kept the bag and binoculars with her. She pressed the call button on her radio. It crackled to life and Sonia's voice came over the line.

"Santa Barbara Police Department, Criminal Investigation Unit, Sonia Rodriguez speaking. May I help you?"

"Sonia, Crane calling. Can you hear me?"

"You're breaking up but mostly I can. Por favor, talk slowly."

"I'm at the Painted Cave. I wanted to confirm a young female who has been dead a day, perhaps two or three. The M.E. and Fred have not arrived. Nobody from Park Service. I know you told the witness to leave the scene, but let the Chief know he was here when I arrived. I'm not sure what that's all about—maybe simply tired of driving. Anyhow, the caller's name is Barclay Stalts," said Robin, spelling out the name. "Mr. Stalts is staying at the home of James and Ana Solarno in Hope Ranch. She's a filmmaker. By the way, his Porsche is not a rental—please run the plate—CA32156Z." She proceeded to provide the dispatcher with the relevant information from his driver's license and registration.

"Gracias Robin, I put the information into the computer and made all of the corrections. Lo siento, I told the Chief it was difficult understanding the caller. Be careful mi'jita! I'll check on the status of the others and run the plate."

"Thanks. Call me on my cell—that line will be clearer." Relieved by the contact, she returned to the Porsche.

Robin took the proffered shoes, bagged them and quickly returned to her car and put them in the trunk.

"Sorry about the delay, Mr. Stalts, let's continue."

"Where do I start? I live up north, but have extended business in Los Angeles, *not* a town where I like spending a lot of time. Jim—his wife is the documentary filmmaker—well, anyway, he called one day and said he and Ana planned to be out of the country for two months and invited me to stay at their house."

"The address on the business card?"

"Yes, that's it. They're in South Africa. Last Wednesday, our production closed down for the rest of the week and I missed being in my own home. So off I went!"

"What kind of work do you do?" Robin enquired, trying to stick to the professional demeanor her job demanded, which meant not letting a pretty face bowl her over.

"I'm a screenwriter, but as I said, L.A. isn't my thing and I've been going back and forth as we work on a project that is underway despite an incomplete script. Unbelievable! Don't get me wrong, I like your fair city, but I'll be glad to return to the Bay area. The drive is wearing me out. Meantime, my assistant has a girlfriend in Santa Barbara, so the arrangement works out for both of us."

"Is your driver's license out-of-date? It's not a San Francisco address."

"That's correct. I mean, my license is correct—I have a terrific place in Mill Valley, north of the city. Anyhow, I guess my personal living arrangements are beside the point. You're probably wondering what I am doing here, finding a body down a ravine and nobody else around. I'm a screenwriter after all—unquestionably, I'd be suspicious."

"You're right."

He looked at Robin curiously. "Well, as I've explained, I went home for a few days to check on things. On my way back to Santa Barbara, I got tired of driving—a bit of a tight fit. Mind you, I'm not complaining, I enjoy tooling around in the Porsche. Anyhow, about the time I was getting an itch, I saw the sign for Painted Cave Road, turned around, and headed up here. I was intrigued by the notion of a cave somebody painted out in the middle of nowhere. When I got here, I pulled off the road and went up the hillside to see the cave." He paused and took a deep breath before continuing.

"After I called 911, the operator told me not to come back until you arrived. Actually, the operator took my information and then passed me along to another. That woman, Sonia, requested that I leave. I wasn't up for driving back and forth over the Pass or into Santa Barbara, so I returned; it wasn't even ten minutes before you showed up. Sorry, I'm not good at following instructions, but I swear I didn't hurt that girl."

"I understand, sir, but you weren't safe if a killer remained in the area."

"Oh shit! I didn't even think about that possibility—only afraid I'd be a suspect."

"That's okay. We're grateful you made the call. Sir, was anyone else here when you first arrived?"

"I'd be more comfortable if you'd call me Bark rather than 'Sir' and 'Mr. Stalts.' You needn't be so formal. Anyhow, no one was around when I parked *or* when I came back from looking at the cave. For that matter, nobody stopped here after I returned from aimlessly driving around. Well, at least that I was aware of. I wasn't even worrying about the killer—in retrospect, pretty stupid. I guess I should've listened to the 911 operator."

"Well, it turned out to be okay but you're right, not such a wise decision."

"I expected more traffic in the area. In any case, as I said, when I parked the first time I followed the pathway up to the barrier they've constructed in front of the cave. Unfortunately, you can't go inside—always has to be someone to spoil things for everyone else. I spent about ten minutes on that side of the road. I was surprised at the sophistication of the pictographs. Pretty cool—I took some pictures. It was dark, so we'll see."

Robin chuckled to herself at hearing the word 'pictograph,' figuring he would also know what petroglyph meant without the need for Wikipedia. Good looking *and* smart. The first time Robin visited the cave, the earnest young ranger explained the experts believed Shamans created the rock art during vision quests, generally in the form of pictographs but sometimes petroglyphs. Too embarrassed to tell the kid she didn't know the difference between a pictograph and a petroglyph, Robin had fired up her laptop the minute she returned home. A thankfully nonjudgmental Wiki informed her that pictographs were rock paintings. Petroglyphs were carvings in stone surfaces.

Getting back on track, she continued. "It would be great if we can examine your pictures, as we may be able to discover something helpful for the case."

"Sure, give me a minute and I'll remove the memory card from the camera."

"I appreciate the offer; however, if you don't mind, I'd like to take the camera with me; the tech will process the card—chain of evidence and all. You should be able to pick it up tomorrow."

"Not a problem—I get it. Man, just like television—grist for the mill." He leaned into the car through the open window and pulled out his camera. She took it with gloved hands and placed it in the evidence bag hanging off her shoulder.

"Thank you. Bark, would you mind if I examine your car, including the trunk?"

"Not a problem."

Other than several empty coffee containers and an athletic bag, nothing connected him to the dead woman. He opened the bag without being asked.

"Thanks for your help." She looked through the bag and returned it.

"Like I said, not a problem. It's in my best interest, I'm sure."

An eagle swooped low over the crime scene and let out an ungodly screech, which Robin found strange. Raptors usually go after live prey and she thought it unlikely that anything alive remained in the area with all the commotion. They both watched the handsome creature repeat the maneuver before settling onto a stark branch of a distant tree.

"Stunning birds, aren't they? Particularly in flight. I'll bet he has the answers. Officer, the cave was intriguing, but I was tired. Your question about seeing the young woman … it's beautiful up here. Great light, so I used my telephoto lens to take pictures of the ravine. That's when I saw what I thought was a human leg and called 911."

CHAPTER 8

Cecilia Hernández:
April 2011

By the end of the fall semester, Cecilia had a full-blown crush on her anthropology professor, which Linda laughingly assured her was worthy of an undergrad. Despite the teasing, maybe because of the teasing, Cecilia signed up for a second course with Dr. Plask when planning her spring schedule. Midway through the semester, he offered her a summer research fellowship.

No longer laughing, Linda suggested she might be getting in over her head, but Cecilia stood her ground, contending nothing was wrong with enjoying the attentions of "a brilliant, handsome, and sophisticated man." Her friend conceded the tall, well-built professor, with his strong patrician features *was* hot but, once again, made a case about his age—figuring him for his early sixties.

Thoroughly annoyed, Cecilia retorted he was younger and that it didn't matter anyway because he took care of himself.

Concerned for her friend, Linda tried a different tact: she argued that rumors abounded regarding Plask and his affairs with students, one that involved an ugly divorce.

Cecilia irritably snapped that the campus was awash in gossip, most of it untrue. She protested that he'd never behaved inappropriately with her.

>>   <<   >>   <<

Cecilia chewed on the inside of her lower lip as she listened to her professor discuss the fellowship. Given she was barely five feet tall and weighed less than 100 pounds, the nervous habit made her look considerably younger than her 24 years. The only makeup she wore was a bit of peach-colored lipstick with the barest hint of glitter, and mascara that emphasized long dark lashes framing large chocolate brown eyes.

Plask stopped to take a breath.

"Professor, should I be concerned about malaria?" As soon as she asked the question, her tawny skin showed a slight flush along high cheekbones.

"Hmm, didn't we already cover the medical issues?" He rolled his eyes, as she had seen him do so many times in class when he was frustrated with a student. "*Of course* malaria is an issue, especially along the coast, but as I've said before, the travel clinic issues effective medication."

He settled back into his chair, swung his feet up on the desk and began discussing the languages used by the Miskito—a native dialect, Creole English, and Spanish.

"Cecilia, you'll be a great help since you speak Spanish. Even after spending years in Nicaragua, I've not managed to master the language. By the way, the layered cut suits such a pretty heart-shaped face," he said with a self-satisfied tone and an approving smile.

"Thank you for the suggestion. It's extremely comfortable," she said, pleased he had noticed.

"Is the expense worrying you? I meant what I said—if you are interested in accompanying me to Nicaragua, my budget covers a fellowship. I always take one graduate student and given your interest in the Miskito culture, the strength of your work, and knowledge of Spanish, I thought you would be perfect for the position. By the way, your last paper was exceptionally well written, which is currently a miracle. And, good job with the lit review."

"I'm interested, just not too sure about—"

"Cecilia, the fellowship would be valuable for your career—you'll be able to get a paper out of the experience; I promise the work will serve you well when you begin the job search process."

"Dr. Plask, I spoke with my parents about your offer. They understand the trip would be good for my career but are concerned."

"Meaning?"

She paused and then decided to tell him the truth. "Well, honestly, they'd rather I don't go."

"Why? I've been working in Nicaragua for decades and am quite familiar with the country. Since the war ended, there's been an influx of investors, tourists, retirees, and the like. Was it your parents' concern that motivated the malaria question?"

She looked away. "Not really."

"Well, then, *what?*" He removed his feet from the desk, leaned forward, pinning Cecilia to her chair with an unblinking gaze and raised eyebrows.

"How will it look?" she asked in a small voice, intimidated.

"I guess I don't understand." Her professor looked around his well-appointed office and then up at the ceiling. He played with the ring on his left hand, a frequent habit of his that she hadn't noticed until recently.

"Cecilia, let's get this straight. I am *not* talking of anything personal. This is a professional relationship—students accompany their professors on research trips all the time. Don't they understand the nature of academic relationships?"

"They, I kn ... kn ... do," she tripped over her words, wanting nothing more than to bolt from the room. She felt her cheeks flushing, but managed to pull herself together despite a pounding heart.

"My parents don't," she ended simply.

"Now then, let your parents know another anthropologist joins us once we get there—Dr. Araya. Here's an idea: you can contact David Pendergrass. He is the graduate student who went with me last year. I can give you his e-mail address, though he might find your concern somewhat peculiar. He currently has a position at Stanford—they were glad to get him given his letters and the co-authorship on the publication that came out of the trip."

"I'm sorry Dr. Plask, I didn't mean to imply you would do anything improper ... my parents were so troubled, I thought I'd better not go. They ask for little from me." By then, Cecilia was sorry she had even raised the subject. She loved her parents but they *were* from a different time and country—this was the twenty-first century, the United States, and academia was something they knew nothing about. They still believed their traditions would ensure her success in life, which was no longer the case, if it ever had been.

Dane took a sip of his coffee and thoughtfully regarded the beautiful young woman sitting in front of him, "Cecilia, I assume you're in the country legally. Do you have a passport?"

"I am, but Dr. Plask, my mother and father aren't. No passport, but it's not about that."

"Good. To be honest, I need an assistant, so it's essential you make a decision quickly. Regardless, *everyone* should have a passport! The process is quite simple: go to the post office with your birth certificate, driver's license, maybe your social security card, and fill out the application. On second thought, you had better check the requirements on the government website—maybe you do not need the social. They even take the passport photos for a small fee. Give the receipt to my secretary and she'll make sure you're reimbursed, even if you decide not to go."

"You're probably right ... getting a passport wouldn't be such a bad idea. Dr. Plask, I want you to know I really appreciate what you are trying to do for me. Maybe you could tell me more about the details of the trip?"

"Sure," he said, leaning back in his chair. "The Miskito Dr. Araya and I study live on the northeastern coast of Nicaragua, though as you are aware by now, they don't pay a lot of attention to formal borders. Anyhow, Araya estimates there are still as many as 40,000 Miskito living in the region, so there is plenty to do. And—"

"Sorry, I meant more information concerning the actual travel plans. Like, how long is the flight from Managua?" She resumed chewing her bottom lip.

"Oh. Well, the trip takes about an hour and a half on a twin engine Cessna to reach what is popularly called the Miskito Nation. My dear, if you keep biting your lip, you'll bleed."

She blushed and stopped. "Ummm … Dr. Plask, I've never flown, never mind on a small plane. Is that the only way to get to the coast?"

"Cecilia, it's time you call me by my first name—no need to be so formal. Believe me, flying is far better than driving. In fact, we drove when I first started with the project, but the trip was difficult and time consuming. It took more than 20 hours to cross some 280 miles of terrain that includes savannahs and jungle crossed by scores of rivers, but did not include gas stations, hotels, or fast food restaurants. Much of the area was dense and inhospitable. The journey was a grueling experience and time is always a factor for us."

"Dr. Plask, I would have to clear the project with Dr. Benson—I need the credits to be applied toward my degree. He approved my paper last semester, but I'm getting a doctorate in psychology, so this research might be pushing it."

"Don't worry about your advisor. A café?"

"Thanks. A coffee would be great … I was up late last night. Studying. Dr. Plask, you may find it difficult to believe, but I don't mean to create complications."

Without a reply or a glance in her direction, Dane Plask walked over to an espresso machine, popped in a pre-measured container and waited while it whirred and chugged before the cup filled with the caramel latté to which Cecilia was partial. Plask placed the fragrant cup of coffee in front of his student with an exaggerated flourish, and then fixed himself a black coffee. Mug in hand, he settled back into the chair behind the massive mahogany desk.

"Okay Cecilia, let me give you some more information," he said, running his long fingers slowly through thick wavy hair, and then lazily tracing the curve of his cheekbone with his forefinger. "*If* you accept the fellowship, you'll need a passport and inoculations. The grant will cover all expenses while in Nicaragua, including airfare. Fellows also receive a substantial stipend."

"That's very generous of you, Dr. Plask."

"I'm sure it'll be worth it. I'm planning to leave the first week of June and come back sometime during the beginning of August. I keep the return date flexible because that is the rainy season in Nicaragua; we'll end the trip early if the rains get too bad. From Los Angeles, we fly to Houston and then on to Managua. We spend a week getting coordinated with Araya and his folks, purchasing supplies, and obtaining permits from governmental agencies. While I am taking care of those things, you will be able to see the sights and do some library research, maybe carry out some interviews with Miskito living in the city. From the capital, we fly to the coast with Araya and his student. I'll get her info—she can show you the city and help you with the other things."

Plask leaned back in the chair, smoothly swung his feet up onto his desk, and drank his coffee. Someone knocked on the door, but he did not answer.

An overwhelmed Cecilia remained silent. She was shaking and afraid to pick up her cup lest he notice.

CHAPTER 9

Doc Genoa Taylor, Medical Examiner: October 2011, Day One

Once Robin sent Stalts on his way, though pissed the park ranger was still a no-show, she felt better able to concentrate on her investigation. She was particularly anxious for the arrival of the M.E., a forensic pathologist. Doc Genoa Taylor's papers on criminality were required reading when Robin was working on her master's, so a job with the noted M.E. as a colleague had been an unexpected bonus. Doc maintained her rep at all costs. Woe to anyone who "frigged" up her crime scene. Robin expected problems when Genoa arrived because she insisted on being in control. Under the circumstances, not an easy task.

As Robin tried to work out the potential dilemma, Doc showed up in the van with her trusty assistant at the wheel: Fred Stinson, a tall, lanky 29 year-old Arizonian, who, despite his relative youth, exhibited an amazing resiliency in the face of his mentor's famed blow-ups—more to the point, he was brilliant and sure to go far. Robin figured any difficulties he might have were worth the experience. Fred pulled in front of the patrol car, efficiently tucking the oversized van into the available space. On their bumper, as it were, the missing Park Service vehicle arrived and parked behind Robin. Alone for far too long, she suddenly found herself in the middle of a plethora of interested parties—some, perhaps, possessing competing agendas. Not having heard from Doug, Robin decided to check in with Sonia to find out where he was in the scheme of things. At the rate folks were arriving, he would have to park in the roadway. Robin figured the good news was that between the four of them they might get Doc down to the body *and* back up the embankment. The downside was so many boots on the ground meant further contamination of the site.

Her cell buzzed.

"Sonia, you read my mind. Anything on the plates?"

"Clean. Not even a speeding or a parking ticket. Mi'jita, how're things?"

"Good. Stalts was cooperative, can't quite see why he would call in his own murder, but we'll see. Sent him on his way for now, but he'll be in tomorrow. Fred just drove up with Doc, as did the ranger. Hon, I wanted to remind you the body is not easily accessible. Doug?"

"Sí. Genoa and I need to get ourselves on one of those weight loss shows! Make us a million bucks while we're at it," Sonia hooted.

"Doug?"

"My boy's on the way. He left Isla Vista about half an hour ago. No problem—he has the six-pack. Tell Genoa to hold off."

"Okay, well I'm going to talk with her and find what she wants to do."

Sonia hung up, leaving her rollicking laugh ringing in Robin's ear. She approached the van and Genoa rolled down her window. A stoic Fred had remained in the driver's seat. A faint smile disappeared as quickly as it appeared.

"Well, Detective Crane, what's facing me in this godforsaken place?" Doc demanded to know. "Nothing in the roadway, so I hope the requisite body is in the cave. Though the path up there seems a bit steep and some of those rocks look ready to tumble, the other choice appears to present an even more precipitous climb. Hell of a drive up here, not a safety railing to be seen. As I get older, I like heights less and less."

"Sorry. Doc, I wish I could tell you the victim is at the cave, but somebody did not want us to find her—body's down the hillside, across the road. I guess there's still a chance we're investigating a hiking accident though it doesn't look that way. I will, of course, leave that determination to *you*."

"Sounds right. Back to the issue at hand—what about getting down there?" Doc drew in her bottom lip and knitted her brow, facial movements making for the stern expression that kept people in line.

"To be honest, getting down to the scene is going to be a bitch, though there's a pathway of sorts over to the side. Anyhow, Doug is on his way and there are the rest of us." Robin said, not believing a word of it.

"Well, I guess I'll find out soon enough because I want to see the body before it's moved. Meantime, bring me up-to-date."

"Sure. When I arrived the caller was here." Robin attempted to keep the irritation out of her voice about the delay of the rest of the team. "Barclay Stalts, a screenwriter from up north—Mill Valley, to be exact. In any case, he was on his way to Hope Ranch where he is staying in a friend's house while travelling back and forth to L.A. According to Stalts, tired of driving, he saw the sign for the cave and decided to take a break. Before leaving, he took pictures across the road using a telephoto—that's when he thought he was looking at a human leg and called 911."

"Do you like him for it, Robin? Very convenient a Hollywood writer is taking pictures of a ravine in an isolated spot and just happens to find a body. Pictures of what? Sounds a bit pat to me," she finished with a rhetorical flourish.

"I agree. On the face of it, he appears suspicious, but other than discovering the body, nothing suggests he is the doer. Regardless, I've interviewed him, his camera and shoes are in my possession, and he'll come in to the PD tomorrow morning. When he does, I'm hoping he'll agree to a DNA sample."

"Well the forensics from the scene, if they're clean of his DNA, may help clear him. *If* he's innocent. Robin, did you search his car?"

"Yep. Didn't find anything. His athletic bag as well."

"You think he'd allow forensics on the vehicle tomorrow?"

"Probably. Though it's hard to tell which request will get him to lawyer up."

"So be it. I'll talk to the Chief. Where is Doug? Or, is Ken coming?"

"Doug's on his way. You'll have plenty of feet on the ground."

"Maybe too many. Anyhow, with Debayle here, we don't need O'Donnell—oil and water. Who's handling this investigation?"

"Chief Bartolo assigned the case to me. My first as primary." Robin tried to keep the pride out of her voice.

"Well, well. Congratulations, girl! Want some advice?"

"From you? Always."

"Robin, all kidding aside, this has the characteristics of a tough case. At one level, you need to keep telling yourself to take things slowly and deliberately, but even so, move as quickly as possible because the first hours are vitally important. Nonetheless, in the end what matters is a successful prosecution. Do not hesitate to ask for help—it will not make you appear weak. Always stay focused on getting justice for the dead. Fred?"

Stinson, hands still on the wheel, nodded his head in agreement.

"Thanks, Doc. I appreciate the advice."

"Enough. Now, let me figure out what we're going to have to deal with."

"Mmmm, Doc, I need to tell you something else."

"Shit, doesn't sound so good already, eh Freddy?" Not even a whisper of a smile from him.

"It isn't," Robin agreed. "Doc, the witness went down to check on what he thought was a body." She added weakly, "He was a medic in Iraq."

"Oh, frig it! Everyone is a CSI now. So much for DNA. Well, Robin, that puts him right up at the top of your suspect list. And you?" she asked sarcastically.

"Me?"

"I guess everyone and their cousin traipsed through my crime scene. I suppose you went down as well?"

"Doc, despite the caller's assessment, I needed to confirm she was DOA rather than injured. You weren't going to be here for a while—hadn't completed the autopsy you were carrying out when Sonia spoke with Fred. I was careful—took notes, photographs, and strung up crime scene tape to indicate the area I had covered and to minimize future disruptions to the scene. Soil samples. Changed gloves as necessary. On the way back up, I found a tube of lipstick. Everything is bagged, labeled, and in the evidence locker. I'll process the contents when I get back to the department."

"Good girl. Good lesson. Fred, it is not enough to know medicine, or, pathology for that matter. Not enough to thoroughly examine a body—you need to work with people who know what in the hell they are doing. Avoid idiots at all cost! In Robin's case, her master's degree in forensics is helpful. In addition, she trained at the L.A. Police Academy, an excellent program, but that is generally not the case. Freddy, my boy, you'll find yourself doing most of the training."

With that advice, Fred bailed out, went around to the back of the van, and began organizing Doc's paraphernalia.

"Well, Robin, time for you to step back and let us get down to business. Anyhow, you'd better go talk with the ranger—he seems more than a wee bit anxious." Genoa opened her door and using her cane and the handle for support, slowly lowered herself to the ground. Robin did not dare assist her—she intended to remain in her good graces.

She left Fred to his job and walked over to talk with the park ranger. "Sorry about the delay. Detective Robin Crane from the SBPD," she said, trying to keep the aggravation out of her voice.

"Pleased to meet you," said the harried man. Genoa had pegged him with her *wee bit anxious* comment. "I apologize for taking so long to get out here, but now that I'm here, I'm sure glad to see you have plenty of bodies on the ground." His hearty laugh broke the tension. "Excuse the unfortunate word-choice! I'm Matt Webster," he said, extending a hand. The hint of a smile originating in his cobalt blue eyes, played around his lips. "We got a call from the SB dispatcher—a tourist found a body out here?"

"Pleased to meet you," Robin said, as she took in the tall, muscular, and tanned ranger who actually removed his hat before returning her handshake. A Marlboro man for the 21st Century stood in front of her—thick and wavy sandy blonde hair, dark brown moustache, rugged—not exactly handsome features, but definitely appealing.

"Yep, to be honest, I'm surprised someone didn't show up earlier," she said tartly.

"I know. I know."

A blushing Marlboro man—truly a guy for the new century, Robin thought.

"Sorry about the delay. Unfortunately, a late arrival at a murder site is the least of my problems. Detective, I don't mean to be rude, but could you bring me up to speed quickly? I understand someone called in a young female. It was difficult getting here and now that I made it, I can't stay—we have a small blaze too close to the Cachuma Rec area and I'm needed there. Well, that is if you don't need me. The fire is probably contained, yet the minute your back is turned, a thousand acres is up in flames. It looks as if you've got everything under control but I guess, like firefighting, you never know—it's still rather dry," he said, shifting his weight from one leg to the other.

"You're off the hook. Go ahead and I'll update you later. Take care."

"I promise to come into town tomorrow. Well, if we get things under control. Robin, I owe you a lunch or something."

"Sure, don't worry about the meal or the investigation. Pretty soon we'll be tripping over each other." She glanced around and it appeared that might actually be the case. Robin proceeded to give Matt the same synopsis she had given Doc.

70

"Thanks, Robin. Here's my card. Sorry I took so long—a stupid delay on my part. Especially since you might have been out here alone with a perp. As I said, I'll try to get to town tomorrow. If I can't, I'll be sure to send someone else."

"That works for me. Be safe." She watched the lanky ranger as he strode to his pick-up truck: about six foot two, well built, in a less defined way than Doug, he walked with a distinctly western swagger. Although stressed, deep laugh lines suggested an upbeat sort. She decided to keep lunch and dinner open, an unexpected benefit of being primary. It occurred to Robin that she could easily get used to her new status. The ranger drove past the parked cars, somehow managed to turn his vehicle around, and headed back down the road with a wave. She returned to the M.E.'s van.

"Hey Robin, what's up with the disappearing Park Service? Taxpayers cut the budget again? He damn sure wasn't much help."

"The budget. There's always that, but the poor guy has a fire to deal with. Somebody will be in tomorrow."

"Fire in the hills—we'd better get a move on. Fred, come over here," she yelled out to her assistant, who was squatting down and scanning the crime scene with Robin's binoculars.

"That's what I thought—better safe than sorry."

Fred walked over and handed Robin the glasses.

"Doc, how about waiting for Doug? That's a pretty steep incline. I kept slipping and had to grab onto small shrubs, which are anything but stable. Poison oak, unfortunately, is plentiful. Sonia says he'll arrive any minute."

"C'mon Fred, let me take a look at what we're facing out here in the hinterlands. Robin seems to be suggesting I can't do my job—you notice she's trying to be politically correct about my weight." Genoa said, glancing in Robin's direction with a raised eyebrow and a smirk.

Mindful of what a hot potato the subject was for her, Robin said nothing, aware that if she did it would kick her in the butt in no time at all. She handed Doc the glasses.

"Awwh, she doesn't get the real you! We're going down there, regardless—even if *I* have to carry you," Fred cackled in the mad scientist way he had when he did speak. Genoa laughed appreciatively.

The oddball pair strolled across the road. Robin trailed behind, but changed course as Doug pulled into the space left empty by Matt's departure. She breathed a sigh of relief.

CHAPTER 10

An Old File:
Day Two

After a good night's sleep, and a relaxed breakfast of granola and fruit with Sean, Robin drove her son to school, red Spiderman backpack in hand. Once he had passed through the front doors, one of a noisy gaggle of children, she headed for work anticipating a lunchless day.

The minute Robin sat down at her desk it started: one fluorescent yellow post-it stuck to the computer screen telling her to update the Chief and another from Doug saying he would be back after breakfast, grease-fueled and ready to go. Not for the first time, it occurred to Robin that she should be sure to lock her door when leaving at the end of her shift. The phone rang: Robin pressed the speaker button and heard an unfamiliar voice.

"Hi Robin. Matt Webster, delinquent Park Ranger."

She definitely had not forgotten. "Good morning, will you be coming in today?" Robin tried to squelch any hint of a hopeful tone. During their brief interchange, Matt had seemed unaware of his hunkiness—a welcome change from many of the men she met.

"Well, actually, that's what I'm calling about." The line went silent.

"Robin, I'm afraid I'm tied up for the rest of the day. Not to be making excuses, but we're short-staffed—I assume you're aware of the cuts. I've got a suggestion—"

"I understand, don't worry. What would work for you?" she said, trying to be accommodating, while hiding her disappointment that the good-looking cowboy wouldn't be riding into town as expected.

"Could you fax an interim report to us? I'm sure you've got the case under control, but I need to get something on file."

"No problem."

The line again went quiet. "Well, I thought we might catch up over dinner tonight."

Surprised, she thought the invite through quickly. "I'd like to, Matt, but it would have to be earlier—supper rather than dinner. During the week I try to be home at a reasonable time for my son."

"That's fine. How about 6:30?" She gave him her address. After a discussion of possible restaurants, they hung up.

The Chief was still waiting for his update. A now thoroughly animated Robin fired up her computer and pulled up the report on the Painted Cave victim, which she judged fairly complete, though that wasn't saying much given the paucity of information. The woman had no identification on her and they had not found a purse, wallet, or cellphone—even after a systematic search of the scene, including the cave and the roadway. Robin considered whether an animal might have dragged off her belongings, but that seemed unlikely. Doug had already submitted the victim's prints and the partial on the lipstick to the AFIS, the acronym for the Automated Finger Print Identification System. Given her age, they doubted she was in the system. Moreover, their victim did not appear to be either the criminal type or military. Rather, Robin thought, she might be a young professional, maybe a student—hip clothes, good manicure, expensive haircut, pearl earring; perhaps a graduate student or, since she seemed slightly older than a typical undergraduate, an Assistant Professor. Doug argued that if a professor had gone missing, they would have received a missing person's report. Based on Robin's hunch, however, he suggested a ride over to USB and City College to see whether anyone could identify a photograph of the victim. She agreed—intent on notifying the victim's family personally before horrified relatives discovered their loss while watching a television report or reading the internet.

Robin went to Sonia's office, folder in hand. "Is Chief Bartolo available to go over the case?"

"Sorry mi'jita. He is not."

"Okay. Here's the report. If the Chief approves, could you fax it to Matt Webster at the Park Service?"

"Sure. You are smiling wide. No secrets, digáme Robin!"

"Thanks. I guess I woke up on the right side of the bed."

"Well, you're blushing clear through those freckles Dougie finds so cute. Something's up!"

"Nope, nothing," she said, and made a quick exit. After refilling her coffee cup in the break room, Robin returned to her desk and began to read the e-mails in her in-box. One from Doc, asking her to drop by. She called Sonia to let her know she needed to talk to the M.E. before submitting the report to the Chief and Park Service.

Freddy told her she would find his boss in the morgue. Robin hated the smell of the morgue with its mingling of antiseptic, death, and decomposition—the coffee sat like lead in her stomach as she walked through the door into the cool room.

"Morning, Genoa. You have something for me?" Focused on the task at hand, Doc finished scrubbing up before acknowledging her presence. "Robin, you're in early. I have a favor to ask. I need an old file—a highway accident that occurred maybe five or six years ago—a young Latina female from SB."

"An accident?" Robin repeated blankly, unable to connect the dots—there she stood in the dreaded morgue, trying to breathe normally, hoping to get information from Genoa about the Painted Cave victim before she and Doug took off for USB, *not* to receive a request to scour through old files. They already had their work cut out for them.

"Yep, a car accident," Doc said. "That is, if I'm remembering correctly. My brain does not always seem to be in gear. Gotta love the aging process! Can you pull the file?"

Robin knew nothing was wrong with Doc's brain because the M.E. had started life with more gray and white matter than she would ever have. "Sure, not a problem. Which record do you want me to retrieve?" Robin asked, anxious to leave. Fred was hosing down the concrete floor but death permeated most of her senses and then some.

"I want to look at a file for a Santa Barbara resident who, I believe, went off the coastal highway in the fog. I am not going to be a big help here—it was somewhere up north. Name of Sarah or Susan. I am even less sure about the last name—maybe Mexican. Give me a minute." She knit her brow. "Never mind, can't find it, but I know the name's in there somewhere."

"Is there a problem?"

"Robin, if you don't mind, I want to look at the file first. It could be nothing and I'm not interested in raising a red flag unnecessarily and tainting your investigation."

"I understand." Anyhow, Robin hoped that would be the case. She apparently was not getting to the university anytime soon and left to check the files.

"Detective!" She turned and saw Fred running in her direction, a piece of paper flapping in his hand. "Doc may have remembered the accident victim's surname. Begins with a C—something like Carrillo, Cabrillo. Well, I guess Cabrillo is the boulevard. Anyhow, she's pretty sure it starts with a C."

"Thanks Fred. I'll do my best. If I locate the file, can you pick it up from Sonia?"

"Sure. Well, back to the dungeon and my personal dragon," he said fondly, a sentiment followed by an outrageous ear-piercing laugh.

Robin tried the electronic databases first because if she could not find what she wanted there, she would have to hit the cabinets, a time consuming process unless she could enlist Sonia's help.

Sonia offered food, no help. The detective took the red rhubarb pastry, filled her cup with fresh coffee, and returned to her office. She left a message for Doug, catching him up. After a good hour, Robin gave up searching the electronic system. She figured that if the file existed, she was off base with the name or incapable of locating it. The Chief had decided the SBPD should go paperless and Sonia was in the process of scanning records in, but generally had her hands full and grumbled to the Chief that his assistant needed an assistant. It now seemed to Robin that the complaint was legitimate. She went back to plead her case more vigorously with Sonia, but again had no luck.

Two hours later and several frustrated calls from Doug, the phone rang again. This time, Sonia was on the line. "Robin, I think I've got what you're looking for. *If* the first name is Sara and the last name is Castillo, her car went off the coastal highway up north in 2005."

"Sonia, you're a wonder! Doc didn't know whether she had the correct name, other than it began with a 'C'. Castillo sounds about right. Thank you! Fred said he would pick it up."

"Not so much trouble, but the Chief needs to hire a temp to get these files scanned in. I'll call Fred. Dougie is waiting for you."

Dougie's waiting! That explained Sonia's change of heart.

"Hon, I owe you!"

"Don't worry, I'll collect. Mi'jita, watch that cute little backside of yours!" She laughed and, bracelets jingling, hung up.

CHAPTER 11

Cecilia Hernández:
Summer 2011

By late spring, Cecilia had gone ahead and applied for a passport despite her continued ambivalence about the fellowship. She had received the crisp blue document at the same time she'd reluctantly started her job search. It seemed early to be engaged in the process, but a faculty member had explained applicants apply for academic positions a year before the start date. He'd strongly encouraged her to accept the fellowship, as it would strengthen her vitae. The discussion got her to thinking about her long-term goal of setting up a non-profit for disadvantaged children. A respected academic position would be an important part of establishing the credentials that would make her effort fundable. This confluence of events pushed Cecilia to take the risk. In the face of her parents' concern, she accepted Plask's offer, contingent on Dr. Benson's approval. Several days later, Cecilia met with her advisor to discuss the research opportunity.

"Cecilia, Dr. Plask called me to discuss the fellowship. Considering your previous work in his classes, I'm inclined to approve the plan, though I want to make it clear that while in Nicaragua, your dissertation research would have to be independent of his study."

"I understand. Dr. Benson, the topic I'd like to pursue is the effect of the economy on gender roles—an extension of last semester's research paper, which was independent of Dr. Plask's work," Cecilia explained, biting at her bottom lip.

Benson did not look up as he made notes on a legal pad. "Sounds reasonable. Tell me more."

"Okay." She took a deep breath. "What I've learned is that among the Miskito, when jobs are scarce, men rely on agricultural work and stay involved in family and community life. Under these conditions, they are more likely to be the decision-makers. In contrast, with a strong economy, men have increased job choices, most of which require them to leave home. Hypothetically, that equation shifts gender roles."

"Interesting. Cecilia, what's the time frame you're discussing?"

"The gender-related trends I'm referring to have been the case since at least the early 1990s—men traveling more because of a national increase in economic opportunities. My research so far shows that under those conditions the majority of males over 13 are away from home for about two-thirds of the year. The Miskito villages *supposedly* have a matriarchal arrangement even though men are generally the breadwinners. Dr. Benson, I want to confirm those data and, if valid, go a step further and investigate the cultural implications of the shift."

"Alright then. What does the literature have to say?"

"Well, women are reported to make the economic decisions, and it is the daughters who inherit the rights to familial land." Cecilia thought about it, and then decided to leave out something Dr. Plask had told her: *Many who believe love magic will help a woman keep her husband and his money practice magia amorosa.* Plask had confirmed what Cecilia had already learned—women might control household management, but they cannot do much without the money their husbands provide. *Magia amorosa* highlights the importance of keeping a man involved in the family and by extension, the community.

It was as if Benson read her mind. "Tell me something about their family relationships?"

Hitting her stride, Cecilia explained that women marry as adolescents and have as many as six to eight children, but since men are gone for such long stretches of time, a significant number abandon their families. "The divorce rate is high. Men frequently protest wives are asking them to support illegitimate children—claiming they have no moral obligation to care for them. Those children are often, but not always, supported by their mother's female relatives. Regardless of the issue of legitimacy, however, daughters tend to remain in the community and gain status. Under these conditions, women are the respected elders or *kukas*, the enforcers of correct behavior in their village."

"So what are you arguing?"

"Dr. Benson, my thesis is still rough, but I believe when the economy is good, Miskito boys rejected by their fathers as illegitimate are at highest risk of becoming outsiders in their community. In contrast, illegitimate girls are integrated under the aegis of their mother's family and more likely to have social and economic power."

The room remained quiet while he made a few more notes and then put down his pen. "All quite interesting," he said, patting and rearranging strands of thinning hair. "Cecilia, I agree the study has implications for psychology, but I will need to review the methodology you intend to use. Nonetheless, approval should not present a problem. I am certain this experience will provide you with important opportunities in the future: Dr. Plask has an outstanding reputation in his field. Your next step is to submit a formal dissertation proposal. Just keep in mind you're working on a psychology degree, not anthropology, so the primary focus is *individual* development, though you can certainly evaluate contextual factors such as the economy."

Two weeks later, Cecilia's dissertation committee approved her proposal with only minor changes. Dr. Plask's administrative assistant processed the appropriate paperwork: with expenses covered, her salary was sufficiently generous that Cecilia made arrangements through her bank to have two hundred dollars deposited into her parents' account each month. In June, Cecilia left for Nicaragua.

Exhausted and queasy from the long and turbulent flight to Nicaragua, Cecilia did not care *where* she was—her relief at having both feet on solid ground eclipsed all other concerns. Once they had cleared customs and retrieved their luggage, Dr. Plask rented a jeep and headed directly to an international hotel in Managua. They drove up to an entrance notable for massive glass doors that framed an enormous crystal chandelier visible from outside. Cecilia was taken aback by the elegance—something she had not expected in an impoverished Latin American country.

When the jeep came to a stop, a young bellhop in a red uniform with gold braiding and epaulets opened the passenger door and greeted Cecilia in English. In Spanish, she replied how pleased she was to be in his country. The comment brought a broad smile of pleasure to the boy's thin face. Meantime, Plask had come around the car and brusquely told the boy to meet them inside with the luggage. He firmly took Cecilia by the elbow and without a word led her through the plush lobby to the reception desk.

In spite of his unhappiness at learning the adjoining rooms he had requested were not available, Plask filled out the paperwork when the clerk offered two rooms located across the hall from each other. He gave the woman his credit card, scrawled his signature on the various forms, and accepted the proffered key cards.

Cecilia, too exhausted to be nervous about checking into a hotel with her professor, took the plastic card he handed her, without knowing what to do with it. She had never stayed in a hotel.

"That takes care of that—we're checked in. How about a drink before turning in? Even for me the flight was damn disagreeable!"

"It's a good thing we're here for a week because I can't imagine *ever* flying again, particularly in a small plane. Dr. Plask, would you mind terribly if I go to my room? I'm worn out."

"Are you comfortable going with the bellhop? There's nothing to worry about, but if you want, I'll accompany you."

"No thank you. I'll be fine."

"I gave the boy a generous tip, so don't worry about the money. I'm off to what is a well-stocked bar—thank the Lord for small favors!"

"I hope you don't mind. It was a pretty terrible experience for a first flight."

"Sleep in tomorrow, my dear. I am having lunch with Professor Araya, but you can meet him another time. I will ask Araya if his graduate student can show you around—get you into the library, etc. However, none of that is important right now. Cecilia, you see in front of you a man desperate for drink and food, in that order. A man off to the bar! Sure I can't interest you in a nightcap?"

"Thank you, Dr. Plask, but I need to call my parents. I bought a calling card."

"Got it. I'll see you tomorrow afternoon. Enjoy your beauty sleep!"

"Goodnight."

When Cecilia and the bellhop reached her hotel room, she handed the white and gold key card to the boy. He opened the door to reveal a lavish suite she would never be able to describe to her parents. Once he set her luggage on the stand, he left with a smile on his face—she had given him five U.S. dollars.

After testing the card and clicking the locks into place, Cecilia opened her suitcase and placed her belongings into mirrored dresser drawers. Finished, she sat on the bed and looked around, amazed to find herself in such a beautiful room, although too tired to enjoy it. She went into the bathroom to get ready for the night. Once she had taken a soothing shower and put on the silky nightgown she had splurged on for the trip, Cecilia only wanted to sleep. Instead, she took out the telephone calling card, picked up the phone receiver and followed the detailed instructions.

>>   <<   >>   <<

Cecilia and Araya's graduate student, Estela Ramírez, got along from the minute they met. The cheerful young Nicaraguan obtained a temporary library card for Cecilia so she could get some research done before they left for the Atlantic coast. She also insisted they tour Managua, go to a beach on the Pacific side, and visit her friends and family. Cecilia enjoyed herself, although the poverty shocked her, particularly when it came to the children.

Their last night in Managua, Dr. Plask invited Cecilia for drinks and dinner at the hotel's upscale restaurant. The grad student had spent the day interviewing Miskito men living in the city, and arrived at the hotel late. Still needing to get dressed, Cecilia decided to call home once she returned to her room for the night. She was excited—she had packed a cocktail dress *just in case*. Linda had wanted to know what that meant, but when Cecilia could not articulate a clear answer, they had gone ahead to Macy's. There, Cecilia chose a beautiful black dress with gorgeous beaded detail work emphasizing the scooped neckline. She hung the dress in the bathroom to steam while she showered.

As Dane had promised, dinner was incredible—local seafood and unfamiliar indigenous dishes. Rather than discussing research, he revealed something of his personal life to her. A gregarious man, Cecilia was surprised to learn his had been a sad and lonely childhood—so different from her own, which although poor was always about emotional stability. Dane's father had walked out on his family when he was a baby. His mother subsequently became depressed and increasingly unable to care for her only child. Social Services eventually took the boy out of his home and put him in foster care.

They sat quietly drinking their wine in the candlelight. Plask put his hand over hers and told Cecilia how beautiful she looked. At the unexpected compliment, a rosy hue suffused her cheeks. The professor laughed gently and told her he did not mean to cause her any discomfort.

He asked about her family, and she talked to him about her brother's death. The waiter had turned over a second bottle of champagne before Cecilia realized it. Her dinner companion convinced her to try an Irish coffee and Bananas Flambé for dessert. When they finally got up from the table, Cecilia held onto a chair for support. Plask put an arm around the young woman, as they left the restaurant. At first mortified, Cecilia was laughing by the time they arrived at the glass-enclosed elevator.

"My dear, I'm glad you're enjoying yourself! We'll have plenty of hard work to do soon enough," Plask pressed the button for their floor with his free hand.

"I need my bed," Cecilia mumbled. Once they reached her room, she slid the key card into the slot, but the mechanism flashed red, which sent her into a paroxysm of laughter. "My key does *not* work! Nodder trip down the elevator," she slurred.

"Give me the card Cecilia—a bit bubbly, are we?" he laughed and squeezed her shoulder. Gave her a kiss on the forehead.

"*Here* you go! Dr. Plask, to be honest, I only uses keys to open a door." She giggled and leaned against the wall while he picked up the dropped card.

Plask opened the door and led Cecilia inside. "Here, my dear, first of all, let's get you comfortable." He deftly settled her on the bed and placed a couple of plump pillows behind her back and head.

"My dear, I know what'll make a difference!"

"And what would that be *Dr. Plask*?"

"Dane. Cecilia, you are making me feel old! *Please* call me Dane."

"Dane it is then. You're the professor, after all!" She took the drink he handed her. "*This* will help?" She laughed and spilled some on her dress. "Uh, oh, I'm taking a shower in my clothes!"

"A drink of whiskey will help, trust me. We need to settle down those bubbles—brown liquids do the trick."

"I, like, get it!" She worked off each shoe and, as she did, sent it sailing through the air before it hit the floor with a soft thunk.

"Honey, let me clean off your beautiful dress before it stains."

>>　　　<<　　　>>　　　<<

The shrill alarm awoke her, or maybe it was Dr. Plask's insistent voice through the door. She flung out her arm, blindly searched for the clock, and pressed the dismiss button. When she sat up, a sharp pain slashed across her forehead and jolted her completely awake. She looked down, surprised to discover she had no clothes on—she searched for her nightgown in the bedclothes, but could not find it. What she *did* find was her beautiful new dress crumpled up at the bottom of the bed.

"Dr. Plask?" she called out weakly. The sound of her own voice cut another swath of pain through her head. So much so, she felt sick to her stomach.

"Just wanted to make sure you're up. We will be leaving the hotel in about an hour. Do you want to go to breakfast? After last night, you must need coffee."

The thought of food made her gag. "No thank you. I'll meet you in the lobby. I have to get ready and call my parents."

"Alright then. I will send someone up for your bag. Cecilia, is everything okay? You don't sound so well."

"I'm fine. Thanks."

"Good. I'm off—a good breakfast is important. We're looking at a long day."

Cecilia waited a few minutes before sitting up on the side of the bed, vulnerable in her nakedness. Her head pounded and she was nauseous. Sore all over. There was a large red mark on her left breast. The previous evening came back to her slowly. She remembered her excitement—the new dress, dinner, good conversation. Once they had returned from the restaurant, she remembered Dr. Plask asking her to call him Dane. She remembered resting against the pillows while drinking the unfamiliar whiskey and answering a question about her brother's illness. Anything after that was a blank. But what Cecilia did know was she was no longer a virgin—she'd had sex with her professor.

CHAPTER 12

University Foray:
October 2011, Day Two

"**O**kay buddy, you** ready?" Robin said, going across the hall-way and popping her head into Doug's office. "By the way, thanks for putting in a good word to Sonia on my behalf."

"No problem. Which file were you looking for so assiduously it took precedence over *our* investigation?"

"Wasn't for me. Doc was somewhat mysterious about the whole thing, but when she wants something, she wants it. I would have been searching all day if Sonia had not come to my rescue. Anyhow, let's head to the university to find out whether the registrar can help us with the identification. I still have this gut feeling our victim is a student—her age, the collegial dress. The fact nobody seems to be missing her could be because she's off at school—perhaps a boyfriend problem run amuck."

"I'm ready, but only if I drive. Robin, I have to get back sometime today. I've got paperwork to finish before the Chief's on *my* case."

"The Chief is not on my case! He simply wanted an update. Besides, he's not in, so I left a preliminary report that I'll probably have to update after we talk to Doc. Sonia will then fax it to the Park Service."

"Thanks, but I drive."

"You're such a chauvinist pig! Shit, don't you get anything out of those bloody harassment seminars the Chief keeps arranging?"

"Yeah, gotta love the pastries—a giant leap from doughnuts! Anyhow, I think those seminars are for Sonia. She'll never understand that in this country the physical characterization of one's colleagues is verboten. Better than the pastry is the view of the hot woman who sits in front of me. A bit shaggy in back, eh Robin? Time for a haircut?"

"You are so last century Doug, a true chauvinist. You can drive, though I am aware I'm rewarding your atrocious behavior. Still, you got me out of the file thing. I swear I might as well be dealing with Sean!"

"Hey, not such a bad thing. How's my buddy?"

"Loving life—he's excited about his birthday and keeps adding to the list. I only wish I had more time with him."

"Sorry, I know being a single parent must be tough," he said seriously. "For Sean as well. I was lucky to grow up in an intact family. Robin, remember I'm taking him this weekend to do guy things. Shoot gulls or something."

"Thank you. That would be great—not the seagulls' thing, but spending time with you. Saturday still okay?"

"Yep. Why, you got a busy social calendar?" he laughed "Seriously, no thanks needed. Little dude and I have a great time together. Well, here we are. Back to business."

>>   <<   >>   <<

Doug pulled into the beautiful USB campus thick with wonderful old eucalyptus trees, Robin's favorite California tree. After a few wrong turns, not surprising given the preponderance of one-way streets, he parked in the visitor's lot and they walked to the building housing the registrar's office.

The large wooden counter was crowded with students clamoring for attention, but Doug quickly caught the notice of the flustered young woman who Robin figured worked as a clerk to defray tuition. She showed the student her badge, a move serving to bring *everyone* in their immediate vicinity to a halt. In the ensuing silence, using his best flirtatious tone, Doug asked to talk with the registrar.

The girl hesitated and then said, "Please wait a minute. I'll find out if she's free." She went to a nearby desk to make the telephone call.

"What are the odds?" Doug whispered.

"Sixty-forty—our favor! Lunch on the line."

"I think you're way too positive, woman—more like sixty-forty and we're on the losing end. Aged angus steak for me."

"Sojourner Cafe."

"Shit, not again!"

After a few minutes of whispering into the phone receiver, the young woman came over to a side wooden gate separating students from staff. "Please come with me, Ms. Lutz will see you," she said, holding it open.

"I win either way," murmured Doug. "What could a lettuce sandwich cost me? Anyhow, my striking good looks are what got us in!"

"Unlikely."

They went down a long corridor until they reached a well-appointed, spacious office. A middle-age woman with blonde hair, expensively highlighted, stood up and came from behind her desk. "Thank you Tanya. I'll take it from here."

"Yes, ma'am." The girl was gone before Robin could thank her.

"I'm Marjorie Lutz, the registrar. What can I do for you?"

"Ms. Lutz, thank you for seeing us on such short notice. Detective Robin Crane and this is my partner, Detective Douglas Debayle—we're from the Santa Barbara Police Department."

The woman shook hands with each of them. "Please take a seat," she said, motioning the two detectives to the comfortable leather chairs situated in front of her desk. "I understand you need our assistance. Is there a problem on campus of which I am unaware? Officers, we'll cooperate in any way possible, though I'm sure you're aware of the privacy constraints we face when it comes to releasing student records."

"We understand the concerns but it may not be a student we're trying to identify. Detective Debayle and I are working on a case involving a possible murder victim. Because she is of college age and has yet to be reported missing, we thought that perhaps she attended school in Santa Barbara and her parents are unaware of her disappearance. I know there are thousands of students at USB, so you might not recognize the picture of the young woman, but we wondered whether it would be possible to identify her through the university identification system. Well, if she's a student here, of course."

Doug asked, "Would you be willing to take a look at the photograph?"

"Of course, though as you've suggested, I know only a small fraction of the students."

"Thank you—we would like to notify her family before they find out through the media. Ms. Lutz, all we have is a morgue photograph, which can be difficult enough, but the poor girl was exposed to the elements before being discovered," Robin warned.

The registrar leaned back in her chair for a good minute without saying a word, but then seemed to have made up her mind, sat forward and took a deep breath. "Detectives, don't get your hopes up because I doubt I'll be much help, but if I don't recognize her, I'll ask someone from IT to search the database for a possible match. Still, you need to understand we do not have anything like facial recognition software. It would be a question of narrowing the field by eliminating possibilities such as sex, hair color, etc."

"We truly appreciate any help at all. Detective, please?"

"This is tough," Doug reiterated. He laid the photograph on the desk in front of the nervous but determined woman.

"Oh my God, this is a tragedy!" She shook her head.

Time can pass so slowly.

"I'm not absolutely sure but I don't think I've ever seen her." Pale and tense, she stared at the photograph. "Hmmm ... a little familiar, but that's probably because I'm surrounded by young people all day—so many look alike—but, honestly, I don't think so. If I can get approval, we'll do what we can to help," she assured the detectives.

"Ms. Lutz, I know this has been difficult, but we have one more request. We would appreciate that the search be kept confidential. We're anxious to avoid any leaks before notifying her family. In addition, we'll leave the photograph with you—you can make a copy for the IT tech doing the search. The victim's height, weight, hair and eye color are notated on the back."

"Here's our contact information." Robin handed the registrar a business card.

"I understand. Again, no promises, but I will do my best. Shouldn't take me long to know one way or another. Do I call the number on the card?"

"Yes, thank you. We'll be waiting to hear from you," Robin said, getting up. She shook the registrar's hand and left her office, relieved to have obtained more than they expected. Before passing through the gate of the main office, Doug walked over to Tanya and thanked her.

As they made their way through the crowded hallways, Robin was surprised to find herself missing the academic life. "Doug, she could have sent us packing under the cover of some university rule or other—I think she'll push the powers that be on our behalf."

"As cynical as I am, I agree she'll do her best to help us out. Still, I expect the legal beagles will cause a problem, though for the life of me I am not sure how we would be violating the law. Teach me not to listen to my father and forsake law school!"

"Doug, Marjorie's got a point—many of the students *are* indistinguishable. Just look around. In their quest to acquire an identity distinct from their parents, they appear to be wearing a common uniform."

"Well, they sure look different to me. But I must be getting old 'cause they're beginning to signal jail bait!"

"C'mon, let's get something to eat and figure out other possibilities if this university thing doesn't pan out. It may be that Doc has information for us."

They drove over to the Sojourner Cafe. There was still construction going on at the Presidio, so it took a few minutes to park.

The friendly host, dressed in shorts and a polo shirt, led them to a table next to the front window and left menus. A waitress promptly brought glasses of cold water. "I'll be right back," she said, hustling off to the kitchen.

"Hopefully, we'll hear from Ms. Lutz by tomorrow, but as cooperative as she is, I expect the inevitable delay generated by the university counsel."

"I agree. Doug, stop making faces while reading the menu. If you keep that up, the waitress will notice and never come back."

"Her loss, I'm a good tipper. Keep bringing me to these granola places and this is what you get Robin. You gotta know by now I'm a *red meat and potatoes* man."

"Well, there's always that, but stop with the faces."

In his *I am so charming* manner: forefinger raised, come-hither smile, a cocked eyebrow, Doug signaled the server who was carrying an order to another table.

She was having none of it. "I'll be with you in a couple of minutes. We're short today."

After about five minutes, she returned. "I apologize."

"Not a problem," Robin assured her. "He's driven to cause trouble."

"Water off a duck's back," was all she had to say. Doug laughed and gave her a wink.

"I'd like the vegan eggplant parmesan and a mango juice," said Robin. "Since my buddy here is paying, the toasted agave almond cake with carob frosting sounds right for dessert. Oh, and a cup of coffee. Sugar, no cream. Thanks."

"And for you, sir?"

"For me, the turkey sandwich on French bread with all the fixings, and tortilla chips. A gazpacho to start. An Arnold Palmer to drink. No dessert. Coffee, black."

"Thank you." She left for the kitchen without having written down the order.

"Okay. Now that chow's on the way, let's get back to business."

"Seriously?"

"Seriously. If we can't identity the victim in the next day or two, we'll have to go to the media. Otherwise, there'll be a leak and we'll lose control over the story."

"Girl, you've got questionable taste in restaurants, but you're right about the reporters. Vultures! Too bad for them because we've got an advantage over the perp as long as the details of the investigation aren't released."

"I'm not only concerned about the tabloids, I'd hate for the family to find out through the media. Doug, we can't release the actual morgue photo because it's too gruesome for public consumption."

"You'll need to get a sketch worked up."

"Right. I'll ask the Chief for approval to have Eddie take care of it."

"Robin, this isn't a criticism, but perhaps we're barking up the wrong tree. This college girl idea of yours—what if she's a professional? Her age and build would appeal to some rich and perverted johns, which might explain the lack of a missing person report."

"Maybe. I sent the photo to the CHP, Park Service, and the FBI. Anything on the fingerprints?"

"Not yet—that could take weeks, although your L.A. contact might make a difference. What if we show the picture to Three-Way? He's probably down by the pier minding the office."

"Good idea. We could also take a drive over to Montecito and see whether Dawn will give us the time of day—she still owe you from the Reynolds case?"

"A visit to Dawn and her girls … sounds worthwhile."

"You are such a low life Doug, I swear!" The couple finishing their dessert at the next table had been glancing over surreptitiously. She figured they would be skipping a second cup of tea.

"Talking about Dawn—how's your love life? Who is it this time? Stephanie? Sandra? Or, how about our esteemed social worker? Laura's name comes up fairly frequently."

"Robin, you know I'm still waiting for you to give me the time of day!"

She laughed. "Yeah, I'll bet! You would starve if we were together. No laundry."

"I guess that's a good possibility. Then, Sean's a definite draw. Anyhow, Laura is married. You know my motto: *Stay away from married women!*"

"I'm being serious now—we had a good thing, but both of us agreed that more was not going to work for us. Doug, you would make some woman a great husband and some child a great father—you should settle down."

"Nope, only have eyes for you. Robin, I'm serious now … I'm always there for Sean, you know that."

She dropped the subject. Other than their discussions about Sean, Robin often found it difficult to tell whether Doug was serious. A while ago, they had arrived at a crossroads in their relationship when the time had come to make a decision: either they would commit long-term and one of them would take another job, or they would give up the relationship. They had decided their current jobs were too important to them and neither was inclined to change professions. Given her history with Stewart, Robin frequently told herself that a friend was more valuable than a lover, especially with Sean getting older. Just as frequently, it seemed, she wished they had taken the other road and stayed together.

93

Robin was finishing off her eggplant when her cell rang. "Hard to believe, but the university is calling. I'll take it outside."

"Go ahead. I'm positive any delay will not affect the quality of your meal," Doug said sarcastically, sotto voce, having long since polished off his sandwich.

A smiling Robin returned to the table in time to save the last of her cake from Doug's roving fork.

"Good news?"

"It is. Kudos to Marjorie ... she actually thinks we might have an answer in the next day or two, one way or another, though a slight hitch developed."

"Uh, oh ...."

"No big thing. They're requiring that the graduate student who agreed to help us out, sign a confidentiality agreement. The kid's name is Dan Sloan. He's willing to put in the hours necessary to get the work done, but wants to talk with his parents before signing anything."

"Great news, unless we have recalcitrant parents; if so, we'll search out another geek."

"Hey Doug, he's doing a good thing here."

"Sorry," he said contritely, and then rolled his eyes.

"Since things are going our way, why not head over to City College?" she said, ignoring the eye roll. "Maybe they'll be equally helpful."

"Let's go for it. Jeez, Robin, we have to do something about your eating habits. This is not good stuff for a growing boy—neither me *nor* Sean—us *men* need red meat and sugar!"

Doug left a hefty tip. They went to the register, paid the bill and left.

>>   <<   >>   <<

The drive over to the community college failed to net them anything other than, "We'll get back to you as soon as possible." They both knew nothing was going to come from that quarter without some evidence and a warrant.

"Robin, let's go talk to Three-Way."

"Okay, but I'm driving this time."

"You go girl!"

They pulled into a free parking spot by the Cabrillo Boulevard pier, and walked over to a picnic table on the beach serving as taxpayer-supported office space for a local pimp, or, professional facilitator, as Three-Way referred to himself.

"Hey Missy Robin, the world treating you good?" Three-Way called out with the Caribbean cadence of his native Jamaica. Thin, wiry, the coal black man had tight cornrows, piercings along both ear lobes, plus several in his nose. The effect paled in contrast with the black lightning bolt, outlined in red, tattooed up his left cheek.

"Well enough Three-Way. Well enough," she responded, shaking his hand.

"And you, my man?" Doug asked, giving Three a high five and an embrace.

"Shaking mon! It's all good. Dougie, my mon, they don't be treating you so good—you come talk to old Tree-Way and I be taking care of you. Missy Robin, *you* would get top billing—all that white skin and blond hair that I's can tell ain't seen no bottle never. Blue eyes that beat out any sapphire jewel I ever see!"

"Three, you are such a smooth talker! This woman is more than you can handle, man."

"Oops, don't want to fool around with your woman, Dougie my mon!"

"Hey, Three—we need help from you," Robin responded, trying to get the conversation back on line. She ignored the ownership comment.

"Dis my office, I'm a working mon, not on the welfare or anyting likes dat. Got sometin dat folds fo dis empty pocket of mine?"

"Not doing this for the love of your friends? How about we keep the fact you are such an upstanding citizen in mind next time you have a close encounter with the law?" Robin proposed.

"Sounding good, sweetheart. How 'bout a Jefferson? What's ya'll got for ol' Tree?"

Doug pulled out two twenties and handed the money and morgue photograph to Three. "Okay man, you got the green stuff and then some. Seen this girl?"

"Mon, someone sure done messed wit dis chick. Sheeit! I had nuting ta do with dis—you knows I treats my girls good." He handed back the photograph and pocketed the cash.

"Three-Way, we're not accusing you of anything. Just wonder if you've seen the girl around?" Robin said, in what she hoped was a reassuring tone. She sat down at the picnic table, which he had painted with all sorts of unrecognizable symbols and started to say something, but then realized the defacement of public property was the least of her problems.

"Okay, Missy, lemme take another look," he said, taking the photograph back from Doug. He set it on the table in front of him and peered closely at the picture of the victim.

Robin was sure the man needed glasses.

"Missy Robin, I neber seen dis girl. Not one of mine. Maybe she be goin' to school around here. De girl got dat look to her. Dat don't mean she ain't making money on da side. Plendy o'dat going on. Bad for my profit line. Got wot I mean?"

"Times are tough. What do I say? Thank you Three-Way," Doug said as he took the photograph back from the man's outstretched hand and gave him a high five in return.

"Thank you," Robin said. "We'll remember you helped us out," she added, knowing that day would be right around the corner. "Anyone else who might be of help?"

"No way. You tinkin' I don't be about my business?"

"Never," Robin rapidly responded before Doug got involved in the endless repartee the two men delighted in. A guy thing—one-upmanship—didn't matter they were pimp and cop.

"Good. All about respect, Missy Robin. Maybe you should be about going ober ta' Montecito to be talking wid dose folks. More da monies ober der … Dougie, my man, ya knowd Dawn. Talk wid dat beaudiful ladee."

"Thanks Three. We're off! Don't want to scare away the business," Doug said seriously.

Once back in the car, Robin laughed. "Even Three-Way thinks she might be a student. Doug, I need to get back and talk with the Chief about the sketch, catch up on my e-mail—damn, I forgot Bark Stalts is coming in today to sign his statement. I'm hoping for a DNA sample and a once over of his car by the M.E.'s office, so it might take awhile. Meantime, why don't you head over to visit the gorgeous Dawn?"

"Sounds like a good idea! I've calls to make and I want to check in on the Ortega case. Man, Robin, I have a bad feeling about the dude from the Isla Vista domestic case."

"Keep me in the loop. Oh, and give Laura my best."

"Smart ass!"

CHAPTER 13

Memories:
Fire, Wine & Romance

After making the sarcastic comment about Laura, Robin realized it was only one of a few she'd made lately. As she sat at her desk, door closed and blinds drawn, she thought about the first time they had been together. It hardly seemed possible that four years had gone by since that cool spring night in 2007. Subsequently, there had been several shifts in their relationship. Now, it wasn't clear to her where it was going. That was particularly the case when shards of jealousy unexpectedly showed themselves. A rather large shard was Laura McCann.

That spring night, Doug had taken her to his parents' estate to meet his parents. After passing through security gates, he pointed out a quaint gardener's cottage, framed with luxurious flowerbeds. That, he'd told her was where he lived.

When she'd commented on the beautiful landscaping, Doug had laughingly explained that a fleet of illegal Latin Americans tended *las flores* with the goal of making the landscape look *natural*. While walking back to the cottage, she had teased Doug about his living arrangement, but he had only laughed and pointed out that the cottage was situated a healthy distance away from his folks, and tucked into a stand of old growth trees, which provided privacy. Still, he had told Robin more seriously, it was not that he didn't appreciate his great life—he did. His mother's incredible decorating skills were evident in the house and even on the patio: amazing teak furniture, tropical plants, and beautiful sculptures. "My father's babies are the water-turned barbecue and bar," he had whispered when she'd commented on his mother's talent. Watching the sunset from the patio had left her speechless. The view of the Pacific Ocean was remarkable; Robin could not imagine living in such opulence. The property appeared to have walked off the pages of one of the English garden books she'd seen displayed à la Martha Stewart in the foyer of the main house.

As they walked along the flagstone path to the cottage, Robin told Doug she'd heard that movie and television stars, authors, and the like lived in Montecito, a detail she had shared with her mother. A dedicated reader of the *National Enquirer*, her mom wanted to know whether Doug had ever been to Oprah's house.

The question had elicited a boisterous laugh from him, one that would always bring a smile to her face.

He had loved the idea that Robin's mother was star-struck and explained that, though he would like to shine in her mom's eyes, O was notoriously private. Of course he should be on the star's A-list but, sadly, his only claim to Oprah fame was that his parents had visited the 23,000-foot mansion when the previous owners listed the property for sale in 2001. Oprah owned 43 acres, which, as he put it, "was a nice spread, even in this neck of the woods."

She assured Doug that he was on *her* A-list. Robin knew that as trite as the words had sounded, she had meant the sentiment. That feeling had not changed—she still did.

They had arrived at the cottage when Doug asked whether she would stay the night. Sean was sleeping over with Francisco, and

Denise would not bring him home until the next afternoon. Robin told him that she could. That she wanted to.

Doug immediately started making plans for a "fire, wine, and romance." When offered the choice to gather wood or build the fire, she had taken the canvas sling he offered and gone outside to the woodpile. After exploring the beautiful garden, Robin loaded wood into the sling.

By the time she returned, a fire crackled. Doug had placed an open bottle of Merlot in front of the fireplace and was sitting on the rug, leaning against the couch; Robin could feel his eyes on her as she stacked the wood in the iron log holder and hung the sling back up on the hook installed in the side of the fireplace. She had felt incredibly self-conscious as she moved about the room but enjoyed his attention.

Robin had wanted to wash up from her trip to the woodpile, but he'd patted the spot next to him. She lowered herself to the floor, took the proffered glass of wine, and leaned against Doug's chest, mesmerized by the dancing flames and his steady heartbeat. His musky warm smell. Her cares had faded away.

She still felt secure with her partner, professionally and personally, though he often drove her crazy. Nonetheless, he continued to play an important part in her life. And Sean's life.

Early on, Doug had avoided sharing much of his personal life with her, yet incessantly poked into hers. That night, intent on learning more about the man who so appealed to her, Robin had pushed to learn new details about his past. Doug had given in, though not without protest, claiming she was spoiling the moment—nonetheless, he laughed and refilled both glasses before settling into his story.

To this day, Robin remembered her astonishment on hearing his revelations. Since then, they had never discussed what he told her that evening, and she sometimes wondered whether he regretted confiding in her.

"Let's see then. My parents, Raúl Enrique and Concepción María Debayle, brought us to the States from Nicaragua when I was four and Julia and Tatiana were six and three. As you already know, unlike their neer-do-well brother, both of my sisters are married with children. You can imagine, as the only son and presumptive heir, the pressure is on for me to settle down. What do you think, Robin, ready for a life-time commitment?"

Robin had laughed at the question and teased him about being *so ready for commitment*! She had assured him *that* would require a few more bottles of wine and an available wedding chapel. Doug had assured *her* that she was easily worth a case of wine and a quick trip to Vegas. He had gotten up and put another log on the fire, and when he sat back down, he'd kissed her on the forehead, stroked her hair, and gently traced the freckles across her cheeks. Even now, she could feel his touch. Nonetheless, Robin was not to be distracted from her mission to circumvent Doug's typical strategy of avoiding discussion of his personal life, and had asked what he remembered about Nicaragua.

"No early memories, but I'm well acquainted with the Debayle clan's past and it's quite the story. Robin, I don't know if you're familiar with Latin American history … my father is a close relative to a man many refer to as a Nicaraguan dictator and, as such, my family led a privileged life for the many years the Somozistas were in power. However, papá recognized the warning signs; by the time the Sandinistas deposed Somoza, he had sold most of his property and transferred the bulk of his money to the U.S. with, it turns out, the convenient help of the CIA. The agency continued to back the Somoza family for a long time, hoping they would regain power. They didn't."

Robin had scooted away, faced him with crossed legs and a frustrated expression. "Honestly, Doug, the CIA—how do you know *that?*"

He had insisted that what he had told her was fact and pointed out that if they were going to make a life together, she needed to know what kind of family she would be getting into. Robin still found it hard to believe: he had been a child and she questioned whether Doug's father had told him that kind of stuff. He agreed that his papi would never have told him anything so personal. Before he said more, he asked her to keep in mind that he'd been a kid at the time. A bored one at that. Doug leaned over and kissed her lightly on the lips before reluctantly continuing his story.

"One rainy afternoon, I rifled through the drawers of papi's desk. I read some personal letters, eventually became bored with those, and rooted around some more. He had locked one of the bottom drawers and, of course, that's the one I had to get into. My father was naïve to the creativity of the young; his bid for privacy was to tape the key underneath the desk. Truthfully, with age I've come to realize that the contents of the locked drawer revealed more than I ever wanted to know about my father and his Nicaraguan connections."

Robin had finally understood that Doug was revealing something incredibly intimate about himself. She asked whether Raúl was aware of what he had done.

Doug had pulled her toward him. He laughed and went on to assure her that Raúl did not know that his son was aware of his business dealings, the intelligence connection, or the bank deposits, but in his gut, Doug knew that one day he would pay a price for the mischief he had gotten into that day. Meantime, for whatever reasons, Doug and his father did not get along so well.

By then, he had wanted to drop the subject, but she was curious to know whether the transition from Nicaragua to California had been difficult for the family. Though she didn't want to irritate him, her need to understand him better won out. Her family had lived in Maryland for generations; in contrast, his parents still seemed very Hispanic, while Doug and his sisters were very American—literally two cultures within a family. Robin had refilled both of their glasses and put another piece of the seasoned oak on the fire. He took a sip of wine, told her this was going to be the last she was going to get, and continued.

"Once papá realized the time had arrived to leave Nicaragua, he checked out properties for his family in sunny Florida and California. After bringing mamá to look at what he had chosen, they settled on Montecito. The estate, which sits on 15 acres and is thick with old eucalyptus, fig, olive, lemon, and orange trees, reminded her of Nicaragua. Here, they have raised their three children.

"Robin, your question about assimilation is a good one. To be honest, I'm surprised that after so many years of living in the United States, my parents and their friends—other wealthy Nicaraguans, some Cubans, and a few couples from Guatemala and El Salvador—all of whom fled their own countries and currently live comfortably in the U.S., still don't feel at home here. I think older Latino immigrants live with the disabling belief they will return to their previous lives. In contrast, their children are assimilated American citizens with no desire to live in Nicaragua, Cuba, El Salvador, or anywhere else in Latin America. Our dreams are about a life of happiness and success in this country.

"I've been down there twice. Once, I went with my sisters to visit one of mami's cousins. My parents hoped we would develop a bond with our extended family and *their* country. While in Nicaragua, much to papi's frustration, I learned it was not my country. Nonetheless, we had a blast with our cousins—fiestas, sunning by the swimming pool, being served by the maids, hanging out with the other privileged kids, and going to the movies. The Sandinistas, noted for their socialist bent, governed, much to the disgust of my parents and their friends, but life was not so bad for those with money who were able to shut themselves away in their gated communities. Still, when we returned to Montecito, I was glad to be home. As a family, we visited once more, but my feelings haven't changed."

Doug, figuring that was enough, more than enough, pulled her closer, and placed their glasses on the side table. They had made love until the ebbing fire drove him, naked and shivering, to get up and add more wood. The fire revived, he handed Robin her wine glass, pulled the comforter off the couch, and wrapped it around both of them.

Considering that he had uncharacteristically bared his soul, he wanted reciprocity. Doug had learned much about her life in Baltimore, but claimed she always avoided telling him how she came by Sean—"bypassing the obvious," he had whispered, holding her tightly.

Even now, Robin could feel him kissing her fingertips—she shouldn't be surprised that she let Laura get under her skin.

Figuring it was only fair, but without going into detail, Robin had explained that everything seemed to be going her way by the end of the Police Academy program, until she had discovered she was pregnant. After a couple of frantic weeks, she decided that having a child would not be so terrible. In reality, the timing was not bad: a ticking biological clock; she had finished her studies and had job possibilities; she and Stewart were pretty much living together. Maybe not the best of circumstances, given her Catholic upbringing, but not the worst either.

He wanted to know about the mysterious Stewart.

Embarrassed, Robin admitted that in some ways her logic had proved flawed. She had discovered she was pregnant at the same time Stewart decided he was too young for so much responsibility. "Too much to do!" was what he had told her. The coup de grâce was that maybe, just maybe, he had not been so monogamous after all. Stewart had been willing to take her for an abortion. Pay for it. Provide financial support if she wanted to see the pregnancy through, sign off if she wanted to go the adoption route. He had been available for everything but a monogamous relationship and fatherhood. Too much wine, too close to their lovemaking, she began to cry.

Doug tried to change the subject, offering to finish his pitiful bio and go on to his next "faux pas—college," assuring her that his story would "bring a smile to your lovely face." He kissed away her tears. She had run her fingers through his hair and lightly pressed her lips against his, tasting her own salty tears. Then, she'd pulled back and told him she was ready for more. In retrospect, it had been a mean thing to do. But she didn't regret it, that night had brought them closer together in so many ways.

He had wanted to stop. Yet, he only laughed and said suggestively, always sensitive to a double entendre, "Sure you don't want more?"

She'd pleaded for him to continue.

"Now an educational history—what's this, a marriage application? Robin, all of these Oprah moments are bound to take us to Vegas.

Anyhow, when the time came to look at potential colleges and universities, my primary motivation was to live independently. My mother's was that her son would remain close by. To be perfectly honest, Latino families can be somewhat claustrophobic, something I would avoid telling mamacita at all costs. My papá, on the other hand, was more interested in reputation than either the tuition or where the university was located. Our dueling motivations resulted in real battles before we settled on Yale. The distance suited me. Ivy League suited him. Only my mother was unhappy. My father's plan was that his only son would complete his undergraduate degree with honors before heading off to law school and a top New York firm. I, however, expected to practice criminal law in a prestigious California firm. Neither of us would get what we wanted.

"My father figured a Yale education would be sufficient to propel me to the top. Unfortunately, fraternity activities and women—not mutually exclusive—were of far more interest than my classes. I applied to the best law schools, but didn't get into a one. Well, in the interest of full disclosure, I did not have top grades or LSATs, though Loyola Law School waitlisted me. In the end, I settled on studying criminal justice at Golden West College in Huntington Beach. By then, papi wanted me to go into the military but I would not have any of it. Finally, *un milagro*; I graduated in the top ten percent of the class. Then, much to papi's frustration and shame, to put it mildly, I applied for a job with the SBPD.

"Chief Bartolo was happy to bring me onto the force—a well-educated local boy, bilingual, an amiable sort, if I do say so myself—he promoted me to detective within two years. Papá didn't care. In more reflective moments, if he has them, my father has to be aware that a big part of our problem is that despite a good education and extensive advantages his only son is a lowly police officer. Robin, I ticketed one of his friends for speeding and my father came to me expecting that I would take care of the ticket. Instead, I laughed—couldn't help myself—told him it was the wrong country and the wrong century. He was angry, to put it mildly. Those resentments continue to simmer."

She had told him she was sorry. He had replied there was no reason to be sorry. Despite the problems with his father, Doug considered himself to be a rarity—a perfectly content man. He loved his work and had found her and Sean. He had a cool place to live, could go about his business with little or no interference, and he had clean laundry. Good meals close by, and a mother who doted on her boy. "What a life! Querida, I deserve a kiss."

They had made love again, with a passion that had left them both breathless, content. When almost asleep under the thick comforter, the embers dying, and limbs entwined, Robin had sleepily asked how this was going to work with the job.

"Querida, we are good. More than good. Let's get some sleep."

Robin shook herself free of the flow of memories, got up, and opened her blinds. As she watched Doug spiritedly talking on the phone in his office across the hallway, she knew their story still had no ending.

CHAPTER 14

A Beautiful Sight:
October 2011, Day Two

Sonia buzzed to let Robin know the receptionist had sent Barclay Stalts to her office. The detective quickly worked out a plan before going out to meet him. She wanted his DNA. Doc wanted his car.

"Mr. Stalts. Thanks for coming in." She extended a hand, which he shook. "Would you like a cup of coffee before reviewing your statement?"

"Sorry about being late, Detective. I would have been here earlier but got caught up with some business. Coffee would be appreciated."

"Cream or sugar?"

"Black, thank you."

Robin stopped at the Sonia's doorway. "Hi, Sonia, could you have someone bring a cup of black coffee for Mr. Stalts when a fresh pot is made? We'll be in Conference Room B."

"No problem!" she said with a wink. "I'm going on break in a few minutes; I will take care of it."

"Thanks. Just for Mr. Stalts. I already helped myself to a cup. The pot was almost empty, but there was too much left to throw away."

Robin led the witness down the long hallway and into the conference room. "Here we are, sir. Sit anywhere you would like. Oh, by the way, the M.E. has a request: because you checked on the victim, Doc was wondering whether you would give us a DNA sample and allow forensics to vacuum your car and check for fingerprints. Honestly, the forensics would serve to eliminate you as suspect given the circumstances under which you found the girl."

The screenwriter did not hesitate. "Makes sense to me. Officer—"

"Robin," she corrected.

Sonia came into the room with a small tray and another surreptitious wink in Robin's direction. She set the coffee mug in front of Stalts, as well as a plate with a huge slice of blueberry pie. Robin hoped that if the screenwriter was at all ambivalent about the swab and car forensics, Sonia's baking would change his mind.

"Sonia. You're one of the operators I spoke with yesterday?"

"I am." She handed him a fork and paper napkin.

"Thank you," he shook her hand. "It was a difficult day and I appreciated knowing you had my back."

"You're welcome." She left the room.

"I'll let Doc know you'll help out. Sonia's quite the cook—enjoy her pie and the coffee—it'll just take me a minute."

"No problem. I've got a script to work on."

>>   <<   >>   <<

Robin returned to find Stalts deeply involved in his work, the pie gone.

"Sorry, it took me longer than I expected. Freddy, Doc's assistant, will pick you up when you're finished here. It shouldn't take too long, but if it's an inconvenience, a loaner car is available. Meantime, here is your statement for review. We'll discuss any discrepancies before you sign it. The pie looked good, I think I'll get a piece and refill my coffee. Can I get you anything? Oh, and if you want to add something significant to your statement, note it at the bottom and initial any changes you make to the text."

"Thanks. Pie's delicious but one piece is enough. No more coffee—I haven't been sleeping. Finding the woman brought back memories of Iraq."

"I'm sorry."

"Thanks." Pen in hand, he began reading the statement. Robin again left the room.

After she returned, Robin powered up her laptop and checked her e-mail while Stalts read and occasionally made a notation. She caught a trace of the Hugo Boss fragrance he had worn the previous day.

Stalts put down the pen. "Alright, Detective—nice job! Only one factual change, though not such a good one. Well, maybe a clarification. Anyhow, as my niece would say, 'it's my bad.' As I told you, I left Santa Barbara for Mill Valley bright and early on Thursday. Friday and Saturday, I was home with my gardener working on the yard. I left my home late Sunday morning, but what I neglected to say was that I had stopped off in Carmel-by-the-Sea midafternoon and decided to spend the night with an old friend. I left next day. I've made a note to that effect at the bottom of the statement, which I initialed."

"Not to worry, Mr. Stalts. Keeping everything straight after a shock is difficult. That's why we recommend witnesses come in and review their statements after the fact. Time you left Carmel Monday?" Robin asked, pen poised, staying low-key.

"Bark. Call me Bark. Monday morning, by about nine, I was back on the road. Stayed up too late, too much wine—probably why I was so tired when I spoke with you."

"Can I get your friend's name and contact information? Also, can someone confirm the time you departed your Mill Valley home?"

"Sure, on both counts. Carmel—his name is Sergio Robiou. Wait a minute." He pulled out his cell phone and gave Robin the phone number. "I guess I'm lucky my neighbor saw me leave the day before.

Here's his number." He handed her a folded piece of paper from his wallet.

Robin wrote down both names and their respective contact information. While doing so, it occurred to her the file Doc requested had something to do with an accident of a student traveling to Monterey, which was not far from Carmel. She would have to remember to tell Doug.

"Would you happen to have the phone number of your gardener with you?"

"Yeah, that's also in my phone. Hang on and I'll write it down." Stalts made a few more notes at the end of the statement and signed his name. He handed the papers to her.

The phone rang. It was Sonia. "Robin, Fred's here for Mr. Stalts. He'll return for the car."

"Perfect timing. We'll be right out."

Robin walked her witness back to Sonia's office and introduced him to Freddy. She fervently hoped Doc's assistant did not scare him off with his erratic behavior.

"Did you like my pie?" Sonia asked Stalts.

"Delicious! Thank you very much."

Robin reached out to shake his manicured hand. "Mr. Stalts, I'll be in touch. Thank you."

"I only hope I've been of help. The poor kid deserves justice." Fred took off with Stalts trailing behind.

"Sonia, please tell Doug I forgot about Sean's dental appointment and have to leave early, but I'll be in early tomorrow. He should call if he has anything for me. Thanks for your help with Stalts." She was relieved the meeting was significantly less antagonistic than the original interview, in part to be sure, due to Sonia's ministrations. Or, could be she hadn't been fair, the screenwriter may have just been tired.

"Glad to do it, Robin. Good looking man!" she said with a wink and a giggle. "I'll give your message to Dougie."

"Chief still out?" Robin inquired, ignoring the implication of Sonia's multiple winks, and the 'good looking' comment.

"At a budget meeting in no danger of ending. But he's got his Blackberry with him."

"Thanks. I need approval for a sketch."

After going to the dentist for a cleaning, Robin dropped Sean off at Denise's house, and arrived home with just about an hour to get ready before Matt picked her up. She started the bath, poured in lavender salts, and went to her closet, anxiously flicking through the few hangers holding clothes appropriate for a date. She didn't want to wear something she had previously worn with Doug. A frustrated Robin then remembered the purple off-shoulder Donna Karan dress she had bought at a Nordstrom sale months ago, aware at the time she was still spending far too much, despite the reduced price. She removed the garment from the nest of tissue in the silver box and carefully laid it out on the bed before returning to the bathroom.

The doorbell rang as a nervous Robin fastened the last strap of her heels; she quickly put on lipstick in front of the hall mirror before opening the door. "Hi Matt, come on in. Be careful not to trip over any ninjago toys—take it from me, the ninja deliver a heavy wallop."

"Robin, you look amazing!" Matt declared appreciatively, and blushed. He extended a bouquet of white tulips wrapped in yellow tissue and tied with a thin silver ribbon. "I'm a little early."

"Thank you, Matt ... on all counts. I love white tulips and I'm ready *and* hungry!"

"What a woman! Not going to keep me waiting and has an appetite. I made reservations at the Wine Cask. Is that okay?"

"Haven't been there since they reopened, so that should be fun. Let me put these beautiful flowers in a vase and then we can go."

"Is your son with his grandparents? I was hoping to meet him."

"Not with his grandparents, unfortunately. I'm from Baltimore. I dropped him off at the sitter's house. She has a child about Sean's age, so he enjoys spending time with them."

"How old is he?"

"Six."

"What about we do something with Sean on Saturday—a hike and picnic?"

"I'd like that." Robin was a goner. Considering her nervousness, she was grateful to remember Doug's mention of gull shooting with Sean on Saturday. "Oops, Saturday's out. Sunday?"

"That works. Why don't we meet up at the Ranger Station at 10? I'll bring the picnic, you bring the toys."

"Great! Sean will like that."

>>   <<   >>   <<

Matt pulled up in front of the restaurant, handed the keys to the valet, went around to the passenger side, and offered Robin a hand, a gesture for which she was grateful, given she was wearing heels. When he put an arm around her, Robin knew she could get used to spending time with this good looking, thoughtful, grounded, and environmentally- and kid-friendly man. The maître d' led them to their table, pulled out a chair for Robin, and then handed each a menu and extensive wine list. He poured water from a chilled clear glass carafe in which wafer thin lemon slices floated. Robin left the wine choice up to Matt and he ordered a bottle of Chardonnay from Mendocino. The attentive server brought the wine to the table and waited for a nod before pouring a glass for each of them.

"I'll be back shortly for your order," she said.

"Thank you. Matt, the wine is delicious."

"Glad you like it. The vineyard has a long history of natural farming practices and great wines keep coming out of the area—a definite win-win! Robin, would you mind business first?"

"That's fine. What's up?"

"The Painted Cave case—I received the paperwork. Thanks. We still haven't received an abandoned car report. Honestly, Robin, I don't think it's out there. Any thoughts?"

Robin scarcely finished updating Matt on the case when their server returned with warm rolls and soft butter. After they had placed their orders, Matt refilled their wine goblets.

"Thank you. Honestly, this is the first time I've felt relaxed all day." She buttered two rolls and handed one to Matt.

"Then let's forget about business, why don't we? We can't do anything else about the case tonight. Robin, I know nothing of you outside of the job. For starters, how did you end up here? Santa Barbara's a far cry from Baltimore—though, to tell you the truth, I've never been to Maryland," he laughed. "I have watched the *Wire*!"

"Sorry to disabuse you of the notion, but the *Wire* isn't exactly Baltimore! However, you *are* correct that Santa Barbara is different from Baltimore. Now that I live on the *West* Coast, being East Coast born and bred is something I generally don't admit to."

"What's the take on California when you're in Baltimore?"

"At home, I avoid talking about California altogether, which isn't difficult—nobody's interested. The key question determining who you are in *Bawlmer* is where you went to high school. In my case, I went to The Catholic High School of Baltimore, an all-girl's school. End of conversation—the discussion never proceeds to where I attended college or my professional life—your high school and neighborhood, in my case Dundalk, are what define you in the city that is my birthplace, the information I gave you lets the the listener know of my blue collar roots."

"Wow, that's interesting. Given the geographic bias, I guess your parents were less than thrilled with your westward migration?"

"To put it mildly. Much to my Baltimore or, as the locals say, *Bawlmer* family's concern, the problem wasn't only that I would be far from home—after all, as far as the natives are concerned, attending school in *Virginia* is far away—their only child was going to California!"

"Other than the obvious, which I guess is the distance—what's their issue with California?"

"Matt, as far as my parents are concerned, I might as well be living on the moon, though I really think they expected California to be worse: drugs, indolence, free love, orgies, new age spirituality, cults, vegetarians, vegans, and on and on and on. I'm not sure where they get their information, but I think Mom and Pop are stuck in the sixties. Worse, they can't let go of their expectations for me to find a job, a boyfriend, marry, and bring grandchildren into the world—all in their own backyard. I tried to reassure them that like all good Marylanders I'll be back in the family-fold in no time, but they are having none of it."

"What's wrong with having a family?"

"Nothing at all, but I wanted to go to graduate school and see the world, so I settled on UCLA. I mailed the deposit the day I received my acceptance letter and a notice of a generous research fellowship *and* a tuition waiver. Three weeks later I was on my way to a Ph.D. in psychology and a new life!"

The server brought their salads and dressed them with parmesan and fresh pepper. She left a small silver carafe of Caesar dressing on the table.

"Mind you, I'm not putting down your final career choice, but how'd you come to SBPD?"

"Well, it's a long story and enough of me. Let's talk about you."

"Nah, you're far more interesting. Puhleeze."

Robin took a sip of water, looked around the beautiful restaurant—it was packed. He'd sounded like Sean and she gave in. "Well, I guess so, given such an intense 'please,' but you'll get the *Reader's Digest* version."

"Here, have more wine. I'm told it loosens the tongue."

"Sounds underhanded to me! Here goes: when my graduate studies were finally ending, I expected to get a great job back in Maryland, but when the time came to apply for a job, I thought twice about my plans. Better late than never, I told my friends." Robin laughed, self-conscious. Aware she was blushing, she hurried along with her story. "Anyhow, my plan was to investigate the early education needs of autistic children, yet when I started looking at academic positions, it occurred to me the classes and internships related to psychopathology were what I'd enjoyed most."

"From autism to killers and crime—I can only imagine how thrilled your advisor was."

"He was actually pretty decent about my last minute career detour and suggested I take a look at the UCLA forensics program and the L.A. Police Academy."

"And your parents?"

"Yep—there were my parents. By then, the pressure was on to return home, but I guess I knew if I did, I'd never leave again, and I wasn't ready for that."

The food runner set down their plates, removed the covers with a flourish, and left without a word. They began to eat.

"Another glass of wine?" Matt offered.

"Thank you. These diver scallops are delicious. Your mushroom risotto?"

"Excellent!"

"Okay, so what *did* you do?"

"Being the overachiever I am, I applied to both the LAPD and forensics program, anticipating a crazy year or two, but thought the extra training and education would be worth it."

"How long did it take?"

"Six months at the Academy. They promised ... let me see if I can remember the exact words, 'a rigorous and demanding training regimen that is a rewarding and life-changing experience.' The most important thing I learned was I am capable of so much more than I ever expected. Luckily, for me, the UCLA program allowed me to use Academy coursework to meet some of my Master's requirements, which made completing both programs more realistic. The career shift paid off—I love my job and I love Santa Barbara."

Once dinner was over, Matt insisted on taking care of the bill. Robin left the tip, and they departed. While the valet brought the car, they stood close together, his arm tightly around her shoulders.

Once on the road, Matt asked, "How about a walk on the beach?"

"Okay, although we'll have to park close by because I can't walk in the sand with heels."

"Oops! You sure?"

"The night is clear and the porichthys glitter under the moonlight. A beautiful sight."

"Wow—porichthys! What a woman!" Matt parked, leaned over, and kissed her. Robin kissed him back.

CHAPTER 15

Alibis:
Day Three

Robin arrived early. The blinds in Doug's office were drawn. According to Sonia, he had already been in and had left to meet Laura McCann. Robin called him on his cell.

"Hey, girl—what's up?"

"Doug, can you come back when you and Laura are finished? Doc's got something for us."

"Sure, but I haven't chased her down yet, so it might take a couple of hours before I return. Oh, and I need to stop by the restaurant where Roberto Ortega *says* he works. Why don't you check in with Doc? Find out whether she has time for us in a few hours. If not, go without me."

"Will do! Bartolo gave me the go-ahead for the sketch."

"Good."

She heard the click at his end and hung up.

>> << >> <<

The phone rang just as Robin finished updating the Painted Cave file with what she had learned from Stalts.

"Hey Robin. Doug. Sorry, about the delay."

"No problem—Doc will see us whenever you show."

"I'll be back in an hour. What are you up to?"

"Processing evidence. Is this what being primary is about? Not the money, not the glory, but the paperwork? By the way, Doug, did I tell you Stalts came in yesterday? I want to follow up on a discrepancy in his statement, but we can talk about that later. I updated the Park Service."

"You go girl."

"Not so much, you dawg!"

"Hey, play nice! You're one to talk. Sonia filled me in on the *hot* park ranger, her word not mine. Also, Genoa's description. Now, *Mr. Hollywood*! Perk of the job?"

"What?"

"Robin, don't take this the wrong way, but you might want to close the door when you've got the call on speaker. Better, don't use it at all. But back to what's important: In the guise of getting a report, you go out with the hottie? What about my boy? Not sounding so kosher to me."

"What do you know about kosher?" Robin slammed down the receiver. Nothing ever got by Doug—the man was an inveterate gossip. She was done with the speakerphone.

While Robin waited for her partner to show, she began checking out Stalts' alibis. At the Painted Cave, he had said he was returning to Santa Barbara from Mill Valley. He *now* claimed he had spent the night in Carmel, which if true, would cover him for Sunday and Monday. Depending on time of death, she still needed to follow-up

Stalts' alibi for Friday and Saturday. She expected tracking down the gardener was going to take time—she had called twice and gotten no answer.

First try, she got hold of his friend, Sergio Robiou. Robiou confirmed that Stalts stopped over at his house—arrived in the afternoon; they'd batted around some ideas for a television show, and had too much to drink. His friend left Monday between 8 and 9 a.m., which Robin figured put the screenwriter near the cave around midday, the time Sonia took his call. Robiou agreed to review and sign a statement Sonia would fax to the Carmel PD. Robin next called Stalts' neighbor, Bradley Swanson. The neighbor said he had seen their person of interest working around the yard on Saturday. On Sunday, Swanson had been outside picking up his newspaper between 11 and 11:30 a.m. when he saw Stalts backing out of the driveway. He had not seen him since then.

"That beauty of a Porsche is pretty hard to miss," he had assured Robin, adding somewhat wistfully, "must be nice to be single." He agreed to go to the Mill Valley station to sign a statement.

Despite the two witnesses, she remained unconvinced of Stalts' innocence. Robiou had not been surprised that a SB detective called him, which got Robin to thinking that Stalts had plenty of time to arrange an alibi. If either alibi failed to hold up, the next step was to consider the possibility that Stalts left the scene, cleaned the car, returned, and made the call, though the time element would be tight. Doc should be able to tell her whether the screenwriter had scrubbed the car. Stalts continued at the top of her list: attractive, hot car, discrepancy in the statement, two of three alibis confirmed—one of those solid, the other shaky, no shortage of opportunities to pick up women, and an argument for DNA at the scene.

Robin plotted the carwashes on a map of the area, hoping for video if he had washed the car at one of them. She wanted to have credit card information pulled, but there wasn't probable cause to do so. She decided to check Stalts' receipts against the timeline after lunch and headed outside to eat and enjoy the California sunshine, cell phone, pen and paper in hand. Sean's birthday was on the horizon, and the days had long since passed when a simple toy made him happy. Each year brought a lengthier list of more expensive requests. Robin would keep that in mind when she negotiated for a salary increase in the spring. After all, she was now primary material with long birthday and Christmas lists and a low bank balance—arguments unlikely to convince a Chief inundated in budgetary woes.

She looked up to see the paunchy, ill-dressed, balding O'Donnell. Once Robin had come to know the recalcitrant detective well, she had decided the grizzled veteran with the gruff personality was partial to her because they were both from the East Coast—he from Brooklyn, she from Baltimore—and both often found themselves disconcerted by California and Californians. Over time, Robin developed a close bond with the man who invariably sported a stain of one sort or another on his shirt and had suffered loudly when the Chief not only banished his cigars from inside the building, but also from anywhere near the entrance. It was with a vengeance that Sonia monitored adherence to the new edict. Although Robin did not smoke, she routinely accompanied Ken to the parking lot while he indulged in his favorite vice.

The old guard divorced cop and the new age single-mother police officer made a habit of going to lunch together once a week. Robin generally ordered a sandwich stacked high with cheeses and vegetables Ken had never heard of, never mind eaten. In contrast, in spite of his high blood pressure, he typically ate a rare roast beef with fried onion sandwich on white bread. Regardless of a multitude of differences, Robin made Ken laugh. For her, he was a generous source of information on crime, crime-fighting strategies and per-haps most important, Santa Barbara politics. Doug Debayle teased her about needing a "Daddy," but Robin was aware that her rapid rise to detective was largely due to Ken's generous, albeit somewhat garrulous mentoring. She liked and respected the Deputy Chief and ignored Doug's caustic remarks.

"Hey, Robin, what are you doing out here by your lonesome?"

"Just thinking how lucky I am. Ken, I could be unemployed, living in L.A. and involved with Stewart—I'm definitely a lucky woman." She took another bite of her sandwich.

"Any more trouble with the so and so?"

"He calls less since you contacted him *and*, Ken, don't deny that you did. By the way, good detecting—I don't know how you located him! Still, despite your help, he manages to make me miserable when I do hear from him, which was last night. Stewart has never once driven the 90-minute trip north solely to spend time with Sean, but when I'm trying to get to sleep, he delights in calling with threats of a trip to court over visitation rights. Those nights, I don't sleep so well. When we left Los Angeles, I was stupid to imagine we could leave him behind."

"Yeah, a drawback to the internet. Robin, you should know that nobody disappears anymore."

"True, but I'm better off than Susana Ortega, Doug's domestic assault victim."

"Kiddo, you're way better off, I have your back. Sorry, but I gotta go. We can talk later."

"Thanks," Robin said, glancing around before giving her friend a quick hug.

"Ken, can you give me just one more minute? It's about a case."

"Sure. What's up?"

"It's the Painted Cave investigation. Don't know what you've heard, but we have a Hollywood screenwriter who called in a murder. He checked to see whether she was alive before we arrived, so his DNA is at the scene. Makes sense—good citizen. Has alibis, which could have been manipulated, we're still following up on those. My question: Why take the chance of implicating himself? What's your experience regarding murderers calling in their victim?"

"Unfortunately, I've got too much of it. Yeah, it's never a big surprise when a dude calls in a dead woman he's been seeing, married to, dating, an ex- of. With few exceptions, he's the soul of innocence, the cops' best friend in solving the murder. It takes a certain amount of arrogance and intelligence, yet maybe because they are so damn arrogant, they actually come to think of themselves as innocent. Denial, Robin, is an *outstanding* defense mechanism. But I gotta go. Talk later?"

"Sure. Thanks, Ken."

>>   <<   >>   <<

Robin let out a yelp of surprise when someone rapped her on the head from behind.

"I'm *baaack*! Ready for Genoa?"

"Jeez Doug ... you scared the hell out of me! How did it go with Laura?" In spite of all her good intentions, Robin asked the question and, worse, followed it with what she belatedly realized was a suggestive laugh.

"Robin, she's *married*—you gotta get your mind out of the gutter! It's a professional relationship."

"Sorry." She wondered once again whether she was jealous—Laura seemed to be an ongoing thorn in her side. It was not so long ago she and Doug had been good together. "Mea culpa," she said, and meant it. "Have you sorted out your domestic?"

"Sorted out? Not really. You know how these cases go ... ambivalence, half-truths, distressed children, and frightened women. Men protesting their innocence. Claims of discrimination. Still, Laura is good at her job, and I have faith in what she can do for the family. Well, that is if *we* can keep the husband in check; with that goal in mind, I stopped by the taquería where the dude said he works."

"Learn anything?"

"That's why I'm late. I was in for a hell of a surprise! It turns out Roberto Ortega works at a restaurant owned by the parents of an accident victim I followed up with when I first started with the PD. Robin, the girl's mother is still grieving, even after so many years—I feel sorry for her. Well, for both of them. A Latino man is all about protecting his family, and this was their only daughter. One son, I think. They are broken. On my way back, I was thinking whoever came up with the ridiculous term *closure* was an ass! Anyhow, I just wanted to make sure the dude worked where he said he did and give him *the eye*."

"The Debayle eye—well, that should do it! Do you think Susana will go back to her husband?"

"Nah, she's filed for divorce. Just wanted to verify employment and give the dude a migraine. Bartolo's not going to want another harassment charge, so I kept the visit low key."

"Hardly sounds low key. Bet you got yourself lunch though."

"Of course. Señora Castillo was at the register and recognized me right away. Talking does not preclude ordering food! Meantime, I saw my guy, so he's on the up and up concerning his job. He saw me. I gave him the eye. I'm anticipating he has the good sense to understand that if he doesn't leave the wife and kiddies alone, I will be all over his ass, and his boss will find out what's up. Incidentally, Robin, it was hot in the kitchen and his sleeves were rolled up. The dude may be sporting a gang tat—at a distance, it looks a hell of lot like Santa Bruja. I'll need to talk with Susana again. That's a whole different matter."

"Shouldn't be difficult obtaining info regarding the tattoo. Oh, by the way, before we go talk with Doc, let me give you a quick update of my meeting with Stalts, the guy who called in the Painted Cave victim."

"Okay, but babe it's going to cost you. Hand over the rest of your sandwich and a slug or two of the water."

"You are an endless pit!"

Doug helped himself to the last of Robin's lunch without another word.

"I'll make this quick. Stalts acted as if he had nothing to hide and appeared legitimately concerned about solving the crime. Less attitude this time around. I told him the victim's death hadn't been judged a homicide, and we're still looking at the evidence."

"Smart. Got a decent alibi?"

"He pretty much repeated the same sequence of events he'd given me at the cave, with one important exception. Stalts had told me, maybe I had assumed, he'd come straight from Mill Valley. Turns out he spent Sunday night in Carmel and left early Monday. Gave me contact information for that friend, as well as for the neighbor who observed him leaving home Sunday morning. He added the piece about the stopover and signed—no request for a lawyer. I contacted the neighbor and friend—their respective PDs are faxing back the signed statements I sent. I asked him about Friday and Saturday, since we don't have a time of death. He left here late Thursday and claimed to be at home Friday and Saturday. I'm trying to reach the gardener he was supposedly working with for those two days, but so far no success, though his neighbor saw him working in the yard on Saturday. I also have his gas and food receipts for the trip. I'm checking on gas stations with car washes near the cave. There is one on the Chumash Reservation. I'll see whether Tyler can take a drive over there—ask to take a look at the tape for the day in question. A couple on upper State we should check on. Haven't gotten to the receipts."

"DNA swab?"

"Uh, huh. Doc took the sample, and techs processed his Porsche."

Doug tossed the sandwich wrapper into the garbage can with his usual accuracy. "Robin, Stalts is a screenwriter, capable of putting together a great narrative."

"I know that. He certainly had time to set up an alibi with his Carmel friend. Doug, I really don't think he's the perp, but he's still at the top of the list, at least for now."

"Good girl. It seems improbable that a Hollywood screenwriter who is driving from San Francisco to an empty house in Hope Ranch forgets to inform a detective he stopped off along the way—for the night. He's tired, takes pictures at a not particularly well-frequented cave, and discovers the body of a beautiful young girl in the area where he is currently living. Call me cynical!"

"Mill Valley, not San Francisco. North of the city. Well … when you put it like that Doug, the story does sound hinky. I'll tell you what, let's wait until the forensics come in and then evaluate where we're at, though he touched the body, so I am not expecting much, unless we get a hit from somebody else. Anyhow, there is still no evidence saying the victim died of anything more than an accident. Meantime, I'll stay suitably suspicious. The car may give up something—maybe that's what she has for us. Let's go." Robin stood up, and the partners walked over to the M.E.'s office.

CHAPTER 16

Preliminary Report:
Day Three

Genoa was reading something at an unbelievably littered desk. Robin rapped gently on the frame of the open door. The only chairs for visitors were stacked high with books and papers. Even the floor was not immune from the chaos.

"You've been here before, don't just stand outside gawking. Come on in, my good Ds, and clear some chairs for yourselves."

"Where do you want these books and papers?" Robin asked.

"Put them under or to the side of the chair. If I need them, I'll find them. My filing system has always been of an easy-going sort!" she chortled.

Doug didn't hesitate—his stack hit the floor with a bang.

Robin sat as directed, but kept the books on her lap. She wondered whether Fred was rubbing off on his boss rather than vice-versa—at this rate, the two of them walking down the hall laughing would send everyone running. She looked around, unable to imagine how the M.E. got any work done amidst the clutter. The room was plenty large, even more spacious than the Chief's office, but in Genoa's world, nature truly abhorred a vacuum: every available space was filled with books, journals, articles torn out of journals, newspapers, all sorts of bones, skulls of varying size, and bottles with body parts, about which Robin preferred to remain in the dark. The collection had not made sense to her the first couple of visits because a medical examiner is required to account for all tissue. One day she had gathered her courage and asked about the weird assortment. Genoa laughed and explained she used them for conferences and teaching purposes, assuring the embarrassed detective she had the necessary permissions.

Robin found it especially difficult to avoid looking at the two eyeballs floating in a large bottle full of an unknown liquid. The container had been placed on a shelf at the same height of Doc's head when she sat at her desk; Robin was sure she had placed it in exactly that position on purpose. In addition to the physical mess, she was convinced Genoa smoked, though she had no direct evidence to support her hypothesis. Nonetheless, a gentle haze persuaded her she was right. She imagined Doc must have a hell of an air cleaner stashed somewhere in the mess, though it did not much matter because Sonia avoided the M.E.'s office at all cost.

"Well, my hard-working Ds, I have a *preliminary* report for you. But, before you take it to the bank or to the Chief, note the carefully articulated word *preliminary*. I am, of course, referring to the young woman discovered out at the Painted Cave, fortuitously spotted by what's his name ... Barclay Stalts. By the way Robin, is that Mr. Hollywood's real name? As you're aware, he spent considerable time in our good company yesterday. 'Grist for the mill,' I was told."

"Probably something like James Smith when he saw the light of day," Doug said.

His response sounded unduly disparaging to Robin, but she gave him a pass—mindful she had stepped over the line with her references to Laura.

Fun and games over, Doc reverted to serious. "The victim was dead 48 to 72 hours by the time Stalts found her. Seventy-two is a stretch—she probably died sometime Saturday. No evidence of rape. So far, we have obtained no forensic evidence from Mr. Hollywood's car to suggest she was with him, though they're still working on it. Prints obtained at the site match the shoes you gave me, Robin. Yours as well. I don't remember any carwashes in the area, but let me know if you pin down a timeline precluding Mr. Stalts from leaving the area to clean the car and return to the scene."

Robin opened her mouth to tell Genoa of Stalts' alibis and the carwash search, but Doc put up a warning forefinger. "If he did the deed and then cleaned the car, you should be able to come up with a witness, given we're looking at a bright red Porsche. So far, nothing at the site or on the body shows he is responsible. Though it is true, we will probably find trace evidence linking him to the victim, which is not surprising since he checked to see whether she was alive. Mr. Barclay Stalts should remain on your list; nonetheless, I think you need to keep looking. Robin, you sent the lipstick to L.A., along with the victim's fingerprints, and fingerprints from the car, right?"

"Doug took care of it. Doc, we're working on other avenues to identify her—right now, we're exploring whether she was a student at USB or City College." She glanced at Doug, "Or, a working woman."

"Both good possibilities. My guess, if a prostitute, she was high end. We have a DNA sample from Stalts. Good-looking guy! Robin, you still single? Apparently, *he* is. Mr. Hollywood asked about you and Fred kept him entertained."

Doug's head snapped up. He shifted in his seat and watched intently as a blushing Robin responded.

"Still single. I guess I missed the cues regarding Mr. Stalts' romantic interest. Tempting," Robin said, with a wink at Doug and a toss of her hair, "but, I'm not going to get involved with a potential perp."

He laughed. "Not giving up much," Doug retorted, stretching his legs. "Anyhow, you may not have heard the news—Robin's got the hottie park ranger on a string."

Genoa chuckled. "You're right, Robin, Stalts appeared genuinely upset to have found the young woman dead and disfigured. But, for now, we'll park the emotion and wait for the science."

"Remember, he's a Hollywood screenwriter!" Doug interjected.

"I guess I don't need to tell you both to keep an open mind as you continue the investigation. Yet, I must say, Doug, your mind may have already snapped shut. Does the guy have an alibi for any part of his timeline?"

Robin answered before Doug made things worse. "Bark seems to be pretty well covered for the time he left his house." The minute she said it, she knew she'd put her foot in it but kept on. "He may have spent the night in Carmel-by-the-Sea and departed for Santa Barbara next morning. I'm waiting for signed statements for each point in the trip. Also, I'm checking out an alibi for Friday and Saturday, as well as canvassing carwashes within a 30 mile radius."

"Bark?" Doug queried, eyebrow cocked.

"Barclay. He said to call him Bark."

"Great. Nothing like keeping a professional distance," he whispered sardonically, kicking the leg of her chair. A batch of folders slipped off the stack of books.

Both women ignored him. "Anyhow, Mr. Stalts gave me two gas receipts and a few from restaurants I'll follow up on. Given the timeline we've got so far, and your findings regarding time of death, I don't think he's our guy, but I'll continue looking into it and get back to you."

"In all seriousness, I agree with Robin—he's probably not the doer," Doug conceded. "But, Genoa, as you so wisely suggested, *we* will keep an open mind."

"Doc, is there an official cause of death for the victim?" Robin asked, given the questions about the screenwriter appeared settled, at least for the moment.

"Victims," the M.E. replied.

"What victims?" Doug asked in confusion. He looked at Robin, who shrugged a shoulder and shook her head.

Looking like the proverbial cat that had shredded the canary, Genoa paused—

"I'm referring to *victims* not victim … the young woman was 12 to 14 weeks pregnant."

Robin looked at Doug, and he responded with a slight pull of pursed lips, a surefire indicator that Doc had caught him off guard.

"I take it you weren't aware of the pregnancy?"

"Absolutely no idea—I guess there'd be no reason for us to know, we don't even know who she is. Well, *that* puts a new light on things," Robin exclaimed.

Doug said nothing. She knew of her partner's soft spot for children; he did not like it when they were entrapped in the evil adults perpetuate so frequently on the young. They'd even had some intense arguments concerning the issue of abortion. He would bend only for rape and incest, and then just slightly.

"Well, she was. Primiparous."

"What does *that* mean?" Doug asked.

"A first pregnancy versus multiparous, meaning multiple offspring. Although we believed our victim had been shot through the temple that was not the case. So, unfortunately, no brass as evidence."

"Doc, you're certainly full of surprises today. What is the cause of death then? I presumed she had been shot because her hair was thoroughly matted with blood in the temporal area of the scalp. Boy, a bad move on my part," Robin said, forgetting Doc had made the same assumption the day before. She felt the eyeballs watching her, and there was not a friendly wink between them.

"Don't feel bad. I'm supposedly a highly esteemed M.E.," she said. "I also thought she'd been shot, but the autopsy results show that's not the case. Instead, a sharp rock probably caused the scalp injury. Head injuries bleed a lot, even after death, but the bleeding then stops fairly quickly."

"Is that how she died? Hit with a rock?"

"Sorry Doug. I can't tell you whether she was hit with something sharp or fell and hit her head on one of the rocks or boulders.

Wouldn't be surprised if someone tried to carry the body down the damn hillside, dropped her and her head hit a rock—getting down the embankment was certainly an experience *I* do not care to repeat! Oh, by the way, Doug, I failed to thank you—nice job you and Freddy did getting me down in one piece and then back up again. *And*, with my pride intact!"

"Anything for you, Doc! Do we have it wrong? A hiking accident and we've let our suspicious natures run amuck?"

"If she died as a result of a hiking accident, I'd expect a car. No abandoned cars, according to Matt Webster," Robin said.

"Nope, my ace Ds!" Genoa said, waving a pen in their direction. "You've got a homicide on your hands. By the way, Robin, given the pregnancy, you need to talk to the DA regarding potential charges. California's fetal homicide law kicks in if the pregnancy is more than seven weeks along. I am confident that the fetus was over 12 weeks at the time of the murder. Our victim wasn't shot in the head and I doubt she was struck with something sharp. She was probably beaten and strangled, but I'm still working on the forensics."

"How did you reach that conclusion?" Doug asked.

"Regarding strangulation—facial petechiae; her remaining eye is speckled due to the hemorrhage resulting from the strangling. Under the turtleneck, her neck was swollen and bruised. Oh, and a dead give-away—her neck is bisected by what is a visible overlapping magenta line, a finding generally consistent with strangulation. We might, and hear me here, *might* be able to get a fingerprint and an imprint of something rectangular—could be from the car, maybe a piece of jewelry. I am sending that section of skin from the neck to the LAPD crime lab. Robin, you have a contact in that lab who will put a rush on this, don't you? Also, the lipstick and DNA samples?"

"Yeah, I called and asked for special consideration. They'll run everything through CODIS. I'll be sure to follow-up the request."

Doug breathed a sigh of relief—he had been convinced all along they were investigating a murder and did not much like being wrong.

"Doc, what can you tell us about the perp from the physical evidence you've examined so far?" Robin asked, finally taking the pile of books off her lap and pushing them under the chair. Doug wrote away in his ever-present notebook. It occurred to her he was always on top of the dreaded paperwork because of his extensive note-taking—another habit to develop. Unlike hers, his notes were actually legible; like his dress, his handwriting was exceptionally neat.

Genoa doodled for a few seconds before proceeding. "At this point I can't give you anything you can take to the bank, but the extent of the overlapping bruising pattern suggests large hands did the deed. Somebody with considerable strength—her neck was broken. Not crushed but snapped. A clean break. There is no question regarding the pregnancy, so find the baby daddy and you will have a DNA match for a suspect. Given the bruising, the break, and the sharp drop-off, I would say it's a safe bet you are looking for a man but, so far, we have no direct evidence of that fact since she was exposed to the elements, and scavengers were at the body. I hope she put up a struggle—a thorough cleaning under the fingernails might reveal something useful. Robin, I'll include that material along with the skin and the DNA sample. Damn, life will be easier when we get our own equipment because L.A. doesn't consider us a priority, unless somebody calls in a favor, which annoys me to no end."

"Anything else indicate a struggle?" Doug asked.

"Well, again, it's complicated to disentangle injuries related to a fall, the disposal of the body, and/or damage done by wildlife, from wounds sustained as a result of murder. In addition to the evidence of strangulation, however, broken finger bones, a fractured hand, and a broken tibia suggest a vigorous struggle and probably serious anger. There is a possibility somebody punched her—the settling of the blood suggests a pre-mortem injury to her face. My guess is if you find a viable suspect, a search of his or her car will give up some useful evidence. That is why I'm not so hot for the screenwriter—his build is on the slight side, there were no injuries to his face, neck, or hands, and there's the question of whether he had enough time to get to a carwash, either before or after he called in the victim. Even if he had managed to do so, given the victim's injuries, it would have taken a pro to leave no evidence without a wash. And, there is no evidence of a wash."

"What about a car accident?"

"I thought about that, Doug, but if the victim died as a result of an accident, it would have had to have been a pretty violent crash. I can't imagine how someone could have then driven the car away."

"Thanks, Doc, you're the best! I guess until we have a suspect, I'll cross my fingers that the DNA from under her nails is a match for the fetal tissue."

"Just doing my job, Robin. I hope you two get the person who did this. It is always sad when a young person's life comes to such a tragic end. Whoever they are, her parents are going to be even more distressed at learning they were to be grandparents and the dreams they surely had for their daughter will never be."

CHAPTER 17

Cecilia Hernández:
October 2011

"**C**ecilia, honey, you're so damn hard on me! All I am asking is for you to give me a few minutes to say my piece. Lord knows I don't want to interfere with your work but in case you haven't noticed, it's a beautiful day for a drive."

"Dane, there's like no way."

"Sweetie, how about a trip to Solvang? California's 'Little Denmark.'" Without waiting for an answer, Plask continued, "You'll enjoy the town's charming Danish architecture and intriguing shops. Ecofriendly before the term became fashionable—lots of people walking and biking."

"Dane, I can't."

"Honey, give me a break. Just a couple of hours—even students get to eat, and distancing yourself from work will clear the mind. Anyhow, you told me we needed to talk."

"Please understand, I can't take off today. And I, like, don't have the time or energy for a serious discussion."

"Communication *is* important, Cecilia."

"*I'm* the one who insisted we talk. All I'm saying is not *now*. Dane, I'm tired and not feeling well. After bombing my last stats exam, I have *got* to ace this one. Worse, my psych paper is pretty much a first draft. And, if that's not enough, I should be doing more for my job search."

"There's a plethora of restaurants, tasting rooms, and bakeries selling authentic European pastries in Solvang, and even a farmer's market—everything right out of the garden. Fresh flowers. We can buy something from there for a picnic. Alternatively, if you decide you have a little time for *me*, how about a fun place for lunch like Bit O'Denmark or Café Angelica. The food is good—no, great! You need to eat. Honey, I'll deliver you back to your house, desk, and laptop before you—"

"A drive sounds enjoyable, but another time ..."

"Well then, we'll go somewhere closer. Anyhow, on second thought, Solvang may be too touristy for you. Let me think of some other options that are not quite so far. Meantime, I'll put together a picnic and we can go for a walk and talk about the baby. I love you sweetheart and I'll support you in whatever it is you decide to do, but I know we can make this work."

"Dane, I don't know what I want. Though I guess that's not true, I *want* to finish my paper and study for my exam. Can't you please let the idea go for now?"

"I understand. Bring your laptop, and you can work in the car. I'll give you some tips on the job search. By the way, Cecilia, I keep meaning to ask you about those clicks."

"Yeah, I'm not sure what's happening. Sometimes the line sounds hollow and at other times I hear clicks. I made a note to call the telephone company when I'm finished. Dane, *please*, can't we see each other next weekend?" she begged, trying not to cry.

There was a loud click; one she knew was not due to problems with the line.

Half an hour later her phone rang. Cecilia gave in on the seventh ring.

"Please hear me out before you say 'no' *again*. Why not work in the car? You'll be in even better shape because you can bounce ideas off of me."

"Well …," she faltered, aware she might have lost the argument by giving him that split second. "Nope. Dane, I appreciate your thoughtfulness, I really do, but I am beyond busy. This paper is like killing me!"

"What's the topic?"

"Biology, Freud, and gender role development. Twenty pages plus references."

"Well, I can't help you with Freud, maybe an anthropological view of gender."

Uncharacteristically strident, annoyance evident in her tone, the tears gone, she struck back. "*Doctor* Dane Plask, you've got your doctorate! *Me*, I am still working on a degree. I've worked hard to get where I am, and my family is counting on me!"

"Okay, okay, I get it. Give me a call when you are finished. *Maybe*, I'll be around."

"Don't be angry with me."

"Call when you're done."

"I will, Dane, but please don't be angry."

"We can work things out, if we deal with this together."

"That's the problem—I'm not sure what I want. I wish you understood that."

"Cecilia, my love, you're upset, but do you honestly think we can have this discussion over the phone?"

"I can't talk. Period!"

"Well, I guess I now understand where I stand in the scheme of things." Plask hung up.

She got up to make a cup of tea. Cecilia was mindful of the price to be paid for standing her ground, but the paper wouldn't get done on its own, and she was unable to deal with life-altering decisions for the moment. Cup in hand, she took the house phone off the hook, put her cell on vibrate, and turned her attention to the computer screen, hoping that with the background research done she could pull an outline together pretty quickly.

Cecilia had learned since Nicaragua that she had made a terrible mistake—one of life's painful lessons: students should not sleep with their professors. The misunderstanding initiating the affair had been her fault, she had led him on and should have left Nicaragua right away, but he had begged her to stay and she had acquiesced.

Things became infinitely more complicated after returning to Managua from the coast. She had gone out to the garden to join Dane and Jorge Araya for a beer, but stopped short when she had overheard a conversation clearly not meant for her ears.

"Cecilia isn't aware of what's going on, and it had better stay that way," her professor had snapped.

Dr. Araya responded with several well-chosen curses in Spanish familiar to Cecilia from high school and later from José, her boyfriend at the time her brother died.

The two men were quiet for a minute. Then, Araya said in a low but intense voice, "Dane, you're a fool. We will end up in a poorly appointed jail cell if you do not get your mind off your prick and back onto business. The Debayle family, though out of power, still has plenty of pull. Believe me, they aren't to be fooled with."

Cecilia turned around and left unobserved. As she sat in her darkened room, thinking about what Araya had said, she decided the two men were somehow involved in drugs. Aware she was out of her depth, Cecilia began thinking about how she was going to disentangle herself from the relationship, even though Dane, in retribution, could cause her trouble with the doctoral committee, never mind her job search. Afraid to tell Dane of her suspicions, she tried to end the relationship, but he just went on as if she had failed to say anything. They had continued the affair after returning to California.

After a month back in the States, Cecilia began feeling tired and sick to her stomach. She was missing too many classes. Her concerned mother asked questions Cecilia would not or could not answer.

She bought a pregnancy kit, which yielded a negative result. She went to the Mission and thanked God. Two weeks later, still unwell, she made an appointment at the health clinic. This time, the news was not so good. Cecilia was pregnant.

She tried to ignore her cell, which was vibrating. But against her better judgment took the call.

"I'll contact you later." Cecilia hung up and went back to work. The phone rang again. She groaned and let it ring but afraid of her lover's temper, she finally answered.

"My love, I know you've got classes on your mind, but don't you think you'd feel better if we talk? Surely this is more important."

"Of course it is. Dane, I don't want to jeopardize my degree or my fellowship. I absolutely need to be in the lab by 4. Estela's calling from Nicaragua at 4:15."

"The only way you are going to jeopardize your fellowship is if I complain about your performance and I won't do that—after all, I managed to extend it. Sweetie, I'll return you to your car by 3:45. Bring the laptop. Think about the invite and get back to me." He once again hung up.

Cecilia complained to Linda of not sleeping at night, never mind the trouble she was having concentrating during the day. At one point, when she accused Plask of dealing drugs with Araya, he'd frightened the student with his reaction. She had been sure he was going to hit her. She wanted out of the relationship with Dane—not to just talk about doing so, but to end it for good. After the last hang-up, Cecilia knew there was no time like the present. Her parents would help her figure things out—they would be happy to be grandparents, regardless of the complications. Determined, she picked up her cell and pressed the green call icon.

"Okay, Dane, you win. I'll meet you in an hour at the fig tree on Montecito Street. I'm having trouble with my brakes, so we'll have to take your car."

"Cecilia, darling, I promise you'll be glad you decided to come with me. Take your car to my mechanic, and I will pay the bill. I can't have you getting into an accident."

"No thanks, I'll take care of my own car. See you soon," she replied tersely and hung up.

>>   <<   >>   <<

Raúl Debayle sat comfortably in his den listening, in real time, to the succession of repetitive conversations between Plask and the girl. Even if he had come up with the scenario himself, it could not have been more perfect than what he had just heard. The recordings from Dane's office would be useful—the shenanigans with his female students, without a doubt, would cause him serious trouble. This particular recording was the decisive factor. The girl who had accompanied Plask to Nicaragua during the past summer was apparently pregnant by the good doctor, who, in addition to sleeping with a student, was quite the bully. The knowledge that a popular professor impregnated his student would not go over well with anyone—the girl's family, the police, the public, or the university. On the other hand, the media would be thrilled. Raúl knew the recording could put an end to Dane's career, which would give him sufficient advantage to get the professor out of his own life, though he knew he had better move quickly. Despite being Latina and Catholic, the girl was ambitious and an abortion was a possibility. She also sounded like she'd had it with him.

Raúl tucked the equipment, CD, and notes into the back of his bottom desk drawer, locked it, and walked out to the patio where Concepción was reading, a cup of coffee by her side. He leaned over and gave his wife a kiss on the cheek, causing her to start.

"Querida, I'm sorry, but a bit of business demands my attention."

"Mi amor, did you forget the cocktail party?" She put down her book and kissed her husband gently on the lips. Forty years of marriage, and she loved Raúl as much as she did the day her brother first brought his classmate home after school.

"Of course not. I will be back in time. Black tie?"

"I'm afraid so. A fundraiser for abused children. Certainly a good cause."

CHAPTER 18

Possible Identification: October 2011, Day Four

"**D**oug, let's go! USB called and Marjorie's pretty sure they've got a hit."

"Wow! Not too bad. Good call on the student thing. Get the car and I'll be right out—need my java."

"Will do."

Robin had no more than driven up to the front of the department when Doug jumped in, travel mug in hand. "Let's do it! If our victim is a college student, maybe the killer's still on campus. Maybe we've got other victims."

"Could be. After I heard from Marjorie, I checked in with my friend at the LAPD crime lab. She got my message and had already put a rush on the forensics. We'll have a report on the fetal DNA and, hopefully, there will be foreign DNA from under the victim's fingernails—with any luck, the forensics will get us to the murderer."

"Not to worry, you done good, girl!"

"Thanks. Doug, catch me up on your other case—the domestic." She swerved around a car as it abruptly stopped to discharge a passenger.

"I'm pretty sure Ortega's sporting a Santa Bruja tat. Guess I told you that. Susana's too afraid to be forthcoming about gang connections but the boyfriend, Stein, has his suspicions."

"So, what's next? I guess I don't understand why you're continuing to pursue it."

"We're looking into possible gang connections—don't want someone taking out a hit on her. And anyhow, for general purposes, we should know what they're up to."

"Shit, a hit? Really?"

"It happens. Too often, we're a day late and a dollar short with these bangers. The other news is Roberto's affiliation with my hometown of Managua. Thought he was Mexican like Susana, but Roberto's parents are Nicaraguans. He is here legally—born in Santa Barbara and not going anywhere, unless we ship him off to jail. His mother died years ago, and his father returned to Nicaragua and remarried. I talked to the Feds to find out what they had on the gang; they sent me to the ATF—should add an E for explosives. ATF put me in touch with somebody over at DEA."

Doug, lost in thought, stopped talking.

"*And?* Did you get anything other than alphabet soup?"

"Yep, but no surprises. Santa Bruja is under surveillance for drug and gun trafficking. Our boy may or may not be involved—dude would not give me anything specific—typical Fed hush-hush investigation. The gang is supposedly running guns down to the North Atlantic coast of Nicaragua, where they then pick up drugs and guns for the return trip. Our burgeoning businessmen are interested in the bottom line."

"I understand drugs coming from South America through Nicaragua to the States, but what's with the going and coming of guns and Nicaragua?"

"Long story, but here's the short version: The U.S. funneled a lot of weapons into Central America during the Nicaraguan conflict. Rumor is the Miskito, who supported Somoza, were involved. They were economically impoverished, so it could be true. Same story for Cuba and the Sandinistas. Guns going down are traded for guns less likely to have history once they arrive on our shores."

"Nice work Debayle! Do I ever tell you how much I admire your detecting abilities?"

He laughed. "Aw shucks, Robin, you're embarrassing me."

Robin pulled up in front of the Admin Building and left the rack lights on.

>>   <<   >>   <<

As soon as they entered the registrar's office at USB, Marjorie Lutz swung open the wooden gate. "Detectives, please follow me. I think we have good news. Well, in a manner of speaking. Dan Sloan, the graduate student who offered to help, is convinced he has a match. We can't be positive because of the state of the young woman in the photograph you left with us, but the resemblance is close enough we thought you should come in. By the way, Dan worked on this pretty much throughout the night."

Robin said, "We really appreciate your cooperation, ma'am, as well as Dan's considerable efforts."

Once seated behind her desk, the registrar handed Robin a copy of a USB identification card.

"This is the student Dan believes is a match for your victim."

Robin jotted down the woman's name, address, and contact information before examining the ID. She then handed it to Doug. "What do you think?"

He looked at the picture carefully before passing it back. "She resembles our victim, but the age seems off."

"Robin, let me take another look." She returned the ID to Doug.

"Dan's right, there's a marked resemblance," he said thought-fully. "Can we keep this Ms. Lutz? I'm thinking our M.E. may be able to help with the identification. Please thank your student for his fine work. We'll contact you as soon as we have some solid information."

"I'd appreciate that. I'll be sure to express your appreciation to Dan—he feels terrible about the dead girl and was invested in finding a match, if she was one of ours."

"Ma'am, Doug's right. Isn't the woman in the photo ID older than the typical undergrad?" Robin asked.

"If they are the same person, her name is Cecilia Hernández and she's a graduate student in her final year, so she would be older than the typical undergraduate. Detectives, I hope you understand we want to proceed slowly. The head of security will arrive shortly. They checked for any type of general inquiry concerning Ms. Hernández and found nothing. Also, I need to advise counsel you're here. We have not called her contact numbers. The counsel advised us to leave that to your discretion."

"Thank you. Ma'am, in which department is Ms. Hernández a graduate student?" Robin, anxious to pursue the lead before security or the legal beagles limited their inquiry, was grateful for the registrar's cooperation and reluctant to push too hard. She scrutinized the photograph and saw some physical similarities between the student and their victim. Still, she was not convinced.

"Cecilia is, was, working on a graduate degree in psychology. Detectives, I was so anxious to show you the photograph that I forgot to tell you we contacted the head of the psychology department to set up a meeting. He could not see you today. Would ten o'clock tomorrow morning work for you?"

"Absolutely. You have been a great help Ms. Lutz. Umm, what's the Chair's name?"

"Dr. Benson; his office is in Slade, room 819."

"Ma'am, is it possible to meet with legal and security in the morning *after* we talk with Dr. Benson?" Robin asked. "The patrol car is out front with the rack lights going—we're on our way to a call but were anxious to look at the photograph."

Doug looked at his partner with guarded surprise but remained quiet.

Obviously caught off guard, the registrar rubbed her temples and thought for a few seconds. She shrugged. "I guess I can rearrange the meeting with the University Counsel and Director of Security."

"We'd appreciate that." They thanked her again and left.

Once they were out of the building, Doug asked, "What was that all about? A call? By the way why *did* you leave the rack on?"

"I wanted to avoid talking with lawyers and security until Doc gets back to us about the photo ID. If it is the same woman, let's see what we can learn about our victim before we meet with Benson. I took down the student's address. Let's get the ID to the M.E. and write up a warrant for her house."

"Thatta girl!"

>> << >> <<

"Good work on getting a preliminary identification on your victim so quickly!" Chief Bartolo congratulated them. "Doc Taylor called. She's pretty confident the USB student is the woman in the morgue."

"Actually, the kudos go to Robin," Doug replied. "She thought our victim might be a student. Surprise, surprise, the university was incredibly cooperative for a change. The best part was when Robin ably sidestepped both the lawyer *and* the head of security."

Robin blushed at Doug's unexpected praise. "Thanks, but it was you who suggested talking with the registrar. Chief, first thing tomorrow we're meeting with the head of the student's department."

"I assume the parents don't know?"

"They don't. That's one of the reasons we wanted to meet. I called the student's personal numbers. There were no answers. I didn't call her parents' contact number; instead, I called the Salinas PD to ask whether there is a missing person's report for a young woman about our victim's age. They don't have one on file; however, someone there knows the family. The Chief is waiting to hear from us. If we find something in the apartment to confirm the identification, I'll request notification. In addition to the parents' DNA, Salinas PD can ask for a hairbrush, toothbrush, and dental records. But we'll wait to hear what Doc has to say before faxing the photograph. Also, I'll talk with Eddie about a sketch, I'd—"

"Chief, what we'd like to do is fly up tomorrow to interview the parents directly."

This was news to Robin, who reminded herself she was the primary. "Chief, I understand the budget's tight but the trip would be worthwhile. I called our contact at the university and advised her that the Salinas police will be meeting with Cecilia's parents and we would get back to her afterward. She has meetings set up for us tomorrow: one with a professor and another with security and legal. Except for the one with the advisor, which is scheduled first, I wouldn't mind skipping the others until we have more information."

"Do the parents speak English?"

"I don't know. Because of that and other cultural issues—according to the Salinas detective, they are in the country illegally—it would be better if Doug and I go as a team."

Bartolo looked at Doug quizzically. "What's percolating in that brain of yours?"

"Honestly? It's different not being primary." He kept his eyes focused on the Chief.

"Well, I'm sure you'll adjust, Debayle. I think your idea to interview the Hernández family is a good one, but I want you to wait another day or two. Let the Salinas police do their job. Robin, make sure to e-mail a copy of the university ID *and* the sketch—morgue photos are tough. If they obtain a positive identification, let the parents know you will be flying up for an interview and to make arrangements for the transport of their daughter's body. Meantime, meet with the young woman's advisor, friends, scare up a boyfriend or an ex-, etc. Examine her apartment. Get the lab tech over to do fingerprinting, collect DNA. Hopefully, out of the multiple lines of investigation you'll acquire evidence that will get you to the perp. Once you have confirmation, there shouldn't be any reason to meet with the USB legal team, other than as a courtesy."

"Sounds good. That gets me to my second request, Chief. With your go-ahead, we'd like to ask Judge Salazar to issue a warrant to search her apartment."

"You've got it. Given Doc's belief that the student in the university identification photo and the Painted Cave victim is the same person, you'll have enough for probable cause. Be sure to note you want to obtain DNA. Oh, and let Salinas know they should hold off until they hear back from you."

"We're on it," Robin said.

"Waiting a couple of days to go to Salinas will give you a better idea of the answers you need when you interview family and friends up there. I guess I do need to tell you that while in Salinas, check out any old or present boyfriends—find the father. Robin, do you have someone to take care of Sean? That will be a long day."

"Thanks, I'm all set. Chief, again, I realize funds are tight, but it'll be worthwhile."

"Hope so." He went back to his paperwork.

The two quietly took their leave. "Doug, I'm going to my office to write up the warrant before calling Judge Salazar's clerk to see if he's in chambers. Once he signs it, we can head to the victim's apartment."

"How long do you need?"

"Thirty minutes. I've got the facts organized."

"Fine, when you're ready, call me and I'll meet you at the car. If it's going to take longer, just let me know."

Robin got back to her desk and quickly shot Ken a text telling him she would not be able to make their Thursday lunch; she'd explain when she saw him. She proceeded to write up the warrant; once finished, she called the Judge's clerk to give him a heads-up. Judge Salazar was in his chambers, so Robin called Doug and they left the building together.

CHAPTER 19

Cecilia Hernández' Apartment: Day Four

"**S**ir, excuse me," I'm Detective Crane, and this is Detective Debayle. We've got a warrant to enter the apartment of Ms. Cecilia Hernández." Robin felt foolish talking to the closed door, but she had seen someone peek through the blinds moments earlier.

Persistence won out. The door cracked open and she showed her badge, as did Doug. Then, to add insult to injury, the man used his foot to prevent it from moving any further.

"Mr. James Wilson?"

"Yep." The grizzled manager stood in front of them rubbing his eyes while with beefy tattooed arms he pulled up the suspenders hanging by his side. It crossed Robin's mind that the grubby red suspenders did not do anything to enhance the sweaty gray T-shirt the guy had worn a few days too long, but they were obviously necessary to hold up his pants.

"A warrant?" The door stayed put. "Weren't me who reported her. Rents on time. Clean. Nice girl. Guess you can't tell. That's the nature of my business," he said with a straight face.

"Do you remember when you last saw Ms. Hernández?" Robin asked, ignoring Wilson's query.

"Lemme think, maybe three days ago." He scratched his jaw, picked at his ear, all the while looking upward, as if the answer could be found on the ceiling. "No—four or five. I gotta tell you, my memory's not so good no more. Age damages the brain, ya know?"

Given the odor emanating from the man, Robin thought he should expand the statement to include booze helping along any age-related brain damage.

"Odd, now you mention it, the girl's always going to classes or her job, or coming back. Shopping. She's a bit of a thing and hauls around a heavy backpack. Sometimes I carry packages for her. What's the problem?"

"Sorry to disturb you, sir," Robin said. "We appreciate your help but aren't at liberty to discuss this matter with you. What we do need is for you to unlock her apartment."

She thrust the folded blue document in his direction. "Court order."

"Sure," he said, carelessly setting the folded warrant on a telephone table. "But when she shows, I'll give her the paper because I don't want to be accused of invading a resident's privacy. I do a good job here," he insisted. "Cecilia's a good girl. Wait a minute." Wilson abruptly closed the door. They heard the lock click into place.

"What do you think?" Robin whispered.

"I think we do a background check on the dude. He's certainly apprised of the comings and goings of the señorita. His comment regarding the cleanliness of her place is hinky."

"True. Bottom line—he's a creep."

"Yet, Robin, creepiness isn't a crime or the jails would be full!"

James Wilson reappeared after about five minutes. He had added an unbuttoned red flannel shirt to his ensemble and held a large set of keys attached to a piece of wood with 'Wilson' printed in black lettering. He locked the door behind him.

Increasingly suspicious about the inside of Wilson's apartment, Robin decided to ask Doug to return. He would be more likely to gain entrance—a guy thing.

"Does Ms. Hernández have a boyfriend?" Doug asked Wilson.

"Never seen Cecilia with a guy. Too busy with school and work." The odiferous manager stopped suddenly at a first floor unit, #22, and Robin almost bumped into him.

"Here we are. Strange, didn't notice they're closed. Cecilia's curtains are always open during the day. The desk faces the window and she likes the sun."

The detectives exchanged a glance. Doug rolled his eyes and cocked an eyebrow. No question, Robin thought, a background search was in order. A little too much information from a man who she figured spent most of the day in front of the television or sleeping on the couch—Doug could request an alibi and scope out the apartment at the same time.

"Thank you, sir. You can leave the key with us. We'll lock up and return it to you when we're finished," Robin said.

"I guess."

Doug shepherded the curious supe toward the door, adroitly removing the numbered key from the ring before returning it.

The apartment was dark, but Robin left the curtains closed in case Wilson decided to hang around outside. She flipped on the light switch and saw an open floor plan with a large but sparsely furnished living room and a small breakfast nook off the kitchen. Several bright bird and floral prints hung on white walls. In the kitchen, yellow poplin curtains, pulled back with artificial daisies, framed a small window. The furnishings and decor looked to be from Ikea. There were several doors along a short hallway coming off the living room. On the left was a tiny bedroom with an even smaller bath; on the right, a linen closet, next to which was a utility cabinet containing a water heater and stacked washer and dryer. Except for books and papers scattered across the large desk in front of the living room window, the apartment was neat. As she looked around, Robin was surprised to note the absence of personal pictures.

"Amiga, we've got something here." Doug swung the end of the cord in her direction. "But surprise, no computer!"

"If she has a laptop, maybe she hid it."

"Huh?"

"I hide mine when I go out. Afraid of a break-in."

"You're kidding me? Robin, that's plain crazy."

"Well, everyone doesn't get to live on their parents' protected Montecito estate!" she said sharply.

"Point taken, I guess. Why don't you look for the computer, since you're familiar with all of the girly-hidey-places? I'll see if I can find anything personal among the papers."

"Alright." An annoyed Robin searched under cushions, under the mattress, in the bedroom and linen closets, under the dresser. She went through all of the drawers.

Robin joined Doug in the living room. "Nada. No computer, no disks, no thumb drive, and nothing else of particular interest either. Nothing in the bathroom or bedroom indicating a pregnancy—no birth control, pregnancy test, prenatal vitamins—guess I should also check for those in the kitchen. No personal pictures, though I did find a camera tucked away in the back of a bureau drawer. I bagged that along with a hairbrush and a toothbrush. The supe is right about one thing—the apartment is neat, nothing but the stuff on the desk out of place. Sean and I could learn from her."

She saw he was chomping at the bit to say something. "Find something of interest?"

"Robin, I've got a passport!"

"Photo?"

"Our girl. No doubt about it."

"That's great—it's always a relief to have confirmation. Now, we can check DMV records for a car. Anything else?"

"Nothing's jumped out at me so far ... then that's often the case with interesting leads, don't you think? The subtle. The test of our profession is to solve the puzzle."

"True ... though when the boyfriend is the perp, the signs are generally more obvious. The lack of personal items may be pointing us to an angry lover."

As Robin returned to the kitchen, Doug added a caveat. "Well, I did find something else, though I guess it's interesting personally rather than professionally."

"Yeah, what's that?" Robin asked distractedly, intent on her search through the kitchen cabinets.

"According to this recently acquired passport our girl spent time in Nicaragua last summer. Not only in Managua, which is anything but a tourist mecca, she traveled quite a distance from the capital—I found a crossed-out visa form stuck in the passport. As her destination, she noted her plan to travel to Managua *and* the North Atlantic coast. We've twice been back to visit family, but never that far afield—don't know of anyone who has."

"If Cecilia's family is from Mexico, I wonder what she was doing in Nicaragua. Did her passport indicate she visited other Latin American countries? Could be she was a mule."

"Nope, just Nicaragua. The issue date is for earlier this year. Still, I guess she might have had another one, which either expired or was lost. Something else to ask her parents, but if a mule, I doubt they'll know much. From the little we've learned, she appears to have been a beautiful woman and a smart and motivated student—doesn't sound like someone running drugs. What a tragedy her life ended as it did. That is, unless she was involved in the underbelly of the beast, then I have to admit I'm a little less sympathetic."

"Anything else related to Nicaragua?"

"Not yet, though I haven't looked through all the desk drawers. I'll skim the books and papers, but for a graduate student there's not much here. Might be more at the university. In addition, we need to access her phone records for the landline. I did find some pictures in the desk. One was in a letter from her brother, apparently written while he was sick. Sounded serious. Also, letters and cards from her parents—mostly her mother. A few from someone who is, or more likely was, a boyfriend. Name of José Santos. Him, we definitely need to follow up. Those have a Salinas return address."

"Good leads. What Bartolo wanted when he told us to delay going until Saturday. Any threats? Implied threats?" Robin asked.

"Nope. Not much correspondence between the victim and Santos, yet from what I read, they sound like friends who cared for each other—no more, no less. Probably something going on once, but they moved on. My guess is she did the leaving and he's the leftee. There is a recent birthday card from the dude—sounds like they've known each other for quite awhile. Nothing bitter. Sort of like us!" He laughed his boisterous laugh and threw up his hands.

Ignoring the personal reference, Robin picked up the gold-embossed blue passport and opened it to the front page. When she saw the photograph, she knew Dan Sloan had gotten the identification right—Cecilia Hernández was the Painted Cave victim. The picture intrigued Robin: the beautiful young woman seemed tentative, her smile forced. Even so, there was an element of excitement—perhaps the eyes. Below the photograph was a small and neat signature with rounded loops and dotted *i*'s. Robin made a mental note that it would be easy to forge. Cecilia described herself as 5 feet and 102 pounds, with black hair and brown eyes. Under race/ethnicity was Latino; occupation listed as graduate student.

"Doug, we need to find the computer. Her laptop might be in the backpack our attentive supe claimed she carried, along with her purse and cell phone. Maybe the stuff is in her desk at the university. We can ask Wilson whether she owned a laptop or a desktop and get a description of the backpack. I wonder what job he was referring to."

"Robin, why don't I try a man-to-man talk with the esteemed Mr. Wilson and find out what he's got for an alibi. Meantime, you can finish searching the apartment."

"Sounds good, I need to catch up with my messages. Oh, and check the DMV for a car."

"Done."

"Doug, don't you find it odd there's no personal pictures on display? I'll go through the stuff on the desk again, but let's take the books, papers, and camera back to the office where we can examine them at our leisure. Perhaps she has a Facebook page—another question for family or Santos."

'We'd better put up some tape or Wilson will be in here like a flash once we've left."

"Right. Please bring the boxes and tape from the car."

"Roger."

After her partner left, Robin checked her voice mail: Marjorie had called only a short time ago; she had arranged the meeting with Cecilia's advisor. After hanging up, she began looking for anything of interest among the student's papers and books. Lost in the task, she started when the door opened. In stomped an irritated Doug, notebook and pen in hand.

"Damn that was frustrating! Wilson was not about to let me into his apartment. Robin, the jerk is hiding something, or he simply lives in a rattrap and is worried his job might be at risk. At this point, there's *nada* to justify a search warrant."

"Doug, if we find the computer, we might get some DNA or other evidence pointing Wilson's way that would justify a search. What about a car?"

"No surprise, after all, she lives in southern California. I have the info for a car registered to the victim. The description given to me by Mr. Eagle Eyes is consistent with what I obtained from the DMV database: a yellow 2002 Volkswagen Beetle. He doesn't remember when he last saw the car. I scanned the parking lot but didn't see it. Her car shouldn't be difficult to miss—yellow, and bound to have a daisy in a vase, a*nother* girly thing. If the vehicle was abandoned out by the cave, whether because it couldn't be driven or was the scene of the crime, it might take some time, but I expect your hottie Ranger will locate it."

"I think so too. Type of computer?"

"He's not positive, but 'pretty sure' he'd observed a laptop on the desk when he last entered the apartment to fix a leaky faucet in the kitchen. A colorful cover—pink, maybe red. He insists he hasn't seen anyone over here for the last four or five days, including Cecilia."

"Is that uncommon?"

"Oh, right! He mentioned Cecilia being gone last summer. She prepaid the rent but according to our erstwhile manager, he didn't know where she went and didn't see anyone at her place while she was gone. But then, he said the drapes were closed."

"Pets?"

"Funny, I asked the same question. No pets."

"Strange, a woman her age not having at least a plant. Even Sean has two plants in his room. Granted, one's a Venus fly catcher to which he feeds hamburger."

"That's my boy ... carnivore all the way."

"Alibi?"

"He's agreed to work up a timeline from the Wednesday before we found the body, until today. But, Robin, it will be one with suspicious holes—our esteemed manager is for sure an alkie. Find anything of interest while I've been out cavorting with the observant Mr. Wilson?"

"Not so much. Cecilia must have taken stuff with her, or she has gone paperless. If that's the case—she carried her computer around— I can't find a thumb drive with her files backed up. Doug, the missing computer, no cell phone, few photos, few papers; this feels personal."

"Has that smell, doesn't it? Particularly given I found the cards and passport in the back of the bottom drawer; they might have been missed if someone cleaned things out. Anything else?"

"Well, the passport may have provided us with a surprising lead. I ran across a notebook from a class taught by a Dr. Plask. He's of potential interest because her notes include details from several lectures on the Miskito Indians living on the North Atlantic coast of Nicaragua. Get this—the professor does research of some kind with those Indians. Can't be a coincidence. Do you know anything about them?"

"Not really, other than the Miskito occupy important mineral reserves and apparently want or wanted to *secede* from Nicaragua. They weren't aligned with the Sandinistas, the political party now in power, because they believe socialists are a godless lot. As I said before, there are plenty of guns in the area. All of which is interesting, Robin, but I can't imagine what the Miskito have to do with her death."

"Don't know, but when we meet with Benson, we'll ask him to steer us toward Plask."

"Sounds right to me. Robin, I'll take another look around the apartment while you get the books and papers together. Oh shit, I meant to bring in an empty file box. Give me a minute."

"Thanks. Once we're out of here, we can post the door and I'll hang the tape. I e-mailed Doc from the car to send a tech over to take care of the fingerprinting."

"Up for a sandwich on the way back to the house?"

"Sure," Robin said.

CHAPTER 20

The Professors:
Day Four

Robin pulled up in front of the SBPD.

"Damn, Doug, I forgot to tell you Marjorie called while you were with Wilson. Benson's secretary tried to intervene, but our new best friend pushed. He'll grant us an audience if we can be there sometime during the next couple of hours."

"Well, it's good to find out somebody other than Sonia is willing to manipulate their boss' time! I'll ask our esteemed dispatcher if she can have someone help us out with the boxes."

"Let's hold off on giving Marjorie a heads-up until we're on our way. Meantime, I'll wait in the hallway while you negotiate with Sonia."

"Okey-dokey."

He sat down on the edge of Sonia's desk. "Mi amor, I'm in a rush—need to talk with a prof at the university before he bails on us. Is there someone available who can log the contents of the boxes from the Painted Cave victim's apartment and then lock them in the evidence room?" he asked in a wheedling tone. "The notebooks are numbered."

"Claro. Get along now."

"Gracias mami. You are the woman!"

Once outside, Robin poked him in the ribs. "It *always* works, doesn't it?"

"Jealous?"

She didn't answer. They got into the car; Robin turned on the rack and merged into the flow of traffic.

"Need directions to psychology?"

"Nah, I've been there for talks. Well, if the Department hasn't moved! Last I heard, they were pushing for more space. Doug, can you call Marjorie?"

"No problem."

"Thanks."

>>   <<   >>   <<

Dr. Benson's secretary accompanied the detectives to his office. In less than five minutes, she had twice declared her boss too busy to see them, but Doug insisted they needed to talk with him. Before she could knock on the opened door, a thin short man with an awkward comb-over and a weak chin told them to come in. After shaking hands and introducing himself in a disconcertingly high-pitched voice, Benson officiously directed Doug and Robin to the two standard blue office chairs positioned in front of his desk—the kind with thinly padded seats and curved metal arms suggesting a visitor should not tarry long.

As she sat down, it occurred to Robin she had forgotten the high esteem many academics accord themselves. Dr. Benson's physical characteristics, alone, should have brought his sense of importance down more than a few notches, but that was not the case. He curtly thanked the secretary who had edged over to the side of the desk and, to Robin's amazement, morphed into Ms. Meekness. She doubted Benson was sufficiently aware of those around him to recognize his assistant's goo-goo eyes. Then, with only a curt nod from Benson, she left, but not before directing a sidelong glare toward Robin and mouthing: *"Don't stay long!"*

"Detectives, our registrar, Ms. Lutz, said you have questions about Cecilia Hernández, one of our graduate students. Per her instructions, which apparently came down from counsel, I have agreed to meet with you. My secretary and I will keep this confidential." Robin believed Ms. Meekness *was* trustworthy. The professor, not so much!

"Thank you Dr. Benson. We appreciate your cooperation," Doug said, before he segued into the purpose for the visit. "Is it accurate to say you're Cecilia's graduate advisor?"

They knew full well Benson was.

"Officer, that question should be easy to answer, but it's a bit more complicated when it comes to Cecilia's program, which I must say is atypical. Originally, I *was* her sole advisor—she's working toward a doctorate in psychology."

What he had said was not making much sense to Robin. She glanced at Doug, and he did not look quite on board either. "Isn't it the case a graduate student is assigned to only one advisor?" she asked.

Benson doodled on the yellow-lined pad in front of him, an effort appearing to occupy his full attention. Robin heard students in the hallway, but other than the sound of the pen, the office remained quiet. They waited him out, a key requirement of investigators, she had long ago learned.

"You're correct." He sounded annoyed. "In Cecilia's case, while she took some anthropology classes, she became interested in a colleague's research. He offered her a fellowship, which meant valuable experience, financial support, and the possibility of professional advancement."

"Name?" Doug asked, pulling out his trusty notebook and pen.

"Name?"

"Of the colleague."

"Oh, right. Dr. Plask. Dane Plask has been doing research with the Nicaraguan Miskito Indians for decades. After she had done well in a couple of his classes, he offered Cecilia the fellowship. She is a smart and motivated student, so offering her the opportunity was a good move on Plask's part, though I have to admit it created complications for us. We ultimately decided the fellowship would benefit Cecilia. The three of us worked up a project she would be able to carry out in Nicaragua that would also meet the requirements of the psychology department. In the end, her research was an offshoot of a paper she'd written during a previous semester."

Confused, Robin sought clarification. "Her degree is in psychology or anthropology?"

The professor answered in an exasperated tone. "Psychology—I'm Cecilia's primary advisor. Since she is carrying out a paid fellowship with Dr. Plask, he serves on her thesis committee. A bit unorthodox, perhaps, but we have made this type of adjustment before, and the arrangement met her needs. Detectives, do you want me to put in a call to Dr. Plask?"

Robin rapidly processed the implications of alerting Plask to their visit.

"No thank you, Dr. Benson. We won't be able to meet with him today, as we have to be somewhere else. Anyway, it probably is not necessary." She decided not to show him the morgue photograph. Otherwise, Robin had no doubt he would be on the phone to Plask the second they left his office.

"What are Cecilia's responsibilities with Dr. Plask?" Doug asked. Robin was relieved to note he stuck to the present tense, keeping Benson in the dark concerning the student's death.

Benson outlined her duties. When he said something about Nicaragua, he drummed his finger on the desk, and then added, "Cecilia hasn't been the same since she returned in August."

"Why so?" Robin asked, surprised that Benson had shared that information.

"I'm not sure, but her work is suffering. On second thought, I guess I was less surprised when I learned her parents were against the trip. Dr. Plask, in his defense, focused on the fact that the fellowship would provide her with an excellent professional opportunity. Of course, he now wonders whether he made a mistake. Cecilia is fairly naïve and never experienced such poverty. Safety concerns also may have been an issue."

Robin wanted to ask about the nature of the relationship between the professor and Cecilia Hernández but decided not to open that door until after they had spoken with Plask. Even though the police had shown up asking questions regarding his graduate student, Benson did not appear too concerned, other than exhibiting some defensiveness about his decision-making process regarding an advisee.

"Why are you here anyhow?" Narrowed eyes, pursed lips, he suddenly looked worried. "Has Cecilia filed a complaint?"

"Not at all, sir. We can't say more at present but do appreciate your cooperation in keeping this visit confidential." Robin wondered why the question of filing a complaint had come to the professor so quickly.

"Thanks for your help, Dr. Benson," Doug said, with only the slightest hint of disdain.

They shook hands and left. Robin glanced back to see if the professor had picked up the phone receiver. Instead, he was once again preoccupied with his monitor. She found it odd he was so easily put off about their interest in his graduate student, a young woman whom he acknowledged appeared to have problems after a university-related trip.

"Robin, let's go over to anthropology and find out what's going on. Man, if Dr. Benson isn't the quintessential nerd—his concern for Cecilia Hernández is damn touching!"

They made their way through a hallway populated with a gaggle of students and exited the building. While they walked along the tree-lined path dappled with sunshine, Robin gave more thought to the interview with Benson.

"Doug, like you, I expected a bit more curiosity from an academic, never mind one who's the advisor of record for a graduate student. An advisor generally has only a few students, and he was pretty blasé in the face of a visit from the police."

"I know nothing about academic relationships, but I do know about personal relationships, and *that* dude is pretty disinterested in his student."

"Or, at least trying to give us that impression," she said.

"Okay, maybe. Robin, let's bypass the secretary this go-around," he cheerfully proposed as they stood outside of the building housing the anthropology department.

"Hate to do anything to piss off Marjorie. Anyhow, we're supposed to meet with legal counsel after talking with Benson, so this is definitely an unapproved detour."

"C'mon partner—we sure as hell don't want to worry about that now. Let's talk with Plask first. We won't give the good Doctor any warning and see what we can shake loose. I'm wondering if somebody alerted Benson to the purpose for our visit."

"Well, it wasn't Marjorie or the student."

"You're right—Marjorie's got our back. Let's go for it."

She hesitated. "Okay, partner, let's go for it!"

They found the directory and headed down the correct corridor. Doug knocked on the door sporting a brass nameplate informing the detectives they had located Dr. Dane Plask. His schedule was posted in a plastic envelope taped to the wall; they had arrived during his student office hours.

"I'm busy. Come back in fifteen minutes," a muffled voice called out through the closed door, more of a demand than a request.

Doug's baritone dropped lower this time. "Unfortunately, we can't do that Dr. Plask."

"Okay, okay. Whoever you are, hang on! I'm finishing up with a student—doing what I'm paid for," he said, a heavy dose of sarcasm easily penetrating the door.

Doug opened his mouth to respond when Robin shook her head. Jaw clenched, eyes widened, he remained quiet.

"Let's find out what happens if we catch him unawares," Robin whispered. "He's raised a red flag in my mind, given the passport, Cecilia's class notes, and the fact he managed to weasel himself into her life as a graduate advisor. He took her to Nicaragua and she returned with problems. Better Plask be unaware the police are cooling their collective heels outside of his office door."

"Got it."

A full five minutes later, with Doug becoming more irritated by the second, the door opened and out sailed a female student, maybe nineteen, a rosy-tinged face, gathering up her waist-length coal black hair. She almost knocked him over. Robin could only imagine what Plask meant by "finishing up with a student." It wasn't pretty.

As soon as they entered the room, Plask said, "I'm not sure what you want, but you're here during office hours and students have priority."

The first thing that came to Robin's mind when she checked him out was what a hit Plask must be with young and impressionable female students; a handsome man with refined features and a full head of silver grey hair sat at the desk in front of them. He projected an air of self-confidence and superiority. She was disgusted: middle age and a professional, he should know better. He appeared to be having difficulty in concealing a smirk at Robin's interest. She knew right away that Doug would be hot on this guy's tail.

The office they entered was at least twice as large as the one they had just left. Instead of Benson's university issue desk, Plask sat behind a massive mahogany desk somewhat at odds with the sleek chair that looked to be a Pollock creation. Both, Robin was aware from surfing on the internet, cost somebody a pretty penny. On a sideboard, underneath a large bay window, he had arranged a Keurig coffeemaker, a slew of ceramic cups, and a milk pitcher and sugar container. There was a microwave above the table and a small brown refrigerator below. Plask evidently brought in some serious funds to the university. An ego wall was devoted to pictures, many of them signed, of him shaking the hands of important personages.

"Dr. Plask?"

"Well, now that you've barged your way into my office, what is it I can do for you?"

Robin did not intend to apologize to the man and Doug sure wouldn't, so she continued. "I'm Detective Robin Crane and this is my partner—we're from the Santa Barbara Police Department."

They showed him their badges and finally had the professor's full attention. "What the hell! All this manpower for a few tickets? Or should I say personpower?" he added sarcastically, looking at Robin with interest.

Despite the supposed outrage, he laughed, but hardly looked relaxed, as he shifted in his chair and twisted the heavy gold signet ring he wore on his left ring finger.

"No, sir, things aren't so bad we're tracking down fines in person," Doug said with a straight face. "We want to talk with you about a student, Ms. Cecilia Hernández."

With just the briefest of pauses and no detectable change in facial expression, Plask answered Doug's question. "Cecilia? She's one of our graduate students."

Ignoring the fact Benson considered her a graduate student in psychology, Robin replied, "Yes, that's our understanding."

Plask sat up straighter. "What *is* the problem officer? Ms. Hernández has never caused any problems. She's a wonderful girl and a dedicated student."

Doug's head snapped up from his notebook. "Sir, we can't give you any details at this point, but your cooperation is appreciated. I'm sure you want to be of help since Ms. Hernández is your student."

Though Benson had missed it, Plask apparently detected the snide undertone. "Officer, I missed your name, and I'd appreciate seeing your badge again."

Doug showed it to him.

Plask barely looked at the badge; instead, he stared long and hard at Doug. "Police or not—I don't appreciate your tone. Furthermore, we are legally required to protect our students' privacy. I'd better have the university lawyer present if you want to ask any more questions."

"We understand," Robin said, inserting herself into the conversation in an attempt to avoid a pissing contest between the two men. "Dr. Plask, I don't believe we want to know anything that'll invade her privacy."

"Well, I certainly hope Cecilia's okay. She is a valued member of my lab and a good person to boot. It was bad enough when we lost Sara."

"Sara?" Robin asked, confused. "Who is Sara?" She glanced at Doug. He remained focused on his notebook.

"Castillo," Plask replied, apparently forgetting he had finished with them. "Sara was an outstanding student who planned to work in my lab. She died in a car accident."

Robin remained silent, caught off guard by the unsolicited information.

Doug's head swung up. "If I remember correctly, the university organized a memorial for her."

"They did. Her death was a tragedy," Dr. Plask said, looking at Doug.

Neither man blinked. Robin might as well have not been in the room.

CHAPTER 21

Forensics:
Day Four

O nce back in her office, Robin found a note from Freddy asking her to call Genoa; instead, she called Marjorie Lutz and left a message apologizing for having become sidetracked—explaining she would provide an update after their meeting with the M.E. She located Doug in the break room talking with an irritated Sonia, put out over something Ken had done. Robin figured the topic probably related to smoking but was not about to ask.

"Hi Sonia. Doug, Doc called. I told Marjorie I'd get back to her after the three of us meet."

"Be good, you two!" Sonia laughed boisterously and took off.

"What's up, Robin?"

"Not sure."

As they walked over to Doc's office, Doug discussed ideas for things he and Sean could do together on Saturday, if they did not go to Salinas: a movie, a play on at the children's theatre, a game in L.A.

"He'd like to do any of that as long as it's with you," Robin assured him, before knocking on the open door. "Hi Doc. Got your message."

"Take a seat. Robin, thanks for e-mailing the university and passport photos. As I've already notified the Chief, I am fairly sure that the graduate student, Cecilia Hernández, is the Painted Cave victim. The forensics should be available soon for confirmation. Meantime, I may have something else for you."

Genoa passed a file folder across the desk to Doug. "Do you remember this case?"

Robin glanced over at her partner; he'd opened the folder and was examining several photographs. He proceeded to read the handwritten notes. She remained quiet.

"Yeah, I do. Sara Castillo studied at City College or USB, don't remember which. Anyhow, she was a tired and an inexperienced driver; her car went off the road up north one foggy night. She was driving up to Monterey, I think. I followed up on the CHP report with a few interviews. Her parents were devastated."

Focused on the medical examiner, he continued. "Doc, this is a pretty odd coincidence."

"Because?"

"Sara's parents are *still* devastated. I talked to them the other day as part of a follow-up on a domestic in Isla Vista—it turned out the dude, the husband, is an employee at their taquería. Even stranger, a USB professor we spoke with about our Painted Cave victim mentioned Sara in passing." He returned the file to Doc. "How does the Castillo accident relate to our case?"

"Well, I had a hunch and asked for the file. By the way, thanks," she said, looking at Robin for the first time.

"None for me. In the end, Sonia located the file and Freddy retrieved it."

"Anyway, the girl's car went off the road, but whether as a result of an accident is debatable. Regardless, the medical examiner up there concluded her death was due to the crash. On the face of it, a reasonable enough assumption—a small car went off a vertical cliff."

"And you?" Doug asked. "Are you saying *I* screwed up the Castillo investigation?"

"No, not at all. That conclusion made sense at the time. Now? I guess not so much. Doug, let's back up, why don't we? After performing the Painted Cave victim's autopsy and reviewing the Castillo results, I believe the girl may have been alive after the crash."

"Doc, the coroner who took care of the autopsy wouldn't deny that. In fact, if I remember correctly, he said she probably didn't die immediately from her injuries."

"I *know*, Doug. What's different now is that I believe Sara Castillo died as a result of asphyxia—from strangulation."

"Can you two let me in on what's going on?" an irritable Robin asked.

"Sorry, Robin. Doug only brought this case to me because he was new to the force and she was a SB resident. I recalled adding notes to the file at the time regarding an unexplained rectangular mark, albeit a faint one, on the girl's neck, and suggesting a distinctive ring may be the cause, though it certainly might have been something in the car. Furthermore, I raised a question about the presence of petechiae. Doug is correct, she was a small girl, and the coroner believed the airbag caused the injuries; however, I was not so certain because of the petechiae. The contusion on the Painted Cave victim's neck brought to mind the Castillo case. Doug, do you remember anything suggesting that someone was at the accident site, other than first responders?"

The room remained silent. Robin, for the thousandth time, reflected on the disconnect between this woman's laser-focused mind and her chaotic office. "Okay, Doc, let's see if I've got this right. Are you saying the cause of Castillo's death was strangulation, and the same killer could have murdered both women?"

"Robin, what I'm saying is a single perp hypothesis is a possibility, one certainly worth exploring. As I'm sure you are aware—I am thinking aloud here—petechiae are the tiny red spots resulting from ruptured capillaries characterizing strangulation. They are often under the eyelids, but also can be found around the eyes or on the victim's face and neck. What is of particular interest in these two deaths is the presence of petechiae above the area of constriction—the eyes, face, and neck of both victims suggest a vigorous struggle and eventual strangulation. Airbag injuries are less focused."

"I don't understand. It was ruled an accidental death. Why didn't this come up at the time?" Doug asked. Robin felt for him—the girl's death had obviously affected him.

"Not my case. The medical examiner up north believed the air bag caused the petechiae. Science has brought us along since then, Doug; we have made great strides in forensic pathology. As I said, I had my questions. In part, that is why the case came back to me, but I am not looking to cast fault here. Times change. I want to get Cecilia Hernández' killer, and if the Castillo girl was murdered, I want to know that as well."

"Even if both women *were* strangled, that doesn't mean there's a link between the two." Doug said a trifle defensively.

"You're right. Like I said, when I saw the mark on your victim's neck and thought through the case, the Castillo death came to mind."

Doug closed his notebook, put his pen in his pocket, stood up, and glanced in Robin's direction. "Doc, thanks for the information. Ready to go?"

"Debayle, sit back *down!*"

He sat.

"Atta boy. What's the matter?" Doc demanded in a no-nonsense tone that even Doug dared not ignore. "Something I can help you with?"

"I'm sure you could. That is, *if* I had a problem," he said, rubbing his jaw, and looking directly at her.

"C'mon on Doug, you and I have history ... give it up! After all, there were others involved," Genoa said.

"You know you're a bossy dame, don't you?"

A flip answer, even for Doug. Only the eyeballs in the jar appeared interested in communicating with Robin.

"Of course—a personality characteristic required for the job. Doug, what's going on?"

"Sorry, I guess the murder of this victim is beginning to feel personal. As I said, I visited the Castillos' taquería yesterday following up on another case. Strange that the ex-husband from the domestic works at a business owned by Sara's parents and, stranger still, her death was mentioned within the context of the Hernández investigation. Apart from all that, I recall her death so clearly. At that time, I was the sole bilingual officer, so the Chief sent me to break the news to her family ... it was damn scary."

Doug continued after a long pause. "Sara was 19 when her car went off the road. It was pretty much the usual accident investigation, except nobody had any idea why she had left town. She worked part-time at the family restaurant and called in to say she would not be in for her shift. She left her wallet behind. Took only a backpack with books, a change of underwear, Snoopy pajamas, and *not* enough cash for the trip. All in all, her decision to leave seemed pretty spur of the moment."

"Well, Doug, having been a college-age woman, most everything is spur of the moment—especially when there's a romantic component," Robin chuckled.

"Yeah, one of her friends suspected as much. It's what I finally told myself, but we never located a boyfriend. I was a rookie and had difficulty dealing with the Castillos' grief." The two women remained quiet.

"Not the seasoned cop I am now," he forced a laugh that trailed off—the wisp of a painful memory. "Sara's mother and father were adamant that their daughter wouldn't have taken off without telling someone in her family. I figured it was grief talking and, truthfully, I didn't look too hard for another explanation."

A fleeting look passed between Doc and Robin. "And both victims studied at the university?" Genoa asked.

"That's what's *really* bothering me. Sara was at City College but in the process of transferring to USB and changing her major from psychology to anthropology, all of which made no sense to her parents. Cecilia Hernández was a psych major who worked with an anthropologist prior to her death. As Robin told you, we met two professors with connections to these women. Neither man was much disturbed the police were talking with them about a student. Benson, Cecilia's advisor, is a nerdy self-involved sort. The other dude, Dr. Plask, is a piece of work—a real shit! Cecilia accompanied him to Nicaragua, and he's the one who mentioned Sara Castillo. Anyhow, they're *both* arrogant jerks, but it could be that's the nature of the beast."

"Dane Plask. I know him. Well, *of* him. We have a mutual friend, a physical anthropologist who helps out with reconstructions. Plask has a reputation as a *lech*. Whether deserved or not, I don't know, but an interesting tidbit to keep in mind."

"I am *not* surprised."

He had Robin's full attention. "What are you thinking?"

"Robin, I don't buy into coincidences easily, which all of this could be, the relationship among Plask and his two students ... a fluke, I mean," Doug said thoughtfully. "But it could be a lead, a slight one, but a lead nonetheless. Ladies, hang on for a few minutes. I want to get something from my office."

Before the two women could catch up on much more than how Sean was doing, Doug returned with a yellowed newspaper article taped to a sheet of onionskin paper. Robin now understood what he had gone to get—he kept a three-ring binder of his cases. She didn't know they even sold onionskin paper anymore.

"Tell me what you see, Robin?" he asked, handing her the brittle discolored page. A beautiful young girl stared at her. She immediately knew what he was asking: Sara Castillo looked younger, but her features were startingly similar to those of the Painted Cave victim. Robin passed the paper to Genoa without comment.

"They could be sisters," the M.E. said softly, returning the page to Doug. "I guess I missed that given the damage done to our victim."

Robin said, "Doug, the resemblance between Cecilia and Sara is unsettling. You will probably think I'm crazy, and it's such a little thing, but the haircut caught my attention. The style is the same as Cecilia's. Most of the Latinas I know keep their hair longer than us white girls, but in addition to the short length, these are high-end sophisticated cuts, which appear at odds with their particular backgrounds. Perhaps I'm engaging in some massively inaccurate stereotyping and, if so, I apologize for my East Coast biases." Robin uttered the last statement hesitantly, anxious not to raise Doug's hackles, but wanting to make her point, aware it is often the little things that turn a case around.

Doug sat up straighter. "The physical similarities *are* incredible— never thought about it until Doc brought up the possibility of a link between their deaths. Genoa, I might not have made the connection even now except Robin and I just saw Cecilia's passport photo and the university ID. The shrine Sara's parents have behind the register includes a couple of pictures."

He opened both file folders and placed them side by side. "Cecilia and Sara were petite, each with the same large dark eyes, a small well-formed nose, and a heartbreaker of a smile. Neither is a woman nor a girl, the physical type many sexual pervs are drawn to. Latinas—legal, but both with parents who came to this country poor and remain here illegally."

"Well, this is certainly interesting, especially given the similar marks on their necks and evidence of strangulation," Genoa said, her chair tilted at a precarious angle.

Doug was excited. "I think we might have something: the physical resemblance, ages, hairstyles, students, and not only students but *psych students*—well, Sara planned to transfer. Doc, if a ring left the mark on our victim's neck, wouldn't the signet or stone be facing outward?"

Genoa leaned forward. "I can't answer that question. Maybe the ring twisted around during a struggle. If so, there should be DNA under Cecilia's fingernails. Doug, you raise a good point. Why that would have happened twice is odd, unless the ring is loose—weight loss or something, although why it wouldn't have been resized during the five years between the two deaths, I don't know. Nonetheless, my honorable Ds, we are jumping ahead of ourselves. Our victim is probably Cecilia Hernández but we need a positive ID. We—"

Lost in her own thoughts, Robin interjected: "Like Doug, I'm not much of a believer in coincidences, but both women though here legally are children of illegal Mexicans and interested in anthropology? What that's about?"

Doug told Doc of their search of Cecilia's apartment, what they had learned from her passport. He was fired up—jaw clenched and face flushed, the case had gotten under his skin. Women are generally pegged as the more emotional sex—Doug was the exception to the rule. After one intense argument, she had demanded an apology. She was surprised when he'd proudly told Robin his volatility spoke to his Latino heritage. There would be no apology forthcoming.

"Well, after meeting Benson and Plask, and given they seem to be a common thread between two dead women who share a lot in common, the next step, I think, is to take a look at the relationship between the professors."

"Nothing to it, Robin. They're both arrogant tools," Doug snickered.

The phone on Genoa's desk rang. Sorry, my good Ds, I have to take this call—details about an FBI seminar I'm organizing. I'll get back to you with more information as soon as I get some."

"The Fibs. Gotta love the Doc!" Doug whispered as they left the room.

CHAPTER 22

Colliding Cases:
Day Four

"**Robin, I know** it's late and you're probably anxious to go home. I'm sure Sean wants to go home, but do you think you'd have a little time to review the Castillo file before you leave? Given our new suspicions, I'd like a fresh pair of eyes. Yours, in particular."

"Of course. Let me have a few minutes to call Denise and tell her I'll be a little longer. Meantime, they can order a pizza."

"I'll tell you what. Why don't the three of us go for pizza? Like old times. That sandwich wasn't enough to carry me this far."

"Sure, sounds good."

Robin went to call Denise and let her know she would be there shortly. She returned to Doug's office.

"Okay Doug—all set. We'll pick Sean up from Denise's. He'll be thrilled—more about spending time with you than the pizza. Though Gino's pizza is a guaranteed hit."

"That's my man!"

"I didn't read the Castillo file before Freddy picked it up, but it was pretty thin. Not surprising, I guess, given her death was judged accidental."

"That's about right, Robin. Here, take a look while I get us some caffeine."

"Thanks, but not for me. I've had enough to keep me going into the wee hours."

After her partner left, Robin opened the folder. Clipped onto the face page were the photographs, which she examined carefully. Robin was of the same mind—the dead woman looked like a sister of their current victim. Enclosed was a summary of the case, Doug's notes, and the autopsy report. She opened a bottle of water and took a long drink before settling into the report. According to the slender file, five years ago, 19 year-old Sara Castillo, a student at the City College, had been driving north along the coast when she died. It was late at night, and a heavy fog enveloped Route 1 up in the Big Sur area. The Highway Patrol believed the car went off the cliff and landed on the beach.

Doug's notes, written in his characteristically neat hand, detailed an interview with Sara's parents: their daughter had called the taquería and told a worker she would not be able to work for the next two nights. She neither spoke with her parents nor left a note, which everyone thought completely out of character. Her mother reported that Sara had been tired lately, perhaps "with a little depression." Mr. Castillo believed his daughter had gone to visit her brother, Johnny, in Monterey. Doug interviewed Johnny Castillo over the phone. He had been unaware that his sister was on her way to his home. He could not imagine "Sarita" taking off without telling their parents or calling him: she was naïve, stuck close to home, and was an inexperienced driver. He was not even in town, having spent the night with his girlfriend in San Francisco—they had gone to a play, followed by dinner.

Sara took no money with her, which perhaps explained why she didn't stop somewhere when the fog rolled in, though Doug had made a note to the effect that lodging along that part of the highway is rare. He'd found Sara's wallet at home—the day before, she had used her bankcard to pay a telephone bill. A surfer and his dog discovered the wrecked car on the beach next morning. Fingerprinting had not been done. The air bag went off but deflated by the time the boy found the car. There were no suspects because there had been no reason to think the girl died of anything more than an unfortunate accident. At the time, Genoa had deemed the autopsy unnecessary. She'd made a note on a Post-it, dated yesterday, regarding the death of the medical examiner who had performed it, so there'd be no way to talk with him as to why he'd made the decision he did. The autopsy report was thorough and included observations of the petechiae and the mark on the neck. Robin paid silent homage to Doc's prodigious memory for details.

Doug returned with fresh coffee and sat down. "Sorry, got held up talking with Tyler."

"Damn, that sure smells good! I read the file—not much, but I guess enough for Genoa, given the thorough autopsy report. Now we've got two USB deaths, with important similarities that might include the manner of the women's deaths—how about calling the CHP who signed off on the report; tell him what's up and pick his brain?"

"Good idea."

"Doug, I'm about to put a kink in your theory that one or both professors may be involved in the Hernández murder and *possibly* that of Sara Castillo. Barclay Stalts did stay over in Carmel-by-the-Sea and, as you know, neglected to tell me of that detour. Sara's destination was Monterey, which is only eleven minutes north. Could be a coincidence but one certainly worth pursuing. Because these are entirely new wrinkles in our investigation, I think we should talk to the Chief. Since you have a relationship with the Castillos, would re-interviewing them be worthwhile? In the process, you might pick up more information on Ortega."

"Mr. Hollywood—you're right, we need to find out more about the man. In fact, all good ideas—worth the price of a pizza! Robin, since we're interested in the two professors, why don't we find out what's going on at the school? I'll check in with the CHP and try to find out more from the Castillos concerning Sara's state of mind before her death."

"What about friends? They might be more forthcoming, know more."

"She had them." Doug said in a clipped tone. "But, at the time, I thought her death was an accident, so I only spoke briefly to one girl. If I remember correctly, she thought there was a boyfriend, but couldn't give me any details. Sara told her she wanted to leave town, but the young woman didn't know why or where she was going. She tried to convince her friend to wait until the morning."

"Doug, we may be barking up the wrong tree, but I think it makes sense to keep the two Profs and Stalts up at the top of our list for now, particularly Plask. He seems pretty unsavory given the student tête a tête we interrupted."

"I agree."

"If we can come up with even one piece of concrete evidence, connecting the two cases, I'm sure the Chief would be willing to let us work up a warrant for Plask's office and home."

"I say this with all due respect Robin, but I'm not sure that's the way to go."

"You've got another idea?" she asked, knowing full well that he did, and it was probably a good one—experience made a difference. It occurred to Robin her role as primary might be getting tricky. He obviously was making an effort to let her run the case, but she too often found herself feeling pressured to follow his lead. A glimmer of resentment, on both their parts, was beginning to show around the edges of the investigation.

"Another option," Doug persisted, "and the one I think most likely to yield something worthwhile, would be to manipulate Plask into a situation in which his defenses are down long enough to make it through his front door to take a look-see. The man is so frigging arrogant we should be able to get him talking. If we go at him directly, we'll hit a wall because the jerk is bound to lawyer up, and he probably has a good one. Benson, I'm not so sure. For him, it'll have to be a different approach."

"Well ..." but aware her partner was due credit, she instead said, "You've got a point. What do you think about dropping in on the good professor after we return from Salinas? Maybe we will learn something from Cecilia's parents we can use to bring down his guard. If we go to Salinas on Saturday, I think I could come in on Sunday, at least for a couple of hours, although I will need to find someone to watch Sean. I know you were going to take him on Saturday, and he'll be disappointed, but it's worth the field trip." Robin made a mental note to cancel the picnic with Matt—too much was going on.

"Saturday *and* Sunday hours! Expecting me to give up my time with the dude! Pushing me, aren't you, Ms. Primary? Comp or over-time?" Doug laughed and sat back, drinking his coffee.

"Why not? Let's do it. I'll make things good with my buddy once we close this case."

The partners sat in a companionable silence, until, out of the blue, Doug proceeded to tell Robin that the idea of women being able to do it *all* was just so much feminist bullshit. Before she could strike back, he had reverted to their weekend plans.

"Robin, how about bringing the little guy to the house on Sunday? My nieces and nephews will be there. Mamacita loves Sean; for her, there can never be enough children around. They can play games on the patio while we are off investigating Plask. You know papá totally has a soft spot for you. He really should have had all daughters because he's incapable of coping with a son. Or, at least the one he has."

"You're sure?" Robin asked, referring to the weekend, not the father-son relationship.

"Absolutely—on both counts! We'll go over to Plask's house late morning—give him time to drink his coffee and do whatever he does Sunday mornings. Catch him in a cooperative mood. Afterward, we'll deserve a good meal! What do you think?" Doug was wound

177

up with his plans—a level of enthusiasm causing Robin once again to wish things could have worked out between them.

"Tactically, it's a great idea. You sure about Sean? I would love to visit your parents, and I have to tell you, I've always had a sweet spot for your father. Way back when, you thought it was all about you!" she laughed. Only later did it occur to Robin that Doug did not join in.

"*Now* you're breaking my heart baby girl—you know how competitive fathers and sons are—oedipal complex and all. Seriously, it will be fine, but to make you happy, I'll give mami a call and tell her exactly what I am now telling you. So, let's go for it."

"Thanks." Robin decided a slice of humble pie would be worth it in the long run. "Doug, your idea of showing up at Plask's house rather than his office is a good one. That way we've got his sweet spot—professor as savior of poor Latina students. Benson, I think, deserves an officious approach."

"Probably. Robin, give me a few minutes to make a call and then we can go get Sean."

"No hurry. I've some things to organize before we leave. I was going to notify the Salinas PD, but on second thought, let's review the case later and I'll call first thing in the morning. I spoke with Marjorie, and she's beginning to feel the pressure, so we have to take care of things at that end. Given a possible connection between Stalts and Santa Bruja via Susana Ortega and Joel Stein, I'll spend some more time following up on his alibis."

"Makes sense. Keep me posted."

Doug returned ten minutes later. "Okay Robin, let's pick up the boy before he thinks he's been abandoned. We'll take my car and I'll come by in the morning; we can drop Sean off at school before heading in to work."

"I'll call Denise and tell her we're on our way." Robin made a note to ask Bartolo about the comp or overtime question. She slipped the Castillo file into her top drawer.

CHAPTER 23

Death Notification: Day Five

When Doug dropped Robin off at the office the next day, the first thing she did was down some aspirin chased with a fair amount of strong coffee. After picking up Sean the previous evening, they had gone for pizza and root beer. Once home, much to her son's delight, Doug roughhoused for a good bit before reading *Harry Potter* until the boy fell asleep. It was like old times: dinner, putting Sean to sleep, sitting up late drinking wine and discussing a case. Robin had known she would pay a price the next day.

>>   <<   >>   <<

Chief Bartolo called Robin as soon as she came in wanting to know where she and Doug were with the Painted Cave investigation. Although he expressed reservations without the DNA report in hand, he gave her the final okay for a Saturday trip to Salinas *if* the victim's parents made a positive identification. It would be comp time; he could not swing overtime.

Robin immediately called Julie Jensen, the Salinas detective assigned to work with the SBPD, and told her she would be e-mailing photos of their victim. Julie assured her they would go to the Hernández home to establish, through visual confirmation, whether the victim was their daughter. While there, she would arrange for dental records and obtain DNA samples. Robin thanked her and asked they be overnighted to Doc. She gave her the address, then requested that the detective call or e-mail if the parents made a positive identification.

After she hung up, Robin scanned the photographs in and sent them to Jensen. She then went to get another cup of coffee and stayed to chat with Sonia. The dispatcher always had something going on. This particular day, she complained about her sister who seemed to be depressed but refused to get help. Robin returned to her office and called Matt to cancel the Sunday picnic. There was no answer, so she left a message apologizing and explaining she had to go out of town for work. She asked to reschedule for the following weekend.

Robin settled back and carefully reviewed the alibis for Barclay Stalts that had come in overnight from Mill Valley and Carmel. Still concerned after reading Robiou's too-pat statement, she wondered whether she could identify a discrepancy between his and Stalts' statements if she spoke with him on the telephone, though Robin realized she'd need his permission to record the conversation, a request that might gum up the works. In the end, it didn't matter, she dialed his number, but there was no answer. She called Stalts' gardener, again no answer. She was going to have to take a different tact with that alibi. She also needed to follow-up on the gas and restaurant receipts but placed those to the side and called Marjorie Lutz.

Marjorie was in a meeting, but her assistant put Robin through to voice mail. She advised the registrar that the M.E. believed the victim was, indeed, the graduate student, Cecilia Hernández. The Salinas PD would confirm the identification. Since she was talking to a machine, she took the opportunity to say that the meeting with the legal department and security would not be possible until early next week because she and Doug were leaving for Salinas to interview Cecilia's parents. She assured the registrar they would continue to keep the university in the loop.

>>   <<   >>   <<

Julie Jensen called Robin back in less than two hours: "Detective, we went out to the Hernández home and showed the photographs to the victim's father. Our visit came as a pretty severe shock, but I'm not sure what we could have done differently. The parents were unaware *anything* had happened to their daughter. Frankly, the mother was hysterical—it's unclear what shape they will be in tomorrow if you still plan to carry out the interviews. The father confirmed the university identification photo and the passport photo are of his daughter. He completely broke down when we showed him the morgue photograph."

"Oh, my god! Julie, I am sorry, I screwed up royally. The Chief approved the expenditure for a sketch, but I didn't follow through after getting the photographs. A morgue photo makes it more difficult for everyone."

"I agree, but it would have been bad no matter how you cut it. These are two loving parents who lost their only surviving child—their son died of leukemia. We took cheek swabs from her mother and father and bagged the girl's hairbrush and toothbrush. The package will get to your M.E. first thing in the morning. I sent the dental records separately. Give me a call if you need anything else. By the way, they speak English, but if you speak Spanish, it would probably help. I tell you, it's a tough break for two really nice people."

"My partner speaks fluent Spanish. Since the death notification has taken place, he will call to set up an interview. If they agree, we'll take an early morning flight. Thanks for everything, Julie. I'll keep you posted." Robin hung up, embarrassed, yet grateful they would not have to do the notification. She had blown it with the sketch—lesson learned.

After updating the Chief and receiving a short but extremely disagreeable lecture about the use of morgue photos with parents, Robin left a message for Doug. She provided a synopsis of her conversation with Jensen and asked him to contact Mr. Hernández and set up a visit for the next day.

An hour later, Doug checked in. "Robin, I spoke with Mr. Hernández and we're on for tomorrow. He was worried for his wife and initially refused to see us, but called back after talking with her. They want justice for their daughter and agreed to meet with us."

"Must have been difficult. Jensen from the Salinas PD said they were devastated. Did you get contact info?"

"Jensen's right about that and, yes, I confirmed the address, etc. Oh, and Manuel wanted more information regarding arrangements for the transport of his daughter's body to Salinas."

"I'll book a flight for us and talk with Doc. Why don't you pick me up here in the morning?"

"Sure, but get back to me about the time. I'm off—working something else." He hung up before she could ask what he was up to.

CHAPTER 24

Grieving Parents:
Day Six

"**You ready, Robin?** We'd better leave if we want to make the plane on time."

"Yep, just need to grab the release forms I got from Doc. Doug, my contact managed to put a rush on things—AFIS sent a report— the victim's prints, those on the lipstick and prints in the apartment are consistent with those on file when Cecilia Hernández completed the fellowship application. There are others in the apartment, which will be useful when we have a suspect. That said, if the suspect is James Wilson, he would have an explanation since he recently repaired a leaky pipe under the kitchen sink. I forwarded the report to the Chief and Doc. Can you follow-up with our hinky manager for his timeline?"

"Sure, I'll pick up the timeline on Monday, or bring him in. The dude still hasn't crooked an elbow to answer the phone."

Robin gathered up what she needed and put it in the small suit-case. Together, they hustled out to the car.

"Let's do it." Doug pulled out of the parking lot and headed toward Fowler Road and the airport.

"You're not around the office much lately. How's the Ortega case going?"

"Moving forward, thanks for asking. I spoke with Susana's boy-friend, Joel Stein. He mostly confirmed what she had told me. But listen to this; you'll never guess who Stein works for."

"I don't know *anyone* involved with your investigation. I'm not even sure why our unit is still involved. Help me out here—I'm trying to get caught up—show interest!"

He slowed down as they came to a stop at the light and at the same time reached for her water, which she grabbed first. Unable to contain himself, he laughed gleefully. "You've got to hear this—Stein works for your Mr. Hollywood!"

Robin almost spit out her mouthful of water. "You are *kidding* me!"

"Honest-to-god truth. Stein works for Mr. Barclay Stalts: screen-writer living in the home of Ana Solarno in Isla Vista. Hope Ranch area. Dude who called in our victim."

"Oh, shit, what's that about? Doug, why am I just now hearing this information?"

"Knew you'd love it! New information, don't worry, I'll keep you in the loop."

"Doug, seriously, this case is getting more complicated by the day. What do you think is going on?"

"I'm not sure, but we need a perp-vic board. It *is* getting compli-cated, and the possible Santa Bruja connection bothers me. Robin, I want to bring Tyler into the Painted Cave case. Maybe we can get some information from Stein about Mr. Hollywood."

"I'll check with the Chief regarding Andy. *You* ask Sonia to set up a board in Conference Room B."

>>   <<   >>   <<

Robin and Doug arrived at the Monterey Regional Airport at 9:20. All they had during the flight were peanuts and Coke for him and cranberry juice and pretzels for her—fare now working a hole through Robin's stomach. She could not imagine how Doug was coping but figured she would find out soon enough. He had told Mr. Hernández they would arrive between eleven and noon, so she stopped at the Golden Tee Snack Bar and picked up a couple of bottles of water and power bars. Doug laughed at her food choices and to provide 'cosmic balance,' as he put it, left to purchase a coke and several chocolate bars, before meeting Robin back at the Enterprise counter.

"Okay, I've got the keys. It's a dark blue Nissan Versa. Let's go."

"Robin, give 'em to me. You *know* I'm the better driver. Besides which, I'm familiar with the Salinas Valley," he assured her, grabbing for the keys.

Laughing, she pulled her arm away. "Forget it Doug. I'm perfectly capable of getting us there in one piece, and the car is equipped with GPS." Partners, she had learned, are a strange breed—in some ways, like a married couple.

Robin had never been to Salinas. All she knew of the area she had learned in high school: home of John Steinbeck, winner of the Nobel Prize for Literature—the author never wrote fiction again after winning the prize. On the plane, Doug had filled her in on the geography: the valley, a region noted for great wineries, begins eight miles from the ocean and rises 52 feet above sea level. Perhaps the most memorable piece of information he had imparted was that the town of Castroville, located in the Salinas Valley, is the Artichoke Capital of the World.

Once they entered the city limits, the GPS lady sent them to East Salinas and finally to a modest Craftsman-style bungalow framed with a traditional white picket fence. The well-tended yard testified to the combined efforts of a dedicated gardener and the mild climate for which the valley was noted, according to Doug. Robin was impressed. Somebody loved flowers: a thick stand of giant sunflowers situated along the length of the fence flowed into an English garden of knee-high asters, marguerite daisies, portho, dahlias, and other color-ful plants sure to attract bees, butterflies, and hummingbirds.

While one entire side of the yard was planted in flowers—beauty for the soul—the other flourished with ripe vegetables—food for the belly. There were stalks of corn, rows of string beans, tomato plants, and fat eggplants with luminous purple fruit hanging off delicate branches. In the front yard, neat rows of lettuce, carrots, and riotous shoots of rhubarb Swiss chard.

Robin pulled into the driveway, parked behind a battered but clean white pick-up, and turned off the key. The detectives sat for a few minutes without saying anything, dreading what was to come—the grief of parents outliving their sole surviving child. A murdered child.

"Well, Robin, let's do this. Something's bound to give. I still think Plask is our man—I was suspicious the minute the student came rush-ing out of his office, even more so after interviewing the self-satisfied jerk! Though I admit, I'm confused by the possibility of a connection between Plask and Ortega, other than both have ties to Nicaragua, and I still have my suspicions about Mr. Hollywood, less so Wilson."

"Yeah, well, some tangible evidence would be good. Could be a serial killer on campus who has nothing to do with Dane Plask, maybe a student who took his classes, or the two cases are unrelated. Whatever, we'll keep looking at Barclay Stalts and Wilson."

"Okay, Robin, but you'll see that Plask is somehow involved in the Hernández murder. I don't believe he's covered his tracks so thoroughly we can't get to him. Now, I guess we have to consider possible connections to Santa Bruja through whatever he's been up to in Nicaragua. On the other hand, we might be looking at crimes of passion—I want to know more about Plask's relationship with Sara and Cecilia. I doubt a serial killer is on campus, unless he or she is a staff or faculty member. A student would have graduated by now."

"C'mon, we need to go in. You've got the Spanish, you take the lead."

"Right, boss!"

Doug received a punch to the arm for the sarcastic crack. The horseplay ended when the front door of the house opened and a middle-age man appeared, his face ravaged with sorrow, shoulders stooped with the weight of what he now faced for the rest of his life.

He approached the car and offered a thin, cold hand to each of the detectives. "Welcome to our home. I am Manuel Hernández, Cecilia's papá. We hope your trip was not too difficult. Thank you for coming. Please enter," he said with an old world charm, stepping aside and gesturing toward his home with a trembling hand.

They introduced themselves before following Mr. Hernández through the gate and up onto the front porch. He pushed open a beautifully carved wooden door, seemingly at odds with the humble bungalow, and motioned the officers into a warmly decorated living room darkened by heavy forest green curtains drawn closed. Manuel offered them seats before excusing himself to get his wife.

Doug settled comfortably into in an overstuffed armchair upholstered in brown velvet. White crocheted doilies covered the arms and the back of the chair—something Robin had not seen since visiting her long deceased grandparents. He kept adjusting them as her grandmother had done. She perched on the edge of a sofa upholstered in brown woven cloth with a design of large flowers in fall colors. A wooden coffee table in front of the couch was devoid of ornamentation except for a small framed picture of a teenage boy, his arm around a young girl; another, of a younger version of the man who invited them into his home. He protectively held a contented looking woman who Robin imagined was Cecilia's mother. She caught herself thinking someone who had caused their nightmare for some egotistical reason had indelibly shattered their happiness. Robin began to tear up at the thought of the pain this family must be feeling—a bad habit of hers. She coughed, effectively putting an end to that particular weakness, a trick she had learned from Ken. Men, he pointed out, at least those of his generation, do not get to tear up.

Robin smelled coffee and something baking, the odors reminding her she was hungry, but nothing bringing *home* to mind. The grocery

187

store was invariably her mother's source of baked goods. Since coming to know Sonia, Robin had learned that the delectability of baked goods was as much in the odor as in the taste. Nothing she would ever tell her mother.

Cecilia's father was talking with his wife in the other room. "Mi amor, la policía han llegado. Tenemos que hablar con ellos. Tal vez podamos ayudar a descubrir el monstruo que ha llevado a nuestra querida hija tan lejos de nosotros."

Doug leaned over and whispered a translation: "He's telling his wife the police arrived and they need to talk with us. Maybe they can help us find the monster who took away their daughter. I can't hear her reply, but this is going to be tough."

Robin was pleased to note her Spanish had improved since moving to Santa Barbara—she had understood the gist of the conversation. Manuel and his wife entered the living room holding hands. Mrs. Hernández was tiny like her daughter and, despite the passage of years, every bit as beautiful: the same thick black hair, though hers was woven through with strands of silvery gray. She wore it pulled back tightly into a traditional braid finished off with a piece of black satin ribbon, unlike her daughter's professionally feathered cut. Pain permeated her lovely face: the surface etched with deep lines, her large brown eyes pools of sorrow, cheeks and throat a deep ruddy shade.

Doug and Robin stood up. Although confident they would find Cecilia's killer, Robin felt in her heart of hearts there was no way to alleviate the pain of these two grieving parents.

"Por favor, please, this is my wife Gabriela. Cecilia's mother," Manuel said. "Mi amor, Detectives Robin Crane and Doug Debayle came from Santa Barbara. Detective Debayle told me on the phone that he speaks Spanish. If we do not understand their questions, he can help us."

Impressed that Manuel remembered their names, Robin extended a hand. "Please accept our sympathy."

Doug added, with characteristic warmth, "Señora, my partner and I are so sorry for your loss. We've been moved by what we have learned about Cecilia's accomplishments. In the midst of your pain, we appreciate your willingness to talk with us."

"Mucho gusto. Thank you for what you are doing for our daughter. Please sit down," Cecilia's mother whispered in a melodious voice, wiping tears from her large brown eyes with the corner of her apron.

"Mr. and Mrs. Hernández, thank you for allowing us to come to your home to talk with you. Doug, please translate?"

"Of course. Señora, podemos—"

"Gracias, but we speak English," Manuel said proudly.

"Officers, can I bring you café? Food?" Gabriela asked.

"Thank you, maybe later," Robin responded. She glanced over at Doug. He gave her the eye, which in the present context, meant she had committed a cultural faux pas. Regardless, she pushed ahead.

"There are questions we have to ask, but please tell us at any time if you want to stop and we can have a café. It smells delicious," Doug said.

"Gracias," the couple said in concert. Manuel got up and opened the curtains, allowing sunlight to pour in—a dark sad room transformed into something out of a picture book: flower boxes thick with bright red geraniums showed through the window, the vibrant flowers embellished by the soft yellow walls of the room.

"Señora, your garden is beautiful. Flowers in the window boxes, at that height, are a lovely idea."

"Gracias. You can take flowers with you," Gabriela shyly offered. "And vegetables."

"Thank you," Robin responded, wondering what the TSA would think of the tomatoes, zucchini, and a sunflower or two tucked into her carry-on. Aware of their limited time, she persisted. "Did you speak with Cecilia regularly?"

"Sí. I'm sorry, yes," Manuel said as he sat down. "Always! Cecilia calls us on Sunday afternoons, sin falta … without fail. We begin to think something is wrong when no call comes on Sunday or Monday or Tuesday. When we call, she does not answer and her mailbag is full." Manuel's voice cracked and his eyes welled up, but determined, he went on: "The Salinas policemen came to talk to us; the fear we could not talk about after they called came true. I do not understand how they knew the dead woman was our daughter."

"The pasaporte and the identification are of Cecilia, but they have another picture and Manuel only can say she looks un poquito like our hija. I do not look," Gabriela said.

She used a corner of her apron to wipe away the tears now trailing down her cheeks and added. "The police say the Doctor thinks the woman in the picture and the one from the school and in the pasaporte are the same. They take the toothbrush of Cecilia for the Doctor to be very sure it is our daughter. A medical test from us. We call our dentist. My husband cannot sleep."

Robin froze at the thought of Manuel seeing the morgue photo, but quickly pulled herself together and explained the passport and university photographs only provided them with preliminary information; they needed a family confirmation. She went on to tell them that Cecilia's fingerprints were on file from her fellowship application and this had convinced Doctor Taylor of their daughter's identity.

"Detective, the doctor calls this morning to say our daughter is treated with great respect. Dr. Taylor puts our hearts at rest. She says you will help make the correct arrangements for Cecilia to come home so she can rest with her beloved brother."

"We will," Robin replied, proud to work with a tough as nails M.E. who was exceptionally tender with families of the deceased. "We'll discuss the arrangements before we leave today."

Manuel put an arm around his wife's slight shoulders while she continued talking in her stilted English. "Sometimes, Cecilia writes to us—cards for our birthday or Mother's day. Father's day. Our daughter always send a present. Many times flowers. They cost too much money, but she say flowers make her happy. Manuel, remember the flowers she send last month? Reina de la noche. Beautiful like our baby." Gabriela shuddered and began to cry. Her husband looked at his wife with consternation.

Doug appeared as uncomfortable as Robin felt, but both recognized they had a job to do. They faced an increasingly intricate puzzle and she had learned long ago that it was never clear where the critical piece would come from.

"Si, mi amor," her husband continued in her stead. "Cecilia sent beautiful flowers—she knew you loved them. Officers, we want the monstruo to be caught."

Quiet settled over the room. Doug fiddled with his tie.

"Can you or your wife tell us anything about what Cecilia has been doing—at school or with her friends?" Robin asked.

"I do not understand."

"Did she have a boyfriend?"

"Manuel, you talk to the detectives," Gabriela said, leaning her head against his shoulder, her dark skin once again flushing. He held his wife more tightly.

Gabriela replied instead. "She does have un novio before she leaves for college, but many years ago. José is sad when Cecilia goes far to school. I think he believes she will not go if she loves him. He is marrying another."

"Did they see each other while she was back in Salinas?"

"Could you tell us his last name?" Doug asked, his pen poised.

"José Santos," Manuel responded.

"Not novios—friends," Gabriela added quickly. "Even if he has another girlfriend, he has dinner with us on many Sundays. When Cecilia comes home, they go to a movie or share meals."

Robin looked at Doug.

"Detectives, José did not hurt our daughter—her mother and I believe he still loves her. But Cecilia no longer feels the same," Manuel said sadly, glancing at Robin and Doug, before looking away.

Robin imagined Manuel to be a father who each day wished his daughter had stayed in Salinas, married José, and given them grandchildren. Much like her own mother. She was grateful Sean was still young and that she could keep him safe; after so many tragedies, she was beginning to be unsure of even that.

"What does her friend do?" Doug asked, intruding on his partner's thoughts.

"José is a mechanic. Officers, we do not want to cause him trouble. It will not be good if police show up looking for him. He is legal, but people here are suspicious of the police and his boss will not like it. José was a friend to our son. He was always a good boy and now is a good man. I've never known him to be in trouble."

"Do you think José will talk with us?" Robin asked. "We could explain to his boss he's not a suspect. We just want to talk with him as Cecilia's friend."

Not that she was going to tell the parents, but young women tend to be murdered by those whom they love or are supposedly loved by, rather than by strangers. In almost every instance she had investigated since coming on the force, when the victim knew the murderer the family initially assured her of his innocence. Still, there was no reason to suspect this young man of Cecilia's murder. They would, of course, check out José's alibi. More than an ex-, a close family friend, he might possess useful information. Robin considered interviewing him a priority after the parents.

"Tal vez. You will have to go to the garage if you cannot wait until his work is over. Officers, José holds no responsibility for this tragedy. The boy came last night to be with us—he is suffering," Manuel said.

"Es cierto," his wife agreed, shaking her head affirmatively.

Doug did not bother translating. He was taking it all down. Her partner was a master at the task, and the notes would be valuable when they got to the prosecution phase of the case. She had once teased him that he should have gone to law school as his father wanted—he would have been a spectacular lawyer. He had responded with a rather unexpected "Fuck that!" Shocked, she had quickly added, "But the legal profession's gain would have been the SBPD's loss." He had said nothing more.

"Did Cecilia talk with you about the university?" Robin directed the question to Manuel.

"Mostly of how busy she is. Her mother and me tell Cecilia she must study hard, but she is young and should enjoy life. My daughter says she has much work. We are not rich and the university costs a lot of money, it is true she has to work."

"What about Cecilia's teachers?" Robin was interested to see the glance that darted between the pair. "We only want to discover who committed this terrible crime."

Manuel continued. We thought the professor was too demanding of our daughter. We expected Cecilia to come home last summer but she stayed to do his work. She would not criticize him—he gave her important chances."

"Have you heard from him?" Doug asked.

"Flowers came from the professor this morning. The card offers sympathy."

"Who is the professor who sent them?" Robin asked. She figured it was Plask and wondered how he had learned of her death.

"His name is strange—we call him the doctor or professor—Cecilia writes it down and puts the paper on the refrigerator. Manuel, por favor?"

Her husband got up and then returned with a folded piece of paper he handed to Doug, who smoothed it out and wrote down the information while he read it aloud: "Dr. Dane Plask, #326 Carlten Hall; Lab: 1.805.555.1793."

The phone rang, startling Gabriela. Her pupils dilated—Manuel squeezed his wife's hand and went to the other room. Left alone, Cecilia's mother began to cry. Robin awkwardly put her arm around the grieving woman's shoulder, wishing she could bring her surcease, but knowing this was not possible. It was terrifying even to go to that place.

Manuel returned. He rubbed his jaw and looked haggard. "José is worried. I said two detectives are here from Santa Barbara."

Shit, so much for the element of surprise, Robin groaned inwardly. "What did he say?"

"I told him you want to talk about Cecilia. We are worried his Jefe will be unhappy. José is not worried. He will talk to you, but his lunch is now."

Surprised, Robin looked at Doug.

"Is it too much of an imposition if we return after talking with José?" Robin quickly asked, fearing the continuation of the interview would be too stressful for the grief-stricken parents.

"This is good," Gabriela replied without hesitation.

Manuel gave Doug the address to the garage. After thanking the couple for their cooperation, the detectives left, their carefully structured day slightly tattered. They walked out of the house and across a yard conveying a joy that no longer existed.

CHAPTER 25

An Ex-Boyfriend:
Day Six

Once in the car, they quickly rolled down the windows to let out the hot air. Doug entered the garage address into the GPS.

Robin took a swig of water. "Yum, exceptionally warm and flavored with BPH!"

As soon as they pulled out of the driveway, up went the windows and Robin flipped on the air conditioning on high—she loved the initial swish of the unnaturally cool air. "Cecilia's parents appear to think Santos is a decent sort, but I guess we're both acquainted with how that goes."

"Yeah, sure are. Mindy Williams."

"That was a terrible case—the poor girl never had a chance at life."

"I remember the son-of-a-bitch as if the case happened yesterday," Doug said glumly. "Mindy's parents *loved* that boy—it's bad enough someone who became a member of their family killed their daughter, but to have done so in such a horrific way is beyond tragic. *Maybe* there is a sliver of understanding if murder is an inadvertent result of an emotional outburst, but torturing someone you claim to love ... no words for that. I thought she would survive. On one hand, Mindy's parents had time with their daughter before she died; yet, day after day, they saw what that monster did to her. After her death, I had nightmares for months. I'll be glad when the damn appeals stop."

"It makes no sense to me that appeals can go on for decades. Each hearing must be another punch in the gut for the family. I guess the horror never ends for the victims."

"I agree, Robin, but let's get back to our current case—thoughts about Cecilia's parents?"

"I can't imagine they played any sort of role in her death. Cecilia Hernández sounds like a good daughter who would protect her parents at all costs, so I doubt they are aware whether anything was up with José Santos or Dane Plask or Benson or Wilson. Or anyone else for that matter, though we didn't get very far with them before this detour to the garage."

"Yeah, bad timing. Never mind, we'll go back—her room may give us something. I agree with you, Robin, I don't think they possess any information concerning their daughter's murder, at least of which they are aware. Given the nature of their relationship with Santos, we might not get any help from them regarding him either."

"Still, as I told the Chief when we tried to obtain approval for this trip, we have so few solid clues. We've really got to turn over every stone."

"Don't you worry, girl. We'll get the doer!" Doug vowed. "I'm sure these are decent and loving people, and I can't imagine how they'll live with their daughter's death. Her loss is particularly tragic given she's their remaining child," he reflected dolefully.

"I won't even go there." Robin shifted gears before continuing. "Regarding our focus on José and the professors as potential perps— on second thought, I guess if Cecilia felt threatened by someone local, someone known to her family, she would have said something to her parents. Well, at least to her mother. On the other hand, if she had concerns about an authority figure, such as a professor, she would have been more circumspect. The letters in her apartment sounded pretty friendly; could be she confided in José."

"I don't know. She may have feared his reaction—hot Latino temperament and all," Doug said with an unruly laugh Robin found disarming.

"If you say so—although distance might make it easier," Robin said, as she narrowly blew through a stop sign.

"Watch the road—you'll get ticketed by the locals! Anyhow, Cecilia's parents are too old school. They wouldn't have approved her trip to Nicaragua if they were concerned about a problem between their daughter and Plask. These are unsophisticated people who wanted their child safely at home. Still, it's a good line of questioning. How can you drink this water? It's close to boiling."

"Yeah, but at least more water than BPH. On a completely different note, it's really beautiful around here."

"Girl, time to take you on a road trip! The state is beautiful—we've got to get you up to San Francisco, Mendocino. Once you're that far, Southern Oregon isn't too much further—the town of Ashland is an exceptional place to visit during the summer—white water rafting, the Shakespeare Festival, great food, outstanding B & Bs," he said, popping in a CD. Shakira accompanied them. "Too bad we can't spend a day visiting the Central California wineries and breweries since we're already here."

Doug made a notation in his notebook. Robin guessed a trip was on the horizon that she would have to deal with when the subject came up.

"Hey, partner, how about stopping for something to eat after we finish up?"

"Sure—if we have time," she laughed, well aware they would stop for lunch, time or no time.

>>   <<   >>   <<

Robin pulled the rental into the far end of the AAA Car Repairs and Body Shop and rolled down her window. At first glance, the garage appeared legitimate. It buzzed with activity, including a soccer mom leaving off her SUV and a man in a three-piece suit picking up a Mercedes. A young woman with two small children was talking intently with a mechanic about a battered red Sentra that looked to be on its last legs. She had Robin's sympathy.

"Well, let's go talk with José without making this into a big deal."

They walked toward the office. "Doug, I doubt there's a need; still, I'm going to lock up the car," Robin asserted, pressing the remote in the direction of the car.

"Okay, but what a shame you white people are such suspicious types!" he retorted. "Probably a lot of good people walking this earth you don't see."

"Shuuut up, you jerk!"

They walked into the office. It had the requisite grungy pin-up calendar, soda machine, and gnarled wooden counter. A soft coating of dust on all surfaces. A grizzled old-timer in overalls and a red flannel shirt with various sized rips and grease stains stood at the register. "Can I help you?"

Robin could not imagine that the man in front of her still worked on cars with their complicated electronics but figured in his day he probably knew his craft better than most. When she hit his age, Robin supposed she would be six-feet under or asleep in a rocker on a porch, drooling away.

"Good afternoon. We would like to talk with José Santos."

"Why?"

"Confidential—won't take much of his time."

"So?"

"He's not in any kind of trouble."

"The man's got work to do."

"Won't take us long."

"Bay three. Make it quick."

"Will do, Boss."

"Watch your manners young lady."

"I apologize."

They rapidly exited through a side door into a bustling garage reeking of grease in the midday heat. "Guess you got put in your place!" Doug burst out laughing. "Good to know the gender-divide is alive and well!" They now had *everyone's* attention.

"Glad we aren't in uniform," Robin whispered. "Though, after our encounter with gramps, it's clear we emanate the aroma of cop regardless of my attempt to look nonthreatening and your spiffy attire. By the way, Doug, what are you doing wearing a purple tie?"

"Lavender. Lookin' sharp, lookin' sharp! You wouldn't expect anything less."

"True."

As they approached the third bay, a man in his late twenties put down a tool. He wiped his hands on a dirty red rag and walked toward them.

"Santa Barbara police?"

"We are. I am Detective Doug Debayle and this is Detective Robin Crane, my partner. You must be José Santos. Thank you for agreeing to talk with us—we won't take too long." Doug, suddenly serious, extended his hand, which the mechanic shook.

"Don Manuel called and said you were coming straight here. I expected you awhile ago."

"Sorry, technology! Contrary to the ads, a GPS doesn't always choose the most direct route, lotta trucks carting vegetables taking their time."

"Max said I can take a break, so if you don't mind, I'll eat while we talk. Behind the garage is a table—most of the guys have finished lunch, so we shouldn't be bothered."

"What about the guy up front?" Robin asked. "I don't think he much wants us here. We only need a few minutes. Don't want to cause you any trouble."

"Don't worry about him; he gets why you're here. Everybody loved Cecilia and we want justice for her," José said, tearing up.

"Max took care of her VW—worked on her car before she left for Santa Barbara—he's always had a soft spot for her. Teased her about the color and the daisy. We'll do whatever we can to help you."

Glaring at Robin, he added sarcastically, "Besides, not all Latinos are running chop shops."

"Soy Nicaraguense. Entiendo," Doug said. "Sorry."

That she understood—her partner got José's resentment. Somebody had been watching them when they had arrived.

Robin scowled at Doug. He raised an eyebrow. This unexpected mix of collaboration and assertiveness on José's part caught her off guard, yet she was relieved they did not have to interview an uncooperative source. Outside, the warm sunshine and slight breeze felt good to Robin. She took a deep breath.

"Thank you, man, we appreciate your help. We're determined to find out who murdered your friend. Robin and I have heard only good things about Cecilia; totally believable after meeting her parents," Doug said in the soothing tone he typically used with a tired Sean. Steady traffic made hearing difficult.

"No thanks needed. Bottom line, I want the son-of-a-bitch caught. Tell me what you need from me. Cecilia Hernández was more than a friend—but I guess I'm not telling you anything new. We were not a couple as we had been during high school, but eventually we adjusted. When she came home, we spent time together. Anyhow, why would someone like Cecilia, educated and beautiful, want to be with a grease monkey like me?"

José did not wait for a reply. "I guess her parents told you I'm getting married. Wait a minute," he said, abruptly taking off for a pristine black pick-up truck, waxed to the nines, silver hubcaps gleaming. He reached into the open window and pulled out a paper bag, which Robin figured for his lunch. She did not flinch. Neither was carrying anyhow—standard protocol when operating in the territory of another PD. He smiled in their direction. Robin figured she'd better not underestimate the man.

They followed Santos to the back of the building and sat down at a battered wooden picnic table replete with cigarette burns and food stains. The hard-packed dirt under and around the table was littered with butts and bottle caps, wrappers, and cans, despite the presence of an oil barrel with a hand-lettered sign declaring it to be a trash receptacle. José pulled a bottle of water and a sandwich out of the bag and set them on the table. Robin thought he had better get to the business of eating his lunch, or Doug would help him out.

"José, when did you last speak to Cecilia?" Robin asked.

"I don't need to think about it—I keep replaying the conversation in my head. The memory makes me crazy and to be honest, is making my fiancée crazy. About three weeks ago, I told Cecilia I was getting married. I had dinner with her parents a week earlier—their son and I were best friends before he died. I wanted to tell them Angie and I were engaged rather than have them hear the news from somebody else—we are close and it was difficult. They ... I ... thought Cecilia and I would marry after she graduated from college, but when she decided to stay in Santa Barbara for graduate school I knew it was over. Still, it's damn hard to let go of dreams."

"I'm sorry," a sympathetic Robin told the distressed man. Even so, she made a mental note to get hold of his phone records.

"José, I'm sorry for your loss, but we have to do this. Do you remember the date?" Doug asked.

"The end of September—if you think it's important I can send you my phone bill."

Robin hesitated, thinking his response was too good to be true and his sad demeanor was meant to throw them off track—suspicious when she didn't get cooperation, yet equally so when she interviewed a too cooperative suspect. Either way, the perps often think they are successfully deluding the authorities.

José continued. "Anyhow, Señora Gabby called Cecilia to tell her I'm engaged. She sent a beautiful card congratulating us—I called her and she was pleased for me but sounded tired and unhappy. Though quiet, Cecilia was always a happy person. I asked what was wrong. She said she wasn't feeling well and had too much work."

"Is it possible Cecilia was not so much tired as sad because you were getting married? Perhaps a dream had ended for *her*?" Robin asked.

"I thought about that," he answered, his eyes welling up. She and Doug remained quiet. Finally, "I maybe even hoped she had regrets. Truthfully, some small part of me did not want my own dream to die. Detectives, I have loved Cecilia since the fifth grade. I still love her, but I also love my fiancée. It makes me not such a good person."

"I understand," said Doug.

"Thank you," he said looking intently at Doug, seemingly surprised by his response. Again, Robin was caught off guard, unsure whether José was a perp playing them and Doug was acting the part, or whether the two men shared a common bond she didn't understand—one of those gender things her partner delighted in referring to.

José resumed his story. "I asked her whether she had a boyfriend, thinking they weren't getting along so well. She said 'not really.' Truthfully, detectives, I didn't believe her. I have known her better than anyone else, except for her parents and brother, and sensed something wasn't right. When I next went to their house for dinner, I asked her mother whether anything was wrong with Cecilia. It turned out she was also worried about her daughter but asked me not to say anything to Manuel. Sadly, I made Señora Gabby worry more and should have spoken with Manuel."

"And you didn't talk to Cecilia after that?" Doug asked.

"No, I didn't. Don Manuel called yesterday to tell me the police thought Cecilia had died. You have to understand, we did not even realize she was missing. Now, it's all about regrets. I could kick myself for being worried, yet not calling her back. Or, going to Santa Barbara. Maybe I would have made a difference." He put his head in his arms and began to weep.

"José, we can talk later if you want." Robin looked helplessly at Doug. Nothing was going the way she had anticipated.

Doug reached out and patted the man's back. "Lo siento, hermano—do you want to talk after work?"

"No, I want to help. *Now*, helping you is all I can do." He raised his head and wiped his eyes with the back of his hand. Another mechanic rounded the back of the building, scoped out the scene in front of him and reversed course. A small yellow stray came sniffing around and José scratched his ears. The dog settled at his feet.

"Could you tell us how Cecilia was the last time you were together?" Robin asked.

"Let me think." He bowed his head.

"Take your time," Doug said. He toyed with his pencil and waited.

Robin wondered whether they should interview the fiancée, although the case for doing so would be easier to make if the woman turned out to be José's alibi. Clearly, the man sitting in front of them still felt strongly about Cecilia. It occurred to her that a girlfriend might have some serious concerns about that state of affairs.

José was getting fidgety, but he then quieted, looked into the distance and responded. "The last time Cecilia and I were together was last summer at her parents' home after she returned from Central America. After dinner we went for a walk—and talked."

"How did she seem to you?"

José furrowed his brow and twirled the water bottle before continuing. "Come to think of it, Cecilia was pretty anxious after she came back."

"Did she say anything about the trip that would explain why?" Doug asked.

"Good question. She didn't say too much. Cecilia thought people were taking advantage of the Indians. I have no idea what is going on in Nicaragua, but I think the experience got her to thinking about her parents' life in Mexico. I told her being sad would not help the Indians, yet her work would—I was trying to be supportive. Instead, I should have listened better."

"What *was* the work about?" Robin asked, still curious about Plask's research.

"I guess I don't really know. I understood the professor she works for has been helping the Indians for many years. That's why I tried to convince her she could make a difference. To tell you the truth, detectives, she didn't want to talk about Nicaragua. Possibly, she thought I wouldn't be able to understand."

"I doubt that," Robin said. "Do you think she was eager to return to the university for the fall semester?"

"I don't think so and *that* surprised me. Not because of anything she said, Cecilia just seemed so unhappy. If only I had asked more questions. What I do know is I let her down."

"I'm sorry," Doug said. "You've been a great help—thank you for being honest with us. We'll do our best to find out why she was so anxious and who hurt her. Oh, by the way José, did Cecilia have a Facebook page, a Twitter account?"

"No. She was too private for social media: Facebook, Twitter, whatever. I should have kept in better contact and then, maybe, I could have helped her."

"José, have you ever heard of Barclay Stalts or James Wilson?"

"Stalts? No. Wilson. Isn't that the name of the manager at her apartment complex? Yeah, that's his name. She thinks he's weird, probably drinks too much, smells, but he's never been a real problem that I know of. Fixes things when she asks. Who is Stalts?"

"Mr. Stalts is the witness who called 911 the day Cecilia was found."

"Why do you ask? Are they suspects in her murder?"

"No. Not suspects—routine queries."

Robin decided to end that line of questioning. "José, I'm sorry to ask you this, but we need the information for the official report. Could you tell us where you were during the last two weeks?" Robin anticipated the question probably would not go over well with their thus far cooperative person of interest.

José's eyes narrowed, his jaw tightened, and through clenched teeth he said, "I didn't hurt Cecilia, I loved her." His reply verged on tightly controlled anger, a distant cry from the emotions they had observed up to now. For the first time, he took out a cigarette and lit up.

"We ask these questions routinely," Doug said calmly. "We're mainly interested in anything you can tell us about Cecilia that might shed some light on what happened to her. We only need to know where you were for our records. And your fiancée."

José again tensed up, but instead of responding, took his time smoking the rest of the cigarette, ground it out, and tossed it into the sea of butts around the table. The sleeping dog didn't budge. They waited him out.

"I don't like your treating *me* as a suspect, never mind my woman, but I want to help. Do you want to see my time cards? They would show I was in Salinas both weeks. Max will vouch for me. In the evenings, I was at home with my girlfriend, Angie Salazar. She works at a local winery in Carmel Valley. Can you check without causing problems for her? I call my mother each night after dinner. You can check my phone records."

Robin breathed a sigh of relief at the apparent shift in demeanor. "José, we probably won't need to talk with Angie for the time being. We do appreciate your cooperation in letting us see your time cards, but we'll need written permission to access your phone records."

"Not a problem," he said, the worry lines on his forehead beginning to smooth out.

"Thank you for your help. We can make a copy of the time cards," Robin offered. "I noticed a Staples store on our way over."

"I'll get them for you," he said, and without another word, stood up and took off around the corner of the garage. The dog got up, stretched, yawned, and went to lie under another tree.

"Well, what do you think?" Doug asked, eyeing José's uneaten sandwich.

"Give me a minute. I want to fill out this release form so we can look at his phone records. Focus. I promise we'll stop and get something to eat."

"I'm focused—hungry, is all."

"Done." Robin put down her pen. "If his alibi holds up, I doubt José is the killer. I don't see how he could have taken off for SB after work, met up with Cecilia, killed her, driven to the Painted Cave, dumped her body down a ravine, ditched her car in some out of the way place, and made it back in time for work. He seems genuinely upset, which is what her parents told us. Doug, I've got the kit with me, but I'm not going to ask for a DNA sample right now."

"Why?"

"I don't think he'll respond well, and I want to continue the interview with the parents. Besides which, we don't have probable cause to require a swab and sure can't tell him about the pregnancy."

"Yeah, I guess I agree with you. José makes an unhappy call to Manuel and Gabriela, and we're done here. I also don't think he had anything to do with her murder but we'll examine the time card and phone records. You can confirm the alibi with your buddy, Max. Robin, let's hold off on the girlfriend for now. I'd hate to cause her problems unnecessarily."

José returned and handed the two time cards to Doug, who in turn passed them to Robin. They showed he had worked the critical days, consistently punching in early and out late—he had even worked the previous two Saturdays. Each day was signed with M something, which she guessed were Max's initials. Nothing looked off to her.

"Thank you," Robin said, putting the time card in her evidence case. "José, would you mind signing this form? It gives us permission to access your phone records. Difficult to tell how long the investigation will take, but we *will* find out who committed this horrendous crime. Here is my card. I jotted Doug's number on the back. Please call if you think of anything that might help. If something feels inconsequential but is bothering you—please call," she appealed, taking back the signed paper.

"I will. Thank you for your help. The numbers are for my mother and Angie," he said, handing Robin a grease-stained piece of paper. "Don't worry, we'll cooperate, but I gotta get back to work. Max's getting irritable, which is never a good thing." He shook hands with both of them—a firm and relaxed handshake, no sweat—all pluses when interviewing a person of interest.

"*Getting* irritable?" Robin asked.

"Just for show—he's a good guy, but please send back the time cards or he will have a fit."

"We'll make copies of the time cards and the release form now and bring the originals back to Max right away."

"Thanks." José picked up his uneaten sandwich, walked over to where the dog was lying in the shade and fed it to the eager animal. He crumpled the wrapper and successfully shot it into the barrel— took a swig of water and left without looking back.

"That sucks!"

"Doug! The poor animal needs food more than you do. C'mon, let's copy the time card and the release for his phone records. Then, we'll get something to eat."

They drove the short distance to the Staples store, made the copies, and returned to the garage.

"Hi Max, thanks for your help. Here are José's time cards. The envelope is also for him," Robin said with a smile and what she hoped was a confident tone.

"Yep," he said, snatching the cards and envelope out of her hand.

"I see you signed the cards."

"That a question missy?"

Robin kept talking, despite the sure knowledge she was raising the guy's ire. "I see José punched in the same time morning and night. Do guys ever punch in for each other?"

"What kind of damned question is that anyway? José is a decent, hardworking guy. Legal."

"Mr. Max, I'm just trying to conduct a thorough investigation."

"Well, you'd better watch your step, missy." He tossed the papers to the side and flipped through order sheets. Max was done with her.

CHAPTER 26

The Investigation:
Day Six

"Hey, Robin, I'm a growing boy who's gotta eat. You, of all people should know that, being my partner and Sean's mother. Grub!" he yelled, pointing to a small stand-alone restaurant they were quickly approaching. The sign was straight to the point: *Pizza and Subs*. It was set back from the road with a few wooden picnic tables and a graveled parking lot. About twenty feet from the rear of the building was a thriving orange grove.

"Come on Robin," he coaxed, "pull over if you want to maintain the peace."

Irritated, she took a sharp turn into the parking lot, gravel pinging the car. "Doug, you're pitiful, you do know that don't you?"

"It'll do you good to order a five-meat pizza. Put some bulk on those skinny bones of yours—you're supposed to have my back; you need strength for the job. Rabbit food ain't going to do it!"

"Doug, in this day and age, a brain is what's generally called for in the solving of crimes, and my brain matter is doing just fine, thank you very much. I'm the one who should worry, all that cholesterol puts *your* brain at risk!" Equilibrium reestablished, Robin laughed as she got out of the car and checked to see whether she had dinged the paint.

"Man, that hurts," he moaned, pitching around with his hand over his heart.

The heat from the noonday sun had come down a few degrees, and there was a soft breeze. Robin watched the man to whom she trusted her life as he strode toward the restaurant. On such days she wished their relationship had grown into more, conveniently ignoring the fact they had consciously put the brakes on because of the job. Once inside the tiny restaurant, she joined Doug in perusing the menu posted on the wall.

"I can't decide between a cheese pizza and vegetarian sub."

"Me, I'm torn between the meat-eaters pizza and lasagna. Then, there's the possibility of a meatball sub."

"Can I help you?" asked the pleasant woman behind the counter, looking from one to the other, before settling on Robin. Her name tag identified her as Rosa.

"Rosa, can you melt the cheese on a sub?"

"No problem," she cheerfully responded. Robin ordered the veggie sub and took a bottle of water out of the old-fashioned red metal refrigerator with *Coca Cola* emblazoned on the front.

Doug, Robin knew, could eat the sub, pizza, and lasagna and then push for a stop at a Dairy Queen. It was a good thing he was dedicated to working out or else he would be a blimp. Instead, after one bout of roughhousing, Sean had told her, "Mr. Doug is ripped." Doug had grinned proudly at Robin and told Sean, "muscles of steel," as he flexed his right arm.

"Señora Rosa, I'd like a medium meat-eaters special and a small meatball sub."

"What do you want on the sub?"

209

"Onions, peppers, and extra provolone. Oh, and a large root beer."

"You can get the soda out of the refrigerator."

"Not a bottle. A fountain drink. I'll take care of the check."

Rosa repeated the order back. Doug paid what had grown to a substantial bill.

"Thanks, but you do know we can put this on the expense account? Things aren't so bad we need to pay for our own food."

"Yeah but, Robin, you're a cheap date. My eating habits don't look so good next to yours, and the Chief gives me grief about my expenses. All I can tell you, woman, is I gotta eat, even if the dollars come out of my own pocket."

They sat at a clean white Formica table situated in front of a broad picture window. Rosa brought over paper plates, napkins, utensils, and Doug's fountain drink.

"Thank you," they said simultaneously.

"You're welcome." Rosa returned to the counter.

"Doug, let's do a quick assessment of where we're at while we wait for the food."

"Sure, shoot." He pulled out notebook and pen.

"Cecilia's advisor, her parents, and her ex-boyfriend all agree she was tired, anxious, and sad. They all believe her state of mind had something to do with school, her fellowship, and/or time in Nicaragua. The consistent factor there is the esteemed professors. Other than still having feelings for José, who was getting married, nobody suggested a boyfriend problem. Moreover, we found no evidence from her apartment pointing in that direction, or to Wilson. Yet, we have a *pregnant* victim. The murder seems personal. Her computer is missing, as are any back-ups, photographs, purse, and cell phone. First thing Monday, I will take care of requesting records for the landline. The time cards, which Max confirmed, provide José with a solid alibi. Cecilia's parents and probably her ex-boyfriend are nonstarters, although we need to examine *his* phone records. Doug, we may need an alibi for the girlfriend—do you agree?"

"I do. I was tempted to probe José for more information, but I don't think we want to present him with a defense based on reasonable doubt *if* he is involved in Cecilia's murder. That said, I agree with you. I don't see how it would be physically possible for José to have committed the crime unless someone is covering for him—the distance between Salinas and Santa Barbara is about 220 miles, one way. Also, don't forget Mr. Hollywood, though we haven't anything on him. Well, yet. Remember to follow-up on the gardener's alibi. I think we should ask Stalts if he knows a Sara Castillo or a Cecilia Hernández and see what we get there. Hopefully, something will come out of the forensics. Mostly, I find it odd Stalts has an indirect connection to a Santa Bruja member through his assistant—a stretch, but we ought to talk with him again. Robin, we've got to locate Cecilia's car, cell phone, and computer."

"Sounds like we're on the same page. Too bad we can't examine José's credit card bills and bank activity for the critical time frame."

"Even our ever so helpful Judge Salazar will tell us to take a hike. We're damn lucky Santos gave us a release for his phone records—we'll take a look at those before causing problems for the girlfriend."

"If José wasn't involved, maybe he'll remember something else Cecilia said or did that worried him. Doug, good idea you had to pay a visit to Plask's home tomorrow. I know you like Plask for Cecilia's murder, but you've got to agree there's not much of anything pointing his way, other than the man's questionable behavior in his office and the fact she seemed unhappy after returning from Nicaragua." Robin removed her utensils from the rolled paper napkin.

"That's true—though he seems to be a pretty fucked up dude, which unfortunately isn't evidence. I know we don't much like Benson, but we've got less on him than we do on Plask."

"Maybe we'll get something useful tomorrow," Robin said.

Rosa brought the lunch to the table on a large tray.

"Perfection! Thanks Rosa," Doug said.

"Enjoy. Let me know if you need anything else."

Looking at his plate, it occurred to Robin that the amount he had ordered was sufficient to feed a small village somewhere in the world. Her sub was perfect: a crisp roll piled high with mushrooms, peppers, onions and melted cheese oozing out of the sides. After taking the sandwich out of the oven, Rosa had added shredded lettuce and thin ripe tomato slices before cutting it in two. Robin twisted off the top of her water bottle, took a drink, and began to eat. Doug was digging into his pizza, which he washed down with gulps of his fountain root beer. Settled in with their food, they put all thoughts of crime on hold as they talked of things that are more personal. She learned Doug and his father were still at it.

>>   <<   >>   <<

Back in the car, the partners again took up the discussion of the murder investigation.

"Doug, thus far all I've learned about Doctor Dane Plask is that he's on a sure path to sainthood at the university—he's considered to be a fabulous teacher, outstanding researcher, someone who always has time for his students, *hot*, and if opportunities aren't available for students, 'the Prof' goes out of his way to increase their chances for success. The caveat, of course, is that I acquired most of the info from the internet—went to sites like *My Professor*. Some of the comments should be taken with a grain of salt, so I looked for trends—the most notable: women are generally the authors lauding Plask. Most of the guys are pretty harsh."

"Shit! All I have to say is that I can't believe he's managed to snow so many."

"It's hardly the whole shebang. Doug, the guy has an outstanding national, even international, academic reputation. He has written four textbooks and a countless number of journal articles. Foundations, as well as the government, seem to like giving him money—a fact the university surely appreciates. His curriculum vitae is an astonishing

38 pages long, which is impressive for an anthropologist, even if it's padded."

"What about Benson? Could be he's flying safely under our radar."

"Well, Benson's an odd duck. Professionally, he's nowhere in Plask's league. The nature of their relationship is unclear. I forgot to tell you, the Chief said to tiptoe around the pair until we discover some concrete evidence. Same thing concerning Mr. Hollywood."

"Legitimate concerns, I guess, but so much political tip-toeing makes my brain cramp," he responded dejectedly. "Enough of work, I'm getting indigestion. No sense in ruining a good meal."

CHAPTER 27

Searching For Justice:
Day Six

Robin once again pulled the Toyota in behind the truck in the Hernández driveway. This time, Manuel was sitting on the porch in one of the two rocking chairs. Doug exited the car and greeted him with a handshake and embrace. They were friends already—she was envious of her partner's ability to negotiate so successfully through his social spheres.

"Señor, thank you for arranging the meeting with José. He was a great help," Doug said.

"José is a son to us. We all want to find the person who did this terrible thing to our Cecilia. Angela understands we need him in our life."

Robin avoided commenting, unable to imagine how any fiancée, special or not, could accept a close relationship between the man she planned to marry and his long-time, beautiful ex-girlfriend and her family.

After they had gone inside and Gabriela joined her husband on the couch, Robin tried to pick up where they left off earlier. "Did you ever visit your daughter in Santa Barbara?" she asked Manuel.

Robin and Doug waited expectantly for an answer, but Cecilia's parents remained quiet.

It was Gabriela who eventually answered Robin's question. Manuel looked down. "We never went. Santa Barbara is far—to travel costs much money and always we have work. Now I am so sad—Cecilia would like for us to visit her university." The grieving woman leaned her head against her husband's chest.

Robin recalled the empty feeling of their daughter's apartment, especially the lack of pictures. She made a mental note to ask whether they should arrange for someone to box and mail Cecilia's belongings. Her parents would need to terminate the lease.

"Have you met Dr. Plask?" Doug asked.

Manuel answered. "No, but he called before Cecilia went to Nicaragua and during her vacation."

"Did either of you talk with him?"

"Both of us. Detective Debayle, to tell you the truth, we worried about Cecilia going to Nicaragua," Manuel said, looking into an irretrievable past. "Our daughter told the Professor about our concerns, and he called us. The Doctor said not to worry; he promised to take care of Cecilia. The experience would be good for her career. Do you agree mi amor?"

"Si, es cierto. He is a kind man."

Robin perked up at that tidbit of information, remembering what Doug had said about Cecilia not going on the trip if her parents did not approve. They did not seem quite on board with the fellowship, but not dead set against it either. A cynical Robin wondered whether they had felt pressured by Plask to go along with Cecilia's decision.

"Do you know why she was in Nicaragua?" Doug asked.

"She works on the professor's project. He pays," a flushed Gabriela answered while retying the ribbon finishing off her braid.

215

Doug took over the lead on that line of questioning. Plask had struck a nerve with him. His jaw tightened and his eyes narrowed ever so slightly. Robin was concerned that eventually his visceral reaction would present a problem for their investigation. She had been intrigued to note that he acted much the same whenever the subject of his father came up. Despite the considerable advantages to the arrangement, Robin still found Doug's decision to live at home odd, given the ongoing animosity between the two men. Then it occurred to her that he was apt to respond similarly to Ken O'Donnell.

"What kind of project? How long did she remain in Nicaragua? Where did they work?" Doug brusquely fired off the string of questions. Manuel and Gabriela glanced at each other.

"Doug, slow down," murmured Robin, but then decided to stay out of it and see where things went. She knew little about Latin America or the cultures of those who come to the United States. He had been primary for years and exceptionally good at his job. She also remembered Doc's advice that accepting help would not reflect badly on her. More important was a successful arrest and prosecution. This was the first case they worked together with their roles reversed, and snags were bound to occur. There was sufficient tension in the room without her pulling rank.

Manuel and Gabriela remained quiet for what seemed to be a long time, yet in reality, probably lasted no longer than a minute or two. Still, the silence was enough to make Robin worry that the connection they'd established earlier with the couple had been lost. Gabriela's nod was barely perceptible, but sufficient for her husband to pick up the story.

"The professor worked with the Indians each summer. He said the work was an important experience for Cecilia."

"Were your fears calmed after speaking with him?" Doug asked more gently this time.

Manuel looked at the picture on the coffee table. When he answered, he did so indirectly. "We worried about her being far from home and living in difficult conditions. We came to this country to have better lives, but we did not protest because the Doctor said Cecilia should go for her profession. She called us from Nicaragua. The telephone calls must have been expensive."

"After Cecilia returned to the States, when did she come home?"

"Two weeks before her classes started. Her last year. ¡Fijate! We are excited to go to her ceremony: 'I am going to be Doctor Cecilia Hernández,' she always tells us," Gabriela said.

Robin was excruciatingly aware of the incorrect tense. The couple would never attend their daughter's graduation. She thought of her own proud parents when she had received her doctorate.

"Señora, how did your daughter behave when she returned home from Nicaragua?" Doug probed, a dog with a bone. Thinking she did not understand, he attempted to clarify the question. "I wonder—"

"To be honest, Señor Debayle, Cecilia is tired. When I ask why, she says life is difficult and she misses her home. They are in Managua for one day before coming back to the United States. She is afraid of the airplane," Gabriela responded.

"Had she traveled anywhere before, somewhere she needed a passport?" Robin asked.

"No. Cecilia never left California."

"I think how the Indians lived bothered her most." Then, Manuel hastily added, "She didn't say that exactly."

Robin looked at Doug, remembering José's comment about something in Nicaragua disturbing Cecilia.

"And what happened when she came back to Salinas?" Doug asked.

"Her papá and I are happy she is home, but Cecilia sleeps a lot and I worry. I think how she acts is normal after such a difficult trip, pero I am worried," Gabriela said. "Manuel says not to worry—she needs rest."

"Did you tell Cecilia of your concern?" Robin asked, aware she was pressuring two very vulnerable parents.

"Cecilia says her papá is right and she is tired. She tells me I worry too much. Pero, I am her mother and I know something is bothering mi hija. Maybe the Indians—pobrecitos, life is hard for them," Gabriela said while crossing herself.

Manuel continued. "We came from México, and life is difficult there for the poor. We came here for our children to have a better life, and we thank God every day for his blessings. Even though our son died, he lived a good life—until the leukemia came. Detectives, I think children living in bad conditions shocked her. Once I took café and tortillas to Cecilia in her room and found her crying. Would it help if you looked at our daughter's room? On *Law and Order* the police ask to visit the bedroom."

"We'd certainly appreciate that," Robin said, thankful they did not have to ask permission to examine Cecilia's personal belongings. She could only imagine what Manuel and Gabriela must be feeling—there was no longer an uninvaded corner in their devastated lives. Yet, she had a job to do. "Did your daughter have a laptop computer?"

"Yes, the little computer is with her. The cover is pink with orange circles," Gabriela said.

"Gabby, we should have a café. Then the detectives can do what they must."

"Café sounds good." Doug responded. "Please call us Doug and Robin. There is no need to be so formal."

"Gracias. Douglas, would you like to see our Cecilia's letters while the women fix the café? We could not bear to read them," Manuel said. He began to well up.

"Thank you, Señor," Robin said. "May we take the letters back to Santa Barbara to review them?"

The room remained silent. Doug scratched the back of his neck with his head tilted left, a sign of discomfort with something Robin did or said—it occurred to her that he was as much a nonverbal as a verbal person. Husband and wife looked at each other. With a barely perceptible nod from his wife, Manuel said he would gather the letters together while Gabby and Robin prepared the coffee.

Doug stepped in. "We appreciate the difficulty of this interview, but we're determined to find whoever committed this terrible crime.

Sometimes the most valuable clues come from the victim's family. Robin, I'll get the evidence bag from the car."

"Thanks, Doug. While you and Señor Hernández take care of the letters, I'll help the Señora with the coffee. Is that okay with you?" she asked Gabriela.

"Sí. Of course," Cecilia's mother responded with an uncharacteristic smile.

Doug went out to the car; Manuel walked up the hallway; Robin followed Gabriela. Once the two women were in the kitchen, the grieving mother seemed a bit more relaxed. The kitchen was sunny with large windows, and window boxes full of flowers and herbs. Long yellow ribbons held back the white pique cotton curtains framing the window. They reminded Robin of Cecilia's kitchen. The wallpaper was a light blue with buttercups scattered about in reckless abandon. In the middle of the room, there was a small oak table and four wooden chairs, bright blue and yellow colored cushions tied onto each seat. On the table sat a white porcelain napkin holder and salt and pepper shakers in the shapes of a chicken and a rooster. Robin imagined Cecilia on her summer break, breakfasting with her parents—smiling and chatting about the day ahead, blind to the evil creeping toward them. Or, perhaps, by that time evil had already insinuated itself into their lives.

Robin shook herself out of her reverie and resumed the conversation. "Señora, is there anything else you can tell me about Cecilia and someone she might have been interested in? Romantically? Mothers are more likely to be aware of what's going on with their daughters than are fathers and, in my experience, try to protect their husbands from things that may be upsetting, which for daughters is usually a man."

Gabriela slowly dried her hands on her apron and without looking at Robin, nodded. "Detective, what you say is true."

"Please, call me Robin."

"I will try. Robin, some things it is truly better only a mother knows of. A father might behave rashly." Her voice dropped to a whisper. "I must speak of this quickly because Manuel would be upset to know I did not tell him."

"Sometimes the critical clue is something people don't think is important. We won't say anything to Manuel without your permission," Robin said, aware she might not be able to keep her word.

"Gracias," Gabriela said, with a gentle sigh of relief. "My daughter is not happy when she comes home *before* going to Nicaragua. Cecilia tells me the trip is an honor and the work will make our lives better in the future. I tell her a daughter can talk with her mother—I always guard her confianzas. I am thinking Cecilia is pressured to go. I ask her not to, but she says is too late—the Doctor needs an assistant. At the end, she says she is being silly."

"Señora, what do you know about Dr. Benson?"

"I do not know of that person."

"James Wilson or Barclay Stalts?"

"I do not know those people." Gabriela busied herself with arranging the coffee cups.

Robin took her lead and silently set about filling the creamer and sugar bowl. "Did Professor Plask and Cecilia speak by telephone after that conversation about him needing an assistant?"

"The Doctor calls one afternoon. My daughter sits at this table while they talk. She thinks I am in the garden, but I am resting in bed—my door is a bit open. Discúlpeme, Dios, but I am worrying and I listen."

"Gabriela, sometimes we do things we're not proud of when we love our children and are worried about them."

"Sí. That is how it is. Cecilia is talking to the Doctor about Nicaragua. I do not know what he says ... I think he is angry. My daughter tells him she does not want to hurt his feelings, he is wrong. Then she tells him not to take a different student to Nicaragua. It is then I understand she does not tell me the truth, so I am worrying. Another person *can* go with the doctor. My daughter apologizes. Later, she will not talk about the trip to me or her father. They leave the country the next week."

"Did she still seem worried?"

"No. She is now excited before she leaves to Santa Barbara, so I do not tell Manuel."

Gabriela opened the oven and removed what looked to Robin like fruit bread. "That smells delicious."

"Gracias. A banana bread. I hope you like it."

"Your husband said Cecilia called while they were in Nicaragua—how did she sound then?"

"Sí. The first call is to say she is safe in Managua. She calls again to tell me she met Professor Araya and a student, Estela Ramírez, who is with him. She likes them very much. Our daughter does not like Managua—the air is dirty from the cars and buses. The city is noisy. Robin, en realidad, I think what bothers Cecilia is many people are poor and some children have no homes. They live on the street, sniffing glue and selling their bodies. The next time she calls, she sounds tired, maybe sick. That day they fly in a small plane to where the indios live. She is afraid."

Robin heard Doug knocking at the front door, followed by the sound of Manuel's footsteps coming back up the hall. Gabriela proceeded to place six empanadas in an enormous black cast iron frying pan, the oil sizzling. Robin waited a few minutes before sticking her head out of the kitchen doorway to ask Doug if he would put the letters in chronological order and make a list of the dates, which he should then sign and leave with Manuel.

"Sure thing," Doug promptly responded.

What a partner, she thought to herself—he understood she needed more time. She again directed her attention to Gabriela, who was carefully arranging the creamer and sugar bowl on the bamboo tray.

"Was there another call?" she asked, intent on seeing the conversation through. In her gut, she knew something important occurred between the student and her professor *before* they had even left for Nicaragua. Once in Nicaragua, something precipitated an emotional reaction in the girl that caused concern among her loved ones after she returned. It may, or may not, have been related to her murder, yet Robin understood knowledge was power and they needed all they could get. Cecilia and her family deserved justice. To be honest, she also wanted to resolve her first case as primary so she would be in line for another. And, then, there was the problem of the never-ending grief she would receive from Doug if she ended up with a cold case.

Gabriela continued talking in a hushed tone as she used a wooden spatula to transfer the empanadas from the hot oil to a plate covered with layers of white paper towel. "Cecilia's next call is not good—it is hard to understand her, and she has trouble hearing us. The other Professor returned to Managua with Estela. My daughter has much work and no friend. She sounds unhappy. Robin, do you have children?"

"I do … a little boy who is six years-old. His name is Sean."

"That is nice for you. Children are the most wonderful thing of life on earth. Your son is now young, but you will learn when Sean is older he will want to protect his mamá. This is what I think my daughter is doing … protecting me."

"Why did you think that?"

"Not what she says, I worried for what she does not say. Her voice is not right."

"I understand." Robin hesitated and then asked, "The next phone call—how long did you talk?"

"Minutos. Professor Plask did not know she called. I think she is nervous … the call cost much money. Robin, my daughter is murdered. I stay awake last night wondering what my Cecilia is not telling me. If I do something different, our daughter could be alive." She had begun cutting the bread but stopped what she was doing and stood still.

"Gabriela, you are not responsible for this tragedy. Were there other calls?" Robin asked, mindful she had better wrap things up

"Robin, the last call … Cecilia is crying and says she misses me. She calms down, but she says something strange."

"Gabriela, can you remember her exact words?"

"I write down the message. She says she will call again. If I do not hear from her, to stop me from worrying, I am to call a phone number—they will help."

Gabriela removed a slip of paper from the battered cookbook lying on the counter. She passed it to Robin; written on the paper was the number *1-806-555-0150, con Doctor Plask en Nicaragua*. Short of breath, Robin's heart dropped a few beats. It was the SBPD helpline.

>>　　<<　　>>　　<<

After having coffee, empanadas, and the banana bread while talking about the garden, Robin again mentioned to Manuel and Gabriela that they needed to terminate the lease on Cecilia's apartment. She wrote down the contact information for the manager, Mr. Wilson. Doug suggested José help them, but to ensure there were no problems he would talk with the manager on Monday. They also discussed the options for getting Cecilia's belongings to Salinas. Then came the most difficult—the arrangements for the release of Cecilia's body. Robin asked Manuel to sign the requisite forms and explained that when Doc gave permission to proceed, somebody from the SBPD might be able to accompany their daughter home to her parents. Robin assured Gabriela and Manuel she would return Cecilia's correspondence within the week. Soon after, Doug told the couple they had to catch their flight but promised to keep in touch with them. After heartfelt thanks and hugs, the detectives left. The door closed behind them.

"What a break—her parents offering the letters, toothbrush and brush, as well as access to her room," Doug said.

"It sure was! I bet we get some valuable information from those letters." Robin could hardly contain herself while backing into the road. "Wait until you hear what else I got."

"Watch it girl! Mamacita will have your beautiful blonde head for doing damage to her baby boy. What's up? You two were in the kitchen whispering away for a long time."

"Gabriela gave me the details regarding Cecilia's calls from Nicaragua. She said her daughter was worried about something before they left, and it became worse once in Nicaragua. I sensed Gabriela was suspicious of Plask—of the relationship between the two. But, that's not all. You'll *never* believe what Cecilia said to her mom during the final call."

"Girl, give it up before you pop!"

"Our victim told her mother that if she became too worried, she should call this number." Robin handed him the slip of paper Gabriela gave her.

"Son-of-a-bitch! It's the helpline. Identifies Plask! Holy shit!"

"Yep."

"Goddamn."

"I couldn't believe it! Now, I'm even more anxious to find the laptop … we'll try to obtain Plask's permission to check out Cecilia's desk, although he has probably erased anything important by now. Oh, I almost forgot, Benson's name is unfamiliar to Gabriela, as is Wilson's and Stalts'. By the way, thanks for staying with Manuel."

"Not a problem—what's an exceptional partner for?"

"What did you learn from Manuel?"

"He wasn't as talkative as Gabby seems to have been. Going through his daughter's letters exhausted the poor guy. They *are* in chronological order and the envelopes numbered. I gave him a receipt—good idea, by the way. Maybe we'll have some luck with the content, though I have to say those I read were pretty white bread. Not much of interest in her bedroom either, but you should take a look at the photos I took, including one of the over-the-top flower arrangement Plask sent." Doug bit into an empanada.

"Oh my god, I don't believe you're still hungry!"

"Between you and me, as good as anything mamacita and Sonia make. Just an appetizer, hijita—dinner is looming. Given you're the boss, it's up to you to be sure my meal is more than coke and peanuts."

CHAPTER 28

Sunday Crossword: Day Seven

Sean got up bright and early on Sunday, excited about going to Montecito, a visit to the Debayle's home invariably special— Doug's parents treated Sean as they did their own grandchildren and he, in turn, felt like one of the brood. Robin, tired from the Salinas trip, was relieved no nagging was needed to get him fed, dressed, and into the car. She and Doug had planned to settle Sean and then drop in on Plask. Concepción agreed to delay dinner until they returned.

>>   <<   >>   <<

Doug knocked on the heavy door of the imposing home set into the foothills behind the Mission. It swung open almost immediately to reveal an incredulous Dane Plask.

"Detectives, what can I do for you?" his calm tone contrasted with his evident surprise at their second unannounced appearance.

Robin began with some trepidation, suddenly concerned that dropping by Plask's house with no warning had not been such a good idea. "Professor, we apologize for just dropping by, especially on a Sunday, but we happened to be in the area and thought you might like to know we've been to Salinas to talk with the parents of Cecilia Hernández."

Doug kicked in. "They asked us to acknowledge your sympathetic gesture—the flowers and card."

"Thank you. Her death was a tragedy—flowers were the least I could do. How is her family doing during this difficult time?"

Robin *tried* to keep the sharpness out of her reply. "Cecilia was their sole remaining child, so I'm sure you can imagine her parents' pain. They only talk about their daughter in the present tense. I can't pretend to conceive of what they're going through."

"Nor I." Doug rubbed his jaw. "Dr. Plask, Cecilia's parents asked us to express their appreciation for the opportunities you gave their daughter."

"Officers, though I have to admit it's unexpected to learn you traveled to Salinas, I thank you for your effort to keep me informed but, alas, I must go. I'm involved with the *Times* and am sure *you've* got crime to fight," he said, his sarcasm palpable. Their person of interest began to shut the door.

"Sorry to bother you, Professor. We thought you'd want to know how her parents were taking their loss," Doug said.

Robin went for it, despite knowing how ridiculous she would sound. "Dr. Plask, I know it's an imposition … if you don't mind, I would appreciate using your bathroom?"

He rolled his eyes. "*Well*, Officer Crane, make it quick. Anyhow, I guess this is the end of the *Times*—I have to get going. I'm meeting a colleague and can't be late." He pointed Robin toward a door halfway up the hallway. Doug asked for water and the two men headed into the kitchen. If she took her time, she knew her partner would score a cup of coffee and, she hoped, some useful information.

Looking to gain time, Robin poked around in the bathroom, flushed the toilet, ran water, and then quietly opened the door. She stopped to admire the beautiful paintings hung along the hall and the amazing examples of indigenous pottery displayed on long multi-level floating black lacquer shelves. As expected, Robin found Doug drinking coffee in the kitchen. She leaned against the counter and took in the modern and expensive decor: stainless and raw steel, bamboo floors, burgundy upholstered chairs, dark wood plantation blinds, black marble counters, and recessed lighting. She thought of Gabriela's warm and cheerful kitchen, flowers peeking through the window. In contrast, Plask's kitchen was cold and egocentric—what she was coming to believe accurately reflected the man.

"Robin, I asked the Professor if he'd noticed any changes in his student's mood after she returned from Nicaragua. He didn't observe anything obvious, other than simple jet lag."

"Now that I think of it, Detective, I remember Cecilia was some-what stressed when we returned to the States. Alternatively, maybe Benson mentioned something to me at one of her dissertation committee meetings. Anyhow, I enquired whether there was some way I might help her. She thanked me and said there was nothing I could do. Cecilia never said so outright but suggested the difficulty was with someone at home."

Robin, caught off guard, blurted out, "A man or woman?"

"Sorry, that's all she told me," he said with a facetious smile. "Officers, I apologize that I can't be of more help. I don't want to be rude, but you'll have to be on your way, as I have to be on mine."

"Sure. Oh, I almost forgot, we'd like to take a look at Cecilia's office." Robin said.

"She doesn't have an office."

"Well, her desk then."

"Nobody's in on Sunday."

"Professor, I'm sure if you'd call over to security, they'd give us access," Doug said.

"I guess you'd need a warrant. Next step, talk with the legal office."

227

"Thank you for your cooperation, Professor. We'll do just that," Doug responded sharply.

Plask shepherded them out of the kitchen into the foyer. As they approached the heavy mahogany door, Doug abruptly stopped and turned around, "Dr. Plask, when we visited you at the university, you mentioned that one of your students, Sara Castillo, died in a car crash. Can you tell us anything that might be helpful?"

Plask tensed and his mouth opened and shut before he collected himself. "Why on earth are you asking *me* about Ms. Castillo?"

"Given Ms. Hernández' unexpected death, we're taking a look at student deaths. Routine procedure, probably nothing—thought perhaps you'd be able to help us out, that's all."

The professor remained quiet. As he ran his fingers through his thick hair, his expensive gold Rolex caught the light. Robin recognized the flashy signet ring from their visit to his office.

"The death occurred a while ago, so I don't remember much. She was a transfer student enrolled in one of my classes. There is no reason I would have had more than a passing familiarity with the girl. Let's see, I was under the impression that Sara was popular—I do recall the crowded memorial. Why would you think the cases are related? It was an accident."

"Probably aren't. Related, that is. Questions we routinely ask when working an unexpected death," Robin said.

"Routinely?"

Doug answered. "It's protocol to check out related deaths. We're looking into accidents, disappearances, assaults, overdoses, and even murders involving female students in the Santa Barbara area because we may have missed something earlier that'll help us understand Cecilia Hernández' death."

Robin picked up a picture sitting on a handsome leather chest made from an old-fashioned luggage trunk and placed to the side of the door. It was of a younger Plask, standing with his arms around two short indigenous men, both sporting rifles, a machete strapped to the waist of one. All were smiling. She glanced up to see Plask watching her. A muscle rippled along his jaw, his mouth pulled tight—looking none too pleased, he reached for the picture. Robin handed it to him.

"I heard you do research in Nicaragua. I have a doctorate in psychology. Isn't it rare for a funding source to stick with an anthropological project for so long?" Robin continued without waiting for an answer. "By the way, were you aware that Doug's family is from Nicaragua?" She had swiftly added the last query, hoping to catch him off guard.

"No. Why would I?"

Doug followed up Robin's question. "I guess you wouldn't, although SB is a pretty small town. My father is Raúl Debaylc. I was born in Managua."

"*Your* father is Raúl Debayle? Well, *that is* a surprise! Didn't catch your surname at my office."

"He is. You've met him?"

"No, but I'm familiar with the name through my association with a foundation for abused children. Are we talking about the same Debayle family related to Somoza?"

"That would be them. Explains why I'm here and not in Nicaragua."

"Well, officers, this has been interesting, nonetheless you need to be on your way. Nothing personal but next time talk to my lawyer—no more informal visits, regardless of how pleasant." He pulled out his wallet, removed a business card, which he handed to Doug. Before they had gone further than a few steps, the heavy door closed behind them with a resounding thud.

Once in the car, they both took a deep breath. "Boy, oh boy, the good Doctor Plask is definitely uncomfortable with our forays into his life. Robin, I'll bet you anything we're in his crosshairs. He sure won't be happy when we show up to examine Cecilia's desk, though I don't expect much there."

"Doesn't matter. Good to keep the pressure on. Interesting he brought up Benson and the possibility of Cecilia having trouble with another man—sounded like he was trying to cover his butt. We need to go at her advisor again. He's been off the radar too long. That was an intriguing response to your Nicaraguan connection!"

"You think! Son-of-a-bitch is guilty of something, and I am going to find out what it is. C'mon, podner, let's get back to the ranch house."

Doug always drove up the winding road leading to his parents' home a little too fast for Robin's taste, sure he did it to rattle her. No sooner had they parked than Sean came running up to the car to tell his mother of the baby kittens. He, of course, wanted one. Luckily, he ran off to play with Tati and Julia's children before she had to come up with an answer. She and Doug walked over to the long teak table covered with a crisp white linen cloth and situated under a beautiful eucalyptus tree, branches trimmed high for the purpose. Raúl and Concepción kissed and embraced Robin. As always, they accepted her and Sean into their lives with the utmost of graciousness—she had learned much about the meaning of family from the Debayles. Concepción called Sean to come ring the dinner bell.

Everyone sat down at the table. After the two maids, dressed in formal black and white uniforms, served the first course, Doug asked his father whether he knew anything about Dr. Dane Plask at USB—specifically, what he did in Nicaragua.

"Met the professor at a party in Managua. Appeared to be a good guy—maybe in Santa Barbara, probably at a fundraiser," Raúl said and shrugged.

"Know what his work with the Miskito Indians entails?"

"Only that he spends summers in Managua. To do what, how would I know? I *am* familiar with the Miskito." With more enthusiasm, he went on to describe the extent of the wood and mineral resources they sat on.

"Why so many questions about Dane Plask, mi'jo?"

"He's a person of interest. Papi, I'm going to tell you something that is *not* for public consumption—Robin and I are looking into the death of a graduate student at the university."

"Person of interest—what in the devil does that mean? I doubt a reputable professor is running around murdering his students," an unexpectedly animated Raúl protested.

"Papi, the man is an egotistical player who fools around with his female students. And," he added, much to Robin's consternation, "there may be other dead students."

"Mommy, who got deaded?" Sean asked anxiously. The other children remained quiet. Wide-eyed they focused on their uncle. Robin envisaged a kitten in her future if Doug kept this up.

"Enough, hijo! You can't talk about such things in front of the children," an irritable Concepción said, shaking a warning forefinger at Doug. "*Raúl*, basta. Por favor."

"Doug, *what* is going on?" Julia asked.

Robin felt chastised. She asked the children if they wanted to make fun drinks with cherries and off they ran, laughing, to the wet bar on the patio. As she juggled glasses, drinks, and red and green cherries, Robin heard Doug and his father having words about respect, secrets, responsibility, and independence. Concepción tried to shush the two men. Unsuccessfully.

CHAPTER 29

Progress:
Day Eight

"**D**oug, the Chief wants to meet about the Painted Cave case. When we're finished, how about reviewing Cecilia's letters?"

"Sure. What's up Robin?"

"Nothing. You know Bartolo—he likes to stay involved. Anyhow, we need the go-ahead to write a warrant for Cecilia's desk."

"Let's go. Sorry about last night. Got hammered by my mother after you left."

"Not to worry; well, unless I end up with a kitten. Did Sonia tell you the university photograph of Cecilia Hernández was released to the media?"

"Anything other than the regular loonies?"

"Maybe. We received two credible reports of our victim driving alone in her yellow VW on Friday, three days before Stalts' discovered the victim. A friend, name of Linda Olsen, called in. Olsen apparently

232

invited Cecilia to go shopping on the Friday of the week she died, but our victim said she couldn't go because she had too much work. Olsen didn't know of a boyfriend, but claimed that Cecilia seemed stressed beyond the demands of graduate school for a month, maybe more. She hadn't been sleeping and had circles under her eyes to prove it. Doug, one of us should talk with Linda Olsen in person. The officer who took the call made a note that she seemed to be holding something back. No calls to suggest José was in town. I asked Sonia to route calls to Andy from now on—Bartolo approved the request to add him to the team."

"Better and quicker response than I expected. Robin, why don't we have Tyler interview Olsen, since the calls will be going through him."

"Good idea. I'll let him know. I already asked him to check out car washes in the vicinity of the Painted Cave."

"Good."

Robin knocked on the frame of the open door. "Chief, you ready for us?"

"Come on in kids. Welcome back from Salinas! Hope you didn't hit too many wineries on my dime."

"I wish," laughed Doug. "Robin's first trip north and not one tasting!"

"How are you doing, sir?" Robin asked.

"Pretty good. Sheila and I took the *Crime Fighter* out to Catalina for the weekend. Wonderful weather! Saw some whales, including a breaching female. I guess the anchovies and krill are abundant this year. Robin, you and Sean should come out with us some time. Doug, you too."

"Thanks. I'll supply the Millers," Doug said.

"You got a deal. Now, Robin, brief me on the trip. Was the flight to Salinas you two managed to coax out of me worth it?"

Doug nodded his head affirmatively, while settling back into his favorite chair—overstuffed brown leather softened by the years.

Robin replied. "Going to Salinas was definitely worth the taxpayer's dollars. Got far more information talking with the family and ex-boyfriend directly than we could ever have gotten over the phone."

"Arguably, the most valuable thing to come out of the trip is the correspondence Cecilia's parents let us take," Doug pitched in.

"I told them we would FedEx back the letters."

"That's fine. Robin, get the expenses to Sonia by the end of the week—those on the department's credit card, as well as out-of-pocket."

"Will do."

"What about the ex-boyfriend? José something?"

"Santos. José Santos," Doug responded.

"A viable suspect?"

"We'll continue the investigation, check out alibis, etc., but for now, Santos is in the clear. There is no way he could have been in Santa Barbara *and* at work—we've got initialed time cards vouched for by his boss. We can obtain a DNA sample if necessary, and we have contact information for a relative and a fiancée to follow up on. Santos was completely cooperative, and has a good relationship with Cecilia's family. A great one—wouldn't you agree Doug?"

The Chief looked quizzically from Robin to Doug. "Why didn't you get a swab?"

"That was my decision," said Robin. "We could have—I had the kit with me, but I decided against it for several reasons. Santos was being surprisingly cooperative, and I didn't want to disturb the flow of information he was providing, particularly given we hadn't finished the interview with the parents. If we had alienated him, there would have been no way we would have been welcomed back into their home. Plus, he had a solid alibi, and we didn't have probable cause to take the sample if he chose not to cooperate. I was also reluctant to tell him about Cecilia Hernández' pregnancy, since Doc has not informed her parents' she was expecting, and I was unsure how he would respond to the information. I didn't want to set the scene for a confrontation between him and Plask."

"I agreed with Robin's assessment of the situation, Chief. We sure didn't want to lose the connection we'd established with our victim's parents. José appeared honestly broken up by Cecilia's murder and willing to cooperate in any way possible. The time cards look legitimate and his boss swears he is a stand-up guy. He met with us on the job and signed a consent form to obtain his telephone records. We're keeping an open mind though."

"I guess I understand why you didn't ask for Santos' DNA sample at the time, but I want you to go ahead and get it now. If he is as cooperative as you say, there shouldn't be a problem. In fact, have the Salinas PD take care of the request. Those results could rule him out as far as the pregnancy. Anything else?"

"Sir, you need an ottoman here." Doug shifted in his seat and winked at Robin. "The Hernandez' agreed something was wrong with Cecilia before she left for Nicaragua, and, even more so when she returned. They wished she wouldn't go. José confirmed what Benson said—she was atypically tired and down. We're going to interview a friend who called in after the media report. She also said that Cecilia had been unreasonably stressed. Robin, tell the Chief what Gabriela said."

"Sure. Gabriela overheard a conversation between Cecilia and Plask: she believed her daughter was not honest with her about all being well with her professor. Still, she did not tell me anything specific, but here's the shocker, kept the best for last—Cecilia gave her mother a number to call in an emergency. You'll never believe this, Chief, it's for our hotline, and she told her parents to say she had gone to Nicaragua with Plask."

"Interesting—clearly all was not well. The pregnancy?"

"We left that to the Doc," Doug replied. "She's going to make the final arrangements for the transfer of the body—she'll tell them then. For now, we've got questions concerning Cecilia's relationship with Plask but no concrete evidence for his involvement."

"Doug suggested we show up unannounced at Plask's house yesterday. Give the professor a song and dance about the Hernández'—how they had expressed gratitude for what he had done for their daughter. We thought a visit might shake him up sufficiently to make a misstep. He *was* shook up—no more visits, talk to his lawyer next time. Chief, you know what's odd? The man has yet to ask what happened to

Cecilia, although he sent flowers, indicating knowledge of her death, I'd guess through university channels."

"This is one hinky dude," Doug interjected. "We mentioned being in the midst of reviewing cases involving other deceased college students, including Sara Castillo, who'd also taken classes with him. *That's* the bit of information ending our friendly chat."

"You and your home visits!" The Chief glowered at Doug.

"Totally by the book! Robin was on board and kept me in check."

"Chief, a good idea—nothing out of line," Robin said defensively, whether of herself or Doug, she was not sure.

"What's this about a Sara Castillo?"

Robin answered. "It's possible Plask was somehow involved in the death of both students. Though to be fair, the original M.E. judged Castillo's death an accident. Doc asked me to pull the Castillo file— she now questions his conclusion. Well, actually, Sonia found it. Chief, she needs help scanning in the files. Anyway, Sara ostensibly died in a car accident, but Genoa remembered a distinctive mark on the girl's neck similar to a contusion on our victim's neck. When the three of us met, Doug pointed out that Sara and Cecilia shared several physical features: generous smiles, brown eyes, dark hair with a modern cut. In fact, they look like sisters, Sara being the younger. Plask wears a large signet ring that may be a match for the contusion. Doc now believes someone strangled both women."

Doug added, "The killer, if it's one person we're talking about, might have been flying under the radar for some time. I went back and re-interviewed one of Castillo's friends; she directed me to another. According to her, Plask spoke with Sara concerning a trip to Nicaragua as a paid assistant. A similar M.O. for Cecilia Hernández; in her case, she did accompany him. The friend recalled Sara as particularly stressed. She had spoken about getting out of town, maybe to visit her brother in Monterey—they were close. But the friend didn't take her seriously because Sara had a number of exams coming up and had already asked for notes because of missed classes."

"Sara died before she had the chance to go to Nicaragua," Robin clarified. "Oh, as a side note—it might not mean anything—Stalts *forgot* to tell me he spent the night in Carmel after leaving Mill Valley, and Sara was driving to Monterey. The towns are only a few miles apart."

"Interesting tidbit to keep in mind, but don't know what it means. Good work guys. Robin, contact me when the forensics are back."

"Will do."

"Chief, it's possible Plask was stalking Sara, and once the opportunity presented itself—thick fog on the highway, no moon, tired, and according to her father an inexperienced driver—he was able to eliminate whatever problem she represented. I think Plask ran her car off the road; negotiating the switchbacks at night and under those conditions is difficult for an *experienced* driver. The son-of-a-bitch just might have run her off the road."

"Doug, you're making some good points. But, bring me some direct evidence."

"We're working on it, Chief. On another note, how about a field trip, a bonding event? Robin needs to get out of the office more—she's never been up north."

"Is that so? Before or after the purchase of an ottoman? Doug, back to the evidence, what did the forensics on Castillo's car show? Any prints or unidentified paint on the bumper, something else helpful for your case?"

"Nothing noted in the file, but I'll contact the CHP officer who investigated the accident. We might find a record of body damage to Plask's car. Should be easy enough to check with DMV to find out what he owned at the time and—"

"Sara owned an older Hyundai, which after going over a cliff was pretty beat up, so I'm not sure what we'll get," Robin said.

"Could be a bit of a reach," the Chief admitted. "And don't forget the wrecker might have damaged the car while bringing the vehicle off the beach."

"True. I am sure the car has been junked. Bound to be a long shot but still worth checking out," Doug said. "I'll check with her parents."

"Guys, I understand why you're hot for Plask; a cautionary note, don't narrow the search for a perp too quickly. You have other viable candidates. Keep me posted."

"Thanks Chief," Robin said, getting up to leave. "Oh, by the way, is there a problem with us contacting the legal counsel at USB for permission to examine Cecilia's desk? Her mother and the manager at her apartment complex said she owned a laptop, which we haven't located."

"If the warrant will move your case forward, go ahead and get it if they won't give you access, though anything useful on that computer has probably long since been erased, if Dane Plask is involved. On another subject, Debayle, what's up with the domestic you handled with Tyler? What a sorry son-of-a-bitch. He was not at all concerned to find himself in a police station—ranting and raving about the Bible and law and order—the show, I believe. 'A man's home is a friggin' castle.' He was not under arrest, so he left in short order, somewhat more sober. Doug, we got a nut job on our hands? Why are you still on this case?"

"Honestly, Chief, I think we need to worry about this dude. He has a Santa Bruja tat, though we have no idea how his social life plays into the domestic. Ortega is not your typical gangbanger: he holds down a job, pays his rent and child support on time, the house is in good condition—that is, until he went after his wife. Payments are up-to-date for his car. On the other hand, Ortega thinks he owns his wife and he figures it's his right to beat on her, according to God, the law, and *Law and Order*. The wife said Ortega believes the youngest is not his. I damn well don't want him talking *CSI* next."

"Another man's baby? Never mind, doesn't matter, he can't whale on his wife."

"She says no, but she's divorcing him and dating another man, so I think we've got something to worry about. Laura is working with the wife and kids. I figured a trip to Ortega's workplace to let him know we've got an eye on him was worth the effort."

Robin interjected. "While at the restaurant, Doug recognized the owners."

"Yeah, how'd I forget that? Ortega works at a taquería owned by Sara Castillo's parents. An interesting coincidence or what? And if that isn't enough, turns out the wife's boyfriend Joel Stein is Barclay Stalts' assistant—the Hollywood dude who called in the body."

"Odd, even in what is still a relatively small town. I'll tell you what—keep an eye on Ortega and talk to Mr. Stalts. When it comes to crime, a coincidence is seldom just that. Debayle, about the restaurant visit, I trust you know what you are doing, but I would not be doing *my* job if I failed to warn you that I do not want any more complaints. Keep that type of hard charging intervention of yours low key. This is a complicated case and I do not want any screw-ups. Same goes for the domestic, Doug. I do not want the Commander on my tail again. Make sure you keep everyone in the loop on that one."

"Right, boss."

"How's it working out as primary?" Chief Bartolo looked searchingly at Robin.

"All's going well, sir."

"If I can put in my two cents, Robin is doing a bang-up job—better than I did on my first case!"

"Good. Get on with it then."

"Later," they said simultaneously and left.

Robin tried to thank Doug for the unexpected compliment, but he was having none of it—her partner was far more comfortable giving her a hard time. He disappeared and then reappeared ten minutes later with two coffees, and they settled in to review Cecilia's letters in the conference room. Earlier, when Robin had tacked up the players and a timeline on the standing bulletin board, the first thing that struck her while looking at the photographs was the inbred nature of the case. She was convinced the events and individuals involved were more than a series of coincidences. Ken agreed when he came in to find out what progress they had made, and she had given him a quick update. Doug remained silent.

Once Doug removed the letters from the evidence pouch, Robin was surprised there were so many—a dozen or more in each of the two packets. He took the top bundle, the most recent, and gave her the other. His trusty notebook was open and her laptop powered up. Sonia had brought in a tabletop copier.

They settled into the task. All Robin heard was background noise through the closed door from the hallway, the rustling of paper as they read the correspondence, the tapping of the computer keyboard as she summarized each piece of communication before copying them and replacing them in the envelopes. They drank their coffee.

After about ninety minutes, Robin looked over at her partner; he was reading the last one. She waited until he had finished.

"Doug, what I have are mostly letters from Santos and a few Cecilia wrote to Plask but, for whatever reason, never mailed. Could be her way of journaling was writing letters. Her parents said they could not bear to read them; I think I'll enclose a note suggesting they wait. They would find the letters difficult right now, perhaps for a long time. Santos' letters clearly indicate he loved Cecilia. They shared a broken heart when her brother passed away and depended on each other for comfort. He made it crystal clear he wanted to marry her, but nothing is remotely threatening in his letters. Rather, he made a real effort to remain her friend and maintain a close relationship with her parents. The letters to Plask, well, they are something else completely. In those, she frequently refers to the content of phone calls. When we finish reviewing them, and after we examine her desk, we can ask the Chief about getting a warrant for his phone records. I want information regarding the incoming and outgoing calls made around the time she went missing. Phone records should also get us her texts."

"So what do the unsent letters say?"

"Let's see ... she had a crush on the man, which he certainly encouraged. I'm really interested in what Linda Olsen has to say. She must know something about the source of our victim's stress. Cecilia certainly was ambivalent about what he offered—something was going on."

"Which was?"

"Offered?"

"Yeah."

"A research opportunity in Nicaragua. She was reluctant to accompany him, although she was not clear about her concerns, other than her parents preferred she not go. He gave the impression he was aware she was troubled, which is consistent with what Manuel and Gabriela told us. I wonder what he might have held over her head. The letters suggest negative ramifications for her career if she did not accept the fellowship. There are also poems and talk of her brother."

"Interesting. I have got a few written by José—same deal, he was accepting of a friendship but in love. Nothing at all to suggest he was a threat."

"Plask?" Robin asked.

"Well, there I hit pay dirt! Like your bundle, several unmailed letters written by Cecilia. In addition, e-mails from the good Doctor she'd printed out. Cecilia *had* told Plask about the pregnancy, but I may need to revise my serial murder hypothesis. Get this, our esteemed professor sounds like a schoolboy in love—he *yearned* to marry our girl. She, on the other hand, wanted to break off the affair. No threats, no reason, just wished to end things, get her degree, and return to Salinas. My guess is if José had held on longer, they would have gotten back together. To tell you the truth, I don't understand the nature of their relationship. Anyhow, this correspondence will get us the warrant for phone records and texts, and if the university doesn't cooperate, the desk."

"Doug, let's suppose Plask killed Cecilia because she tried to end the relationship. Why would he have killed Sara? I'll grant you he's a jerk, but as you've said repeatedly, jerkiness is not a crime, and we don't have anything suggesting a sexual relationship between Sara and Plask."

"Yeah, well, that was also true for Cecilia, until the autopsy and these e-mails. Robin, we need Plask's DNA to determine whether there's a match with the fetal tissue, though given the content of the letters it's pretty clear he believes he's the baby's father. Do you have any ideas about what was going on with Sara Castillo that might have resulted in her murder?"

"Honestly, I don't know. It's certainly a hole in our theory but that doesn't make it dead in the water. I'm still suspicious that two of Plask's students are dead—attractive women he spent time with, made promises to, and in the case of one, took to Nicaragua."

"No argument from me. Taking female students to Nicaragua, alone, makes Plask suspicious in my book, but something else is off with this guy. If we find out what that is, we'll be a lot further along."

"What do you mean?"

"Robin, his home is decidedly upscale, one not purchased on a public university professor's salary."

"You're probably right. Maybe Sara intended to report him to police or university officials—she may have learned something about what he had been up to in Nicaragua and confronted him. He, in turn, threatened her. She's frightened and heads up to Monterey to the safety of her brother. Plask pursues her. I don't know, Doug, we've got no end of options."

"Robin, as much as I hate to say this, I guess we'd better stick to making a case for Plask's involvement in the death of Cecilia Hernández. Meantime, we'll keep our eyes open for evidence pointing us toward him for Sara Castillo—something, despite the passage of time, both women held over him. Honestly, and I *hate* to admit this, we have to consider the possibility we are being overly suspicious. Sara could have been depressed, tired, and unable to see the road, a stressed college student who went off the cliff in her little Hyundai. By the way, where in the hell is Cecilia's car? There's Doc's idea we are looking at strangulation as cause of death. And the contusion on the neck—we've got to get hold of Plask's ring."

"Still no report of an abandoned car. Matt scheduled a fly-over to get a better look. No car, no computer, no cell. Camera—oh, the pictures on the memory card from Stalts' digital camera are mostly standard tourist fare, what look to be friends, maybe family. None of our vic. I will add the ones of the Painted Cave to the board. Cecilia owned an older Nikon, but there was no film."

"A flyover—my-oh-my! How's our hottie Ranger?"

"Forget it. Doug, I've been thinking ... I know you and your father have problems, but would you try talking with him again about Plask? If he doesn't have any useful information, perhaps he'd be willing to make some calls."

"I guess so. Why not? Though he sure as hell wasn't much help on Sunday. Robin, papi has been gone from Nicaragua for a long time, but you're right, he may be able to point us in the direction of someone who can provide us with useful information."

"Thanks. If you'll take care of that, I'll check the city records for Cecilia Hernandez' car, which could be at the impound lot or ticketed somewhere. I'll find out what Plask drives and get Cecilia's letters in the mail, so when Doc speaks with her parents she'll be able to tell them the originals are on their way back."

"Sounds good. Querida, I'll copy what I read so you can return them, but then I'm leaving. I'm going to see James Wilson to get his timeline for the days in question and talk with him about terminating the lease. Then, I need some serious sleep, unless we have to act on something I get from our pal."

"Thanks and nighty-night."

CHAPTER 30

Confrontation: Day Eight

Doug dreaded the discussion he was about to have with his father but knew Robin was right—he should try again. There was no reason why Raúl couldn't contact someone in Nicaragua to help them out. He found his father on the patio with a drink and a book. The sun was setting.

"¿Dónde está mami?"

"She's taking a nap."

Doug went over to the bar, took a beer out of the refrigerator, and settled into an armchair across from his father. "Papá, we need to talk."

"Of course, mi'jo. A problem?"

"Work-related. We got into it over this already. I don't want to fight, but Robin and I could use your help. We really need to find out more about Professor Dane Plask's activities in Nicaragua. I was thinking that if you still have contacts, say the adoption agency

244

you used to help, you could talk to them. Remember when Ronnie stayed with us—he spent most of the time under the dining room table before he went to his foster family? I wonder what happened to him."

"How would I know? What is it exactly that you want to know Douglas?"

"It's an investigation; we're not sure what we're looking for. Anything related to Plask."

The two men sat there nursing their drinks. Doug thought that his father was looking pale and tired, and remembered his mother's cautionary note the previous Sunday about his father's health.

"Douglas, I'm going to be truthful with you. You may not like what I have to say and I do not even know if this will help. I am sorry to say, I was not being honest with you. I've known Dane Plask for years."

"Thank you. I appreciate your help," Doug said, as calmly as possible. He had suspected his father was keeping secrets, but self-satisfaction would not bring justice for Cecilia Hernández or for her family and friends.

"Okay hijo, but remember you asked the question."

"I'm an adult—not to worry," he said, not believing it himself.

"This goes back a ways. Douglas, when I was with the Somoza government, we had heard there was a team of anthropologists that had been studying Miskito culture for decades. For political reasons, I arranged for a meeting with the man heading the project."

"The Miskito on the North Atlantic coast?"

"Yes."

"What was your interest in the Miskito?"

"The Somoza family needed allies to protect Nicaragua from the Communists."

"Communists? You mean Sandinistas. How could the Miskito help?"

"Sandinistas were receiving support from the Castro regime to spread Communism."

Doug decided he had better leave politics out of the discussion—he would never get anywhere on that front. "How was an anthropologist going to be of value?"

"He'd established strong ties with political leaders that we'd hoped would be useful, but he was concerned about jeopardizing his relationship with the Miskito; said he wasn't interested and refused to get involved. It wasn't Plask—this was before his time." Raúl took a long drink. "I miss a good cigar. Fidel will outlive us all."

Doug's world had gotten smaller. Quieter.

"Pops, how did Plask become involved?"

"You have to understand, Doug, our political success was at stake. The professor we had spoken with planned to retire, so I recruited one of his graduate students. *That* was Dane Plask. When he took over the project, Dane agreed to feel out the Miskitos about their attitudes toward the current government and keep us informed. In turn, we offered to help him with expenses and offered compensation going forward. I knew nothing about the actual research he was doing, if that is what you are asking. Still don't."

The two men sat without saying anything. That was more information than his father had ever shared with him about his professional life in Nicaragua. Noting his father's increasing pallor, Doug decided to back off. The revolution was long over and he was not sure how this information related to the two dead students.

"Thank you. Papi, I'm going to take a siesta—haven't been getting much sleep."

"Sorry I couldn't be of more help, hijo."

"You made the effort, and that means a lot to me. This information may yet turn out to be important." Doug got up, wavered, and then lightly kissed the top of his father's head. He left for the cottage without saying anything more.

CHAPTER 31

A Tightening Noose:
Day Eight

After Doug left, Raúl went back into the house. Not finding his wife, he entered the study, sat at his desk, and pondered his next move. There was no way around it—he loved his son. He dialed Plask's home number. Nobody answered, so he reluctantly left a message that he hoped made it clear he was done with his tormentor.

About an hour later, just as he and Concepción were finished getting ready for an awards dinner, the phone rang. Dane was on the line and, with no preamble, demanded "half a million" if Debayle wanted him out of his life. Raúl told Plask he would have to call back.

"Sorry, mi amor. Business. I won't be long." He gave his wife a kiss. Every time he thought he was finished with Plask, the man returned with his hand out—a recurring bad dream. Now, with Doug asking questions and Robin involved, the professor had become a nightmare.

Raúl returned to his study and called Plask back. After a short but intense argument, Dane assured him that he was leaving town; it would be a permanent parting of ways. Raúl hung up. He did not buy the, *I am leaving town* assurance; rather, he expected Plask would continue trying to suck him dry. Regardless of how much money he paid out, his secret would eventually be revealed. He held his head in his hands, still finding it difficult to believe his son was a policeman. Though Doug had seemed satisfied with their conversation, he knew that until there was an arrest for the murder of the young woman, his son would undoubtedly be back with more questions. Raúl thought he heard his wife through the door he had neglected to close all the way, but realized exactly how on the edge he was when he got up to look and nobody was there. His cardiologist had told him to reduce the stress in his life. *Fat chance*, he had replied. He went upstairs and told his anxious wife he was ready to leave.

After the dinner and what felt like endless speeches, Raúl had complained of not feeling well. When pressed, he admitted to chest and stomach pains. Concepción wanted to take him to Cottage Hospital, but he adamantly refused, attributing the discomfort to too much food and drink. Afraid to worry Julia and Tati, she called Doug, but his phone was turned off. In the end, a friend drove the couple home. After relaxing in the living room for an hour, Raúl insisted he felt better and promised to schedule an appointment with his cardiologist first thing in the morning. Shortly thereafter, his wife fell asleep and Raúl returned to his study to call Plask. A volley of heated words passed between them before it dawned on Debayle that his Mercedes was still at the hotel; reluctantly, he decided to use his wife's car.

"A 2:30 meeting at the regular place."

"Hope Ranch, I don't think so Raúl. Middle of night, middle of nowhere—I am not meeting you there at that hour! What kind of idiot do you think I am?" Plask's voice came through the line loud and strident.

"Dane, if you want the money, you have no choice. But, be warned, your days of receiving payouts are over. I am done, you son-of-a-bitch, and if you threaten me again, the university and the scientific community are going to know what you've been up to. The police are already asking questions."

"You idiot, I'm not a fool! I know that your son is on the force. You're right, he is hot on my tail, but believe me, you have just as much—if not more—to worry about. Why in the hell would you think I'd agree to meet you after midnight, never mind in an isolated area?"

"Dane, you're being ridiculous, it's not the first time we've met there. What do you think is going to happen?" Raúl demanded in a low voice. "Come on hombre, be sensible. We both live and work in Santa Barbara and a murdered professor is not anything I need in my life, *especially* given my son is on the police force. Listen to me and listen damn carefully. You are a well-respected university professor with a good lifestyle, which I am sure you want to preserve, whether in this country or in Nicaragua. You had better believe that you won't be so well-respected when they arrest you for the murder of a student. Maybe you are not aware of it, but you have quite the rep with the little girls. That might have been okay a few decades ago but it isn't politically correct today."

"You shit! You know that I didn't kill anyone. Is that what is going on, you fed some bullshit information to your son? Raúl, you asshole, you're *fucking* setting me up!"

"Just saying there are going to be plenty of questions for a man who diddles children ... gets one pregnant."

"You fuck!"

"Maybe. But that's not what this is about, is it? Plask, I am willing to give you half of what you want. A quarter of a million will get you far in Nicaragua. If I hear from you again, mi amigo, you will have something to worry about. You do *not* want to cross me. It is time to find another revenue source or tighten your belt. I'll see you at 2:30, the promontory off of Marina Drive."

"Shit! Debayle, I'm leaving a letter for my lawyer, so don't pull anything."

"C'mon, be sensible. Plask, you're beginning to lose it."

CHAPTER 32

Forensics Are In:
Day Nine

Sean was grumpy when he woke up and grumpier still when Robin took him to school. She was convinced there was an ear infection in their immediate future, but he emphatically denied his ears hurt. After attending a meeting about an upcoming fundraiser for the school music program, she drove to USB to meet with Dean Mann, who, according to the unexpectedly helpful legal counsel, was the go-to person if she wanted to examine Cecilia's desk. Robin had been relieved to learn it would be unnecessary to serve the university with a warrant—Doug would once again be surprised. Each time they needed to interact with the university, he was sure they would raise havoc in the name of academic freedom. Meantime, he had gone to talk with Barclay Stalts about Ortega, given the connection between Joel Stein and Susana Ortega.

>>   <<   >>   <<

It was midmorning before Robin made it back to her office. She unloaded two boxes containing the contents of Cecilia Hernández' desk and carried them into the conference room. Sonia followed her with a report from Doc and a generous slice of warm apple pie. In response to Robin's queries, the dispatcher told her that Dougie had arrived a few minutes ago. Gordito was still fielding calls about the Painted Cave case.

Robin went to her partner's office and knocked, eager to catch up. "Yeah? Come in."

"Blinds drawn, didn't know you were in. Sugar from Sonia," she said, handing him the plate without waiting for an answer.

"Thanks, Robin."

"You look terrible. What's the matter?"

"Got some sleep, but not enough. I'm coming down with something."

"You and Sean. I'm sure he's got a percolating ear infection. Get anything useful from your father?" Robin asked the question reluctantly, fearing another confrontation.

"Papá was surprisingly cooperative, but I didn't push too hard. Given the bonding experience, I think there's more to be had. Big surprise, Robin, it turned out that my father was not truthful on Sunday. He, and this *was* a shocker, knows Plask from Nicaragua," Doug said, with thinly disguised sarcasm.

"Jesus, what could they have to do with each other?" she asked, not meeting his eyes, the tension in her voice reflecting his.

"Robin, I told you some things about my family that night I had plans to haul you off to Vegas, but I left out important stuff. Now, I think I'd better come clean." Doug began to dig apples out from under the pie crust with his fork, and then replaced them, one by one. Robin waited him out.

He took a deep breath and continued. "In Nicaragua, my father was a member of the Somoza government. He used Plask to recruit the Miskito Indians for their cause, and though he didn't say so directly, I suppose that meant money and guns for political and military support."

"Wow," Robin responded, not quite sure what to say, unsure what the information meant in terms of their case. Doug abruptly changed the subject.

"What about Cecilia's desk—did we need a warrant?"

"Nope, even though Dean Mann wasn't too happy about us chasing down his professors, he allowed me to remove her belongings. Not much there that's helpful. Seems Plask beat us to the punch."

"Shit! What happened?" He lifted his head and rubbed his jaw with his thumb, looking none too happy.

"The good Doctor packed up Cecilia's belongings and left the boxes in the Dean's office because, apparently, there's been some 'reshuffling of space in Dr. Plask's lab.' As I said, there's not much, no laptop or back-ups but, truthfully, I looked through them quickly. I pushed Mann to call Plask. He did. Our prof claimed he did not know anything about the laptop and, according to him, she didn't use a desktop. I'm still hoping we'll find something that will help our case. The IT guy can take a look at it. Oh, and one of the forensics reports is in. Everything's in the conference room."

"Good! Let's go take a look. Find the victim's car yet?"

"Matt left a message. Still no sign of the missing VW."

"Robin, I've been thinking. We've been assuming she was in *her* car—she could have been in the *killer's* car, and he disposed of hers afterward."

"So if that's the case, where is it?"

"Any number of places. As I said, it could be in SB collecting parking tickets or at the impound lot. Did you make those calls?"

"I did. It's not in the system as ticketed. I left a message at the impound lot, but am still waiting to hear back from them."

"It could have gone to a chop shop *or* is on its way to Latin America intact."

"Good ideas. Tough possibilities to investigate."

"Just stick with me girl. Another reason to look at Santa Bruja—the rumor is they are big in the chop shop industry. Give it up already. What's in the forensics report?"

"No surprises, but hard evidence is always appreciated by a jury. And the Chief. The DNA results confirm what we already know from the photo identification and fingerprint analysis—our Painted Cave victim is definitely Cecilia Hernández. We now have a genetic analysis of the fetal tissue, so we can identify a baby daddy if, *when*, we find him. Cecilia used the lipstick and only her fingerprints were on the tube. Doug, the tube came from somewhere, maybe a purse. She wouldn't have been carrying it in her hand, although it may have fallen out of a pocket."

"I still say this has to be personal. Anything else?"

"Get this, Doug. They used reflective ultraviolet photography to examine the patterned contusion on her neck. The lab agreed with Doc that it is *similar* to the contusion on Sara's throat—well, as far as they could tell from those autopsy pictures we sent. My understanding is that a contusion, which involves trauma resulting in broken blood vessels, changes over time: it increases in visibility the next day because as skin dries it becomes more transparent. Bottom line, they couldn't come to any strong conclusions from the same-day photographs we gave them. But, they've got a dandy new software program, and if they had an object to compare—such as the ring Plask sports—they *might* be able to determine more conclusively whether or not it made the mark."

"What did the ring look like again?"

"At his office and home the Professor was wearing a heavy gold signet ring on his left ring finger—not round or oval, but rectangular. Pretty fancy for a class ring. He twists it around with the thumb on the same hand when nervous. Or, at least that was my take."

"Girl, you're sounding like a psychologist! I'll take a better look next go around. Anything more?"

"Well, about Doc's hypothesis that Cecilia Hernández and Sara Castillo were both strangled, that's a bit more complicated. The lab corroborated Doc's conclusion that *Cecilia* was strangled. Using Sara's autopsy photographs and the coroner's notes, they somehow examined the superficial and deep tissues of the neck to track the force vector that may have produced the injuries. Despite the technology, Doug, they couldn't determine definitively whether *she* had been strangled."

"What about the family?"

"Doc called Manuel personally and confirmed Cecilia's murder. She said it was difficult telling Manuel about the pregnancy. He, of course, was devastated. Oh, she let him know her letters were on the way back. José called to say he'll accompany Cecilia's body to Salinas, and he and Cecilia's friend, Linda Olsen, will pack up the apartment. Linda had called Manuel and Gabriela to offer her condolences and wanted to help in some way. We can get the DNA sample the Chief wants then. Andy spoke with Olsen, and she will be in for an interview tomorrow afternoon. Has an exam today."

"It's a good thing that José is making the trip because I wasn't sure how I was going to find the time to go to Salinas. I'm pursuing a lead in the Ortega case, but let him know I'll be at the airport. Robin, if you need help with Sean tomorrow, I can pick him up in the morning, ear infection and all. Mamá will be thrilled to nurse him."

"If he's sick, I'll take you up on your offer."

"No problem. I'll let her know what's going on."

"Thanks. The Chief was interested in the commonalities between the two students, physical and otherwise, but doesn't believe that's part of the equation right now. I would love to examine his phone records, texts, car and get an impression of the ring, but that will probably have to wait. Whatever you can get from your father to strengthen our case would be great. I guess I really don't understand their connection or, for that matter, what has been going on in Nicaragua."

"Same here."

"You know, Doug, I don't totally trust the Dean. He seemed more concerned about the school's rep than the students entrusted into his care. My guess is that Plask brings in some serious bucks, which I still think is strange. I looked at some of his publications and can't figure out why everyone's so hot and heavy over this research of his. Funding comes mainly from foundations, some from the feds. I can only access the governmental grants. The deal between him and your father, it's long over?"

"When the Sandinistas came into power, truthfully, papi and his cronies took the money and ran. Plask wouldn't be of any use to them, which means he shouldn't be a threat."

"Well, I want to know about his funding sources—following the money might help us understand what he's hiding—what the women might have had over him, even though he seemed to have feelings for Cecilia. Doug, I'm worried that Plask might take off."

"If he does, we'll have a hell of a time extraditing him from Nicaragua, particularly the Miskito nation, which has a less than opti-mal relationship with the current government. And let's not forget to factor in limited SBPD resources. I bet that Plask has been tucking away a good bit of cash somewhere, and would not be at all surprised to learn that he has bought a home in Nicaragua. It would have cost him a pittance compared to property costs in California. He'd be liv-ing the good life, and we'd have us another cold case."

"All good points. When we bring Plask in, maybe we can find something that will get us to his financials and the paperwork on any properties."

"Robin, let's keep building our case. Bartolo is going to worry about the university coming down on us in the name of academic freedom."

"I guess." She had not gotten that impression from the Chief but didn't say anything.

"I'll see what else I can get from papi. Have to leave anyway—I'm feeling punk. Oh, I got the timeline from a shifty Wilson. Tacked it up on the board. Shouldn't be a problem terminating the lease, he's got someone he wants to move in ASAP."

>>　　<<　　>>　　<<

The phone rang as soon as Robin unlocked the door of their apartment. Sean beat her to it, so she went to change. From her bedroom, she could hear his enthusiastic "Mr. Doug," "ice cream," and "Montecito." After a few minutes, her son hollered that Mr. Doug wanted to talk to her.

She took the call in her room. "Hi Doug, Sean's sure revved up!"

"It's all in the promise of ice cream! Robin, if Sean isn't feeling well in the morning, mami will take my boy. Otherwise, we'll stick with the original plan and I'll pick him up after school tomorrow afternoon."

"Okay. How are—"

Doug hung up before she finished the question.

CHAPTER 33

Latent Prints:
Day Ten

A packed day in front of her, Robin apprehensively woke her son. Sean insisted he was okay though she knew that what he really wanted was to have Doug pick him up from school, and to spend the night at the cottage. In the end, she decided not to second-guess her child and off they went, backpack and lunchbox in hand.

"Sean, have fun with Mr. Doug when he picks you up after school. I'll call you to say goodnight," Robin promised as children converged on the building from all sides. "Come on, give mommy a kiss!" Not waiting, she leaned over and kissed him on the cheek.

"*Mom*, not here!" Sean protested, scrunching up his face and wiping at the offending spot.

"Have fun with Mr. Doug," Robin laughed. As she drove off, a wave of love for her little boy washed over her.

>>   <<   >>   <<

Robin left a message telling Doug that Sean was in school. She then spent hours calling around in search of the yellow VW but had no luck locating the vehicle. Hoping to find out what Doug had learned about chop shops, she checked his office a couple of times, but he had not returned or even called in. Frustrated with her lack of progress, she called Salinas.

Robin made it through the Max barrier at the garage and José came on the line. He breathed an audible sigh of relief when Robin told him that for the present there was no need to talk with his mother or fiancée. She again offered her condolences and let him know that Doug would pick him up at the airport, adding that her partner had spoken with the manager and had the key for Cecilia's apartment. She thought José was crying as he mumbled his thanks and gave her his flight plans.

Finished with her e-mails and telephone calls, Robin stopped by Andy's office, but a post-it said he was out, and she then remembered the Linda Olsen interview was later in the day. She went to see whether Doc was available to discuss the forensics report.

Robin rapped on the doorframe of the M.E.'s office

"Detective Crane, come on in. I only have about ten minutes, but they are *your* minutes."

"Thanks Doc, I'll make it quick. Just one question, at least for now."

"Sure. If it takes longer, we can talk later."

"You sure you can't take time out to eat?"

"Wish I could, but I'll have to take a rain check. An autopsy of a pedestrian, father of two, killed by a texting teenager."

"Sorry. For you and the pedestrian. Less so for the texter."

"It's such a waste—we need a more stringent law against texting and driving, particularly when it comes to kids. What did you want to know?"

"I wondered about the partial print on our victim's throat? There's nothing in the report."

"Oops. I was in a hurry and probably sent over my summary. I'll scan in the original as soon as I return. Sorry, but they did not get anything on the partial. Skin, as I remember warning you, is difficult."

"Do you mind explaining why?"

Without a word, Doc picked up the phone and punched in a few numbers. "Freddy, come here for a few minutes. Unscheduled seminar."

Freddy popped into the room in what seemed like seconds, but stopped short at seeing Robin. "Oh. Hi."

"Hi Freddy, how are you?"

"Busy."

"Won't hold you up for long," Doc said sarcastically. "The detective asked for an explanation regarding the difficulty of getting prints off of skin. Freddy, want to answer the good detective's question?"

"No, that's okay."

"Freddy! Look at it as experience for testifying in court."

"Okay, then." Doc's assistant stood there as if in a trance for almost a full minute, apparently gathering his thoughts. "Robin, I guess I am going to subject you to a quick course on the complications of obtaining latent prints from skin, starting with the elementary: I am sure you remember that a fingerprint is a reproduction, in sweat, of the raised ridges. Sweat is 99% water. The rest of the residue consists of amino acids, fatty lipids, and salt, as well as contaminants. It's disappointing, but not a surprise that we didn't get a viable print from our victim because there are so many factors that affect the *quality* of a recovered print. So, for example, if there was already dirt on her neck, the fingers remove dirt instead of leaving an impression. For the same reason, it's also difficult to get a print if the skin is sweaty. In the Painted Cave case, there were signs of struggle due to either the killer or scavengers but in any event, factors that could have removed or distorted prints. He continued for several more minutes, providing a detailed but clear explanation for the fragility of prints."

"Good job, Freddy. Robin, the processing issues are also complicated, but I have to go, and Freddy has to get back to whatever he was doing." The sarcasm in Doc's tone was once again evident.

"Thanks." Robin said to both of them. The M.E.'s assistant responded with an abashed smile and fled.

Robin returned to her office. As soon as she opened the door, the flashing light on her phone caught her attention. After accessing her calls, she heard a message from the dentist's assistant reminding her of her appointment in the morning; another from her mother wanting to catch up; and from Doug: "Just to let you know, I'll pick up Sean after school. Your boys are going for ice cream as promised, and then to Montecito. Have fun with the dentist in the morning! Oh, and mamacita, we want new brushes for our pearly whites." He hung up. Nothing about the case.

O'Donnell stopped by and hustled her off to lunch, explaining he couldn't make it on Thursday. Robin was glad to see him: Stewart had left another nasty message and she planned to ask her friend for help in putting an end to the harassment. She still suspected Ken of taking matters into his own hands after the bruising incident, and though the intervention hadn't put an end to the problem, it at least had caused Stewart to back off. For awhile, at least.

>>   <<   >>   <<

Plask contacted Debayle yet again.

"Raúl, I've got the cops on my heels. Your son and that bitch will be at my office and house with a warrant next. I promise I will expose you and take my chances, *or*, you can pony up the rest of the money. After that it's over—I'm out of here."

"You bastard, I told you, nada más!"

"Raúl, my man, you shorted me—only half of what I needed. Do not be such a hard ass. You know you have it. After this, we'll go our own ways."

"Dane, if you threaten me one more time, I'll kill you and feed your worthless body to the sharks," Raúl said quietly and hung up.

Twice, Dane had accused Raúl of looting his country and leaving his compatriots behind to suffer, while "your kind" lives the good life. Raúl knew that a desperate Plask wasn't about to let go and, given Doug's profession, there were few options. Moreover, he and Concepción still hoped their son would marry Robin—she and Sean were already a part of their family and he did not want that possibility jeopardized.

His wife had invited the professor to their home for a Christmas party one year because he was on her charity's donor list. After that, Plask figured that a million or two was a drop in the bucket to a man he deemed a thief, and if he could not get Raúl to give him the money willingly, Debayle knew the man would figure out a way to expose him. It occurred to him that Dane might actually be planning to leave the country this time—he'd never been so aggressive in his demands. The anthropologist owned property in Nicaragua; it would not be long before the police would suspect he might flee and confiscate his passport.

Time was short. Debayle was pretty sure that Plask did not have proof for any claims he might make—he'd been exceptionally careful in his dealings with the academic, but there was no doubt about it, the bastard could make his life miserable. During the last year, Raúl had painstakingly concocted a plot to deal with the man who had become his nemesis. He had spent several months audiotaping both Plask's office and home; once he thought he understood what was going on, he put a plan in place. It was just in time because the walls were rapidly closing in.

Raúl called his old military buddy in Nicaragua, Col. Roberto Ortega Sr., hoping all the while that he didn't regret what he was about to do, yet sure that under the circumstances he had no other options. He then called Plask and told him he would meet him with the other half of the money Friday night at 11:30, same place. Debayle explained that it was going to take another day to get that amount together after the last withdrawal.

Without hesitation, he again told Plask he would kill him if he came back for more.

CHAPTER 34

Concerned Partner:
Day Eleven

The dentist had discovered a substantial cavity and Robin was late getting to work. She knocked on Doug's office door, but there was no answer. A call to his cell went to voicemail; his message assured her he would contact her in short order. She checked her own messages, relieved to find he had called to report Sean was at school and they'd had a great time. Nothing else. She wondered whether Doug was avoiding her but, if so, could not imagine why.

Robin decided to risk talking to Sonia about her concern. The dispatcher was on the phone but signaled the detective to wait.

She hung up just as Robin turned to leave. "Hola, chica. What can I do for you?"

"I hate to bother you, Sonia. Sorry about the lisp, just came from the dentist. Have you spoken with Doug?"

"Pobrecita. The dentist is terrible! No. Funny you ask—I am thinking that I am missing my boy. Last time I spoke with Dougie was yesterday morning. He said he had things to do and would not be back. Por qué?"

"I'm not sure. I can't seem to catch up with him—just one machine talking to another. Sonia, we're working the Painted Cave case. Doug left to look into chop shops as a destination for the victim's car and thought Santa Bruja might be involved. Coincidentally, Roberto Ortega, the guy who terrorized his family in Isla Vista last week has a Santa Bruja tat. Honestly, I suppose I'm concerned."

"Relax, mi'jita. I'll tell Dougie to call you next time we talk."

"Sean stayed at Montecito last night. I called at bedtime, but when I asked to speak with Doug, he was on his cell. He dropped Sean off at school this morning, so I guess there's nothing to be worried about."

"Robin, you know Dougie goes off sometimes. Not worry mi'ja. Oh, I forgot, Gordito was looking for you. He's got information he thought you'd be interested in from an interview he did yesterday."

"Thanks, Sonia." Robin returned to her office, not feeling particularly reassured about Doug.

>>　　<<　　>>　　<<

Robin's day seemed to be nonstop. She had not gotten far with Wilson's alibis before she had to leave to pick up Sean. Andy called and, though still hung up in the field, wanted to tell her that an initial interview with Linda Olsen had gone well. Apparently, the graduate student was suspicious of Plask's involvement in her friend's death but afraid of accusing him publicly. They had arranged to meet first thing in the morning to talk further.

He'd not been able to get hold of Doug either.

Instead of waiting for her partner to get back from wherever he was, she went ahead and met with the Chief to bring him up-to-date on the case. She asked about bringing Plask in for questioning; getting a warrant for a DNA sample, telephone records, and texts.

Bartolo laughed when she told him of Doug's concern that the university would take strong steps to protect their own. "Robin, I think you have enough to bring him in, but to be safe, let's wait until morning to find out what Doug came up with. If Santa Bruja is involved, then that might be something else altogether. Don't concern yourself with possible fallout—I can cope with academic grumbling and manipulation. Anyhow, there's always the *Crime Fighter*, Susana and I can quickly escape from any negative political and media attention!"

"Sounds good."

"What's this about not being sure of Doug's whereabouts? Is that correct?"

"Yes. No. Well, Doug left a message this morning. He's not answering his phone and has not been in today. Sonia reminded me he's gone off like this before and not to worry, but it's difficult not to—though, admittedly, he's been under the weather."

"He's probably working on other things."

"Chief, I'm sure you're right. I think I was concerned because he is looking into the possibility that the Hernández car ended up in a chop shop. He thought Santa Bruja might be involved." She did not want to say he had been out of touch.

"I'm sure he's okay. Poking around dangerous hombres takes time. Come see me in the morning. Meantime, try and corral your anxiety."

"Yes sir."

CHAPTER 35

Tragedy Strikes:
Day Twelve

Friday was a difficult day. Doug called in sick. Then, besides struggling with the Painted Cave investigation—although Linda Olsen's testimony would be a plus—a new case in their district sent Robin's anxiety level skyrocketing. A young boy had gone missing from the park across from the Mission and his whereabouts remained unknown despite an almost immediate Amber Alert. If Sean had not been so insistent that he *had* to attend his school friend's birthday sleepover, she would have kept him safely by her side. As it was, he was unhappy she planned to pick him up first thing in the morning. Robin returned home after dropping him off at the party, dulled her anxiety with two glasses of wine, and watched *Homicide: Life on the Street* before getting ready for bed. Just after turning out the light, her cell phone rang; she was confused when a man identifying himself as Joel Stein apologized for disturbing her. He went on to explain he had been waiting for Detective Debayle to call him back, but so far nothing.

"Mr. Stein, I don't understand why you've called me."

"I guess … it's that I couldn't reach him. Aren't you his partner?"

Wide-awake now, she pulled herself together. Aware of Stein's connection to Stalts and Doug's domestic—his concerns regarding chop shops and gun trafficking, Robin decided not to take any more time asking pointless questions. "Do you have an emergency?"

"To be honest, I'm not sure. Detective Debayle said to call if anything came up. He was concerned about Susana and the children."

That sounded right, Robin thought. "Did her husband threaten her?"

"No. I'm sorry. I don't know why I'm bothering you."

"Sir, it would be better all-around if you'd just tell me what's on your mind."

"Okay … Roberto called and said he couldn't take the children this weekend."

"Isn't that a good thing?" Robin tried to keep the annoyance out of her voice.

"Well, instead, he wanted the kids tonight. I hesitate telling you this because Doug and Laura told Susana not to let Roberto come to the house because a court order is in effect."

"Don't worry about that. Joel, just tell me what happened?" Robin pushed, increasingly anxious given Doug's recent disappearing act.

"Sorry. Well, Roberto came by to pick up the older children. As promised, he stayed on the porch. This is the thing, to make sure we were safe, I sat by an open window with the curtains drawn. Ortega was unaware I was in the house, but I had a baseball bat and my cell set to 911. He remained outside talking on the phone while Susana got the kids ready."

Robin willed Stein to get to the point. "Why's that important?"

"Well, I'm not sure it is. But here's what's bothering me. While on the phone, he referred to 'the professor' and 'money' several times. Actually, what he said sounded like cash for him *and* the professor, whoever that is," Joel said. "Once, he said 'Dean.' Before hanging up, I heard, 'He won't be bothering you anymore.' Officer Crane, Roberto Ortega is a seriously scary man. Detective Debayle asked Susana if he had gang connections. She refuses to talk about the Santa Bruja, but I believe that he does." All of a sudden, he stopped talking.

"Go ahead, Joel. I'm listening."

"Roberto repeated directions to a meeting place in the Hope Ranch area of Isla Vista. Twice. I wrote them down the second time. As soon as he left, I called Doug. As I already told you, he didn't answer or return my call. The second time I called, I left the details. That was two hours ago."

Robin knew in her gut that something was terribly wrong. Painfully, she recognized her mistake in ignoring the nagging feelings haunting her for the last couple of days. "Mr. Stein, are the children back?"

"Yes, yes. Roberto returned in less than an hour. Susana said he was in a rush, which for some reason worried me, so I took everyone to my boss's house. Thank god, Mr. Stalts is in L.A. Doug spoke with him the other day and my boss won't be happy if he finds us here."

"Mr. Stein, I'm at home. Give me the address for Mr. Stalts' home, and we'll contact Laura immediately. Do not leave the house under any circumstances, and tell Susana *not* to use her cell phone. Sir, we'll need a statement, so officers will bring you to the SBPD. Now, where did Roberto go?"

Once Joel gave her the convoluted directions, Robin understood why Ortega asked the caller to repeat them twice. She repeated her instructions, hung up, and called the department. Hesitant to ask the Chief to come in and then find out she didn't have a problem, Robin instead asked the night dispatcher to have Bartolo contact her when he checked in and to send Andy Tyler to pick her up at home STAT. Once the call went out, she requested two patrol officers to bring in the Ortega family and Joel Stein. She gave Stalts' address to the dispatcher and requested he notify Laura McCann. Robin assured the dispatcher she would be in as soon as possible to take a statement from

Mr. Stein. Meantime, he needed to arrange lodging for the family and keep them under police protection. After hanging up the phone, she threw on some clothes, removed her gun and mag light from the safe, and dashed outside to wait for Andy. It was only minutes before he showed up, lights flashing.

Robin sprang into the car and told a confused Andy to head toward Hope Ranch. As they sped along, tires squealing and siren wailing, Robin told him about Stein's call. She released the retention on her holster and checked that her magazine was in place. Once they'd located the general area, Andy turned off the siren and lights and followed the directions she gave him. When he spotted car lights about two hundred feet ahead, he pulled off the road and parked.

The two detectives moved cautiously toward the lights, guns hot. Robin was struck by the silence, pierced only by the chirping of crickets and the ocean's dull roar. They looked at each other. Andy nodded, and they moved closer in tandem. Still nothing. Robin slowly stood upright and peered in the direction of the car. Blinded by the headlights, she couldn't make out anything. There did not seem to be anyone around, but they maintained their crouched positions and, guns drawn, identified themselves. Not getting a response, Robin moved peripheral to the lights. Her heart skipped beats when she recognized the car.

She saw the body sprawled on the sand ....

"Oh, good Jesus, Doug—it's *Doug*. Andy, call in an officer down," Robin whispered the words with an urgency she'd never before felt.

Convinced nobody else was in the area, she holstered her weapon and dashed over to where her friend and partner lay on the hard-packed sandy ground.

Doug's face was leeched of color. She could find no pulse. There was a devastating wound in the left side of his chest, his black leather jacket, silk shirt, and lavender tie blood-soaked. His beautiful brown eyes were open but empty. Yet, it was not until Robin looked up and absorbed Andy's forlorn expression that she knew they had arrived too late. Doug's right hand, resting at his side, clutched his service

269

revolver. Suicide crossed Robin's mind but she just as quickly ruled it out. Doug loved life too much. Andy's voice came from miles away—she could not process the words.

She had to pull herself together. Doug would demand it of her.

"Andy, have the dispatcher contact the Chief and Doc. Send out anyone they can spare. Ask the Chief to pick Sonia up on his way in. The rack will be on to make it easier for them to locate us. They should move Stein, Susanna Ortega and her children to the safe house right away. If at all possible, Laura McCann should stay with them."

It occurred to Robin the news media would soon get hold of the story. She wanted to touch his cheek. Instead, she forced herself up and walked off a few steps to call Doug's sister, Julia.

CHAPTER 36

Shock Sets In:
Day Thirteen

The sun was coming up over the horizon when Robin and Andy, emotionally and physically exhausted, walked into a department that, at first, appeared eerily devoid of human activity. Looking around, she spotted the Chief and most of the Criminal Investigation Unit through the window of the conference room. Robin walked over to a weeping and disheveled Sonia, eyes red and swollen, and took her in her arms. Neither woman said anything. Soon afterward, she fled to her office.

As she sat huddled at her desk, protected by the closed door and shades, she struggled to block out thoughts of Doug's body lying cold and abandoned in the morgue; fought the urge to take a blanket to cover him, as she did with Sean late at night—as *he* had done with Sean. Tell him she loved him—the job should not have come between them. Sean—she called Denise. After hearing of Doug's death, her sitter told her not to worry; she would pick up Sean first thing in the morning from the sleepover and keep him at her house as long as needed. Robin went to join the others, wondering how she was not to worry. The mood in the conference room was somber; the expressions of bafflement, anger, and sadness on the faces of Doug's colleagues and friends bore into her heart. Ken came up behind Robin and put an arm around her. She couldn't move.

The Chief, standing at the vic-perp board, saw them outside the doorway. "Robin, Ken, take a seat and we'll brief you." He waited until they were settled before continuing. "I interviewed Joel Stein and Susana Ortega and put them in protective custody—Laura agreed to stay with them for the time being. Honestly, we're a bit lost here. Actually, a lot lost and could use your help. Robin, do you have *any* idea what the relationship is between Dane Plask, a suspect in the murder of one student, perhaps two, and Roberto Ortega, a perp from a domestic? Those were his most active cases, the ones he was most concerned about—we've clearly missed something of importance."

She was finding it hard to breathe. "Well, to be fair," Robin finally got the words out, still standing and now looking at Ken rather than her boss, "Joel only heard Ortega refer to 'the professor,' though admittedly, he mentioned a word sounding like 'Dean,' and so may well have been referring to Professor Dane Plask. 'Money to be delivered to the professor,' perhaps Roberto served as the middle-man, but I've no idea who Plask might be blackmailing, if he is." She glanced at Bartolo and recoiled.

The Chief's intense stare and the muscle rippling along his jaw belied his previously gentle tone. "What in the hell was Doug doing out there? Dispatch has no record of a call, or *anything* from him advising he was on his way to Isla Vista. His name isn't even on the duty roster."

Light-headed, Robin could hardly catch her breath but went on in a low, almost inaudible, voice. "Joel Stein left some directions on Doug's voice mail. He must have acted on that information, yet for the life of me, I cannot figure out why he didn't call me. Stein called my cell after Doug failed to return either of his two calls, and I contacted the dispatcher. Andy reached my place in less than ten minutes."

"Did you and Tyler see anything or anybody suspicious when you first arrived?"

"No. Nobody. Nothing," she said more forcefully.

"We didn't pass anyone on our way in," Andy said from the far side of the table, darting a quick glance in Robin's direction. He persisted. "Chief, whatever went down happened well before we arrived. The forensics unit took a cast of the two partial sets of tire tracks, but I don't think we'll get much—someone made a considerable effort to erase tracks and footprints. It's as if somebody, probably more than one person, lay in the trunk of a car, or the bed of a truck, sweeping the area as they drove away. Something gangbangers might do. Shit, Chief, I just don't know."

A red-eyed and wan Sonia shook so hard when pouring coffee that Ken took the pot from her and set it in the middle of the table. Once she'd left the room, they heard her patiently answering what seemed to be an endlessly ringing telephone. At one point, she came in with message slips for Robin: one from Marjorie Lutz; another from Laura about Susana being scared; Matt called—he wanted "to be there for her." Sonia told Robin there was an urgent call she needed to take.

Robin excused herself, sure Sean had learned of Doug's death. She closed her office door and picked up the receiver. Instead of her son, a weeping Concepción was on the line and her heart dropped.

"Mi'ja, Julia called to tell us Jesús has taken Doug to heaven. How did this happen?" The distraught woman did not wait for an answer. Robin could not give her one.

She began to wail, a sound that gave Robin chills. But quickly pulled herself together. "Robin, Raúl suffered a heart attack—you should come to the hospital."

"Oh my god, Concepción, I am so terribly sorry. Are the girls with you?"

"They are coming. Mi'ja, your letter is with me, but why is Doug mailing you a letter?" she sobbed.

Robin was unable to process the news that Doug wrote her a letter, or that his father might die. "Concepción, I'm going to hang up and leave right now."

She returned to the conference room and told the gathering of Raúl Debayle's hospitalization. The Chief asked Ken to drive her to the hospital.

Once they'd parked and reached the waiting room, Ken left to join the detectives and patrol officers down the hall. They had come hoping to find their friend and colleague alive and remained to support Doug's family.

When Julia caught sight of Robin, she uttered a cry and ran to take her into her arms. "My god, what happened?"

Doug's sister ushered Robin to the seat she had just vacated, and a frightened Concepción grasped her hand. The three women looked at her expectantly.

"I don't know … we don't know," Robin faltered, feeling physically weak and utterly baffled. She had no idea what to say, but saying nothing wasn't an option.

"Julia, I was at home, not with Doug; he went to meet somebody by himself." She clutched Doug's mother's small hand, a hand so fragile with age that she worried about hurting her, but held it nonetheless, finding comfort in the physical connection.

"Concepción, I'm sorry, but this is an ongoing investigation and I shouldn't be talking with you of what happened. I *can* tell you Doug was trying to bring the killer of a young girl to justice."

"Did he suffer?" Julia whispered, before looking away. Concepción bowed her head and fingered the rosary beads in her other hand, her lips moving.

"I don't think so. I am so sorry. Please, how is Raúl?"

Tati answered. "Papá is still in surgery, but they are 'cautiously optimistic.' The doctor came out to talk to us about ten minutes ago. He said mamá should go home, yet she doesn't want to leave. She needs to rest—this is too much. We can return when he's out of recovery." Tati sounded as if she was talking to herself; she had lost the argument.

"I think rest is a good idea—Concepción, you need to take care of yourself, Raúl will need you. I can't stay too long. Julia and Tati, do you want to go to the cafeteria while I sit with your mother?"

"Thanks, Robin. Mami, can we get you a coffee?"

"A tea would be nice. Robin, this is the letter from my Douglas," she said, removing a folded manila envelope from her purse. Her daughters looked confused. Robin dropped it in her bag without a word, but not before she had glimpsed her name and address on the front of the envelope, written in Doug's neat hand.

"Thank you."

After Doug's sisters left, Robin put an arm around his mother, aware that with her son dead and her husband in critical condition, there was little to say or do to make a difference. The knowledge that Doug wrote her a letter right before his death left her perplexed and anxious to examine the contents.

Julia and Tati eventually returned with two trays laden with coffee, tea, sodas, a variety of sandwiches and cookies. They pressured Robin to eat something, so she took a small black coffee and an oatmeal cookie, insisting she needed to leave but would stay in touch with Julia and return later.

"Mi'ja, you and Sean are familia, please embrace him for us. Give him our love."

"I'll be sure to do that." She hugged Doug's mother and sisters and turned to leave. Ken was standing outside the door. As they walked down the hospital corridor, Robin handed him Doug's envelope for processing. They returned to the department in silence. Once back, she asked Sonia to tell the Chief they had something important to show him and would be in her office with Ken. When Bartolo came in, Robin gave him an update on Doug's parents and then explained the bagged envelope sitting on her desk.

She gloved up and removed the envelope from the bag. Inside they found an unlabeled CD and a folded page of yellow-lined paper with Doug's handwriting. At a nod from the Chief, she slipped the

275

CD into the computer. She started when, instead of Doug's voice, Dane Plask's voice came through the speakers.

"What the *hell*? Chief, that's Plask!" She did not recognize the voice of the woman to whom he spoke but in seconds was able to identify her.

In an atypical coaxing tone, Plask addressed the unhappy young woman as "Cecilia."

"How would Doug have gotten this recording?" Ken prodded a dazed Robin.

"I don't understand. Jesus, Ken, I just don't understand," she sat down heavily. "Did this get him killed?" She handed the letter to the Chief.

He scanned it and handed the letter back. "This is addressed to you, Robin—looks like Doug wrote it after Stein called. *You* should read it."

She took the page, swallowed, coughed a few times, and began to read it aloud:

Querida, there is not much time. Joel Stein left a message sounding like a hand-off of money from Ortega to Plask is in the works for tonight. In case things go south, you need to be aware of what's up. I discovered papá has been tapping Plask's phone: The CD suggests the prof is involved in Cecilia Hernández' death. He bullied her into going with him that day, and easily could have carried her down into the ravine if they went to the cave. You and the Chief are for sure asking how I got to this point—Bartolo probably has a few well-chosen words! Well, I eavesdropped on a conversation between Plask and papá. Later, when I confronted him, he admitted Plask has been blackmailing him. About

what? I don't know. Roberto Ortega is supposed to deliver a final payment tonight. What is Roberto Ortega's role in this? Papá explained that his father, Ortega Sr., is an old pal from Nicaragua who arranged for his son to transport the money and, more importantly, to scare Plask good so he wouldn't be back with an open hand. Papá claimed he was trying to protect me—what a bunch of crap! I am hoping you never read this but if you do, get the son-of-a-bitch! Robin, you know I love you and Sean. Tell my boy I am always there for him,
*   and, of course, always yours, Doug*

"Robin, put out a goddamn APB for Plask and Ortega *now*," the Chief ordered as he stalked out of the room.

>>   <<   >>   <<

The day after Doug's murder, the Texas Marshals arrested Professor Dane Plask in Houston as he stood in line for an early morning flight to Managua. The substantial amount of cash in Plask's possession provided credence for the telephone conversation Stein heard on Susana's porch. An invoice found in his wallet showed he had checked in boxes, which turned out to contain scientific papers, books, and computers. Tyler discovered Cecilia Hernández' backpack, laptop, phone, purse, personal papers, photographs, and two thumb drives in one of the boxes. She could hear Doug saying, "We hit pay dirt!"

A surprised Robin discovered that Cecilia's computer was intact. Her e-mails made it undeniably clear that Plask had pressured the young woman to accompany him to Nicaragua and later, not to end the relationship. His threats, although subtle, were interpreted by the

277

graduate student to mean she should worry about her future. From the beginning of the relationship, she apologized for accusations he contended were unfounded. Though, at one point, Cecilia had struck out at Plask, broaching what seemed to be a long-festering unease about an overheard conversation in Managua. Apparently, she had suspected Jorge Araya, a fellow anthropologist, and Plask of engaging in an illegal business deal, possibly drugs. When she brought the matter up after their return, they had had a *serious* altercation, but when she again referred to it in an e-mail, he laughed off her distress and claimed she was worried over nothing more than a heated discussion about the research project: Araya was angry with him for not spending more time looking for funding. In reality, Plask insisted, Araya, a gay man, was simply jealous of their relationship. Robin was amazed the young woman accepted what sounded to her like patently absurd explanations.

Cecilia complained in another e-mail about losing control over her life, accusing Plask of pressuring her to cut her hair to appear younger—arguing she would not remain young forever. Robin looked at the picture of the graduate student and then pulled the Castillo file out of her drawer and examined Sara's photograph. The grad student had a point—despite the modern cut, both women could be young girls. Plask might be good-looking, intelligent, and charismatic, but he was much older than his two female students.

Exhausted, Robin felt like she had lost her bearings—each step cost her and she couldn't think clearly. She decided to go by the hospital and check on Raúl's condition. If Doug's mother and sisters had left, she would call Julia and let her know she would be at home for a couple of hours of sleep before picking up Sean.

CHAPTER 37

Bereavement

S ean wanted to attend Doug's wake and funeral, but Robin thought he was too young. Her son pleaded and cried. Her heart breaking for him, she discussed the situation with Ken, and he offered to accompany them; he and Sean could go elsewhere if the funereal events proved difficult for the boy. Reluctantly, she acquiesced. Her concern had been unwarranted at the wake as Sean spent most of the time playing with Doug's nieces and nephews and the adults fussed over him. Robin imagined Doug proudly saying, "That's my boy!" Next day, after the funeral mass and burial, Concepción invited them back to Montecito. Ken claimed he had work to do and asked Robin to drop him off at the department.

A nervous Robin maneuvered up the winding roadway leading to the Debayle home; her heart pounded as memories washed over her of the wild rides she had so often experienced with Doug driving up the same road. Robin finally pulled onto the grassy area to the side of the driveway. Incapable of catching her breath, she sat frozen behind the wheel, slow to realize Sean was out of the car. Only gradually did she become aware of Concepción's approach. Doug's mother gave Sean a one-armed hug and without a word, handed a glass of white wine through the open window to Robin. She asked Sean if he wanted to see the kittens, and hand-in-hand they walked off in the direction of the house. Long minutes passed before Robin got out of the car and went to be with Julia, Tati, and their husbands.

She had just accepted a second glass of wine when she noticed Sean walking in her direction holding a large woven basket with both arms, an unexpected grin on his face. Concepción looked abashed and avoided Robin's questioning look.

"Mommy, can I have a kitty? Puhleeze," he pleaded. "They are almost all gone."

"Robin, lo siento. I told Sean he can visit whenever he wants." Concepción added apprehensively, "I promised I would not give this one away."

Sean placed the basket on the grass in front of his mother and with the care of a practiced magician, slowly pulled back the top to reveal a midnight black kitten curled up asleep on a plush white towel.

"Sweetie, I don't know. I've never had a cat; I'm so busy—you're in school." By then a small group clustered around the scene.

"I'll take care of Mr. Dougie. I promise, I promise. Puhleeze." He gazed at Robin beseechingly as he tenderly stroked the kitten.

"Mr. Dougie?" Robin glanced toward Concepción, who had tears in her eyes. She looked away.

The murder of a well-known detective, as well as the subsequent rumors of a connection between two dead students and their popular USB professor, quickly made local and even the national news. One of the journalistic pack camping outside of the SBPD accosted Andy and asked if he would comment on the fact that both of Plask's victims were Latinas. He tossed a "*No* comment!" over his shoulder and promptly bumped into Robin. They walked into the building together.

"Sorry, Robin. Damn vultures. Doug was right on, they *are* vultures! What do you think?"

"Think?"

"The vulture's question regarding the students being Latinas?"

"I'm not sure. Although the two women are not from the same geographic area, their parents are in the country illegally. I guess it's not unreasonable to believe that families fearful of deportation are less likely to make waves, *even* if it means their daughters will not get justice. Andy, be careful what you say to them. Well, I guess, you would be better off not to talk with reporters at all. We have no evidence of Plask's involvement in Castillo's death, and while we have some for the Hernández murder, it's purely circumstantial. We need to remain cognizant of the fact that he or the university might sue."

"Got it! Thanks."

After she left Andy, Robin went to ask Sonia to put all noncritical calls through to voicemail so she would be able to get something done. Unsaid, but understood, was that she found it too difficult to deal with the constant telephone calls and was unlikely to get much done, despite the screening process. Both Barclay Stalts and Matt Webster were put through. Stalts was concerned for his and Joel Stein's well-being. His assistant admitted to having been at his boss's home with Susana Ortega and her children. To be fair, an irritable Robin reminded herself after hanging up, Stalts also called to thank her for what the SBPD did to get the family to safety. While listening, she heard Doug giving her grief vis-à-vis *Mr. Hollywood*. Matt left another message to say he was worried about her. Conflicted, Robin did not return the ranger's calls.

During those fleeting moments when she managed to be honest with herself, Robin knew she mourned more than a colleague—in love with Doug, it was now too late to undo the choices she'd made. Chief Bartolo assured her she did not bear responsibility for Doug's death and, as a department, they needed to move forward. She did not believe him on the first count and did not really care about the second. Doc had an open door and a cleared chair for anyone who wanted to talk, yet Robin could find no words. Ken quietly worked the case and made himself available for her at every turn. A shattered Sonia told the Chief she had to leave her job. His assistant no longer came in with empanadas or generous slices of pie. "Cooking," she said tearfully, "brings back too many memories of my boy." Each time Sonia referred to *her boy*, the reality of her own son's loss tugged at Robin. Doug's death had devastated the child. Often, while she tucked in an anxious Sean at night, he told his mother not to be sad. He assured her that Mr. Doug would be back from vacation soon and would pick him up after school. They would go to Montecito, spend time with Mami and Papi Debayle, eat dinner under the big tree, and play with mama cat and Mr. Dougie. Sleep in the cottage. Robin's heart broke as she realized her son was too young to understand death and she, his mother, was inadequate to the task of comforting him.

Robin, Ken, and Andy threaded their way through the same painful maze their colleague had found himself a part of during his last days. A thorough examination of Doug's computer, texts, e-mails, office, and home, failed to reveal anything that could answer the Chief's question regarding Plask's leverage over Raúl Debayle. Even his notebooks were unhelpful, despite his compulsive note-taking.

The investigation finally began making progress when Raúl's health improved; a state of affairs that brought a small measure of relief to the team. After reading the letter Doug left for Robin, Debayle reluctantly confirmed to Ken and Andy that in an effort to get rid of Plask, he had electronically monitored the professor's office and home after having heard rumors of his affairs with female students. Later, he had bribed Wilson, the complex manager, to access Cecilia's apartment so he could bug her home phone. Through the phone tap recordings, he had learned of the graduate student's pregnancy, and realized that the information would be a boon because there would be DNA evidence of her connection with Plask. Robin was not surprised to learn of Wilson's involvement, as limited as it might be. Bartolo had him detained for questioning. The squirrelly manager, when brought in, admitted to accepting money for leaving the apartment unlocked. He was promptly charged.

As much as Ken pushed, cajoled, and played on Raúl's guilt about his son's death, he was unable to obtain an explanation for Plask's blackmail scheme. Eventually, though, Debayle admitted to making arrangements through Ortega's father, an old friend living in Nicaragua, to have his son deliver the hush money to Plask *and* to ensure the extortion ended. He vehemently denied ever speaking to Roberto himself.

A pair of L.A. detectives located Ortega's truck at LAX. Forensics showed the single bullet killing Doug came from the Glock 40 found in the glove compartment of the truck. One print, Ortega's, was discovered on the weapon. On the other hand, the crime lab determined Doug's gun had not been fired and there was no gunshot residue on his hands. No one really thought his death was by suicide; still, late one night, she admitted to Andy that she had experienced a sense of relief when the report came in.

The D.A. issued a warrant for Roberto Ortega Jr.'s arrest for first-degree murder, but by then he was believed to be in Nicaragua. The U.S. State and Justice Departments submitted an extradition request to the Nicaraguan government. Andy bitterly referred to the move as a 'crock,' convinced of a Santa Bruja connection. He argued they would protect one of their own, even as far away as Nicaragua.

Robin found it excruciatingly difficult to watch Ken's videotaped interview of Raúl while in the hospital. Doug's father admitted to gambling with the life of an innocent young woman to escape from Plask's blackmail scheme. She was incapable of imagining how he would live with the knowledge that he had put into motion events culminating in the death of his son. There were so many layers to Robin's pain, she found it increasingly difficult to cope. Doug was dead; Robin had cared for Raúl; she and Sean had felt part of the Debayle extended family. It was all gone.

>>   <<   >>   <<

Robin was reading Ken's e-mail update on the case when her phone rang. "Criminal Investigation Unit, Detective Robin Crane, Santa—"

"Good morning Robin. I was wondering whether we can meet to discuss where we're at with the case."

She did not have to ask who the caller was or which case he was referring to. More likely, what the Chief really wanted to know was how she and Sean were doing—she could not imagine he was anything but up-to-the-minute with the investigation.

"Good morning, Chief, I can be in your office in about fifteen minutes, but I don't think Ken's around and he's been working on the financial piece. I'd just started reading his update when you called."

"That's okay. I met with him while you were out. Ken is busy with the missing child investigation. He knows you're bringing me up to speed on other aspects of the case. Fifteen minutes then." The phone clicked. Robin pulled up her own notes and read them over before printing the update.

Fifteen minutes later, she knocked on the Chief's door, file and notepad in hand.

"Come on in Robin and take a seat."

She avoided the leather chair Doug typically sat in. Blocked out Doug's frequent request to the Chief for an ottoman. His more recent request for a wine-tasting excursion.

"Here's the update." She handed him the file folder.

"Thanks, I'll look it over. But first, Robin, how are you and Sean doing?"

"We're fine, sir. Thanks for asking." She shifted in her seat and took a pen out of her pocket. She wanted him to get on with it.

"Robin, I'm not saying this as your boss, but as your friend. Don't hesitate to call either Susana or myself at home if we can be of any help."

"Thank you, sir. I will. Right now, work is what I need."

"I understand completely."

"Chief, let me give you a rundown, minus the financial piece Ken is covering and, I guess, already discussed with you."

"He did. The three of you—I'm including Detective Tyler—are doing a fine job with an investigation that is tough in so many ways, but I guess I don't need to tell you that. Okay, Robin, let me have it."

"Plask claims Raúl Debayle murdered Cecilia Hernández to set him up. When Ken confronted him with that accusation, Raúl demanded to see the evidence. He's furious, to put it mildly."

"What evidence do you have?"

"We have none."

"That's what I thought." He made a few notes. "Go on."

"Well, Plask continued accusing Raúl of the murder; however, when we played the audiotapes yesterday and showed him Cecilia's e-mails and letters, he began to waver, but in the end asked for his lawyer. That shift has triggered some significant wheeling and dealing between his high powered attorney and the D.A., who informed Plask's lawyer that she has sufficient evidence to successfully indict his client on extortion, a second degree murder charge for Cecilia Hernández' death, and an involuntary murder charge for the death of her fetus. Multiple murder charges, she told me, mean the death penalty is on the table."

"Robin, I spoke with the Commander and the D.A. yesterday. My understanding is that with public pressure mounting and an election coming up, she has offered to take the death penalty off the table if Plask pleads guilty to the murder charges, with the caveat that the Hernández family agrees with the deal. Have you spoken with them? Manuel Hernández told the D.A. they trusted you and wanted to discuss the offer with you. Apparently, he and his wife are really upset by Doug's death."

"Mr. Hernández did call me—earlier this morning. They spoke with José Santos, and between the three of them decided they didn't want to go through a trial and, 'If the man who murdered their daughter and grandchild would spend the rest of his life in jail,' they would agree to the deal."

"Good. Let the D.A. know."

"Will do."

CHAPTER 38

Justice—Of A Sort

"**Robin, come with** me. I've got coffee and something for you to eat." Ken took her firmly by the elbow before she had time to protest and led her out of the building to a bench in the shade.

"And *why* am I being strong-armed?" Robin said irritably, before sitting down and picking up the coffee with *R* on the lid. "Sorry, I'm wretched to be around."

"It's okay. Just wanted to see how you were doing. Find out what's going on with the case from your end. But first things first, here's a bag of tasty pastries."

She took out a warm flaky chocolate croissant and handed the bag back. "Thanks, Ken. I mean it."

"I know. I know. Robin, were you in court this morning?"

"Yeah. I looked but didn't see you."

"Couldn't go. I'm still working the missing child investigation."

"Got anything? It's been awhile now."

"Nope, nothing. Robin, don't just hold that—you need to eat more."

"Remind me of what happened." She took a small bite of the croissant under Ken's watchful eye.

"Mother and child were at the park across from the Mission. She received a business call and took it while walking through the rose garden. Three or four minutes later, she hung up and her son was gone. The soccer ball he'd been playing with was still there. We've re-interviewed the ex-, neighbors, and what seems to be a long string of babysitters. But that's not why we're here. Robin, what happened in court this morning?"

"Ken, Dr. Dane Plask, under oath, confessed to the murder of Cecilia Hernández, though the son-of-a-bitch characterized his graduate student's death as an accident, which true to form, he blamed on her."

"How in the hell did did the a-hole argue she was responsible for her own death?"

"Plask claims they got into a fight on the way up to the Painted Cave for a picnic, though that's an area where you might go hiking but isn't the first place most people would think of for a picnic. Anyhow, Cecilia threatened to get an abortion and wanted to end their relationship. According to him, he was driving along a switchback area when she hit him—they skidded, he panicked, lost control, and hit a tree. Given he drove away, the forensics don't quite back up that story. Didn't find any trees bearing witness to a crash, nothing from the few people living up there. Some security cameras but nothing there either. Not surprising, too much time has gone by. Anyhow, Plask acknowledges that he knew of the pregnancy at the time. As you know, the prosecutor took the death penalty off the table, with the agreement of the victim's family, in return for his plea."

"What did he admit to regarding the extortion charge?"

"Well, Plask supposedly came clean about his motive for black-mailing Doug's father. Ken, the flip side of getting this information is that it makes things even more painful for Doug's mother and sisters. If that's even possible."

"I'm sorry about that, Robin, but it's you and Sean that I worry about. Did you believe him?"

"It's difficult to know what to believe, particularly because I think he's in a strange sort of denial regarding Cecilia's death. Anyhow, about the extortion—according to Plask, during the early 80s he had heard a rumor from a Miskito mother that Raúl Debayle sometimes took boys from the tribe to the United States. Initially, Plask regarded the claim as gossip but subsequently confirmed the rumor: He had encountered other women who had praised Colonel Debayle, convinced children taken to the United States would have a better life, would 'become rich.' Maybe come back and help their families. He swears he doesn't know what happened to the children."

"We need to follow up on *that* claim. How are *you* doing, it must have been difficult?"

"I don't really know, Ken. It's going to take time to sort out my feelings about Doug's father. While I listened to Plask's testimony, however, some things Doug had said began to make sense to me. Once the Sandinista Party came to power, Plask no longer received money from the Debayle government. With influence peddling no longer lucrative, he had to find another way to finance his work and, probably more importantly, maintain his elevated standard of living. Plask ostensibly went to Raúl and threatened him with exposure regarding the Miskito children. According to the professor, prospective parents paid upward of fifty thousand dollars on the black market for children with the appropriate paperwork. Little boys, for reasons I don't understand, are less likely to be missed. I can't quite remember what you got from the financial consultant. Is there anything helpful … I wish we could get some corroborating evidence for child trafficking."

"Maybe, some of this you might already know, Robin, so stop me whenever you want. Some of what he found may confirm what Plask admitted to. When we asked about the source of *his* money,

Plask's explanation was that despite his relative youth when he first met Raúl, the Nicaraguan research project had been ongoing for decades. A steady influx of U.S. dollars meant those with a say in tribal affairs listened to him—same as he apparently swore to in court. The Nicaraguans set up an offshore account in the British Virgin Islands into which substantial sums were deposited, and purchased a property for him in Santa Barbara. The title had originally been in the names of Plask and a corporation, but after five years reverted to him alone. In return, *they* had expected his active cooperation and complete discretion. Plask's lawyer claimed that if he had failed to comply, significant repercussions, financial and otherwise, would have resulted. When I pushed for more details, the lawyer would only say the CIA was involved. When pressed further, he admitted Plask had no direct evidence for the claim, yet maintained that Raúl Debayle had frequently alluded to the organization. I've spoken with the agency, but they profess no knowledge of either man's activities. I'd love some substantiating evidence for all of this because I agree with you: I think we're looking at a human trafficking case."

"Remind me about the bank accounts?"

"The details are in the file, but big picture—the consultant located several bank accounts in Raul Debayle's name in the U.S., Canada, and the Virgin Islands, and assured me there would be more. Despite the significant amount of money he apparently gave Plask over time, the sum of money remaining in his accounts was staggering. He also put substantial property and one sizable bank account in Concepción's name, but we've concluded that she had no knowledge of her husband's business activities. Robin, I know you care for the woman, but I find it difficult to believe she continues to maintain Plask set up her husband."

It was not clear what charges, if any, the prosecutor could level against the two men on child trafficking, so the Chief and D.A. advised the FBI and IRS of the purported scheme, hoping a federal investigation would yield useful information. The State Department notified the Nicaraguan government of the case, and authorities there initiated an investigation of Plask's partner in Managua, Professor Jorge Araya.

Ken told Robin that he believed that Sara and Cecilia had somehow learned of the human trafficking and the knowledge put their lives in peril, although in Cecilia's case Plask had developed feelings for the young woman—his DNA was consistent with the fetal DNA. Once Raúl learned Plask was talking, he lawyered up. The D.A. refused to prosecute either Plask or Debayle on trafficking without more evidence.

Bartolo tried a new tactic and assigned Tyler to head a task force charged with locating the Miskito children. They had thus far had no success, though as he told Robin in confidence, the idea of taking children out of loving well-to-do homes in the U.S. to return them to the Miskito Nation was something nobody cared to do, so she was not too surprised about the lack of progress.

The Chief and the D.A. eventually concluded Plask was unlikely to be charged for Sara Castillo's death—the lab, using post hoc analysis, was unable to match the mark on her neck with Plask's ring. Neither Sara Castillo's wrecked car nor the car Plask drove at the time she died were located. All the detectives had were their suspicions.

One overcast day, Robin went to the taquería to talk with the Castillos, expecting them to be upset and angry that the D.A. would not be charging Plask for the death of their daughter. Instead, the grieving parents told her they had found peace with the decision. They felt that Doug, in some way, had already achieved justice for their Sarita—the man they believed to have killed her would be locked away for their lifetime and for his. They had added a picture of a smiling Doug to their daughter's memorial behind the cash register. Shortly afterward, Robin left the taquería and ran for her car. She broke down.

Robin believed Doug knew going out to Hope Ranch that night was risky, given money was on the line and Roberto Ortega was involved. But she also knew Doug was all about justice and, as

Andy had pointed out in his eulogy, it was just like him to stay on the job until the end, regardless of the cost. Doug was also about family. Robin could only imagine his distress as he tried to be a good son *and* achieve justice for two young women, one pregnant. Robin hoped that out of such horror, the Castillo and Hernández families continued to derive a measure of comfort in knowing so many cared about their daughters, and that Plask would spend the rest of his life in prison. Yet, instead of a sense of relief, Robin found herself wishing Doug had figured out how to solve the case *and* protect himself. She missed him terribly.

EPILOGUE

June 2012

Mr. Dougie had become an integral part of the Crane family. No longer a kitten, the plump and contented black cat still slept curled up each night on Sean's pillow—an abiding comfort for which Robin was grateful.

They, including Mr. Dougie, made regular visits to the Debayle home for several months after the funeral. With Raúl in prison for illegal wiretapping and income tax evasion, and the D.A. threats of additional charges as an accessory in his son's murder, Robin felt her presence was painful for the adults.

An indictment came down for Roberto Ortega but the authorities still had not located him. Andy Tyler's task force continued investigating the whereabouts of the trafficked children, but they had had little success. Still, Robin called Doug's mother each Sunday; Julia or Tati picked Sean up every other week to spend the day in Montecito with

Concepción. That, Robin knew, was what Doug would have wanted. She could not bring herself to visit Raúl in prison.

Matt Webster continued calling Robin to see how she was doing. He didn't push. He listened. He hung up when she wanted off the phone. He sent clusters of white tulips held together with curling silver ribbons, always accompanied with a note saying: "I'm here for you." Eventually, Robin agreed to go for a walk. More followed, and then one day, hungry, they went to lunch. Afterward, she'd felt conflicted and pulled back. When she finally returned a call, Robin explained it was too soon: Sean still hurt, and she did not feel comfortable bringing anyone else into his life. Matt said he understood. Late at night, the grieving woman realized the fear was less for her son than for herself.

Many months passed before Robin acceded to Matt's repeated urgings to spend an evening together. After dinner they walked on the beach holding hands when, unexpectedly, a laughing Matt pulled her along with him into the glistening moonlit ocean. Enveloped by warm waves and the arms of a caring man, Robin caught a reassuring glimpse of her future.

ACKNOWLEDGMENTS

Detective Crane and company would certainly not exist without the considerable efforts made by my dedicated readers: Barbara Crain, Sergio (Macho) Rivera, Mike Bamberg, Mary Keating, Mary Bamberg, and Ann Marie Jusczyk.

I owe an enormous debt of gratitude to Barbara Crain for the editing of this book—a tedious process carried out during a difficult time—there is really no adequate way to thank you for your patience and dedication to getting it right. Special thanks to Mary Keating, Esq., for your legal expertise, to Detective Rob Hankard Jr. for generously sharing your knowledge of police procedure and experience, and to Lisa Smith, Esq., for your thorough legal and editing contributions. Special thanks to Sean Smith for your generosity in allowing me to use your name and your thoughts about the imprint. I am indebted to family and friends for their support, especially, Sharon Bamberg, Grace Robiou, and Mike and Marianne Moran. My everlasting gratitude goes to the Doctors, Nurses, the ICU staff, Housekeeping, Physical Therapists, and Nutritionists of Brigham and Women's Hospital and the Spaulding Hospital for Continuing Medical Care, Cambridge, all of whom worked so hard to keep my son alive.

To my cherished children, Morgan and Lisa. To the kids who I am so grateful to have in my life: Rachel, Sean, Santiago, and Natalia.

I recognize Carol Anstett for the back cover photograph (2013). I would like to acknowledge the following sources for background information: the Painted Cave area: Bryan Conant and Jan Tinbrook, Ph.D; the Miskito Indians of Nicaragua: Laura Herlihy Hobson, Karl Offen, Michael Olien, and Dennis Phillips. Susan Stonich, the BBC News, and *The New York Times*. Full references are available at www.robincranemysteries.com. Because this is a work of fiction, I have taken some liberties with the history of Nicaragua and the culture and history of the Miskito, as well as the structure and function of Santa Barbara Law Enforcement agencies. I hope all will understand. Any errors are mine and mine alone.

ABOUT THE AUTHOR

B A Smith received her doctorate in psychology, taught and carried out research at the Johns Hopkins University for twenty years, during which time she studied healthcare delivery in Costa Rica, as a recipient of the Fulbright Senior Scientist Award. She is a proud mother and grandmother. Smith has lived in Central America and across the United States but currently calls Maryland home, where she is at work on the next novel in the Robin Crane series, *Floater in Baltimore Harbor*.

EXCERPT

Floater In The
Baltimore Harbor

A Robin Crane Mystery

Chapter 1

Baltimore City Police Officer, July 2013

The radio crackled as the dispatcher came on the line. "Rossi, Crane, got a domestic for you: 2044 Eastern Avenue. Anonymous caller. No previous calls for the address. Out."

"Affirmative. Will comply. Out."

Greg flipped the lit cigarette out of the window, turned on the siren and rack lights, and off they sped toward Fells Point through the darkened but not quiet streets of Baltimore—cameras at many of the corners keeping careful watch over the clusters of kids paying them no mind. She wondered how often the flashing blue lights served for target practice. Robin closed the windows and released her seatbelt. Rossi never used his. The call brought back the memory of the Isla Vista domestic Doug and Andy investigated—brought back the painful memory of Roberto Ortega.

"Hey Rossi, City detectives generally go out in marked cars. In Santa Barbara, we used unmarked cars. What's that about?"

"Yeah, our detectives worked in unmarkeds until a few months ago, when an order came down from the brass requiring they use patrol cars. The powers that be are trying to keep the public mollified—they're demanding transparency and visibility."

"Sure gives the criminals the advantage," she objected. "I'd think they'd be worried about public safety. The safety of the police."

"Yeah, well you're in Baltimore. Won't be the first thing that'll make you scratch that pretty head of yours—blonde hair, blue eyes, and *hot*—you're certainly going to be a stand out on the streets where we'll be hanging out."

Shades of Sonia Rodriguez, Robin thought—so much for the East Coast-West Coast distinctions she and Doug used to laugh about. The SB dispatcher, known for her inappropriate comments, frequently referred to the detectives as skinny, fatty, and Chinese looking, depending on their physical characteristics. She'd also provided other nuggets, such as a repeated advisory for Robin to watch her backside, when sending her out on a call. Greg Rossi, as a partner, would provide her with a far greater challenge. It occurred to her it might be a good idea to invite Ken O'Donnell to Baltimore for a visit. One ride-along and Ken would set his old Brooklyn buddy straight in a millisecond. Since it was unlikely her friend and colleague would be riding into Maryland anytime soon, there was always the option of requesting a transfer to another district, although that was probably a less than optimal way to continue her career in a new city. Still, she was not up for overt sexism on the job in a city that apparently presented sufficient challenges without personnel issues.

It was her first night with her new partner. She'd introduced herself to Greg Rossi, tall and paunchy, with curly gray hair, a strong jaw line, and settled facial expression daring someone to cross him. He, in turn, gave her the once over. She knew from a colleague that the old-time tough and impatient cop had twenty-two years on the job, fourteen of them in Baltimore and the rest in Brooklyn, New York. The area of the downtown Central District they were assigned included the touristy Inner Harbor, the newly developed upscale Harbor East, and quirky Fells Point—a smorgasbord of problems.

Once in their car, Rossi described his expectations pretty clearly. Given he had "seniority and the tactical know-how," Rossi informed her he'd be "first in, with her as back-up." Training apparently didn't count for much with him. Or previous experience for that matter, she thought irritably, as he continued to set limits for every conceivable situation. "Partner-in-training," he kept referring to her.

Rossi pulled up to the address the dispatcher had given them, moved forward, and parked in front of the darkened house two doors down. Robin didn't need to be told it never paid off to be in the line of fire. Once out of the car, the blue and red flashing, they heard what sounded like a man and woman yelling from inside the row house. Despite the volume, as far as she could tell, not a single neighbor was in evidence. Nobody even peeking through a curtain.

"Greg, just an FYI—I speak some Spanish. Understand more," Robin said, aware of the high concentration of Latinos living and working in the Fells Point neighborhood.

"Good, but follow my lead."

"Of course." It was all she could do not to add a sardonic "Sir."

Once on the porch, Rossi whispered, "I don't know how you're used to doing it, but in Baltimore, we put an ear to the window before knocking. That way, we can listen to what's being said or done inside. The guys call the front door the fatal funnel. And gals." He threw the last two words in with the barest hint of sarcasm.

"I'll call for back-up."

"Go ahead. Can't understand what they're saying inside; sounds pretty fucking heated. We'll wait for reinforcements to arrive before we go in. Pure shit dealing with domestics—can be a friggin' nightmare! I'll take gangbangers any day—they're more predictable."

She moved away from the porch and called in. In less than five minutes, another patrol car pulled up.

"Okay, let's go inside. Those two can stay out here." Rossi signaled the arriving officers accordingly, approached the door, and stood to the left side. Robin positioned herself to the right. Both had released their guns.

Greg rapped hard on the door and stepped back. "Baltimore police. Open the door and step back. That's an order."

No one answered, though the screaming had stopped. "Crane, go ahead," he said, with a thrust of his jaw in the direction of the door.

She knocked. "Baltimore police here—Officer Robin Crane. Please open the door so we can talk."

She pulled back, ambivalent about the bright porch light. It was quiet. After a long minute, she heard the lock turning and waited apprehensively for it to open. During those tense moments, Robin remembered a discussion she and Matt had in Santa Barbara one night over dinner. Although he had never been to Baltimore, he had "watched the *Wire*!" She had laughed, arguing that the popular series did not exactly represent Baltimore, as so many people have come to believe. As she stood anxiously waiting to find out what was going on behind the closed door, Robin figured she might have to take back her assessment. Later, she had discovered the man who was now her husband had seen the series *twice* and wanted to watch it a third time with her—his "Bawlmer girl."

The door opened to reveal a terrified couple holding hands—pupils dilated, mouths clenched, stances rigid. The man had a strained but probably pleasant face under other conditions, wire-rimmed glasses, and straight black hair on the longish side. He wore faded blue jeans, a long-sleeved purple Flacco football jersey, and upscale Nike sneakers.

Slim, he looked like a runner to Robin. The woman was shorter but equally thin. Large barrettes held her luxurious curly chestnut brown hair back from her face. Dark brown eyes and dark skin, she looked Latin American to Robin. The woman was breathing rapidly.

"Sir, you come with me," Greg pretty much ordered, rather than asked. "We had a call about the racket coming from your home."

"We're sorry. Officers, nothing wrong is going on here. A normal husband-wife disagreement," the man insisted. He let go of the woman's hand, crossed his arms, and stood at the threshold, resolutely looking over their heads.

"*Sir*, I'm not saying anything is wrong. But we want to keep things that way, so how about we go outside and talk." Greg took hold of the tense man's elbow and firmly led him out of the house to the small seating area arranged on the sidewalk to the left of the stairs.

Rossi signaled the officers standing by the second car. "Davis, keep Crane company. Santiago, you stay put."

Once Rossi finished hollering directions, Robin directed her attention to the woman who now stood in the doorway biting the cuticle of one of her thumbs. "Ma'm, I'm Officer Crane. I'd like to talk with you for a few minutes." Robin showed the trembling woman her badge. "Please don't be scared, you aren't in trouble, we want to make sure everything is alright. Do you mind if I come in?"

The young woman nodded her head. Robin and the officer she assumed was Davis entered the tiny foyer and wiped their feet. Stairs went straight up to a second floor. Robin saw a living room to her left and assumed further back there was a dining room.

"Ma'am, why don't we sit at your dining room table and talk?" Without waiting for an answer, she led the way. The shades were drawn, the house dimly lit. Robin walked through the front room into the dining room and waited until the woman sat. She then pulled a dark green upholstered chair out from the wooden table, sat down, and surreptitiously looked around. The only other piece of furniture in the clean and orderly room was a dark wooden sideboard with three slim drawers above two cabinets. On top, sat a clear glass vase of silk irises, several framed photographs, and a lamp. Robin took out a notebook and pen from her jacket. Davis remained leaning against the wall. He said nothing.

"Let's begin with your name, why don't we?" Robin asked.

"Marisol Jimenez. Officers, can I get you something to drink?" the still scared woman asked. Robin noticed her bleeding thumb where she'd been chewing at her cuticle.

"No thank you," Robin said. She looked over at Davis; he shook his head.

"We're both good, thank you. Ms. Jimenez, we received a call about the noise coming from your home. Are you okay?"

"I'm fine. I'm sorry, officer—I guess we got kinda loud."

"Ma'am, do you mind telling me what's going on? We'll be on our way if you're all right, but we do not want to return. You should know, if multiple calls come in over time for this address, there's the possibility you could be issued a citation for acting in a disorderly manner that disturbs public peace. Not so good—the ticket is five hundred dollars and your landlord can be charged. Another report—the charge is doubled to a thousand and your property owner is going to have a problem on his or her hand. But first, ma'am, are there children in the house?"

"No, just the two of us. Me and my husband, Jimmy."

"Have you been hurt in any way?"

"Hurt—no way! Jimmy would *never* hurt me."

"Well, ma'am, then why all the yelling?"

"We're married. Officer, married people fight," she said tersely, and began chewing on the cuticle of her other thumb.

"True. But not usually loud enough for a 911 call, though we don't show any other calls for this address."

"Sorry," she said apologetically. "I guess I lost my temper. You're correct; the police have never been here."

Robin tried again. "Anything you want to tell us?"

"Not really." Marisol sighed, hesitated, and it took almost a minute before Robin seemed to make her mind up about something.

She swallowed and began, "Jimmy's sister and her daughter have been staying with us. His sister's a problem, always has been, but I put up with her because she's family. Her daughter, that's different. I love my niece. I'm an aide at the St. Vincent DePaul Head Start; I love children and we haven't been able to have any. Anyhow, his sister wanted money and I didn't want Jimmy to give it to her. In the beginning, my husband sided with me, which made her furious and when she gets angry, it's something to behold."

"And where are your sister-in-law and niece? By the way, what are their names?"

"Brenda and Joey. Well, most of the yelling was *about* them. She said she was leaving, Joey started crying—she's an 11 year-old girl who has been very happy living with us. She, Brenda, screamed at Jimmy— told him in no uncertain terms that any brother who threw his sister and niece out on the street was a son-of-a-bitch because he knew she didn't have money. My husband wasn't throwing her out—he doesn't like fighting and he loves his family, so what did the dumb lug do?" Marisol did not wait for Robin's answer. "He actually gave her most of next month's rent money. I swear Brenda is going to put *whatever* he gave her up her nose."

"Where did Brenda and Joey go? The daughter's name is Joey, correct? A nickname, I take it?"

www.robincranemysteries.com
basmith@robincranemysteries.com

www.ingramcontent.com/pod-product-compliance
Lightning Source LLC
Chambersburg PA
CBHW030028180626
46810CB00001B/259